Emil Reisch, Wolfgang Helbig, James Fullarton Muirhead, Findlay
Muirhead

Guide to the Public Collections of Classical Antiquities in Rome

Volume 2

Emil Reisch, Wolfgang Helbig, James Fullarton Muirhead, Findlay Muirhead

Guide to the Public Collections of Classical Antiquities in Rome
Volume 2

ISBN/EAN: 9783337382841

Printed in Europe, USA, Canada, Australia, Japan

Cover: Foto ©Andreas Hilbeck / pixelio.de

More available books at **www.hansebooks.com**

GUIDE

TO THE PUBLIC COLLECTIONS OF

CLASSICAL ANTIQUITIES IN ROME

VOL. II.

THE VILLAS, THE MUSEO BONCOMPAGNI, THE PALAZZO SPADA, THE ANTIQUITIES OF THE VATICAN LIBRARY, THE MUSEO DELLE TERME

BY

WOLFGANG HELBIG

THE ETRUSCAN MUSEUM IN THE VATICAN, THE MUSEO KIRCHERIANO, AND THE PREHISTORIC MUSEUM AT THE COLLEGIO ROMANO

BY

EMIL REISCH

TRANSLATED FROM THE GERMAN

BY

JAMES F. AND FINDLAY MUIRHEAD.

LEIPSIC: KARL BAEDEKER

1896

CONTENTS.

Villa Albani.

Most recent catalogue: *Morcelli, Fea, and Visconti*, Description de la Villa Albani (Rome, 1869).

At the end of the walk leading to the left from the entrance to the villa, along the wall, stands, —

705 (864). Meta, with decorations in relief.

> The extreme top and the lowest part of the cone have been restored.

The reliefs surrounding the lower end of the cone represent a Satyr and three Bacchantes dancing to the music of a woman playing on a cithara. All five figures are of the type so frequently affected by the neo-Attic workers in relief (comp. Nos. 556, 578, 785). The projections higher up were intended to hold garlands, four of which are represented in relief. Near the top the sculptor has added a club and a pedum, which are apparently fastened to the cone by a broad band, and are probably symbolic of tragedy and comedy ,comp. Nos. 271, 272). The supposition that this monument was the meta of an actual circus is contradicted by the small size of the cone and by the fact that the figures bear no relation to racing. It is much more likely that it formed part of a sepulchral monument and indicated the goal or termination of the earthly life. The frequent representation of scenes from the circus on Roman sarcophagi (comp. Nos. 336-339) shows how well-known this form of allegory was to the public of the imperial days. Sarcophagus-reliefs also furnish numerous analogies to the sepulchral significance of the scenic attributes and the Bacchic dance (comp. No. 432). It is, however, by no means certain that another explanation may not be the right one. Thus it is possible that some ancient Roman, on retiring from public life, may have erected the marble meta in his villa as an emblem of the close of his military or political career.

Zoega, Bassi rilievi antichi di Roma, 1, 34. Comp. *Braun*, Ruinen und Museen, p. 611, No. 1. *Hauser*, Die neu-attischen Reliefs, p. 87, No. 4.

In the small Colonnade to the left of the main building, —

705A (48). **Head of a Youth.**

> The point of the nose and fragments of the curls are modern.

This has rightly been recognized as a copy of a work by an artist of about the same period as Pheidias. The hair is, however, more freely treated than was usual at that period. The execution is poor.

Furtwaengler, Masterpieces of Greek Sculpture, p. 103. note 1.

Portico of the Main Building.

706 (51). **Sitting Male Figure,** freely restored.

The body belongs to the type usual in seated figures of Zeus. The laurel-crowned head (nose restored) is ancient but can hardly have belonged to the same figure, as the whole of the neck, connecting head and trunk, is of modern workmanship. It betrays a superficial resemblance to the head of Augustus.

Clarac, IV. Pl. 912A, No. 2334A. Comp. *Bernoulli*, Römische Ikonographie, ₁I, 1. p. 32, No. 22.

707 (52). **Term of Hermes.**

> The nose and lips are restorations.

The shaft bears three epigrams, two in Latin and one in Greek. The last gives the name of the donor and expresses the devout wish that the god may be gracious to him and his. The Latin inscriptions enumerate the various functions of Mercury, both of them mentioning that he was the founder of the palæstra. This point of view seems to have suggested the formation of the head and neck, the broad and vigorous features and powerful muscles of which resemble those of Heracles.

Corpus inscr. gr., III, 5953. *Braun*, Ruinen und Museen; p. 620, No. 7. *Kaibel*, Epigrammata græca ex lapidibus collecta, No. 816.

708 (61). Seated Female Figure holding immortelles in her hand, freely restored.

Found in the Via Baccina, between the Quirinal and the Esquiline. The nose, lips, and ears are restorations.

The poorly executed head would seem, from its style and the arrangement of the hair, to belong to the time of Hadrian or the Antonines, while the body, to judge from its admirable workmanship, probably dates from the beginning of the Empire.

Clarac, v, Pl. 956, No. 2456. Comp. *Braun*, Ruinen und Museen, p. 618, No. 4. *Bernoulli*, Röm. Ikon., II, 2, p. 249.

709 (66). Circular Basis, with Hecate (?) and the Seasons.

The reliefs represent the Seasons and a goddess holding two torches, the latter probably representing Hecate in her capacity as goddess of the moon (comp. No. 619). The maiden immediately behind Hecate, holding a bunch of ears of corn and poppies in her left hand and a garland in her right, represents Summer. The following figure, whose attributes are a basket and a kid, has usually been taken for Spring but is more probably meant for Autumn. Next comes Winter, laden with the spoils of the chase; while last of all is Spring, the fold of whose garment seems to have been filled with flowers. As the procession of the Seasons is opened by summer, it would seem that this composition must have been designed in a region in which summer was regarded as the beginning of the year. This may have been Attica, where the year began with the month of Hecatombæon, corresponding to the latter half of July and the first half of August.

Zoega, Bassi rilievi, ii, 94. *Millin*, Gal. myth., Pl. 26, 92. *Hirt*, Götter und Heroen, T. 4, 33. *Guigniaut*, Rel. de l'ant., Pl. 184, 250r. *Conze*, Heroen- und Göttergestalten, T. 89, 1. Comp. Ann. dell' Inst., 1861, pp. 209, 210, 1863, pp. 294 et seq. Archäol.-epigr. Mittheilungen aus Oesterreich, v (1881), pp. 43, 44. *Herrmann*, De Horarum apud veteres figuris (Berlin, 1887), p. 32. *Hauser*, Die neu-attischen Reliefs, p. 103, No. 36.

710 (67). **Double Herma,** freely restored.

This herma presents the portrait of the Hellenistic poet described under No. 469, along with another portrait, which we may assume to be also that of a poet.

Comparetti e De Petra, La Villa Ercolanese dei Pisoni, T. iv, 3, 4, pp. 38 et seq.

711 (74). **Puteal, with the Eleusinian Deities (?).**

Pentelic marble. Upper part restored. We know that this is a puteal, and not a base, from an ancient drawing in which the central cavity is shown (Jahrb. des Arch. Inst., vi, 1891, p. 160, No. 37; comp. vii, 1892, p. 86, No. 10a, p. 86, No. 13).

The reliefs on the Puteal, which is a work of the neo-Attic school, are usually explained by a reference to the Eleusinian myth. The woman and the girl leaning against her are taken for Demeter and her daughter Persephone; while the figure to the right of this group, resting the right hand on the stump of a tree entwined by a vine, is supposed to be either Dionysos or Iacchos, the mystic bridegroom of Persephone, waiting for his bride. Another view sees in the reliefs the reunion, in the presence of Dionysos, of Demeter and Persephone, on the return of the latter from the lower regions. Both of these hypotheses, however, encounter the difficulty, that the figure whose hand rests on the tree seems to be decidedly feminine in outline; and indeed it is unmistakably a woman in several better preserved replicæ. The three dancing maidens are either Nymphs or the Horæ. It has been pointed out that either of these would harmonise

with the symbolisation of nature involved in the Eleusinian Mysteries.

A sketch of this monument is given in the Codex Pighianus
(Ber. der sächs. Ges. der Wiss., 1868, p. 203, No. 106). *Zoega*, II. 96.
Comp. Arch. Zeitung, xxxii (1875), p. 86. *Friederichs-Wolters*,
Bausteine, No. 2144. Archæol.-epigr. Mittheilungen aus Österreich,
v (1881), p. 54. *Overbeck*, Kunstmythologie, III, p. 509, No. 13,
pp. 514, 515. *Hauser*, Die neu-attischen Reliefs, p. 32, No. 40,
p. 140, p. 141, No. 3, p. 144, No. 4. Jahrbuch des Arch. Instituts,
IV (1889), p. 259.

712 (79). Seated Female Figure, freely restored.

The attitude and treatment of the body correspond
to those of a well-known statue in the Capitoline Museum (No. 460). On the cubical support below the seat
are represented three amply draped female figures, one
of whom holds a cup. The head is ancient (except the
nose), but it is doubtful whether it belongs to this body.
The arrangement of the hair would indicate a portrait
of the time of the Julian emperors. Its identification with
Agrippina the Elder is groundless.

Clarac, v, Pl. 932, No. 2367A. Comp. *Winckelmann*, Mon.
ant. ined., I, trattato preliminare, p. 48. *Braun*, Ruinen und Museen, p. 618, No. 5. *Bernoulli*, Römische Ikonographie, II, 1, p. 184,
No. 12.

713 (87). Seated Figure in Armour.

The restorations include the head, the neck, the outstretched right arm, the outer half of the upper part of
the left arm, the index-finger of the left hand, the lower
end of the staff in the left hand, nearly the whole of
the back, the legs, most of the chair, and the plinth.
The restorer, in order to make them look antique, has
furnished the head and neck with artificial weather-
marks and staining ('patina'). The features are those of
Augustus.

The reliefs on the cuirass show two Victories standing by a burning thymiaterion, or incense-holder; while
below are personifications of the Earth (comp. No. 5) and
the Sea, the former with a lapful of fruit and a horn
of plenty, the latter with a dolphin on her left knee.
The style of the execution and the arrangement and sub-

ject of the ornamentation of the armour point to the
second half of the first century of the Christian era.

Clarac, v, Pl. 936B, No. 2386A (published as a statue of
Claudius). Comp. Bernoulli, II, 1, p. 32, No. 23. — For the cuirass,
see Zoega, II, 111. Bonner Studien (Berlin, 1890), p. 16.

On the rear-wall, —

711 (58). **Head of Ptolemy,** last king of Numidia and
     Mauretania.

The nose and the herma are restorations.

Comp. No. 33.

In the niches stand six freely restored **Figures in
Armour** (Nos. 715-720), all with ancient heads, which,
however, in most cases, probably do not belong to the
figures to which they are attached.

Comp. Braun, Ruinen und Museen, p. 619, No. 6.

715 (54). Figure with a head of which the entire upper
part, including the right eye and the nose, has been
restored. The features recall those of Tiberius. The head
does not seem to have been carved by the same sculptor
who made the body, and it is of a different kind of marble.
In both cases, however, the execution seems to point to
the time of the early emperors.

Clarac, v, Pl. 936A, No. 2354C. Comp. Bernoulli, II, 1, p. 148,
No. 13. Bonner Studien, p. 11.

716 (59). Figure with the head of Lucius Verus nose
restored. The body dates from the first century of the
imperial period. On the armour are represented two
short-skirted Victories, one holding a burning thymiaterion (comp. No. 713), the other placing a ball of incense in the flames.

Clarac, v, Pl. 936A, No. 2459C. Comp. Bernoulli, II, 2, p. 206,
No. 3. — For the bas-reliefs of the cuirass: Zoega, II, 110. Comp.
Bonner Studien, p. 13.

717 (64). Figure with the head of Trajan, of which,
however, only the upper part, including the eyes and the
root of the nose, is antique. The body seems to belong

to a somewhat earlier era, perhaps that of the Flavian emperors. The cuirass bears no ornamentation but is girt with the cingulum, or general's sash.

Clarac, v, Pl. 936D, No. 2415B. Comp. Bernoulli, ii, 2, p. 76, No. 1.

718 (72). Figure with the head of Marcus Aurelius (nose and neck modern). The trunk dates at soonest from the time of Hadrian. The uppermost relief on the armour is a head of Medusa, below which are two griffins and a thymiaterion — the latter group unfortunately cut in two by the cingulum. At the foot is a scheme of leaves.

Clarac, v, Pl. 936B, No. 2449B. Comp. Athenische Mittheilungen, xvi (1891), p. 149. Bernoulli, ii, 2, p. 166, No. 4.

719 (77). Figure with the head of Antoninus Pius (nose and most of the eye-sockets restored), which seems to belong to the body. The cuirass is devoid of ornament.

Claruc, v, Pl. 936B, No. 1442A. Comp. Bernoulli, ii, 2, p. 141, No. 2.

720 (82). Figure with the head of Hadrian, of which the skull, the forehead, and the outer half of each eye are modern. The head and trunk seem to belong to the same statue, though they are now united by a modern neck. The reliefs on the armour represent a youth clad in a lion's hide (Arimaspes?), grasping the neck of a griffin with each hand. They are carefully executed but devoid of character.

Clarac, v, Pl. 936A, No. 2420B. Comp. Bernoulli, ii, 2, p. 103, No. 5. For the cuirass, see Zoega, ii, 109. Bonner Studien, T. iii, 1, p. 4.

Room at the left end of the Portico.

721 (19). Caryatid by Criton and Nicolaos.

According to Piranesi (Vasi e Candelabri, ii, subscription of T. 68), who claims to have been an eye-witness of its discovery, this Caryatid was found in 1765, along with Nos. 834 (628) and 837 (726) — now in the so-called Caffè — in the Vigna Strozzi, on the Via Appia, adjoining the Tomb of Cæcilia Metella. Two other Caryatids had be·n discovered in the same vineyard in the time of Sixtus V. (comp. *Winckelmann*, Geschichte der Kunst, xɪ, 1, § 14). The restorations include the nose, the lower lip, the chin, the right arm, the lower part of the left arm (with the thyrsos), various pieces of the calathos, the neck, the drapery, the feet, and the outer parts of the plinth.

An inscription on the back of the calathos, or basket-like object borne by the head, names the Athenians, Criton and Nicolaos, as the sculptors of this figure. Both the style of execution of the figure itself and the shape of the letters of the inscription indicate the Roman empire as the period in which these artists must have flourished. The design of the figure, which seems due to an earlier artist, probably of the Hellenistic era, is obviously borrowed from a work of the golden period of Attic art. Very possibly this may have been a type of Pallas produced in the third quarter of the fifth century B. C., in which the ægis lay transversely across the breast, in the position here occupied by the nebris. Our Caryatid thus shows, if not in the treatment of details, yet in the general conception and plan, a certain kinship with those of the Erechtheion at Athens (comp. No. 1. The length of the body, which seems disproportionate to that of the legs, leads us to conclude that this figure, or at any rate the original which it imitated, was intended to occupy a lofty situation. The addition of the nebris may be explained by the supposition that the building for which the Caryatid was executed was connected with the cult of Dionysos. If our figure belonged to the same building as Nos. 831 (628 and 837 (725) — as seems probable from the fact that they are all three of the same height and were found in the same place —, it sheds a curious light on the taste of the architect, who could combine these figures in a decorative whole. The Caryatids in the semicircle of the so-called Caffè differ from that which bears the names of Criton and Nicolaos, not only in their less assured pose and more slender forms, but also in the pettier and more restless style of their execution.

The type of head and the disposition of the drapery are different in all the three figures; and in No. S37 (725) traces of an archaic style may be observed in both. Figures of so unlike a character must needs have produced an inharmonious effect as bearers of one and the same architrave. To convince oneself of this, it is only necessary to glance at Piranesi's attempted restoration.

Gerhard, Antike Bildwerke, T. 94, 2. Brunn und Bruckmann, Denkmäler griech. und römischer Sculptur, No. 254. All the other references are given in Friederichs-Wolters, Bausteine, No. 1555, and in Loewy, Inschriften griech. Bildhauer, No. 346. Comp. Arch. Zeitung, XLI (1883), p. 203. Jahrbuch des Arch. Instituts, v (1890), p. 93. — For the restoration: Piranesi, Vasi e candelabri, II, T. 68.

722 (20). **Relief from a Frieze**, supposed to represent Capaneus.

> The restorations include the nose, the right quarter of the slab, pieces of the shield and the lower part of the left leg, and the rocky ground.

A fine-looking man, of dignified bearing, marked out by the wide fillet on his head as a king or a priest, has fallen on one knee and with one hand stretches out his shield, while the other clutches at his neck, in which he has obviously just received a wound. The theory that it represents Capaneus, struck by lightning as he is about to scale the walls of Thebes, is untenable. Capaneus must have worn a helmet at least, in addition to the chlamys and shield, and would show his character by his expression of defiance. It is more probable that the man, whoever he was, was attacked unexpectedly by his enemies while unarmed, and had just time to seize his shield. The murder of Agamemnon, for example, would answer the conditions. The style indicates an original of the end of the fifth century B. C.

Zoega, I, 47. Overbeck, Gallerie, T. v, 6, p. 128, No. 45. Baumeister, Denkmäler des klass. Alterthums, III, p. 1759, Fig. 1480. Comp. Welcker, Alte Denkmäler, v, p. 200. Abhandlungen des arch.-epigr. Seminars der Universität Wien, VIII (1890), pp. 141, 142. Bie, Kampfgruppe und Kämpfertypen, p. 91. On the representations of Capaneus: Benndorf, Das Heroon von Gjölbaschi-Trysa, p. 193.

723 (18). Head of Vespasian.

721 (23). Head of Titus.

> The restorations include the bust, the pedestal, and the end of the nose of each.

These two portraits show clearly the family likeness between father and son, and yet also indicate their difference of character. The head of Vespasian, both in form and expression, reveals a certain degree of severity, while mildness is the distinguishing characteristic of the Titus.

> Bust of Vespasian: *Bernoulli*, Röm. Ikonographie, II, 2, T. IX, p. 22, No. 1. — For the bust of Titus: *Bernoulli*, II, 2, p. 33. — For the two portraits: *Braun*, Ruinen und Museen, p. 625, No. 12.

725 (16, 726 (24). Caryatids.

> Found in 1761 at Monte Porzio, along with two other Caryatids (Nos. 727, 728) now in the room to the right of the portico (p. 12). The Dionysos of the Vatican (No. 327) was found in the same place, and the reports of the excavation are cited in its description (vol. I, p. 233). In all four Caryatids the head-baskets, the front of the feet, and the plinths are modern. The ancient heads remain only in Nos. 725 (16) and 728 (97), in the one of which the nose and chin, in the other the point of the nose have been restored. The arms are all modern, except the left arm of No. 726 (24).

The modern restorer has completed the four figures as Canephoræ, or detached basket-bearers. But this conception has been shown to be false by the discovery at Eleusis of the torso of a colossal Caryatid (Fig. 33), which, with its lost companions, seems to have formed the model of the Roman sculptor. The head of this figure still bears the χίστη, or round, bandbox-like object which plays so conspicuous a part in the cult of Demeter; and above this is a fragment of a calathos see p. 8), the purpose of which was undoubtedly to support an architrave. Both in the Eleusinian and the Roman examples the diploïdion of the drapery is confined by bands, the intersection of which is covered by a brooch bearing a mask like that of Medusa. The architectonic symmetry of the four Roman Caryatids is impaired by the varying position of the

Fig. 33.

arms. Three of the figures hold both arms above their
heads, while in the fourth (No. 726) the left arm hangs
by her side.

No. 725 (16) in *Cavaceppi*, Raccolta di statue, III. 28. *Gerhard*,
Antike Bildwerke, T. 94 (right); Prodromus, p. 337. *Clarac*, III,
Pl. 442, No. 807 (left). — No. 726 (24) in *Gerhard*, Ant. Bildwerke, T. 94 (left). *Clarac*, III, Pl. 938F, No. 807A. To the references given in *Friederichs-Wolters*, Bausteine, No. 1558, must
be added Arch. Zeitung, XXXVII (1879), p. 66, No. 390. — For the
Caryatid of Eleusis, see *Michaelis*, Ancient Marbles in Great Britain, p. 242, No. 1. Comp. Athenische Mittheilungen, XVII (1892),
p. 137.

Room to the Right of the Portico.

727 (91), 728 (97). **Caryatids from Monte Porzio.**
See Nos. 725, 726.

No. 727 (91) in *Clarac*, Pl. 442, No. 807 (to the right).

729 (94). **Relief of a Victory sacrificing a Bull.**

The head, left arm, right forearm, and the upper part
of the right wing of the goddess are modern, as are also
the head and neck of the bull.

The restoration is a mistaken one. Other and better-
preserved examples show that the goddess held the
muzzle of the ox with her left hand, while dealing him
the fatal blow with her right hand in the shoulder, just
above the spot where the trickling blood is shown in the
present example. The composition, which appears in
frequent examples and with many modifications, seems
to be a development of a group in relief in the balustrade
of the Temple of the Wingless Victory at Athens (comp.
No. 161).

Zoega, II, 60. *Lajard*, Recherches sur le culte de Vénus,
Pl. XI, 3, p. 176. Comp. Arch. Zeitung, VIII (1850), p. 207. *Brunn*,
Geschichte der griech. Künstler, I, p. 418. Ann. dell' Inst., 1865,
p. 143. *Friederichs-Wolters*, Bausteine, Nos. 1440, 1441. Journal
of Hellenic Studies, VII (1886), pp. 273 et seq. Rheinisches Museum,
XLII (1887), p. 515.

Interior of the Main Building.

To the left of the staircase, —

730 (9). Rome seated on trophies, a relief.

> The restorations include the index-finger of the left hand, the upper part of the staff held in the same hand, the right arm (except the elbow), the whole of the right leg, and the helmet crushed by the right foot; also, apparently, the neck, the right shoulder, and the upper part of the right breast. The only ancient portions of the circular temple in the background are the piece of the podium in direct connection with the goddess and the column-base seen below her elbow. The head, with the nose, lips, and parts of the helmet restored, is old, but does not belong to the body. It seems too small in proportion and is essentially similar to the emotional Pallas type described under No. 107.

The relief obviously belonged to a public monument of victory, probably of the Hadrian period. The figure of Rome may be completed from coins, where she is seen supporting a Victory on her outstretched right arm and holding a spear in her left hand.

Zoega, I, 31. Comp. *Braun*, Ruinen und Museen, p. 627, No. 15.

Adjacent, —

731 (11). Tombstone of Tiberius Julius Vitalis.

The bust of the deceased, who was obviously a butcher by trade, originally occupied the middle of the stone, the right side of which is missing. His name is inscribed on the lower part of the bust. To the left is a full-length figure of the deceased, in the act of splitting open a swine's head with a cleaver, while other portions of the slaughtered animal hang above him. The inscription MARCIO. SEMPER. EBRIA ('Marcio the constantly intoxicated') in the middle of the slab is difficult to explain. Perhaps it had originally nothing to do with the tombstone but was added by some one in mockery of a tippling lady of his acquaintance.

Zoega, i, 28. Berichte der sächs. Ges. der Wiss., 1851, T. 13, 1, pp. 352 et seq. Corpus inscr. lat., vi, 2, No. 9501. Jahrbuch des Arch. Instituts, iv (1889). Arch. Anzeiger, pp. 101, 102. Athen. Mittheilungen, xvii (1892), p. 202, No. 2. *Daremberg et Saglio*, Dictionnaire des antiquités, i, 2, p. 1159.

On the first landing of the staircase, —

732 (SS5). Fragment of a Frieze with the Sons of Niobe.

The entire left half of the slab has been restored; also the right arm, the right leg below the knee, and most of the left leg below the knee of Artemis, the right forearm of the dead Niobide, and other unimportant parts.

The old part of the relief shows Artemis, about to speed an arrow from her bow; a son of Niobe, on his right knees, throwing back his head in an ecstasy of pain, and grasping with his right hand the wound in his neck; and, finally, the back of the head, the upper part of the right arm, and the left arm of another son of Niobe, who is already dead. Better-preserved replicas show that the last lay across a rock, with his head and arms dangling. The figures show a character similar to Attic types of the best period (5th cent. B. C.); and it is by no means unlikely that the relief is a reproduction, with some re-arrangement and modification, of the representation of the legend of Niobe with which Pheidias adorned the throne of the Olympian Zeus.

Zoega, ii, 104. *Stark*, Niobe, T. iii. 3, pp. 173-175. Berichte der sächs. Gesellschaft der Wissenschaften, 1877, T. v, 2, pp. 76, 78-81. *Baumeister*, Denkmäler des klass. Alterthums, iii, p. 1680, Fig. 1760. Comp. *Friederichs-Wolters*, Bausteine, No. 1867; Jahrbuch des Arch. Inst., ii (1887), p. 172. *Hauser*, Die neu-attischen Reliefs, p. 74, No. 105. *Furtwaengler*, Masterpieces, pp. 43, 44.

733 (SS9). Relief of the Giant Sinis.

The restorations include the left arm (except the hand) and the upper left corner of the slab with the ends of the two outer branches of the tree.

A powerful and savage-looking man, with a defiant stare, is represented seated on a rock and encircling with his left arm a tree growing alongside. His left hand holds his right knee. A serpent is crawling up the rock. The most likely explanation of this figure is that it represents Sinis, the terrible giant of the Isthmus of Corinth, who tied travellers to the tops of pine-trees which he had bent to the earth by his prodigious strength and then killed them by letting the trees spring back to their original position. Theseus put an end to his life and his ravages when passing the isthmus on his way from Troizene to Athens. The left side of the slab, now lost, probably represented Theseus in the act of talking with Sinis before the beginning of the combat. Possibly the relief belonged to a cycle celebrating the feats of Theseus. The figure of the giant is not only most happily conceived but is also marked by extreme vigour of execution.

Römische Mittheilungen, I (1886), pp. 247-252. A survey of the bibliography referring to this bas-relief is given in *Milani*, Il mito di Filottete, p. 89, note 3.

734 (590). **Colossal Comic Mask**, relief in rosso antico.

This mask was apparently fixed to the wall of a bath, where the holes in the mouth-piece served for the admission or escape of heated air.

Beschreibung Roms, II, 2, p. 511, No. 5. *Braun*, Ruinen und Museen, p. 631, No. 20.

On the second landing, —

735 (591). **Relief of Thanatos (?).**

The restorations include the neck, the left forearm and attribute, the left leg, the right foot and the rocky ground below it, and the gable which rises above the frieze with its vases and garlands. A vertical strip at each end of the slab, including in each case the outermost column with the section of the frieze above it, is also modern. The head, which is of an Apollo type, is ancient (except the nose), but does not seem to belong to the figure.

A graceful winged youth stands in a languid attitude, with his legs crossed, before a building adorned with pilasters. The most obvious interpretation sees in it a personification of Thanatos or Death. If this hypo-

thesis be justified, the left hand must have held an inverted torch, the emblem of death (comp. No. 185), while
the relief probably comes from the façade of a tomb. The
amphora, which stands on a lofty pedestal beside the
figure, may refer to the libations in honour of the dead.

Zoega, ii, 92, Beschreibung Roms, iii, p. 511, No. 6.

**736, 737 (593). Two Reliefs of the Puellæ Fausti-
nianæ.**

The so-called Puellæ Faustinianæ were the bene-
ficiaries of the fund, established by Antoninus Pius in
honour of his deceased wife Faustina, to provide poor
girls of free parents with annual grants of grain or money.
Marcus Aurelius established two similar endowments,
one on the marriage of his daughter Lucilla with Lucius
Verus (164 A.D.), the other after the death of his wife,
the younger Faustina (175 A. D.). These two reliefs
seem to refer to the earlier foundation of Marcus Aurelius. The first represents the distribution of the grant.
The girls draw near a platform, on which stand the empress and a younger female figure. The former, who may
be recognized as the wife of Marcus Aurelius by the profile (so far as it remains) and by the arrangement of the
hair, pours the grain out of a cylindrical vessel into the
lap of the girl nearest her. The features of the other
figure are undistinguishable, but we may assume that it
is Lucilla, playing the part of Proserpine to her mother's
Ceres. The other relief shows a procession of girls, some
of whom hold garlands, moving from right to left, or
in the opposite direction to those in the first relief.

Zoega, i, 32, 33. Comp. Ann. dell' Inst., 1844, p. 20. *Braun*,
Ruinen und Museen, p. 632, No. 21. On the empresses in the character of Δημήτηρ νέα: Corp. inscr. gr., i, No. 1073, ii, No. 2815;
as Δηὼ νέη; iii. No. 6280, B 6.

Over the third landing, —

738 (595), 739 (599). Two Reliefs of Dancing Girls.

These two reliefs, obviously intended to form pendants to each other, were used to fill the panels of a wall,

thus serving a decorative rôle usually performed by paintings. That to the left shows a girl advancing and playing
on the tambourine, a favourite subject of neo-Attic art.
The girl on the other slab seems to be hovering in the
air rather than dancing; she is playing on the cymbals.
It has been contended that the first figure is derived from
a type of Aphrodite of the fifth century B. C., discussed
under No. 915. If, however, this be the case, it must be
assumed that this motive had been represented and modified in painting before being used in relief; for the drapery of the two figures now before us is rendered in an
undisguisedly pictorial manner.

Magnan, La città di Roma, I, T. 67, 68. *Zoega*, I, 19. Comp.
Welcker, Alte Denkmäler, IV, p. 152, p. 156, note 16. *Hauser*,
Die neu-attischen Reliefs, p. 13, No. 11. Fünfzigstes Programm
zum Winckelmannsfeste der Arch. Gesellschaft zu Berlin (1890),
pp. 117, 118.

740 (902). **Relief from a Tomb.**

> The ruins of the tower-like tomb which this relief
> helped to adorn may still be seen in the Vigna dei Sereni,
> to the right of the Tivoli road. All the heads, both of
> men and animals, are modern. The restorations also in-
> clude the left hand and the right forearm of the man to
> the left; the left hand, the larger part of the mask, and
> the left foot of the youth; part of the thyrsos (from the
> bow upwards); and other unimportant parts.

As reliefs of this kind generally stand in an intimate
relation to the occupants of the tombs they decorate, we
shall probably make no mistake in identifying as the deceased the figure to the left of the table, clad in tunic
and mantle. The youth standing opposite to him, clothed
in a tunic only and holding a large theatrical mask with
both hands, seems to be a servant. On a table between
the two figures stand a hoop garnished with little rings
and a bird. The latter, placed on a small square pedestal, is probably to be interpreted as artificial, not
alive. A thyrsos leans against the table, while on the
ground lie a goat and a hare (or rabbit), the latter to the
right of the principal figure. The round object above the

hare seems to be a discus or quoit. Though several of
the details in this relief cannot be explained with absolute certainty, the general purport of it is plain. It
represents the favourite pursuits of the departed Roman.
The thyrsos, the goat, and the mask show that he honoured
Bacchus, not only as the country gentleman's deity but
also as the representative of the dramatic art. The hoop
and the discus typify the gymnastic exercises and games
with which he improved his muscle. The animal couched
behind him, if a hare, testifies to his love of the chase;
if a rabbit, it probably means that he kept rabbits as pets,
a custom known to have prevailed in Italy as early as
the time of Varro.

The entire mausoleum with the bas-relief is reproduced in
S. Bartoli, Antichi sepolcri, T. 48. The bas-relief alone: *Zoega*,
I, 25. *Penna*, Viaggio pittorico della Villa Adriana, III, 52. Comp.
Braun, Ann. dell' Inst., 1840, p. 135; Ruinen und Museen, p. 634,
No. 23. — For the hoop: *O. Jahn*, Ad Persii Sat., III, 51. Berichte
der sächs. Gesellsch. der Wiss., 1854, p. 255, note 51. — For
the rabbit, see *Hehn*, Kulturpflanzen und Hausthiere, 4th ed.,
pp. 371 et seq.

Upper Floor.
First Room.

711 (918). Statue of a Satyr with a wine-skin.

> Restorations: the point of the nose, the thumb and
> forefinger of the right hand, the mouth of the wine-skin,
> the legs, the trunk of the tree, and the plinth.

The Satyr, as is shown by his faltering gait and inane
smile, is drunk and consequently is allowing the good
liquor to escape from the skin. The statue obviously
served as a fountain-figure, and the wine-skin was tra-
versed by a channel for a jet of water. Comp. the statue
of Silenus, opposite (No. 924 of the Museum.

Clarac, IV, Pl. 740C, No. 1730. Comp. *Friederichs-Wolters*,
Bausteine, No. 1505.

712 915). Eros bending his Bow, a freely restored
statue.

Clarac, iv, Pl. 644B, No. 1471C. Comp. *Schwabe*, Observationum archæologicarum particula, i (Dorpat, 1869), p. 1A.

743 (909). Base or Altar, with Apollo and his attributes.

The idyllic character of the rustic chapels and the sacred groves connected with them furnished, from the Hellenistic period onwards, numerous motives both for poetry and for the plastic arts. The front of this stone represents a sanctuary of that kind dedicated to Apollo and consisting of an architrave borne by two Corinthian columns. Beside the columns grows a laurel tree, the branches of which extend above the architrave. In front stands Apollo, grasping the strings of his testudo, or lyre, with his left hand, and holding the plectron in his right. Beside him rests his quiver, one compartment of which holds his arrows, the other his griffin-headed bow. The vase standing on the architrave is presumably a votive offering to the god. The left lateral face of the block represents a richly ornamented tripod, on the foot of which perches a raven, a bird sacred to Apollo. On the right face are shown a pitcher and a cratera, vessels of libation such as frequently occur in monuments of this kind. At the back (at present concealed from view) is a griffin, looking backwards, another animal sacred to Apollo. As the upper part of the block is wanting, it is impossible to decide whether it is a base or an altar.

Zoega, ii, 98. Comp. *Braun*, Ruinen und Museen, p. 640, No. 28. — With regard to the rustic sanctuaries and the sacred trees, see *Helbig*, Untersuchungen über die campanische Wandmalerei, pp. 297 et seq.

744 (906). Statue by Stephanos.

Found in 1769 (Anecdota litteraria ex MSS. cod. eruta, iii, Romæ, 1774, p. 468). The restorations include the entire upper part of the skull, a great part of the hair-fillet, the curls on the forehead, the end of the nose, the right arm, the front of the left forearm and the front of the right foot, the toes of the left foot (except the little toe), and a large part of the plinth.

The inscription on the stump informs us that this statue is a work of Stephanos, a pupil of Pasiteles. The school of which it is the fruit can be traced through three generations. It begins, so far as we know, with Pasiteles, a contemporary of Pompey, who worked in a great variety of materials (marble, silver, bronze, gold, and ivory) and also distinguished himself as a writer on art. His pupil Stephanos, whose activity extended into the first century of the Christian era, we know by the present statue and by a passing reference in Pliny (Nat. Hist., 36, 33). Menelaos, a pupil of Stephanos, is known by a group in the Museo Boncampagni (No. 887). The importance and artistic skill of this school have recently been often greatly over-rated. The artists who composed it dealt more in reproductions than in original creations. They copied types of the most diverse epochs and sometimes went so far as to mix in one and the same work the most incongruous materials. Thus they would give to the figures they copied heads which had nothing to do with them, and would combine, in more or less mechanical groups, figures which were originally entirely independent of each other. The type of head in this statue of Stephanos, the shape of the body, with its high shoulders and abnormally vaulted breast, the attitude, and the whole effect may be explained in the most natural manner, if we assume that it is a copy of a Greek original of the middle of the fifth century. The only claim to originality that can be made in favour of Stephanos is that, voluntarily or involuntarily, he has toned down and smoothed away the crude freshness with which the surface was treated in the archaic original. As the statue shows close kinship with the sculptures of the Temple of Zeus at Olympia, and as it suggests the worker in bronze by the sharply defined edges of its planes, it seems not unlikely that the original which Stephanos reproduced was a bronze statue of the Peloponnesian school. Like the sculptures of Olympia, it doubtless owes its origin to the Peloponnesian art before Polycleitos, a period of which Agelaïdas of Argos is for us the chief representative. It may possibly represent the ideal figure of a successful athlete. The fillet round the head would fit in admirably with this hypothesis. It is easy to imagine that the hands held the strigil, oil-flask, sponge, or other articles used in the palæstra.

Ann. dell' Inst., 1865, Tav. d'agg. D, pp. 58 et seq. *Kekulé*, Die Gruppe des Künstlers Menelaos, T. II, 2, pp. 20 et seq. *Overbeck*, Geschichte der gr. Plastik, II³, p. 413a. *Baumeister*, Denkmäler des klass. Alterthums, II, p. 1191, Fig. 1391. The best reproductions of this statue are found in Arch. Zeitung, xxxvi (1878), T. 15, pp. 123 et seq., and in *Brunn und Bruckmann*, Denkm. griech. und röm. Sculptur, No. 301. See also *Friederichs-Wolters*, Bausteine, No. 225, and *Loewy*, Inschriften gr. Bildhauer, No. 374. Comp. Athenische Mittheilungen, IX (1884), pp. 250 et seq. Römische Mittheilungen, II (1887), pp. 98, 99. Fünfzigstes Programm zum Winckelmannsfeste der Arch. Gesellschaft zu Berlin (1890), pp. 117, 118.

In the middle of the room, —

745 (905). **Seated Figure of Apollo.**

The restorations, made by Cavaceppi, include the head and neck of Apollo, both his hands, his right knee, his left foot, the serpent, the tongue of the lion, and a few other unimportant parts. Cavaceppi, in accordance with a frequent custom of his, has, in order to give the new head an appearance of antiquity, broken off the nose and then stuck it on again.

Apollo is here represented as the Pythian God, seated on a tripod, with the Delphic omphalos as his footstool. In his right hand he may have held a cup, in his left a twig of laurel. The tripod and omphalos are covered with a coarse, net-like woollen covering and the omphalos is encircled with a broad ribbon. The object in low relief between the omphalos and the stand of the tripod is obscure. Some authorities take it for a lustration vase; others see in it a padlock, used for fastening the cover of the tripod and omphalos. Below the tripod couches a lion. The part of the covering at the back of the tripod (to the left) shows a smooth, parallelogram-shaped object in low relief, of which no one has succeeded in offering a satisfactory explanation.

Müller - Wieseler, Denkmäler der alten Kunst, ii, 12, No. 137. *Overbeck*, Kunstmythologie, iv, pp. 231 et seq.; Atlas, xxiii, 30. To the bibliography given by Overbeck must be added *Guigniaut*, Relation de l'antique. Pl. 75, No. 280 e, and *Braun*, Ruinen und Museen, p. 699, No. 92.

Fifth Room, on the side facing the garden-wall, —

746 (960). **Relief-Portrait of a Man.**

     The left side and the upper part of the background have been restored.

In the 16th century this relief belonged to Cardinal Jacopo Sadoleto (d. 1547), who believed it to be a portrait of Persius, the satirist. It is scarcely necessary to offer a serious refutation of this belief, which prevailed universally down to the time of Winckelmann. Aulus Persius Flaccus died in A.D. 62, before reaching the age of thirty, while our head is the portrait of a man of a much more advanced time of life. Besides, Persius undoubtedly followed the custom of his time in having a smooth-shaven face, instead of wearing a full beard. The delicate but somewhat dry execution of the relief points to the time of Hadrian or the Antonines. The chaplet of ivy on the head by no means necessitates the supposition that it is the portrait of a poet. On the contrary, it may just as well be a symbol of the 'New Dionysos' (comp. No. 221), in which case the head might be a portrait of a victorious sovereign or general.

     The earliest reproduction of this relief is found in *Fulvius Ursinus*, Imagines, p. 46. *Bellori*, Illustrium philosophorum, poetarum, rhetorum, et oratorum imagines, T. 58. *Zoega*, ii, 115. Comp. *Winckelmann*, Geschichte der Kunst, xi, 3, § 6. *Braun*, Ruinen und Museen, p. 676, No. 60.

747 (957). **Relief in palombino** (comp. No. 454).

     Discovered, it would appear, in the 16th century. At the Palazzo Farnese in the 17th century.

This relief belongs to the same category and suggests the same remarks as the Tabula Iliaca (No. 454). In the upper part Heracles is depicted, resting on a huge lion's skin and holding the scyphos in his left hand, while Satyrs and Bacchantes sport around him. The hero has evidently been disturbed in his repose by the indecent conduct of a Satyr behind him, from whose attacks a Bacchante is trying to protect herself with her thyrsos. Heracles turns himself heavily and with an expression of annoyance towards this couple, while a youthful Satyr seizes the opportunity to take a hearty draught from his scyphos. Nearly all the figures are indicated by inscriptions. In the lower part of the relief we see Nike about to pour out wine for a draped female figure, holding a torch in her left hand. Behind this woman steps forward Heracles, extending a cup in his right hand to share in the liberality of Nike. In front of Nike stands a burning altar, adorned with reliefs of Apollo playing the cithara and two Muses, Graces, or Horæ. The scene, therefore, takes place in a sanctuary of Apollo; and the particular sanctuary intended is, as we learn from the inscription on the tripod-stand in front of Heracles, the Theban temple of the Ismenian Apollo, of which Heracles was the priest (δαφναφόρος) when a boy. It is hard to determine whether the torch-bearing woman is Alcmene, the mother of Heracles, or a priestess of the Ismenian Apollo. The prose inscriptions on the pillars enclosing the lower part of the relief and the hexameters on the plinth give a résumé of the labours of Heracles.

O. *Jahn*, Griechische Bilderchroniken, T. v, pp. 6-8 (where all the earlier bibliography is collected), pp. 39-53, 61, 62-64, 68-75, 78 et seq., 82, 83, 84 et seq., 88, 89, 123. Comp. *Roscher*, Lexikon der griech. und röm. Mythologie, I, p. 2251.

748 (953). **Herma of Quintus Hortensius**, with an inscription.

Found about 1767. The nose and parts of the ears, upper lip, and chin are restored.

According to the inscription on the breast, accepted by the best epigraphists as undoubtedly authentic, this herma represents Quintus Hortensius (114-50 B.C.), the foremost orator of Rome before Cicero entered public life and long the rival of the latter. It is, unfortunately, a very mediocre work and probably gives us no very complete idea of the great lawyer it represents.

Bernoulli, Römische Ikonographie, T. VI, p. 98. Ann. dell' Inst., 1882, Tav. d'agg. L, pp. 61-70. *Baumeister*, Denkmäler des klass. Alterthums, I, p. 704, Fig. 762.

749 (952). Bronze Statuette of the Apollo Sauroctonos.

Found in a vineyard below the Church of S. Balbina.
The tree and lizard are modern.

Although the execution of this statuette leaves much to be desired 'the legs, *e.g.*, being too large), it deserves attention because made of the same material as its original, the Apollo Sauroctonos of Praxiteles. Comp. No. 194.

Rayet, Mon. de l'art antique, II, Pl. 47. *Baumeister*, Denkmäler des klass. Alterthums, III, p. 1400, Fig. 1550. Comp. *Winckelmann*, Geschichte der Kunst, VII, 2, § 21, XI, 3, § 17 (with the commentaries of Meyer-Schulze); Mon. ant. ined., II, p. 46. *Braun*, Ruinen und Museen, p. 676, No. 61. *Friederichs-Wolters*, Bausteine, No. 1214 (where it is erroneously stated that this statue is published in *Winckelmann*, Mon. ant. ined., T. 40, and in *Clarac*, Pl. 486A, No. 905E). *Overbeck*, Kunstmythologie, IV, p. 235, No. 3.

750 (951). Bust of Isocrates, with an inscription.

The end of the nose and the shoulders are modern.

That this portrait was originally in the form of an ordinary bust is shown by the fact that the cartouche is enclosed by raised edges — a phenomenon never seen in an ancient herma. The hermetic form it now bears was given to it by the modern restorer, who wished to make it a match to the above - described herma of Hortensius (No. 748). The two portraits have, however, nothing to do with each other, differing both in the kind of marble and in the method of execution. The expression of the well-formed head of Isocrates (436-338 B.C.) shows most distinctly his constitutional timidity, which prevented him from delivering his orations in public and confined his activity for the most part to the teaching of rhetoric and the composition of epidictic orations for others.

Visconti, Iconografia greca, I, T. XXVIIIA, 3, 4, p. 324. *Baumeister*, Denkmäler des klass. Alterthums, I, p. 762, Fig. 813. Comp.

Ann. dell' Inst., 1882, pp. 61-63, 68. *Brunn und Arndt*, Griech.
und röm. Portraits, No. 135. Comp. Ann. dell' Inst., 1882, pp. 61-
63, 68.

751 (949). Bronze Statuette of Pallas.

> Formerly belonged to Queen Christina of Sweden.
> The right arm and the plinth have evidently been
> restored.

This statuette reproduces one of the types derived
from the Athena Parthenos of Pheidias. It differs from its
famous original in the ornamentation of the helmet, the
shape of the ægis, the arrangement of the drapery, and
the attitude (comp. particularly No. 870). The effect is
injured by the fact that the lower part of the statuette
has been broken off and very clumsily re-united with the
upper part.

> *Causeus*, Romanum Museum, I, sect. II, T. XVI. *Montfaucon*,
> L'antiquité expliquée, I, 1, p. LXXIX, 3, p. 319. *Claräc*, III, Pl. 457,
> No. 845. *F. Lenormant*, La Minerve du Parthénon (extr. from the
> Gazette des Beaux-Arts, 1860), p. 28. Comp. *Braun*, Ruinen und
> Museen, p. 677, No. 62. Abhandlungen der philol.-hist. Klasse
> der sächs. Gesellschaft der Wissenschaften, VIII (1883), p. 576d.
> It is not the case that this statuette has been reproduced in the Codex
> Pighianus (Ber. der sächs. Ges. der Wiss., 1868, p. 181, No. 26):
> Monatsberichte der Berliner Akademie, 1871, p. 461, No. 2.

Over the door, —

752 (948). Relief of a Satyr and a Mænad.

> The restorations include the lower part of the Mænad
> (from the girdle downwards), the lower part of the Sa-
> tyr's left leg, and the legs of the panther, except the
> upper part of the right fore-leg.

A horned Satyr and a Mænad are performing a wild
Bacchic dance; between them is a panther. The Mænad
brandishes a thyrsos with her right arm, held high above
her head. The Satyr holds in his right hand a staff surrounded with three disks, which apparently is one of the
wands used in the game named cottabos. With his left
arm he swings a wine-cup, through the handle of which
he has passed his forefinger, as was usual in this game,
when the wine was thrown out of the cup. The cottabos

differs considerably from the form familiar to us from
bronze examples of it that have been preserved and also
from the paintings on Attic vases; but this may be explained by the fact that our relief dates from a period
in which the game of cottabos had long been out of fashion, so that the artist had no clear idea of the implements
used in it. The band on the upper part of the relief,
adorned with boucrania, rosettes, and pateræ, suggests
that it may have formed part of a frieze.

Müller - Wieseler, Denkmäler der alten Kunst, II, 53, 544.
Philologus, XXVI, T. IV, 4, p. 237, where the entire bibliography is
given in note 148. *Baumeister*, Denkmäler des klass. Alterthums,
II, T. XVIII, Fig. 931, p. 848. Comp. *Friederichs-Wolters*, Bausteine,
No. 1883. Römische Mittheilungen, I (1886), p. 242. *Hauser*, Die
neu-attischen Reliefs, p. 108, No. 44.

752 A (945). Alabaster Figure with Bronze Head of Pallas.

> Head and body are both ancient, but do not belong
> to one another. The sphinx and griffin on the helmet
> are modern.

This admirably executed head reproduces a type of
Athena, created by an artist of the Pheidian school,
which is best represented by a statue in the Hope Collection. It shows, however, certain slight modifications
of this type, as, *e.g.*, in lacking the side-locks and showing more of the ears.

Clarac, Pl. 462 C, No. 902. Comp. *Furtwaengler*, Masterpieces,
p. 78.

753 (942). Statuette of Diogenes.

> The restorations include the nose, both arms from
> the biceps downward, nearly the whole of the left leg,
> the lower part of the right leg, the feet, the stump, the
> dog, and the plinth.

The whole movement of the body shows that the
figure rested on a staff held in the left hand. Its identification with Diogenes is probably correct. On the one hand
the statuette exhibits the same physique and stooping
form as an authenticated relief of Diogenes (No. 809), of

which, however, the head is modern. On the other hand
it agrees perfectly with the traditional conception of this
philosopher. The surly and satirical expression, the keen
and observant glance, the unkempt hair and beard, the
poorly nourished body, unimproved by the exercises of
the palæstra, — all these traits admirably suit the man
who ruthlessly carried out in daily life the theory of An-
tisthenes (see No. 284) that the absence of desire is the
highest good, who held himself above the ordinary conven-
tions of society, and who was styled by Plato 'a Socrates
run mad'. The careful realism with which the body in
particular is executed proves that the original was not
produced in the lifetime of Diogenes (d. 323 B.C.) but
more probably in the time of the Diadochi. It is hardly
likely that Diogenes exhibited himself to the public in a
state of utter nudity as in the statuette; he probably wore
some rags at least. The sculptor, however, represented
him as naked in order to express even in the forms of
his body the individuality of the cynic philosopher.

To the bibliography given in *Friederichs-Wolters*, Bausteine,
No. 1323, must be added: *Schuster*, Ueber die erhaltenen Porträts
der griech. Philosophen, T. I, 7, 7a, p. 11, No. 7; Berichte der sächs.
Ges. der Wiss., 1878, p. 136, No. 492; *Baumeister*, Denkmäler des
klass. Alterthums, I, p. 428, Fig. 475, 476.

754 (936). Veiled Statuette of Pallas.

The right arm and the drapery that covers it have
been restored.

The goddess stands holding her shield against her
breast with her left hand, while her raised right hand
probably rested on a spear. She is covered with a chiton,
provided with an *apoptygma* or upper fold; this covers
her head and envelops the whole body except the right
arm, which protrudes through the opening at the side.
As the image of Athena Polias was veiled during the
Attic Plynteria and Callynteria, some authorities have
explained the statuette by a reference to this custom. This
interpretation, however, is contradicted by the fact that
the goddess is here represented as standing still, while

the image of Athena Polias seems to have been in a position of attack. The hypothesis that the statuette represents the image of Athena Sciras, which was covered with whitewash during the Scirophoria, is also untenable; for the peculiar veil of the figure before us is certainly not at all the same thing as a coat of whitewash. For the time being the statuette remains an archæological riddle.

Clarac, III, Pl. 457, No. 903. *Gerhard*, Ges. akademische Abhandlungen, I, T. XXIV, 3, p. 245, p. 357, No. 3. *Braun*, Ruinen und Museen, p. 677, No. 63. *Bernoulli*, Ueber die Minervenstatuen, p. 30. With regard to the Athena Polias: *Roscher*, Lexikon der Mythologie, I, pp. 687, 688. *Michaelis*, Alt-attische Kunst, note to p. 8. Jahrbuch des Arch. Inst., VIII (1893), p. 145.

755 (933). Bronze Statuette of Heracles.

Formerly in possession of the Giustiniani. The rock on which the club stands is, perhaps, a restoration.

This statuette is one of the examples which reproduce the same original as the Farnese Heracles. It is, however, favourably distinguished from that colossal work by the more sober rendering of the muscles. The Albani figure is also free from that air of physical weariness which the sculptor of the Farnese statue has so strongly emphasized. The hero rests, but does not appear utterly exhausted. The right hand is placed on the hip, not, as in the Farnese Heracles, behind the back; the left arm does not hang limply down the club, but is held out a little in front, and probably contained some such attribute as the apples of the Hesperides. The original dates certainly from the fourth century B.C. The attempt to ascribe it to Lysippos is confronted by the difficulty that the conception has no striking analogy with any work positively known to be by that master, while many of the replicas show a much less realistic handling than his. The execution of the Albani bronze is so admirable that it seems reasonable to ascribe it to a Hellenistic master.

Galleria Giustiniani, I, 13. Beschreibung Roms, III, 2, p. 515, No. 3. *Stephani*, Der ausruhende Heracles, p. 162 (414), No. 4. *Roscher*, Lexikon der Mythologie, I, p. 2173.

756 (964). Æsop.

The front of the nose and the right shoulder have been restored.

The statues of Æsop are not portraits in the strict sense of the term; like the busts of Homer (comp. Nos. 480-482, 495-497) and the Seven Sages (comp. Nos. 278, 279), they are products of the artist's imagination. The master who created the type now before us held fast to the popular tradition that Æsop was deformed; while in the head he has endeavoured to express the character of the ancient Greek fable, which presented all manner of human experiences in the guise of witty and significant anecdotes. Burckhardt has happily characterized the work before us as an ideal epitome of the witty hunchback. The well-formed forehead shows an unusual intelligence, while the fine vertical and horizontal folds with which it is seamed indicate the mobility of the skin that covers it. The eyes are those of an acute and attentive observer of the world around him. The effective treatment of the pupils is especially noticeable; these are not represented, as was usual in the later Empire, in a mechanical manner, but are indicated by a few light, well-calculated strokes of the chisel. The ironical expression that plays round the finely-formed lips is softened by a certain air of good-nature. The interest excited by the intellectual head reconciles us to the audacity of the artist in representing the deformed body in a state of nudity. The conception and the style of the work prove that this type cannot date farther back than the time of Alexander the Great. It has therefore been suggested that it may have been created by Lysippos or his pupil Aristodemos, both of whom are said to have made statues of Æsop. The intense realism of the work under review would better suit the younger of the two masters; but as the artistic individuality of Aristodemos is entirely unknown to us, it is impossible to prove his connection with it.

Visconti, Iconografia greca, T. XII, vol. I, pp. 153-160. Mon. dell' Inst., III, T. XIV, 2; Ann., 1840, pp. 94-96. *Baumeister*, Denkmäler des klass. Alterthums, I, p. 35, Fig. 38. Comp. *Burckhardt*, Der Cicerone, I⁵, p. 152g. *Friederichs- Wolters*, Bausteine, No. 1324.

Second Room, on the side next the garden, —

757 (991). **Two Fragments of Ancient Reliefs.**

The modern parts of the fragment to the left include the upper part of the skull, the nose, the chin, both hands with their attributes, both legs from the middle of the thigh downwards, the end of the chair-back, and the support of the chair in front. The only ancient parts of the fragment to the right are the lower half of the figure (from the hips downward), the end of the left hand, and the lower two-thirds of the thymiaterion; and these have been freely retouched by the modern restorer.

As these two fragments were found at Tivoli about 1770 at the same time and in the same place, the well-known engraver Piranesi, who sometimes also did a little amateur sculpturing, had the curious notion of uniting them (though obviously having nothing to do with each other) into one whole, placed in a modern frame. The fragment to the left formed part of an early-Greek relief, which still shows many traces of the archaic style. It represents a seated female figure, under whose chair couches a hare; but it is impossible to determine whether it was a votive relief or a tombstone. In the first case the figure would represent Aphrodite, with the hare, an animal sacred to that goddess; in the other case it would simply be a portrait of the deceased, with a household pet. The fragment to the right belonged to an archaistic relief representing a female figure, probably Pallas, advancing towards a thymiaterion (comp. No. 713).

The two bas-reliefs in their present condition: *Raffei*, Saggio di osservazioni sopra un basso-rilievo della Villa Albani, diss. II (Rome, 1821), pp. 21 et seq. *Percier et Fontaine*, Fragments antiques de sculpture, Pl. 3. — For the early Greek fragment: *Zoega*, II, 112. *Müller-Wieseler*, Denkmäler der alten Kunst, II, 24, 257. *Roscher*, Lexikon, I, pp. 399, 410. — For the archaistic fragment (restored): *Quatremère de Quincy*, Le Jupiter Olympien, Pl. I, 1, p. 20. Comp. Beschreibung Roms, III, 2, p. 536. Arch. Zeitung, XXIX (1872), p. 138, note 6. *Kekulé*, Das akademische Kunstmuseum in Bonn, p. 14, No. 39b. *Bernoulli*, Aphrodite, p. 51, No. 49, p. 61. *Hauser*, Die neu-attischen Reliefs, p. 62, No. 90, p. 128.

758 (993). **Education of Dionysos,** fragment of a sarcophagus-lid.

The infant Dionysos throws his arms round the neck
of the Nymph on whose lap he is sitting, as if afraid of
being transferred to the Nymph standing in front of him
with outstretched arms. The charming and perspicuous
composition betokens an admirable original. Behind the
Nymph holding out her arms is another, also looking at
the infant Dionysos. Farther to the right is Silenus, advancing with a mixture of delight and astonishment to
greet the young god. Over his back is seen the upper
part of a youthful Satyr. The female figure at the left
extremity of the fragment, with her back turned to the
principal group, shows that there must have been at least
one other relief on the sarcophagus-lid, relating to the
birth or education of Dionysos (comp. No. 443).

Zoega, II, 73. Comp. Ann. dell' Iust., 1842, p. 28. *Braun,*
Ruinen und Museen, p. 667, No. 53.

759 (985). **Tomb-Relief of an Athenian Knight.**

Found in 1764 in the Vigna Caserta, not far from the
Arch of Gallienus. Pentelic marble. The restorations
(very unskilfully done) include the nose and lower lip
of the standing figure, and the right ear of the horse.

This work is one of the grandest and most beautiful
Greek tomb-reliefs in existence. It is easy to understand how the art-loving Romans transferred it from
Attica to Rome. It is uncertain whether it commemor-
ates one warrior, or several who fell in the same battle.
The size of the slab would well accord with the latter
supposition. The relief represents a youth, who has just
sprung from his horse and holds the rearing animal with
his left hand, while with his right he raises his sword
to deal the fatal blow to his fallen enemy. The latter
tries to protect himself with his left arm, enveloped in
his chlamys. The bridle-reins of the horse and the brandished sword were added in metal. The head of the knight
is not a portrait but an ideal Attic type. The artist has

not paid attention to the condition of life of the subject farther than to represent him, not as nude, but clad
in the chiton and chlamys. the appropriate dress of the
Athenian chivalry. Behind the front of the horse the
relief is very deeply hollowed out. This device makes
the movement of the noble animal appear clearer and
more lifelike, without transgressing the law, observed in
all reliefs of the best period, that the figures should not
project beyond the original plane of the marble block
on which they are carved. This relief seems to belong
to the transition period between the art of Pheidias and
that of the Second Attic School. The sentiment is still
very soberly expressed. It shows itself only in the somewhat compressed lips of the youthful warrior and in the
mouth of his foe, half opened as if to emit a cry of dis-
may. On the other hand the fluttering chlamys of the
victor is draped with an audacity that recalls the frieze
of the Halicarnassian Mausoleum.

Zoega, 1, 51. For the rest of the bibliography, see *Friederichs-
Wolters*, Bausteine, Nos. 1004, 1122. Comp. *Von Wilamowitz-Moel-
lendorff*, Aus Kydathen, p. 85. *Bie*, Kampfgruppe und Kämpfertypen, p. 105.

760 (9SS). Procession of the Gods, an archaistic Relief.

> The restorations include the lower left corner of the
> slab, with the lower part of the altar, and part of the
> right foot and the front of the left foot of Hermes.

Two gods and two goddesses advance towards a burning altar. The leader is Hermes, bearing in his right
hand a simple wand instead of the customary caduceus;
and he is followed by Pallas, Apollo, and Artemis. It
is highly probable that this relief was continued, at least
towards the left, and bore other deities advancing to meet
those named above. The nicety of the archaic style is
strongly exaggerated. The folds of the mantles of the
gods and of the upper part of the drapery of the goddesses
are especially artificial.

Zoega, II, 100. Comp. Ann. dell' Inst., 1860, p. 452. *Hauser*,
Die neu-attischen Reliefs, p. 34, No. 43.

761 (984). Relief of Quintus Lollius Alcamenes.

During the 17th cent. this relief was in the house of a certain Ippolito Vitelleschi (*Reinesius*, Syntagma inscript. latinarum, p. 465, No. 134).

Among the numerous attempted explanations of this relief the most probable is that the seated figure to the left, described by the inscription above as Quintus Lollius Alcamenes, decurio and duumvir, has, with the stylus in his right hand, either just added, or is just about to add the inscription (*titulus*, *elogium*) to the waxen bust (comp. Nos. 673, 674) of his dead son, held in his left hand. The woman in front of Alcamenes, presumably his wife, holds a box of incense (*acerra*) in her left hand and with her right throws a grain of incense into the flame of a burning thymiaterion (comp. No. 713). While her husband occupies himself with the bust of the lost child, she burns incense in his honour.

Zoega, 1, 23. Comp. *Braun*, Ruinen und Museen, p. 668, No. 56. *Benndorf und Schoene*, Die antiken Bildwerke des lateranischen Museums, p. 209.

762 (980). So-called Relief of Leucothea.

The restorations include the nose, lips, and the thumb and forefinger of the right hand of the seated woman; the right hand and the left forearm of the child; and parts of the face and the left hand of the nearest of the three standing women. Part of the ribbon held by the last is also modern.

The former view, which saw in this relief a representation of the education of the young Dionysos by Leucothea, scarcely requires refutation at the present stage of archæological science. All authorities now recognize it as a tomb-relief, in which the deceased is depicted as a happy mother, seated in a chair and caressing her little daughter. A relative or servant hands her a ribbon, either for her own decoration or that of the child. The two other smaller female figures are either older daughters or servant-maids; their outstretched hands seem to express their delight in the gaiety of the little one. The wool-basket below the chair indicates that the deceased was a thrifty and diligent housekeeper.

Though executed in a somewhat formal style, this relief shows a wonderfully delicate feeling for nature. This is illustrated, *e.g.*, in the organic treatment of the right wrist of the tallest of the three standing figures. It is not easy to determine with precision the school to which the monument belongs. The general style recalls that of the archaic Attic reliefs; but, on the other hand, it has also points of contact with a relief found in the island of Paros and with another from Thasos. The chair, the footstool, and the wool-basket were evidently decorated with colours; in their present colourless state, they contrast unpleasantly with the careful and minute plastic treatment of the human bodies, the hair, and the drapery.

Müller-Wieseler, Denkmäler der alten Kunst, ı, 11, 40. *Baumeister*, Denkmäler des klass. Alterthums, ı, p. 383, Fig. 420. *Brunn und Bruckmann*, Denkmäler griech. und röm. Sculptur, No. 228. *Collignon*, Histoire de la sculpture grecque, ı, p. 278, Fig. 141. All the other references are collected in *Overbeck*, Gesch. der griech. Plastik, ı⁴, pp. 230, 231, Fig. 59, p. 296, note 164, and in *Friederichs-Wolters*, Bausteine, No. 243. Comp. particularly Sitzungsberichte der bayerischen Akademie der Wissenschaften, 1870, ıı, 2, pp. 211, 212.

763 (982). Fragment of a Frieze, with two Bacchantes and a Dwarf Silenus.

Formerly in the Palazzo Mattei.

Two women, holding each other by the hand, follow a dwarfish Silenus, playing on the double-flute. The solemn bearing of the two Bacchantes forms a marked contrast to the grotesque figure of the flute-player. The entire relief has been worked over by a modern hand, so that it is difficult to determine all the original motives. The semicircular object in the right hand of the first woman seems to be the remains of a tympanon or tambourine. The animal that the second woman drags after her now appears as a dog; but this form is cer-

tainly to be attributed to the restorer, since all analogy
demands that it should be a roe-deer.

Zoega, ii, 102. Comp. *Braun*, Ruinen und Museen, p. 666,
No. 52. *Hauser*, Die neu-attischen Reliefs, p. 59, No. 82.

764 (977). Relief of the Rape of the Tripod.

> The restorations include the front of Heracles' nose,
> his right arm, the lower part of his legs, the lower part
> of Apollo's legs, and insignificant fragments of the tripod.

This relief represents a scene frequently met with in
monuments of this kind. Heracles is carrying away the
tripod he has stolen from the temple of Delphi and is
overtaken by Apollo, who tries to regain the sacred
utensil. As in most of the reliefs of this nature, the
sculptor has imitated the archaic style. Comp. No. 377.

Zoega, ii, 66. *Welcker*, Alte Denkmäler, ii, T. xv, 28, pp. 299
et seq. All other references are collected in *Stephani*, Compte-rendu
pour 1868, p. 47, No. 83, and in *Overbeck*, Kunstmythologie, iv,
p. 406 B³.

765 (979). Satyrs treading out grapes.

Two young Satyrs, holding with both hands a ring
made of cord or of leather, swing themselves round in a
circle, while treading out the grapes with which the vase
below them is filled to overflowing. To the left dances
another young Satyr, playing on the double-flute and
beating the time with his left foot on the rustic pedal
(κρούπεζα, scabellum). To the right advances Silenus,
bringing another basketful of grapes. The fact that the
objects in the vat and in the basket look like egg-shaped
balls, and not like grapes, is doubtless due to the care-
lessness of the stonecutter. In other and more carefully
executed monuments, reproducing the same composition,
they are clearly characterized as grapes.

Zoega, ii, 87. *Müller-Wieseler*, Denkmäler der alten Kunst,
ii, 40, 476. *Welcker*, Alte Denkmäler, ii, T. vi, 10, pp. 113 et seq.
Baumeister, Denkmäler des klass. Alterthums, iii, p. 1564, Fig. 1627.
Comp. Beschreibung Roms, iii, 2, p. 235, No. 6. Bull. dell' Inst.,
1843, p. 91. *Braun*, Ruinen und Museen, p. 666, No. 51.

766 (975). Archaic Greek Statue.

The restorations include the nose, the left arm, the part of the drapery raised by the left hand, the bare part of the right arm, the hanging ends of the mantle, the feet and lowest part of the legs, and the plinth.

This statue, the surface of which has unfortunately suffered much from too vigorous cleaning, is a Greek work of the sixth century B.C. In pose and style it specially resembles statues found on the island of Delos, which evidently stand in relation to the art of Bupalos of Chios. It reproduces a type frequently employed by early Greek art in the representation of female deities and votive figures (comp. No. 593). The outstretched right hand undoubtedly held a flower. The slight protuberances above the ears appear to have served as supports for a metal diadem, now lost. The hole bored vertically into the top of the head contained the shank of the bronze disk (μηνίσκος), placed over the heads of statues to protect them from the weather and the birds (comp. Nos. 200, 201). The sculptor has accentuated the main features of his composition with great, sometimes even with exaggerated, sharpness, and this suggests that it was intended for some lofty situation, such as the angle of a pediment. In such a position it would be necessary for the fold of the apoptygma, or upper part of the chiton, to be cut as deeply as it is, in order to produce a proper effect as seen from below. The use of figures such as this for the adornment of pediments in archaic times is proved by those in the decoration of the temple of Athene at Ægina. The statues by Bupalos and his brother Athenor, which Augustus placed in the pediment of the temple of the Palatine Apollo (Pliny, Nat. Hist., 36, 13), doubtless belonged to the same category.

Clarac, iv. Pl. 770B, No. 1922A. Mon. dell' Inst., ix, 3; Ann., 1869, pp. 104-129. *Conze*, Heroen- und Göttergestalten, T. 37. Comp. *Bernoulli*, Aphrodite, p. 40, No. 1. — For the figures from Ægina: *Brunn*, Beschreibung der Glyptothek, No. 70, a, b, No. 74, o, f. — On the art of Bupalos: *Collignon*, Histoire de la sculpture grecque, i, pp. 141 et seq. — On Pliny, Nat. Hist., 36, 13: *Robert*, Archæol. Märchen, p. 120. *Collignon*, Op. cit., p. 143.

767 (976). **Relief of Eros in the guise of a Satyr.**

> The restorations include the left arm and almost the whole of the left leg of the Eros, the front part of the thyrsos, parts of the cratera and table, most of the base of the latter, a narrow strip at the right edge of the curtain, and a large piece at the lower right corner of the slab.

If this composition is, as seems likely, of Hellenistic invention, we have before us one of the most ancient examples of a custom which became extraordinarily common in Græco-Roman art — *viz.* the custom of representing Amoretti as the actors in scenes drawn from mythology or from daily life. In this relief Eros appears as a member of the Bacchic thiasos and furnished with a Satyr's tail. He is playfully teasing a panther, by thrusting his thyrsos at it and pushing out his left foot, on which the animal lays its paw as if to stop its motion. The background is occupied by a motive often met with in Hellenistic reliefs, consisting of a curtain hanging from a tree, in front of which is a cratera on a table with feet in the form of lion's claws.

> *Zoega,* II, 88. *Müller-Wieseler,* Denkmäler der alten Kunst, II, 40, 479. *Schreiber,* Die hellenistischen Reliefbilder, T. LXII. Comp. *Braun,* Kunstvorstellungen des geflügelten Dionysos, p. 5; Ruinen und Museen, p. 668, No. 54. *Schreiber,* Die Wiener Brunnenreliefs aus Pal. Grimani, p. 96, No. 52; Abhandl. der phil.-hist. Classe der sächs. Ges. der Wissenschaften, XIV (1894), p. 461.

768 (970). **Statue of Pallas.**

> Found at Orte (Horta). The restorations include the helmet, the nose, almost the whole of the right arm, the left forearm, the lower part of the legs, several of the serpents on the ægis, the wings on the head of Medusa, and the loose ends of the apoptygma.

This statue, which represents the goddess in the altitude of the Palladium — brandishing a spear in her raised right hand —, is, in the main, archaic in its forms. Many details, however, such as the head of Medusa on the ægis, are treated in accordance with a more liberal style of art; and therefore it is impossible to accept the formerly current opinion that the statue is an archaic Greek original. It is, moreover, also difficult to recognize in it an inexact copy of an archaic Greek work, more or less modified by the freer style of art, or even an archaistic statue executed·in harmony with the principles of Greek art. The statue before us is marked by an extraordinary contrast between the skilful representation of the epidermis and the ignorance shown in the treatment of the human body and its proportions. So pronounced a contrast is unknown in Greek art, but finds many analogies in Italic, and especially in Etruscan art. The idea thus suggests itself that this may be a Roman reproduction of an ancient Etruscan bronze. On the one hand the religious traditions of the town of Horta, situated on the south frontier of Etruria, may easily have occasioned such a reproduction; while, on the other hand, we have to remember the lively interest in Etruscan antiquities shown by the Romans of the last century of the Republic and the first of the Empire. It is enough to recollect that in the time of Horace Epist., II, 2, 180), Roman amateurs of art were especially addicted to collecting Etruscan bronze figures.

Winckelmann, Mon. ant. ined., T. 17, II, pp. 18, 19. *Clarac*, III, Pl. 462D, No. 842B. *Müller - Wieseler*, Denkmäler der alten Kunst, I, 9, 34. Comp. *Braun*, Ruinen und Museen, p. 663, No. 47. *Bernoulli*, Ueber die Minervenstatuen, p. 6. Bull. dell' Inst., 1870, pp. 35, 36. *Friederichs - Wolters*, Bausteine, No. 445. Ἐφημερίς ἀρχαιολογική, 1887, p. 137.

769 (967). Relief of Dancing Girls.

The restorations include most of the crowns of both dancers, the left hand of the figure to the left, both hands, the left foot, and the lowest part of the right leg of the other dancer, the rocky ground, and parts of the architectural background. That the restorer has correctly reproduced the original form of the crowns is proved by some remaining fragments of the old ones.

This relief represents two short-skirted damsels, executing a mimic dance in front of a building adorned with two ranges of pilasters. The subject of the dance seems to be the wooing of a lover. One girl stretches out her arms to the other, as if in desire or supplication. As both the hands of the second girl are modern, her attitude is not certainly known, but it seems to have expressed refusal of the other's demands. In other monuments (comp. No. 816) dancers of this kind are crowned with chaplets of upright reeds. In the case before us this adornment is exchanged for curious-looking crowns, apparently formed of metal bands. The originals of these figures, which occur so frequently in ancient monuments, are now supposed to be the Dancing Laconian Women ('saltantes Lacænæ', Pliny, Nat. Hist., 34, 92) of Callimachos. This artist flourished mainly at the time of the Peloponnesian War and was distinguished for his careful attention to details.

Zoega, I, 21. *Visconti*, Museo Pio-Clem., III, Tav. b, II, 4, p. 257. Comp. *Welcker*, Alte Denkmäler, II, pp. 146 et seq. *Braun*, Ruinen und Museen, p. 668, No. 49, p. 696. *Stephani*, Nimbus und Strahlenkranz, p. (471) 111, note 2; Compte-rendu pour 1865, p. 60, No. 3, pp. 63 et seq. *Hauser*, Die neu-attischen Reliefs, p. 97, No. 21. Jahrbuch des Arch. Inst., VIII (1893); Arch. Anzeiger, p. 76. *Furtwaengler*, Masterpieces, pp. 438, 439.

770. Fragment of a Frieze, with reliefs of Aphrodite (or a Nereid) and Eros.

> The restorations include both legs of Eros, the right claw of the sea-dragon, and the head and fore-legs of the sea-horse.

Aphrodite or a Nereid, borne over the ocean by a sea-horse, has grasped the arm of a hovering Eros with her left hand and draws the struggling boy after her through the air. To the left are a sea-dragon and a dolphin, disporting themselves in the waves.

Percier et Fontaine, Fragments antiques de sculptures, Pl. 21. Comp. *Braun*, p. 668, No. 55. *Bernoulli*, Aphrodite, p. 406.

As Rome does not contain many Etruscan urns, it may be interesting to glance at four specimens kept in this room (Nos. 771-771'. The cinerary urns of Etruria, rectangular in form and adorned with reliefs, date from the second and third centuries B.C. and are, with a few

isolated exceptions, the products of a more or less inferior art-industry. The reliefs usually represent scenes of
Hellenic mythology; and their composition seems also
to rest in all essentials on Greek models. The execution,
however, especially in the reproduction of faces and
costume, shows many national traits, while figures from
the Etruscan demonology are often introduced into the
Greek compositions. The covers bear portrait-figures of
the persons whose ashes are contained in the urns. The
heads are often lifelike and full of character, making the
impression of successful portraits, while the bodies are
generally neglected and sometimes very maladroitly foreshortened. The four examples in the Villa Albani seem
to come from Volterra, as they are made of a variety of
alabaster quarried in the neighbourhood of that city.

771 (992). Rape of Helen.

To the left is the Trojan ship, with a sailor in Phrygian dress. On a seat hard by sits Paris, waiting for Helen.
Two servants carry towards the ship a cratera stolen from
the house of Menelaos. Farther to the right is Helen,
making some resistance to the two Trojans who are leading her to Paris. Behind this group is another companion
of Paris, holding an oar in his left hand.

Brunn, I rilievi delle urne etrusche, I, T. 18, 4.

772 (981). Battle of Centaurs and Lapithæ.

Zoega, I, p. 182. *Braun,* Ruinen und Museen, p. 670.

773 (978). Orestes at the Altar of Delphi.

Orestes, his drawn sword in his right hand, kneels
on the altar with one knee, and is attacked by five Furies
armed with swords and torches. To the left of the altar
is Pylades, recoiling in terror from the Furies.

Brunn, I rilievi delle urne etrusche, I, T. 83, 17.

774 (968). So-called Echetlos.

An Attic legend relates that at the battle of Marathon a man armed with a plough-share appeared, slew

many of the Persians, and then vanished. In obedience
to an oracle the Athenians worshipped this warrior as a
hero, under the name of Echetlos or Echetlaios. On this
tradition is based the attempt to identify with Echetlos
the chief figure on this urn, representing a man striking
a fallen warrior with a plough-share. This figure, however, seems more probably an Etruscan demon of death,
who is accomplishing his work of destruction in the
thickest of the fray, the fierceness of which is symbolized
by the Furies at both ends of the relief.

Zoega, I, 40. *Inghirami*, Monum. etruschi, I, 2, T. XIII. Comp.
Ann. dell' Inst., 1837, pp. 264 et seq. *Gerhard*, Prodromus, p. 41,
note 112. — For the bibliography of the legend of Echetlos, see
Roscher, Lexikon, I, p. 1212.

Third Room, towards the garden, —

775 (994). Fragment of a Colossal Relief of Antinous.

Found in 1735 in Hadrian's Villa, near Tivoli (*Ficoroni*, in *Fea*, Misc., I, p. CXXXXIII, No. 51). The restorations include the thumb, forefinger, and middle finger
of the right hand, almost all the left hand with the garland, and the lowest section of the part of the body
covered by the drapery.

As a fragment of a ribbon has been preserved above
the ancient part of the left hand, the restorer was probably justified in placing a garland in it. But this detail
hardly helps us to recognize the subject of the relief; for
we do not know whether Antinous was represented alone
or in a group. This fragment is one of the best specimens of sculpture we possess from the time of Hadrian,
clearly illustrating both the qualities and defects of the
plastic art of that period. The bodily forms and the moral
character of Antinous (see No. 295) are alike admirably
rendered. The execution shows both elegance and care,
but there is a certain lack of spontaneity, especially in
the modelling of the flesh. In order to facilitate trans-
portation, the back of this relief has been hollowed out.

Borioni, Collectanea antiquitatum romanarum (Rome, 1736),
T. IX (without the restorations). *Winckelmann*, Mon. ant. ined.,

T. 180, II, pp. 235-237. *Penna*, Viaggio pittorico della Villa Adriana, III, 55. *Dietrichson*, Antinoos, Pl. v, 12, p. 189, No. 21. *Baumeister*, Denkmäler des klass. Alterthums, I, p. 85, Fig. 89. *Brunn
und Bruckmann*, Denkmäler griech. und röm. Sculptur, No. 368. —
For other references, see *Friederichs-Wolters*, Bausteine, No. 1663.

776 (997). Statuette of a Panisca.

> The restoration of the horns was justified by traces
> left on the head. Further restorations include the tips
> of the ears, the left forearm, hand, and flute; the right
> hand, the lower part of the left leg, the lowest part of
> the right leg, and the plinth. The face has been slightly
> retouched by a modern hand.

This statuette is apparently a reproduction of some
excellent original of the Hellenistic period. The artist
has very cleverly surmounted the difficulty of uniting the
body of a young girl to the legs of a goat, by adroitly
covering the line of transition with a fold of the nebris.
The position of the legs and head betrays unmistakably
the animal side of a Panisca; it is easy to see she can
jump and use her horns. The puffed out cheeks indicate
that the restorer has done rightly in placing a flute in
the hands.

> *Clarac*, IV, Pl. 727, No. 1732. For other references, see
> *Friederichs-Wolters*, Bausteine, No. 1508. Comp. also Ann. dell'
> Inst., 1846, p. 240.

Large Room.

777 (1019). Statue of Zeus.

> According to Clarac (III, p. 34) this statue was found
> in Hadrian's Villa, near Tivoli. The restorations include
> the right arm with the staff, the left hand with the thun-
> derbolt, fragments of the drapery, the right leg below
> the drapery, the left leg from the knee downwards, the
> plinth, the greater part of the eagle (that portion of the
> right wing which touches the drapery is antique), and
> the lower part of the tree-trunk. The head (nose restor-
> ed) is antique but does not belong to the statue and seems
> too small for the body.

The carefully executed statue to which this body
belonged, represented Zeus in a calm attitude. The right

hand probably held a sceptre, but it is not likely that the attribute in the other was a thunderbolt. The mantle, apparently cut in a circular shape, extends from the left arm across the back and legs, while its right end is caught up in front and thrown over the lower part of the left arm. The general arrangement of the drapery and the treatment of the folds remind us of the Menelaos group (see No. SS7). This conception of Zeus must have been a popular one, for there are three other replicas besides the one before us. In comparing this with other types of Zeus reproduced by Græco-Roman art (comp. Nos. 245, 294), the head attached to this body strikes us by its peculiarly mild expression and by the greater smoothness of the hair.

Clarac, III, Pl. 401, No. 678A. Overbeck, Kunstmythologie, II, p. 141, Fig. 15; comp. p. 88, No. 21, p. 140, No. 40.

778 (1018). Alto-Relief representing a Distribution of Grain by Antoninus Pius.

The restorations include the nose, both hands, the lower part of the legs, and the feet of the emperor; the emperor's footstool and one leg of his chair; the head of the goddess behind the emperor and the attribute in her left hand (the end in her fingers ancient); the nose, the left hand, two fingers of the right hand, and part of the baldric of the figure resembling an Amazon. The head of the emperor has been broken off, but certainly belongs to the body with which it has been re-united.

Although the left side of this relief is missing, its meaning can be made out by similar representations on coins. Antoninus Pius is seated on a sella curulis, superintending an extraordinary distribution of wheat. The woman standing on the podium just behind the emperor is Abundantia or Felicitas. The restorer has placed a caduceus in her hand, but the traces left on the upper part of the left arm and the curved end between the figures indicate that the original attribute was much more probably a cornucopia. The Amazon-like figure at the right end of the relief is either Dea Roma or Virtus, the goddess of manly courage (comp. No. 416). As she

wears no helmet and is just about to take off her belt,
she may typify the peaceful mood of the emperor. On
the missing left portion of the monument were depicted
figures receiving bounties from the emperor.

Mon. dell' Inst., IV, 4; Ann., 1844, pp. 155-160. Comp. *Braun*,
Ruinen und Museen, p. 644, No. 31. *Purgold*, Archäol. Bemer-
kungen zu Claudian und Sidonius, p. 27, note 3. *Bernoulli*, Röm.
Ikonographie, II, 2, p. 146, No. 78.

779 (1014). Relief of the Divinities of Delos.

The restorations include part of the pillar to the left;
the right hand and elbow of Leto, the part of the mantle
hanging below her right elbow, and a great part of her
figure between the right hip and the knees; the end of
the nose and the right hand of Apollo; the end of the
nose, most of the left hand, and fragments of the wings
of the Nike.

Apollo advances, in the dress of a cithœrodos, holding his lyre in his left hand and extending a cup in his
right to receive the draught poured out by Nike from the
pitcher she holds aloft. Behind Apollo are his sister Artemis, with a torch in her left hand, and his mother Leto
(Latona), with a sceptre. Adjoining the Nike is a base
adorned with a relief of the Hours or the Graces; and
behind Leto is a pillar, bearing a tripod. The background
is occupied by a Corinthian temple, rising above an
enclosing wall and decorated with a frieze representing
a chariot-race. This has been taken, with much probability, as a free rendering of the sanctuary of Delphi. The
graceful archaic forms, which characterize the figures of
the four deities, are not in the style natural to the sculptor of this relief, but are an artificial imitation of an older
fashion. He has involuntarily fallen into a freer style in
his treatment of the flowing drapery of Artemis. Moreover the Corinthian order, shown in the temple in the
background, did not come into vogue until after the close
of the archaic period. It is, however, none the less probable that this relief, like other similar ones that have
come down to us, goes back to an archaic original, so far,
at least, as the figures of the four gods are concerned. This

may have been a votive relief, dedicated by a lyre-player
who had won a prize in the Pythian Games, and representing the victory-giving god instead of the victorious mortal.
The assumed existence of an early Greek original is
confirmed by a fragment recently acquired by Baron Barracco, which belongs to a relief representing the same
theme and consistently reproducing the peculiarities of
the late-archaic style.

Zoega, II, 99. *Schreiber*, Die hellenist. Reliefbilder, T. xxxiv.
Brunn und Bruckmann, Denkmäler griech. und röm. Sculptur,
No. 344. For other references, see *O. Jahn*, Griechische Bilder-
chroniken, pp. 45-50; *Stephani*, Compte-rendu pour 1873,
pp. 218 et seq.; *Overbeck*, Kunstmythologie, IV, pp. 259 et seq.
Comp. Abhandlungen des arch.-epigr. Seminars in Wien, VIII
(1890), pp. 24-27. — On the Barracco fragment, see *Barracco et
Helbig*, La collection Barracco, Pl. xxxiii a, p. 34.

780 (1013). Alto-Relief of a Youth and his Horse.

> The restorations include the head of the youth (with
> the features of Antinoos), his neck, his right arm, and
> his left foot; the head and neck of the horse, the knee
> of the right fore-leg, and the lower part of the right hind-
> leg; and the whole of the architectural background, ex-
> cept a piece to the left, below the horse, and the lower
> part of the pilaster to the right.

A vigorous youth stands, with his horse, in front of
a wall divided into sections by fluted pilasters. With
his left hand he shoulders a staff or a lance, while his
outstretched right hand doubtless held the metal reins of
the horse. Behind the young man is the lower end of
his scabbard, executed in very low relief. The composition resembles that of an Argive relief and is undoubtedly inspired by a Greek model; the execution,
however, points to the Roman period. Originally the
relief adorned a tomb. A similar relief was attached to
a tomb on the Via Tiburtina and was drawn by Bartoli
in situ. The identification of this latter relief with the
one before us is, however, a mistake, as the youth and
horse were placed differently and turned in the other
direction.

Braun, Ruinen und Museen, p. 643, No. 30. Comp. *Fried-länder*, De operibus anaglyphis in mon. sepulcr. Græcis, p. 43, § 3. *Dietrichson*, Antinoos, p. 192. *Furtwaengler*, Sammlung Sabouroff, I, Einleitung zu den Sculpturen, pp. 36 et seq. — For the Argive bas-relief, see Athenische Mittheilungen, III (1873), T. XIII, pp. 287 et seq. *Friederichs - Wolters*, Bausteine, No. 504. *Furtwaengler*, Masterpieces, p. 230. — For the mausoleum, see *Bartoli*, Antichi sepolcri, T. XLVII.

781 (1012). Statue of Pallas.

According to Clarac (Text, III, p. 189) this statue was found in Hadrian's Tiburtine Villa. The restorations in-clude the nose, the lips, the back of the head, the muzzle of the dog's skin on the head, the right arm and shoulder, the left forearm, the front of the left foot, parts of the ægis and the drapery, and most of the plinth.

The effect of this imposing statue is marred by the fact that the restorer has made the right forearm, pro-jecting from the drapery, too long. We have obviously to do with the copy of a Greek original belonging to al-most the very best period; and the treatment, especially of the folds, seems to indicate that this was a work in bronze. The body is short and thickset. The right arm was supported by a spear; the left hand held another attribute, perhaps a cup or an owl. It has hitherto been assumed that the head-covering was a lion-skin, but that it is rather that of a wolf or of a dog, is proved not only by the absence of a mane at the back of the cap but also by the fact that the extant portion of the muzzle indi-cates that it must have ended in a point. This curious headgear has, accordingly, been very properly recognized as the 'Cap of Hades' (Ἄϊδος χυνέη), which is sometimes shown in ancient art as made of dogskin. Its presence here shows, further, that this statue is the product of a cult in which Athena stood in close relation to Hades, as, *e.g.*, was the case in the sanctuary of Athena Itonia at Coroneia. The forms of the head indicate that the artist was inspired by an early Peloponnesian type, which, however, he has developed and modified with considerable independence. A recent critic has seen in this statue a mixture of the styles of Calamis and Pheidias and has suggested that it may be by Praxias, a pupil of Calamis and a contemporary of Pheidias.

Clarac, III, Pl. 472, No. 898B. *Braun*, Vorschule zur Kunstmythologie, T. 70. *Brunn und Bruckmann*, Denkmäler griech. und röm. Sculptur, No. 226. *Furtwaengler*, Masterpieces, p. 55, pp. 78-81, Fig. 29, 30. To the bibliography in *Friederichs-Wolters* (Bausteine, No. 524) must be added *Baumeister*, Denkmäler des klass. Alterthums, p. 215, Fig. 169, p. 216, Fig. 170; *Roscher*, Lexikon der Mythologie, I, pp. 696, 697; Athen. Mittheilungen, xv (1890), p. 30; *Amelung*, Florentiner Antiken, pp. 9-14.

782 (1011). Relief of Ganymede and the Eagle.

The restorations include the head and left arm (hand ancient) of Ganymede, the body and right talon of the eagle, almost all the rocky ground, and the whole of the background.

This charming and harmonious composition represents Ganymede, seated on a rock and holding a cantharos for the eagle to drink from. The eagle has placed his left claw on the edge of the cantharos, while Ganymede holds his right hand under the head of the imperial bird.

This relief is cited by *Winckelmann*, Pierres de Stosch, p. 59, No. 173. This example, and not that at St. Petersburg as *Stephani* assumes (Compte-rendu pour 1867, p. 192), seems to be figured in *Bartoli*, Antichi Sepolcri, T. 110 (also in *Barbault*, Monum. ant., Pl. 22, and Les plus beaux monuments de Rome, Pl. 25), where it is wrongly called a mosaic. Comp. *Braun*, Ruinen und Museen, p. 645, No. 33. Bull. dell' Inst., 1870, p. 7. *Overbeck*, Kunstmythologie, II, p. 547d.

783 (1009. Relief of Dædalos and Icaros.

The ancient parts of this relief were found, along with No. 388 and fragments of other reliefs, on the slope of the Palatine overlooking the Circus Maximus. All of these reliefs evidently decorated the walls of a room in the Palace of the Cæsars (Bull. dell' Inst., 1870, pp. 65, 66). The following are the only ancient parts: the right foot of Dædalos, the lower end of the support of his work-table, a piece of the floor below the table, the figure of Icaros from the top of the forehead to the middle of the thighs (nose, left eye, right arm, and left hand modern), the root of the left wing, the upper part of the pillar on which Icaros leans his left elbow, a part of the wing standing beside him, and the wall in the background. The restoration, however, is undoubtedly accurate, as it has been made in accordance with a better-preserved replica also in the Villa Albani (No. 807).

This relief, which must reproduce an admirable original, hits off, in the happiest way, the idiosyncrasy of the two personages represented. Dædalos is working at the wings which are to free him from his imprisonment in the Cretan Labyrinth and carry him back to his fatherland. A sharp contrast to the absorbed earnestness of the father is afforded by the figure of his son Icaros, who stands in front of Dædalos, already equipped with his own wings and supporting with his right hand the one under construction. The indifferent expression and listless attitude of the young man shows that he has no adequate conception of the importance of the enterprize before him. The hewn stone wall at once indicates with clearness the nature of the scene of action and forms an unostentatious background, in perfect keeping with the requirements of plastic art.

Winckelmann, Mon. ant. ined., T. 95, ɪɪ, pp. 129, 130. *Millin*, Gal. myth., Pl. 130, 488. *Hirt*, Götter und Heroen, T. 34, 290. *Guigniaut*, Rel. de l'ant., Pl. 198, 702. *Braun*, Zwölf Basreliefs, T. xɪɪ. *Schreiber*, Die hellenist. Reliefbilder, T. xɪ. Comp. *Winckelmann*, Geschichte der Kunst, vɪɪɪ, 2, § 28. *Zoega*, ɪ, pp. 207 et seq. Ber. der sächs. Ges. der Wissenschaften, 1861, p. 336, note 162. *Roscher*, Lexikon der griech. und röm. Mythologie, ɪ, 1, p. 937.

784 (1008). Relief of Heracles and the Hesperides.

In the sixteenth century this relief was preserved on the Monte Giordano, where it was drawn by Pighius (Berichte der sächs. Gesellschaft der Wissenschaften, 1868, p. 183, No. 39). The upper part and the left third of the slab, including the top of the tree above the serpent and almost the whole of the Hesperide to the left, are modern. The only ancient portions of the latter figure are a piece of the left arm and the lower part of the left leg, with the drapery covering it. The nose of the Hesperide to the right and most of the rocky ground are also modern (comp. Arch. Zeitung, xxxɪɪ, 1875, p. 64).

This admirably composed relief seems to reproduce an Attic original of the end of the fifth century B. C.

Its subject is a version of the myth of the Hesperides, especially current in Attica, according to which Heracles obtained the golden apples, not by violence but with the connivance of the daughters of Atlas. The hero is comfortably seated on a rock, using his lion-skin as a cushion, and converses with the Hesperide in front of him. He leans with his right arm-pit on his club, while with his left hand he dangles his quiver by its strap. The confidential terms on which the Hesperide evidently is with the youth convinces us that she will not refuse him the branch of the apple-tree, which she presses to her side with her left arm. The other Hesperide, standing behind Heracles, seems, to judge from the antique part of her left arm, to be about to pluck another branch. No danger threatens the hero on the part of the serpent which guards the apples; for it hangs motionless from the branches of the tree, perhaps lulled into sleep by a magic charm.

Beyer, Hercules ethnicorum (1705), T. 12 (without restorations, after the drawing by Pighius). *Zoega*, II, 64. *Braun*, Zwölf Basreliefs, T. XI. Comp. *Gerhard*, Gesammelte akad. Abhandlungen. I, p. 52, No. 5, p. 83. *Braun*, Ruinen und Museen, p. 646, No. 35. Ann. dell' Inst., 1871, p. 154. *Roscher*, Lexikon der Mythologie, I, pp. 2227, 2228. Abhandl. des arch.-epigr. Seminars in Wien, VIII (1890), p. 134, note 1. Röm. Mittheilungen, IX (1894), p. 72.

785 (1007). Fragment of a Relief of a Bacchante.

> The restorations include the face, the neck, the left arm, shoulder, and breast, half of the right foot, the toes of the left foot, and parts of the drapery. The slab has been cut into an oval form by a modern hand.

A Bacchante advances in frenzy, carrying the hind-quarters of a goat in her left hand and holding a sword with her right arm, bent behind her head. This fragment is one of the best replicas of this frequently occurring type (comp. Nos. 556, 578).

Zoega, II, 106. *Percier et Fontaine*, Fragments antiques de sculptures. Pl. 23. Comp. *Hauser*, Die neu-attischen Reliefs, p. 15. No. 16.

Above the doors, —

786 (1005), 787 (1006). **Pair of Trophies, in high relief.**

Their ancient position was evidently similar to their present one — *i.e.*, under an archway. They probably adorned the two corresponding passages of a triumphal arch. The weapons and armour composing the trophies are grouped with great clearness and taste. Both Roman and barbarian arms are recognizable. Thus the short, thick horns and the two-edged axe are undoubtedly of barbarian origin. A scorpion is represented on a square shield.

Zoega, II, 113. *Percier et Fontaine*, Fragments antiques de sculptures, Pl. 18. Comp. *Braun*, Ruinen und Museen, p. 645, No. 32.

Next Room.

788 (1034). **Herma of Theophrastos.**

> In the sixteenth century this herma was preserved in the Palazzo Massimi, whence it passed into the possession of Dr. Mead, an English physician resident in Rome. On the death of the latter, it was acquired by Cardinal Albani.

The inscription on the shaft informs us that this herma represents 'Theophrastos, the son of Melantas of Eresos' (on Lesbos, who succeeded Aristotle as the head of the Peripatetic School. We see before us a dignified head, wearing just such a superior smile, as would beseem a professor holding a comfortable post and quite conscious of his own ability. The portrait shows that Theophrastos did not shave his face, as began to be the vogue in the time of Alexander the Great, but adhered to the older fashion of letting the beard grow. This detail is worth remembering in discussing the so-called statue of Aristotle in the Palazzo Spada No. 954). The execution is careful but somewhat dry.

Visconti. Iconografia greca. I. T. XXI, 1, 2, p. 245. *Schuster*, Über die erhaltenen Porträts der griech. Philosophen, T. III, 4, p. 19. *Baumeister*, Denkm. des klass. Alterthums, III, p. 1764,

Fig. 1848. — For the earlier bibliography, see Corpus inscr. graec., III, No. 6064. Comp. *Braun*, Ruinen und Museen, p. 651, No. 39. Berichte der sächs. Ges. der Wissenschaften, 1878, p. 137.

789 (1033). Head of Sappho.

> The end of the nose, the lower part of the neck, and the herma are modern. The surface has suffered severely from ruthless scouring.

The identification of this beautiful head is vindicated by its resemblance in profile and headdress to a portrait of Sappho on the earlier coins of Mytilene. It also harmonizes with the idea of the Lesbian poetess that we form from her own poems and from the most authentic traditions. The deep skull and the vigorous features betoken an unusual amount of feeling, will-power, and capacity. The expression of severity is softened by the languishing look of the almond-shaped eyes, of which the left seems slightly less open than the right. The massive chin and the full under-lip reveal a strongly sensuous nature. An attempt has recently been made to bring this type into relation with a statue of Sappho by the Athenian sculptor Silanion (comp. No. 265).

Jahrbuch des Arch. Instituts. v (1890), T. 3, pp. 151 et seq. *Overbeck*, Geschichte der griech. Plastik, II⁴, p. 12, Fig. 136. *Brunn und Arndt*, Griechische und römische Porträts, Nos. 147, 148. *Furtwaengler* (Masterpieces, pp. 66 et seq.) contests the above identification, sees in the head the type of a being connected with Aphrodite, and ascribes its invention to some artist in close relation with Pheidias.

790 (1031). Relief of Orpheus and Eurydice.

> The restorations include both feet of Orpheus, the right foot of Eurydice, and half of the right forearm and the right calf of Hermes. Other replicas, in which the right hand of Hermes is preserved, show that the restorer has given it the correct attitude. He should, however, in compliance with the rules observed in Greek reliefs of the best period, have executed it in much lower relief (comp. No. 759). The relief is carved in Pentelic marble.

According to the beautiful Greek myth, Orpheus, after the death of his wife Eurydice, descended to Hades, charmed the rulers of the underworld by his music, and obtained their permission to lead his wife back to earth, on condition that he should not look round at her until he had crossed the threshold of Hades. Orpheus, unable to resist his longing to see Eurydice, failed to observe this condition; and Eurydice had to return to the world of shades. This last moment is the subject of the relief before us. Orpheus, recognizable by his Thracian bonnet and by the lyre held in his left hand, has just looked round. Eurydice places her left hand tenderly on his shoulder, while he holds her left wrist with his right hand. But Hermes, the conductor of souls, already approaches and lays his left hand on the right arm of Eurydice, to lead her back to the underworld. In every respect the composition breathes the spirit of the best Attic period. The emotional expression is attenuated as much as possible, and indeed is scarcely apparent in the heads. Our comprehension of the scene is mainly due to the significant motions of the characters, which not only clearly pourtray the exact moment chosen by the artist, but also suggest both what has gone before and what will follow. The effect of the relief was doubtless heightened by the use of painting. This is clearly seen in the leathern tags of the boots of Orpheus, which are very slightly indicated by the chisel. This relief is not an original work; and several defects are noticeable in it. Thus the left calf of Hermes is out of drawing, and the right thumb of Eurydice is too short. The example in the Museum of Naples has greater claims to be an original. This latter is more severe in its forms and is fresher in execution than the relief at the Villa Albani, while its general character corresponds more closely to that of Attic sculpture about 410 or 130 B.C. The example before us, however, to judge from the Pentelic marble in which it is carved and from the style of the execution, must also be an Attic work. The original was probably a votive offering in commemoration of the victory of the author of a tragedy on the subject of Orpheus and Eurydice. Comp. No. 635.

Zoega, I, 42. *Roscher*, Lexikon der griech. und röm. Mythologie, I, 1, p. 1422. For other references, see *Friederichs-Wolters*, Bausteine, No. 1198, and Abhandlungen des arch.-epigr. Seminars in Wien, VIII (1890), pp. 130 et seq.

791 (1040). **Head of Socrates.**

Found in 1735 in the so-called Villa of Cicero near Tusculum (Bull. della commissione arch. comunale, X, 1882, p. 224. No. LXIII). The herma has been restored.

This head is the finest portrait of Socrates that has come down to us. The high moral and intellectual character of the man is admirably expressed in spite of the unprepossessing features, while the vigorous execution is instinct with life. The style, particularly the realistic treatment of the skin, the hair, and the beard, points to an original dating at soonest from the time of Alexander the Great. Comp. Nos. 464-466.

Schuster, Die erhaltenen Porträts der griech. Philosophen, T. I, 4, pp. 8 et seq. *Baumeister*, Denkm. des klass. Alterthums, III, p. 1683, Fig. 1764. Comp. *Welcker*, Alte Denkm., v, p. 96. *Braun*, Ruinen und Museen, p. 652, No. 40.

792 (1036). **Head of Hippocrates.**

The end of the nose, the back of the head, the ears, and the herma are modern.

The identification of this head, based on an inscribed portrait of Hippocrates, known to us from coins of Cos, seems well warranted. The head may be considered as the ideal type of an able and benevolent physician. The keen glance and the motion of the half-opened mouth are especially characteristic. One would say that the celebrated physician was about to make a diagnosis and that he was lending the most vivid attention to the symptom which would place him on the right track. The execution is poor and dates at soonest, to judge from the mechanical treatment of the pupils, from the time of the Antonines. Hippocrates flourished at the end of the fifth, and the beginning of the fourth century B.C.; but the style of this head is much more realistic than was usual in works of this period. We must, therefore, conclude, either that it is a portrait modified in a realistic direction by an artist of a later date, or that it is a freely treated invention of this later period.

Baumeister, Denkm. des klass. Alterthums, I, p. 694, Fig. 752. Comp. Beschreibung Roms, III, 2, p. 543. *Braun*, Ruinen und Museen, p. 653, No. 41. Berichte der sächs. Ges. der Wissenschaften, 1865, pp. 51, 52. *Brunn*, Griech. Götterideale, p. 105. — For the coins of Cos, see *Imhoof-Blumer*, Porträtköpfe auf Münzen hellen. Völker, T. VIII, 30, p. 68.

Colonnade to the right of the Main Building.

793 (103). Statuette of a Dancing Bacchante.

The restorations include the neck, both arms with the cymbals, the head on the nebris, the lowest part of the right leg, and almost the whole of the plinth. The head (nose restored) is ancient, but it is doubtful whether it belongs to the body.

This figure is marked by its graceful movement and makes a charming impression in spite of its careless execution. It is hard to say how the arms should be restored. Perhaps the left arm was bent above the head, while the right arm was extended downwards and held an inverted thyrsos. Comp. No. 936.

Clarac, IV, Pl. 694 B, No. 1656 D. Comp. *Braun*, Ruinen und Museen, p. 680, No. 66.

794 (106). Satyr with a Boy on his shoulders.

This group has been freely restored and ruthlessly cleaned. It reproduces the same motive as No. 397, but in the reverse position.

Gerhard, Antike Bildwerke, T. 103, 2; Prodromus, p. 346. *Clarac*, IV, Pl. 704 B, No. 1656 D. Comp. Berichte der sächs. Ges. der Wissenschaften, 1878, p. 117. *Roscher*, Lexikon der griech. und röm. Mythologie, I, p. 1124.

795 (112). So-called Head of Numa.

The nose and the shaft are modern.

The current appellation of this head is based, first on its alleged resemblance to portraits of Numa on Roman coins of the republican period, and, secondly, on the fact that the mantle is drawn over the back of the head, the traditional arrangement during a sacrificial ceremony (comp. Nos. 319, 330) and therefore supposed to be especially appropriate for a portrait of the legendary king to whom was attributed the organization of the Roman forms of worship. The resemblance, however, is very superficial; and none of the coins represents Numa with his head covered in this way. A more plausible theory sees in it a head of Hades, a deity to whom not only the general character of the head, but also the hair falling over the brow, seems appropriate. Several undoubted images of the god of the lower world represent him with his mantle drawn over the back of his head.

Visconti, Iconographie rom., I, Pl. I, 5, 6, p. 28. Comp. *Gerhard*, Prodromus, p. 18, note 11. *Braun*, Ruinen und Museen, p. 682, No. 69. *Bernoulli*, Römische Ikonographie, I, p. 14.

796 (119). Herma of Dionysos.

The end of the nose, the rim of the left ear, and several fragments of the curls are modern.

This herma is akin to that discussed under No. 692, but shows somewhat softer forms and approaches more closely in this regard to the manner of the later artists of the Second Attic School. The locks above the temples are modern and probably take the place of bunches of ivy-berries, as in No. 692, or of small horns, as in other reproductions of this type.

Comp. *Visconti*, Mus. Pio-Clem., IV, Pl. 58, note 3. *Braun*, Ruinen und Museen, p. 682, No. 70. *Amelung*, Florentiner Antiken, p. 21. See also the bibliography cited under No. 692.

First Room beyond the Colonnade.

797 (131). Sarcophagus, with Relief of the Marriage of Peleus and Thetis.

Found in 1722, in a vigna not far from the tomb of Cæcilia Metella.

Peleus and Thetis, the latter attired in bridal veil, sit side by side, while various gods approach them bearing wedding-gifts. Just in front of the bridal pair is Hephæstos, holding a buckler in his left hand, while with his right he hands Peleus the famous sword. From the position of the legs it is easy to see that this god is lame. Behind Hephæstos is Pallas, bringing a Corinthian helmet and a spear as her gifts. Next come personifications of the Seasons, each with her characteristic offerings (comp. No. 709. Behind the Seasons is Hesperos (the evening star), represented as a boy with an inverted torch, showing the way to Hymen, the god of marriage. Hymen carries the nuptial torch, still unlighted, on his left shoulder, while in his right hand he holds a pitcher, probably as a symbol of the bride's bath. The warm clothing of this deity, consisting of a double chiton, a mantle, hose, and shoes, seems to refer to winter, which the Greeks regarded as the proper season for marriages. At the left end of the scene is an Eros, trying to expel a recalcitrant goddess from the nuptial procession. This group is hard to explain; but it may, perhaps, be Hera, who, after concluding the marriage *(Juno pronuba)* and leading the procession to the house of the bridegroom *(interduca)*, is removed by Eros at the moment when Hymen enters the bridal chamber. The reliefs on the ends and lid of the sarcophagus typify the relation in which Thetis, as the daughter of Nereus, stands to the sea. On the left end is an Eros. bestriding a dolphin and holding a sunshade; on the right end are Poseidon and a sea-dragon; on the lid is a mask of Oceanos, flanked by marine monsters. The sarcophagus is one of the best that has come down to us, and its execution is extremely careful. The reliefs on the principal face, though made up of borrowed motives, are distinguished both by the clearness of their arrangement and by the harmony and skill with which the whole field is occupied.

Robert, Die antiken Sarkophag-Reliefs, ii, T. i, pp. 2 et seq.

Second Room.

798 (144). Colossal Statue of Dionysos.

> The restorations include a piece of the forehead, the
> nose, the lower part of the beard, both forearms, frag-
> ments of the hair and drapery, and most of the plinth.

This statue is a rude Roman copy of an archaic Greek
original, which was doubtless the sacred image in some
sanctuary. According to the invariable usage of archaic
art, the god is represented as clad in a long chiton, and
with his hair and beard conventionally arranged. The
head is encircled, not by an ivy-wreath, but by a fillet, an
attribute given to Dionysos also in the statue No. 327
and sometimes in vase-paintings of the severe style. The
one hand may have held a cantharos, the other a vine or
an inverted thyrsos.

> *Winckelmann*, Storia delle arti del disegno, trad. *Fea*, i, T. xiii,
> p. 181 (Geschichte der Kunst, vol. iii, chap. 2, § 12), iii. pp. 433,
> 434. *Quatremère de Quincy*, Le Jupiter Olympien, Pl. i, 4. *Clarac*,
> iv, Pl. 770B, No. 1907B. *Roscher*, Lexikon der griech. und röm.
> Mythologie, i, p. 1102, Fig. 5. Comp. *Braun*, Ruinen und Mu-
> seen, p. 683, No. 72.

Third Room

799 (151). Terracotta Relief, representing the Build-
ing of the Argo.

> According to an oral tradition. this relief, like Nos.
> 802 and 803 in the same room, was found at the Palazzo
> Caserta, near S. Maria Maggiore.

This relief represents Pallas in the act of putting in
place the mast and sail of the ship Argo, in accordance
with a version of the legend of the Argonauts adopted
by a Latin poet. She is assisted by a bearded man, whom
some authorities take for Tiphys, the steersman of the
Argonauts. Another bearded man, wearing the pileus
and exomis of the artizan, and wielding a hammer and a
chisel, is working at the lofty prow of the vessel. This
is supposed to be Argos, the builder of the ship. On a
column behind Pallas is perched her sacred owl. On the

date and purpose of terracotta reliefs of this kind, see vol. I, p. 449.

Zoega, I, 45. *Millin*, Gal. myth., Pl. 130, 147. *Guigniaut*, Rel. de l'ant., Pl. 198, 639. Comp. *Braun*, Ruinen und Museen, p. 684, No. 74. Berichte der sächs. Ges. der Wissenschaften, 1861, pp. 332, 333. *Blümner*, Technologie und Terminologie der Gewerbe, II, pp. 336, 337.

800 (183). Fountain Rim, with reliefs of Vintage Scenes.

> The two masks of Satyrs, which close the openings of the rim, are the corner-pieces of an ancient sarcophagus-lid and have been placed in their present position by a modern hand.

The concave exterior of this fountain-curb is adorned with a clearly composed but carelessly executed relief. In the middle are three naked youths, grasping each other by the hand and treading out the grapes in a vat. A fourth youth is emptying a basket of grapes into the vat, while a fifth brings another heavy basketful for the same purpose. To the right of the principal group is a youth pouring must from a pitcher into a basket, while to the extreme right is another, pouring must from a basket into one of those earthenware vessels *(dolia)* in which the ancients kept their wine (comp. No. 809). Baskets used in this way were, as we are informed by ancient writers, carefully pitched. In the background is the wine-press properly so called, in which, after the treading process, the last drop of juice was squeezed from the grapes.

Zoega, I, 26. *Panofka*, Bilder antiken Lebens, T. 14, 9, p. 31. Comp. *Welcker*, Alte Denkmäler, II, p. 119. *Braun*, Ruinen und Museen, p. 686, No. 78. *Friederichs-Wolters*, Bausteine, No. 1917.

801 (178). Relief.

> The edges of the relief and two triangular portions in the upper part of the background are modern, as is also the left forearm of the standing figure.

A matronly form, sunk in meditation or melancholy, stands before us, laying her right hand on her shoulder. Artemis hastens away from this figure, grasping with her right hand the quiver slung over her back. The hole bored in the left hand probably served for the insertion of a metal bow. The motives resemble Attic types of the early years of the fourth century B.C. It would be rash to offer any decided explanation of the subject, as the scene is evidently incomplete. One suggestion is that it represents Leto ˋLatonaˋ, grieving over the insult offered to her by Niobe, while Artemis starts out to avenge her mother.

Braun, Ruinen und Museen, p. 685, No. 75. *Stark*, Niobe, p. 175, note 1.

802 (173). Terracotta Relief of two of the Seasons.
Comp. No. 799.

This slab bears personifications of Autumn and Summer. The first holds a small basket of fruit on her left hand and draws a kid towards her with her right. The attributes of Summer are a bunch of wheat-ears and poppies and a garland of flowers or fruit. The personifications of Winter and Spring occupied another slab, now missing. Comp. No. 709.

Zoega, ii, 95. Comp. Ann. dell' Inst., 1861, pp. 206 et seq., 1863, pp. 294 et seq. *Hermann*, De Horarum apud veteres figuris (Berlin, 1887), p. 32.

803 (168). Terracotta Relief of Silenus and Eros.
Comp. No. 799.

Silenus, who has obviously drunk ˋnot wisely but too wellˋ, stumbles into the arms of Eros, who looks amusedly into the old man's face. The movements of the drunkard are represented with great truth to life. Silenus places his left hand on one of the wings of Eros, oblivious of the fact that so delicate an object can hardly be much of a prop; his right arm hangs limp by his side, as if he had some vague idea that it might serve to support him in case of a fall. In front of this group dances a fair Bacchante, beating a tympanon, and evidently the object of Silenus' attention before he was overcome by wine.

Zoega, ii, 79. *Guigniaut*, Rel. de l'ant., Pl. 108, 428b. *Müller-Wieseler*, Denkm. der alten Kunst, ii, T. 42, 510. Comp. Rheinisches Museum, vi (1838), pp. 602, 603. Ann. dell' Inst., 1841, p. 293, note 2. *Braun*, p. 686, No. 77.

804 (169). **Relief of Dionysos and Pan.**

The only part of this relief which is undoubtedly ancient is the fragment, formerly in the possession of Winckelmann, comprising the upper portion of the bodies of Dionysos and Pan and the hand on the breast of the latter. Between 1860 and 1870 another fragment, which till then had been immured in the garden-wall of the villa, was combined with the Winckelmann relief. This latter represented a female figure, dressed in the skin of an elephant and hastening towards Dionysos with a gesture of supplication; she is evidently a personification of India, a country conquered by the god of wine. But both the type and the execution of this figure make a distinctly modern impression; and this fragment is not improbably an attempted restoration of last century. This attempt was considered a failure; the modern fragment was again separated from the ancient one, and has quite recently again been rejoined to it as above noted.

The female figure may be modern, but the outstretched, ancient hand proves that some such form was represented before the god in an attitude of worship or supplication. It remains uncertain whether this personage was, as the modern restorer has assumed, a personification of conquered India, or an Indian prince making his submission to Dionysos. In any case the god, as is shown by his bent head and outstretched right arm, receives the suppliant favourably. Beside him stands his armourbearer Pan, holding the shield of the god in his left hand. His face, in harmony with his function, wears a truculent and warlike expression.

The ancient fragment is reproduced in *Zoega*, ii, 75; *Guigniaut*, Rel. de l'ant., Pl. 108bis, 458b; *Müller-Wieseler*, Denkm. der alten Kunst, ii, T. 38, 445. Comp. *Braun*, Ruinen und Museen, p. 695, No. 88. *Graef*, De Bacchi expeditione Indica (Berolini, 1886), p. 47, iii, 30.

805 (174). **Relief of a Woman crowning a Man.**

The head of the man and the left forearm of the woman, with the crown, are modern.

The movement suggested by the ancient part of the outstretched arm of the woman shows that the restorer has probably done right in showing her in the act of placing a garland on the head of the man. It is impossible to give a more definite explanation, as the man holds no attribute and we do not know whether his head is ideal or a portrait. Assuming that it is the latter, we might surmize that the man is being crowned, in return for some public service, by the personification of a town or nation. The style resembles that of Attic art of the fourth century B. C. The fact, however, that it is in Luna marble and its dry execution show that it dates from the Roman period. It is not easy to decide whether the artist has copied a definite Attic model or has merely imitated the Attic style.

Ann. dell' Inst., 1871, Tav. d'agg. II, pp. 213 et seq. Comp. *Bernoulli*, Aphrodite, p. 91, No. 39. *Friederichs-Wolters*, No. 1868.

806 (171). Colossal Mask of a Water God.

Most of the bust and fragments of the garland, hair, and beard are modern.

As the mouth evidently served for the passage of water, it is clear that this mask decorated a fountain. It does not show the melancholy yearning mood usually seen in water-gods, but rather a gloomy, almost fierce expression. Both hair and beard seem saturated with water.

Braun, Ruinen und Museen, p. 684, No. 73.

807 (164). Relief of Dædalos and Icaros, in rosso antico.

Found in the kingdom of Naples. The restorations include the upper part of the slab, with the point of the wing standing on the ground, the head and right hand of Icaros, and the upper part of the wing on which Dædalos is working.

This relief is a replica of No. 783. The figure of Dædalos was almost wholly missing in the latter, and was restored from the relief before us. On the other hand Icaros is much better preserved in No. 783, and we can detect an error which the restorer of the present relief has made in his figure. Here, as there, the youth should have his wings on — an addition which is shown to be necessary, among other things, by the straps over his breast. The vacant space over his head was harmoniously filled by the wings.

Zoega, I, 44. *Roscher*, Lexikon der griech. und röm. Mythologie, I, 1, pp. 934, 937. For the rest of the bibliography, see *Friederichs-Wolters*, Bausteine, No. 1872.

* 808 (165). **Landscape in Fresco.**

> Found between 1760 and 1770 near Roma Vecchia, on the Via Appia.

To the left are some peasants driving a herd of cattle over a bridge, approached by a gateway topped by a lofty pediment. More in the foreground is a shepherd, with a pedum, driving the cattle still lingering in or near the water to join the herd. To the right is another group of peasants, paying their devotions to a sacred tree, behung with ribbons and garlands. Behind them is an altar, formed of two rough-hewn slabs of stone; against the altar leans a large torch. In the background are some villas and a lake (or the sea), with two ships. The composition is permeated by the idyllic spirit which came into vogue in the Hellenistic period and was introduced at Rome along with other growths of Hellenistic civilisation. In harmony with the same tendency, the painter has represented the architrave and pediment of the gate as overgrown with weeds and bushes. Such a detail as this testifies to the romantic delight which both the Hellenistic and the Roman public took in the sight of picturesque ruins.

Winckelmann, Mon. ant. ined., T. 208, II, pp. 281-283. Comp. Geschichte der Kunst, VII, 3, § 10. *Braun*, Ruinen und Museen, p. 690, No. 84. *Helbig*, Untersuchungen über die campanische Wandmalerei, p. 99. *Woermann*, Die Landschaft in der Kunst der alten Völker, p. 242.

S09 (161). **Relief of Diogenes and Alexander the Great.**

> The restorations include the left margin of the slab, with the rear of the temple and the dolium; the whole of the figure of Alexander except the right hand; the head, right forearm, and most of the stick of Diogenes; the head and part of the right hind-leg of the dog.

The subject of this relief is the famous anecdote, according to which Diogenes, when asked by Alexander the Great whether he could do anything for him, replied: 'Yes, you can stand out of my sunlight'. According to the tradition, the abode of Diogenes is one of the large earthenware vessels *(dolia)* in which the ancients kept wine (comp. No. S00), oil, and grain. The modern idea, that Diogenes lived in a wooden tub, is a mistake; for in antiquity casks of this kind were confined almost wholly to the barbarian races and were not used in the classical lands, except, perhaps, just on their borders. It is related that an urchin once threw a stone at the tub of Diogenes and damaged it considerably. The sculptor seems to have had this incident in mind, for a piece is broken out of the edge of the tub, and a crack runs back from this point over its body. The swallow-tail-shaped objects adjoining this crack evidently represent the leaden clamps that the ancients used to repair fractures in vessels of this kind. A lean and mangy dog, crouching on the tub, alludes to the Cynic (or dog) philosophers, of whom Diogenes was the chief.

> *Winckelmann*, Mon. ant. ined., T. 174, ii, p. 229. *Zoega*, i, 30. *Schreiber*, Die hellenistischen Reliefbilder, T. 94. Comp. Ann. dell' Inst., 1841, p. 293. Rheinisches Museum, iv (1846), pp. 611 et seq. *Schreiber*, Die Wiener Brunnenreliefs aus Pal. Grimani, pp. 7, 63, 97, No. 101.

S10 (157). **Relief of Polyphemos and Eros.**

> The edges of the slab and the whole of the lower part of the relief are modern. The line of fracture runs almost horizontally through the middle of the right calf of Polyphemos and through the fore-leg of the goat. Other restorations are the right arm of the Cyclops (with the

plectron), parts of his lyre, the head, neck, and right arm of Eros, and the head of the goat. The restoration of the animal as a goat seems correct, since the treatment of the skin negatives the supposition that it is a ram.

This pictorially treated relief refers to the story of the love of Polyphemos for the Nereid Galatea. The uncouth Cyclops, holding a rudely made lyre in his left hand, sits on a rock, against which leans his club, and looks downwards in the direction pointed out by the Eros standing behind him. The beauteous Galatea is evidently disporting herself in the waves below. Polyphemos smirks at the sight of the beloved Nymph, but there is vexation mingled with his smirk, because he cannot reach the object of his desire. According to the myth the Cyclops had only one eye. Ancient art, however, generally, as in this case, took the liberty of adding two normal eyes to the Cyclopean orb in the centre of the forehead; otherwise the visage would have been a simple monstrosity, entirely incapable of any expression. From a cavity in the rock on which Polyphemos sits a goat looks up at its master, as if wondering at his behaviour.

Zoega, II, 57. *Schreiber*, Die hellenistischen Reliefbilder, T. LXV. Comp. *O. Jahn*, Archæolog. Beiträge, p. 416. *Braun*, Ruinen und Museen, p. 688, No. 22. Symbola philologorum Bonnensium, pp. 368, 369. *Schreiber*, Die Wiener Brunnenreliefs aus Pal. Grimani, p. 96, No. 56.

811 (154). Relief of a Sportsman and his Horse resting in a wood.

The restorations include the upper and the lateral margins of the slab, the left forearm of the hunter, the head of the herma, and the head of the horse, the adjoining portion of its neck, and most of its right fore-leg. The hunter's head is ancient, but can hardly have belonged to this body.

This relief is a product of the idyllic spirit that prevailed both in poetry and the plastic arts from the Hellenistic period onwards. It represents a sportsman, resting from the fatigues of the chase in the midst of a forest. The man stands besides his horse, which is

covered with a panther-skin, and lays his right hand on
the pommel of the saddle. The landscape-background
is handled with great detail. On the rocks behind the
huntsman is a herma, the leaning position of which is
apparently another appeal to the romantic interest in
picturesque ruins taken by the Hellenistic and Roman
public (comp. No. 808).

Guattani, Monumenti ant. inediti, 1787 (Maggio), T. II, pp. 41
et seq. *Zoega*, I, 37. *Schreiber*, Die hellenistischen Reliefbilder,
T. LXXVI. Comp. *Braun*, Ruinen und Museen, p. 687, No. 79.
Schreiber, Die Wiener Brunnenreliefs, p. 96, No. 78.

512 (149). Relief of a Sacrifice.

Formerly in the possession of the Vitelleschi. The
restorations include the upper margin of the slab, with
the rocky vault below it, and the lower third of the slab,
with the lower part of the three personages represented
and most of the altar (right upper corner ancient). The
nose of the principal figure is also modern.

An old woman, whose wrinkled face is represented
with great character, solemnly revolves round an altar,
apparently throwing grains of incense into the flames with
her right hand. Her left hand, stretched out behind her,
holds a plate of fruit, while a pitcher hangs from one of
its fingers. To the right stands a girl playing the tambourine, while another girl sits in front of her and plays
on the flute. The music that accompanies the sacrifice
indicates that it appertains to the worship of Cybele or
to some other cult originating in Asia Minor (comp.
No. 436). The execution is very careful.

Bartoli, Admiranda, T. 47. *Barbault*, Les plus beaux monuments de Rome, Pl. 32, p. 52. *Zoega*, II. 105. *Schreiber*, Die hellenistischen Reliefbilder, T. LXVI. Comp. Bull. dell' Inst., 1845, p. 7;
Ann. dell' Inst., 1847, p. 290. *Braun*, Ruinen und Museen. p. 687,
No. 80. *Schreiber*, Die Wiener Brunnenreliefs aus Pal. Grimani,
p. 8, p. 96, No. 79.

513 (146). Attic Votive Relief.

The three heads are modern, and also the right foot
and left heel of the worshipper. Pentelic marble.

To the right stand Asclepios and Hygieia, the latter laying her right hand on her father's shoulder; to the left, on a smaller scale, is a worshipper. The style, and the fresh, though slight, execution, indicate the fourth century B. C.

Jahrbuch des Arch. Instituts, II (1887), p. 107.

814 (147). Attic Votive Relief.

The right margin of the slab, with the square altar, is modern. Pentelic marble.

The small mound shown in the lower (and ancient) part of the right side of the slab is the form of altar used in the cult of the heroes. The missing part of the slab, therefore, probably bore the figure of a hero and has been wrongly restored. The ancient part of the slab, to the left, represents a maiden, with a cup in one hand and a pitcher in the other, who is advancing to pour a libation to the hero. Behind her stand three worshippers. To judge from the style, this relief also dates from the fourth century B. C.

Zoega, I, 18. Jahrbuch des Arch. Inst., II (1887), pp. 109, 195. Comp. Bull. dell' Inst., 1845, p. 4; Ann., 1845, p. 248.

Fourth Room.

Below the statue of Heracles in the second niche, —

815 (190). Fragment of a Relief of Satyrs lifting up the trunk of a tree.

As this relief has been freely restored and covered with an artificial patina, which makes it difficult to distinguish between the old and the new parts, strange misinterpretations have hitherto been made of its subject. To the left are two Satyrs raising the trunk of a tree, perhaps to hang on it a trophy commemorating a victory of Dionysos. One Satyr, of whom only the rump and tail are ancient, supports the burden on his back, while the other clasps the tree with both arms and tries to lift it into a perpendicular position. Between these two Satyrs stood a third, of whom only the left side of the breast and the left arm have been preserved. To the right is a fourth Satyr, raising his right hand to strike the back of a figure that is escaping with grotesque gestures. The legs and almost the whole head of this latter figure are modern; but enough remained of the ancient head (right eye, right half of the forehead, and a horn) to allow Pan to be recognized in it. He has evidently been interrupting the Satyrs in their work and is being chased from the scene. The idea that the Satyrs are busied with the club of Heracles is controverted by the character of the object they are lifting. A close resemblance to the left side of this slab is shown by the reliefs on some ancient lamps, which represent three Satyrs erecting a herma of Dionysos. The trunk before us is, however, too long and too knotty to serve as the shaft of a herma.

Braun, Ruinen und Museen, p. 695, No. 86. Berichte der sächsischen Gesellschaft der Wissenschaften, 1878, p. 131, note 1. — One of the lamps is reproduced in *Müller-Wieseler*, Denkmäler der alten Kunst, II, 49, 615.

In the niche of the window to the right, —

816 (199). **Triangular Candelabrum Base, with Dancing Girls.**

Formerly in the possession of the Giustiniani.

On each face is represented a girl with a crown of reeds (comp. No. 769), advancing in rhythmic movement on the points of her toes. An altar of unhewn stone, with fruit and a fire, stands in front of two of the girls; while a reed-like plant grows before the third. One of the maiden raises both her hands in prayer; the second holds a dish of fruit in her left hand; the third inclines her head and raises her hand to her brow, apparently to express adoration of the divinity. The execution is excellent; but the surface of the relief is sadly weatherworn.

Zoega, I, 20. *Welcker*, Alte Denkmäler, II, T. VII, 12, pp. 146 et seq. Comp. *Winckelmann*, Versuch einer Allegorie, ed. Dressel, p. 35. *Braun*, p. 695, No. 87. *Stephani*, Nimbus und Strahlenkranz, p. (465) 105, No. 14, p. 111; Compte-rendu pour 1865, p. 60, No. 2, pp. 63 et seq. *Hauser*, Die neu-attischen Reliefs, p. 96, No. 19.

Fifth Room.

517 (213). Frieze-Relief in Phrygian Marble (paonazzetto).

Found in Hadrian's Villa, near Tivoli.

This relief furnishes another striking proof of the disastrous influence on sculpture exercised by the taste for variegated marbles that grew up in the time of Hadrian (comp. Nos. 233, 441, 514). The sculptor has reproduced fine motives, borrowed from an earlier art; but these are far from producing their due effect, the clearness of the forms being everywhere marred by the dyes of the marble. The middle scene represents Dionysos aided by two Satyrs to ascend his chariot, which is drawn by panthers. The Satyr standing beyond the chariot, holding the thyrsos and cantharos of Dionysos, seems to be almost wholly modern. Above the panthers rises a Bacchante, carrying a basket of grapes on her head. In front of her marches a Satyr, with a pedum over his left shoulder and a rhyton in his raised right hand. To the right of the central compartment are an ædicula, enshrining a Bacchante with a tympanon, and a framed relief of a Satyr with a torch. The corresponding shrine and relief to the left are by the modern restorer.

Cavaceppi. Raccolta di statue, III, 33. *Zoega*, II, 78. *Penna*, Viaggio pittorico della Villa Adriana, III, 56. Comp. Beschreibung Roms, III, 2, pp. 307, 308. *Braun*, p. 697, No. 89.

518 (201). Group of Theseus and the Minotaur.

Found in 1740 at Genzano, in the Cesarini grounds (*Fea*, Misc., I. p. CLII, No. 70). The restorations include the right forearm and club and the lower part of both legs of Theseus (right foot ancient), also the left horn and ear, the right forearm down to the wrist, and the left heel of the Minotaur.

This group is mediocre in execution, but has certainly been inspired by an admirable original, which is found reproduced on Attic coins and was perhaps a group on the Acropolis of Athens. The figure of Theseus, dealing a blow with all his vigour, forms a most effective contrast with that of the Minotaur, who has sunk on one knee and is already on the point of death. The bull's head of the monster is charged with character. The expression is full of pain; the eyes are beginning to glaze and stiffen in death; the tongue lolls from the mouth.

Clarac, iv, Pl. 811A, No. 2071B. Comp. *Welcker*, Alte Denkmäler, ii, p. 302. *O. Jahn*, Arch. Beiträge, p. 266. *Braun*, Ruinen und Museen, p. 700, No. 94. Arch. Zeitung, xxv (1867), pp. 31, 32.

819 (207). Colossal Mask of Silenus, in relief.

> The nose, lips, and other unimportant parts are modern.

This mask presents a type of Silenus, crowned with wild ivy and treated in a decorative style. The fall of the hair and beard proves that it was intended for a horizontal position. It served, in fact, like the so-called Bocca della Verità in the wall of S. Maria in Cosmedin, as the mouth of a drain, and furnishes a striking example of the artistic taste which the ancients expended even on objects meant for the humblest uses. The water escaped through the nostrils, the mouth, and the holes bored in the eyes and ears.

On the Bocca della Verità, see *Matz-Duhn*, Antike Bildwerke in Rom, iii, No. 3617.

Sixth Room.

820 (216). Relief of Hypnos.

> The nose, and the body from the lower edge of the upper garment downwards, are modern.

Hypnos or Sleep, usually represented as a youth, here appears as a warmly-clad old man, sleeping as he stands leaning on his staff. If it were not for the wings on his feet and head, one would take him for a genre figure.

Zoega, ii, 93. *Hirt*, Götter und Heroen, T. xii. 107. *Müller-Wieseler*, Denkm. der alten Kunst, ii, 70, 874. *Conze*, Heroen- und

Göttergestalten, T. 94, 1. *Baumeister*, Denkm. des klass. Alterthums, ɪ, p. 707, Fig. 770. Comp. *O. Jahn*, Arch. Beiträge, p. 208, note 10. Ann. dell' Inst., 1869, p. 33. *Winnefeld*, Hypnos (Berlin and Stuttgart, 1886), pp. 19, 20.

821 (217). Greek Tomb Relief.

> The nose, the right hand, the feet, and the margin of the slab are modern.

The youth, whose tomb was adorned by this relief, is indicated as a regular visitor of the palæstra by the strigil (comp. No. 31) and the oil-flask held in his left hand. The head is not a portrait but an ideal type; and, like the style of the somewhat careless execution, points to the Attic art of the fourth century B. C.

Visconti, Museo Pio-Clem., ɪɪɪ, Tav. b, ɪɪɪ, 5, p. 239. *Zoega*, ɪ. 29. Comp. *Friederichs-Wolters*, Bausteine, No. 1018.

On the outside-wall, above the door, —

822 (223). Cover of a Sarcophagus, with a Battle Scene.

The principal figures in this relief are two warriors advancing in their bigæ to attack each other. From the ground between them emerges the bust of a female figure, raising her hands in astonishment or grief — a motive resembling various representations of Gæa. No positive interpretation of this sarcophagus has so far been offered. It might be the combat of Achilles and Memnon, or that of Æneas and Turnus, or the fratricidal duel of Eteocles and Polynices.

Zoega, ɪɪ, 55. Comp. Bull. dell' Inst., 1864, p. 263, No. 2. Arch. Zeitung, xLɪ (1883), p. 191.

Let into the garden-wall, to the right of the door, —

823 (226). Fragment of a Relief of Heracles.

This fragment belonged to a large relief, the composition of which seems to have been invented by Hellenistic art. The subject forms an ancient parallel to Gulliver's adventures among the Liliputians. The gigantic form of Heracles reclines on a lion-skin, his scyphos in the left

hand. A tiny Satyr or Pygmy stands on tiptoe on the top
rung of a ladder he has placed against the vessel, without the hero's noticing it, and drinks the wine within.
Comp. No. 747.

Zoega, II, 69. Wiener Vorlegeblätter, series III, T. XII, 4.
Schreiber, Die hellenistischen Reliefbilder, T. xxx. For the rest
of the bibliography, see *Stephani*, Der ausruhende Herakles, p. (377)
125, No. 4, pp. (380) 128-(381) 129.

In the alley leading to the so-called Bigliardo, between the fourth and fifth tree, to the right, —

824 (276). Sepulchral Ara of Quintus Cæcilius Ferox.

Originally in the house of an apostolic secretary
named 'Rigetius' (Righetti?). On this point, and for the
subsequent owners of the monument, see Corpus inscript.
lat., VI, 1, Nos. 2188, 2189; Jahrbuch des Arch. Instituts,
VI (1891), p. 164, No. 62a.

The inscription on the face of this ara informs us
that it was erected by Marcus Gavius Charinus in honour of his son Quintus Cæcilius Ferox, who had died at
the age of fifteen years, as usher of the College of Priests
charged with the cult of the deified Vespasian and Titus.
The monument cannot, therefore, date earlier than the
year 81 A.D., in which the apotheosis of Titus took
place. On the right lateral face of the ara is a female
figure, whose left foot rests on the wheel of Nemesis,
while her left hand appears to hold a scroll. The inscription over her head (FATIS · CAECILIUS · FEROX ·
FILIUS) shows us that she personifies fate. The Ferox
named here is obviously the boy interred below the ara.
It cannot now be determined whether he himself desired
that his tombstone should be adorned with a figure of fate,
or whether the selection is due to his father. On the left
lateral face is inscribed SOMNO · ORESTILLA · FILIA,
below which is a figure of the god of sleep, here obviously meant to typify eternal sleep. The sculptor has
represented him as a winged boy, sleeping as he leans
on an inverted torch. Orestilla was evidently the daughter of Charinus and the sister of Ferox. Whether she

was alive or dead when the altar was erected cannot be determined. The palæography and accentuation of the inscription, as well as the style of the reliefs, point to the pre-Hadrian epoch.

A drawing of this ara is given in the Codex Pighianus (Ber. der sächs. Gesellschaft der Wiss., 1868, p. 208, No. 135), and there is a sketch of the right lateral face by Heemskerk in the Jahrbuch des Arch. Instituts, vi (1891), p. 164, No. 62a. In Zoega (i, 15) the earlier bibliography is collected (p. 63, note 14). Müller - Wieseler, Denkmäler der alten Kunst, ii, 73, 941. Comp. Gerhard, Prodromus, p. 259, note 64. Stephani, Der ausruhende Herakles, p. 30 (282). Braun, p. 699. No. 93. Ann. dell' Inst., 1869, p. 33. Corpus inscr. lat., vi, 1. Nos. 2188, 2189. — On the Sacerdotal College of the Flaviales, see Ephem. epigraphica, iii, pp. 211 et seq.

Let into the wall to the left, —

825 (291). **Frieze of Cupids.**
Formerly in the Palazzo Giustiniani.

The composition is skilfully put together of charming motives, most of which are due to Hellenistic art. In the middle two Cupids are taking their places for a wrestling-match, while the umpire stands behind them (comp. Nos. 573–575. The palæstra, in which the scene occurs, is typified by the vessel of sand on the floor comp. Nos. 337–339, 634. Five other Cupids are spectators of the contest. One stands to the left of the wrestlers, placing both hands on a pillar, which supports an amphora and three palm-branches, apparently the prizes for the victor. Three other winged boys are grouped on the base and margin of a large basin, to the right of the principal group. Another Cupid, standing behind this group, reveals in the movement of his hands the intense interest he takes in the outcome of the contest. The two-handled vase in front of this figure, the pitcher on the table behind him, and the garland hanging above him are probably other prizes. The right side of the relief is bounded by a herma, such as the ancients used to erect in their gymnasia comp. Nos. 561–565. The left side of the relief falls into two scenes. A Cupid opens

one of the cists used in the mysteries of the Bacchic cult,
and thereby releases the snake coiled up within. Another
Eros close by falls on his back in alarm at this sight;
while two others, farther off, regard the scene with cau-
tious curiosity, one kneeling in a huge basket of fruit,
the other crouching on the ground. A fifth boy stands on
the back of the last-mentioned and takes as much fruit
from the basket as his arms can hold. A second and
smaller basket of fruit serves to fill out the field. The
scene at the left end of the relief represents a Cupid hid-
ing behind a colossal mask of Silenus and thrusting his
hand through its open mouth. A companion is terribly
frightened by this practical joke. In the background is a
large torch, garnished with ribbons. The motive of the
boy and the mask is also known in figures in the round
comp. No. 552 .

A drawing of this frieze is given in the Codex Pighianus (Be-
richte der sächs. Gesellschaft der Wiss., 1868, p. 219, No. 189).
Galleria Giustiniana, II, 128. Zoega, II, 90. Comp. Beschreibung
Roms, III, 2, p. 533. Braun, p. 700, No. 95.

In the portico of the Bigliardo, —

526 (308 . Cast of a Relief of Heracles, Peirithoos, and Theseus.

> The original has been transferred to the Museo Tor-
> lonia in the Lungara. The undoubted restorations include
> the heads of the central figure and the figure to the right; a
> large piece near the middle of the slab with the left fore-
> arm of the youth standing on the left, the right arm of
> the middle figure from the biceps downwards, the piece
> of the rock on which the right hand of the latter rests,
> and the lower part of the quiver; further, the right knee
> of the central figure. with the part of the leg above and
> below it; the right forearm of the youth standing to the
> right, the upper end of his staff, the lower end of his
> sword, and the part of the mantle below it. Comp. Arch.
> Zeitung, XXXVII, 1879, p. 65, No. 287.

Theseus and Peirithoos descended to the Underworld
to carry off Persephone, but were chained by Pluto to the
rock on which they had sat down to rest. When Herac-

les came to Hades a little later, to fetch Cerberus, he succeeded, according to one version of the legend, in free-

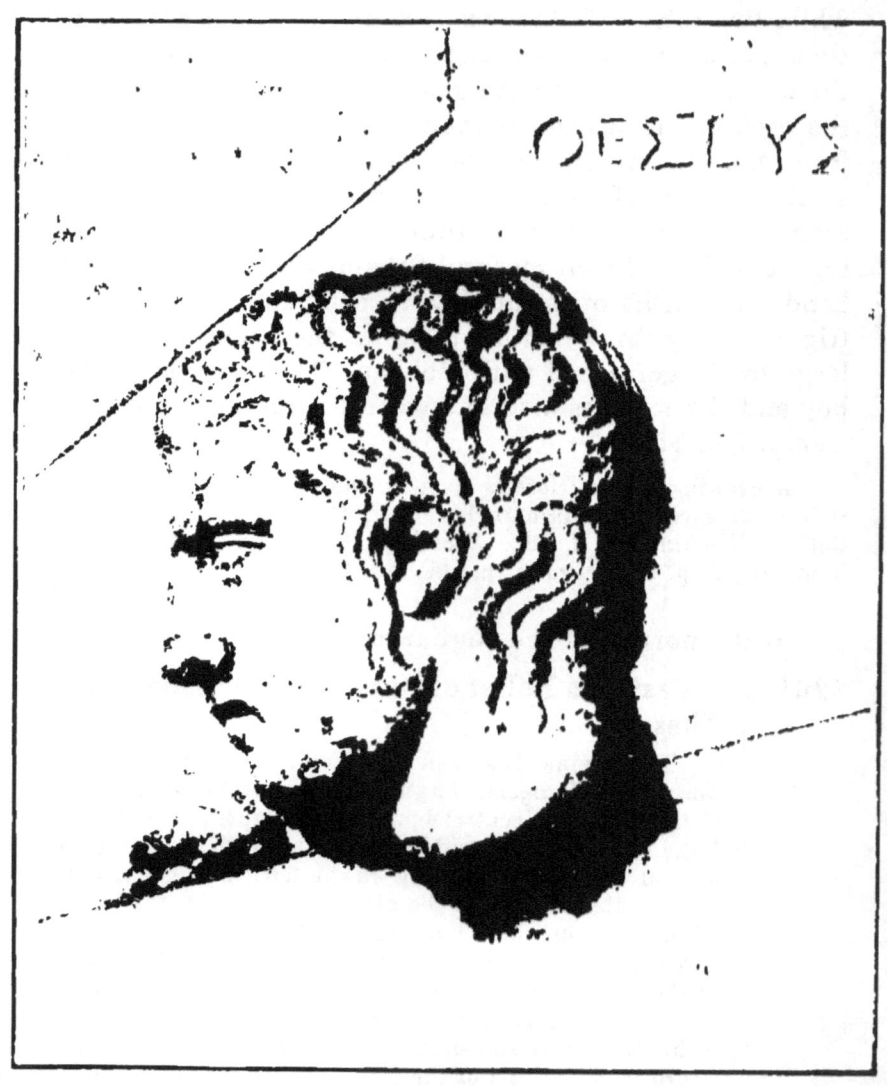

Fig. 34.

ing both the heroes, or, according to another version, Theseus only. Our relief seems to follow the second version of the myth. To the right stands Theseus, already liberated and ready to depart, holding a sword in his left hand and resting his right on a long staff. We know the type of his head from the fragment of another relief of the same scene, now in the museum of Berlin Fig. 31). The features express the grief of the hero at having to abandon his friend Peirithoos. The latter is seated in the centre, the position of his legs showing that he is still chained to the rock. His head was obviously turned, with an expression of woe, towards Heracles. The latter, recognizable by the club in his right hand and the bow and quiver at his feet, is making an effort to free Peirithoos also. As the left arm is modern, we cannot be sure of its attitude; but in all probability it held the right arm of Peirithoos in an attempt to detach him from his rock. This relief belongs to the same category as Nos. 635 and 790. It is probably a copy, executed in Athens, of an Attic original, which was doubtless a votive offering dedicated by a choregos or poet in commemoration of a dramatic victory. The replica before us was evidently painted, for the soles only, and not the straps of the sandals, are plastically represented.

Zoega, II, 103. I monumenti del Museo Torlonia riprodotti con la fototipia, T. XCIII, No. 377. *Baumeister*, Denkmäler des klass. Alterthums, III, p. 1796, Fig. 1880. Monumenti antichi pubblicati per cura della reale Accademia dei Lincei, I (1892), pp. 673-686, plate No. 2, where the entire bibliography is collected. Comp. Römische Mittheilungen, VII (1892), pp. 110, 111, 112.

Bigliardo.

First Room.

827 (317). Replica of the Stephanos Statue (No. 744).

The execution is slighter than that of No. 744, and the crude freshness of the archaic style has been still more obliterated.

Ann. dell' Inst., 1865, p. 62. *Kekulé*, Die Gruppe des Künstlers Menelaos, p. 25, No. 1.

828 (322). Statue of Dionysos or a Satyr.

> The restorations include half of the right forearm
> with the bunch of grapes, the left forearm with the cup,
> the front of the feet, and unimportant fragments of the
> accessories. The head (nose and chin modern) is antique
> but does not belong to the figure. The upper part of the
> body has been freely worked over.

The nebris shows that this is a statue either of Dionysos or of a Satyr, but as the head of Dionysos does not
belong to it, it is impossible to say which. The accessory
details deserve attention. The stump on which the figure
leans is entwined by a thick vine-stem. On one of its
top-branches stands a wingless boy, seizing a bunch of
grapes. On a lower branch kneels an Eros, handing down
a basket of grapes to a bearded and goat-limbed Pan,
who advances eagerly to receive the burden. Similar
scenes were also treated by the ancients in the round.

Beschreibung Roms, III, 2, p. 536. *Braun*, Ruinen und Museen, p. 706, No. 96. — On Eros in scenes of vintage, see Arch.
Zeitung, XXXVII (1879), pp. 170 et seq.

Second Room.

829 (336). Fragment of a Puteal or of a Circular Base.

> All the heads are modern except that of the Satyr
> putting his arm into the amphora, and there are other
> unimportant restorations.

Three Cupids are represented, one riding on a bull,
another on a goat, and the third on a panther. All three
animals are fantastically provided with horse's necks. In
front of the bull stands a goat-legged Pan, drawing water
for it out of a lofty amphora, while two Satyrs give drink
to the goat and the panther. The Satyr at the left edge
of the fragment, dipping into an amphora, was evidently
coupled with another animal in the missing part of the
relief.

Zoega, II, 89. Comp. Beschreibung Roms, III. 2, p. 495, No. 8.
Braun, Ruinen und Museen, p. 702, No. 98.

Caffè.

Semicircular Portico.

To the left, —

830 (594). So-called Head of Alcibiades (plaster cast).

> The original has been transferred to the Museo Tor-
> lonia in the Lungara. The left frontal bone, the nose,
> the lower lip, parts of the upper lip and ears, and the
> bust are modern.

Comp. No. 91.

I monumenti del Museo Torlonia riprodotti con la fototipia,
T. xvii, 67. Comp. Ann. dell' Inst., 1866, p. 229, iii.

831 (601). Statue of a Nude Warrior.

> Both forearms and the hilt and lower end of the sword
> are modern. The middle of the sword is ancient. The
> helmeted head (crest, vizier, nose, and lips modern)
> seems to be the original, but has been broken off and
> re-united with the body.

The motive of this figure is evidently derived from
that of the Doryphoros of Polycleitos (comp. No. 58,
with which it agrees in attitude and proportions. The
type of the head, however, is changed; and the left hand,
instead of shouldering a spear, grasps the pommel of the
sword with which the young warrior is girt. The right
arm seems, like that of the Doryphoros, to have hung
empty by the side.

Clarac, v, Pl. 833 C, No. 2064 A. Bull. dell' Inst., 1873, p. 10.
Jahrbücher des Vereins von Alterthumsfreunden im Rheinlande,
viii (1873). p. 36. note 2. Ann. dell' Inst., 1878, p. 9, note k.
Bayerische Sitzungsberichte, 1892, p. 674. *Furtwaengler*, Masterpieces, p. 230.

To the right, —

832 (609). Portrait-Head of a Roman (plaster cast.

> The original is in the Museo Torlonia. The front of
> the nose, the chin, fragments of the ears, the neck. and
> the bust are modern.

This head represents the same individual as No. 29.

I monumenti del Museo Torlonia, T. cxxx. 508.

To the left, —

533 (610). **Head of Aratos (?).**

Part of the forehead, the nose, the shoulders, and the shaft are modern.

The identification of this head with Aratos is based on its resemblance to a portrait on the coins of Soli-Pompeiopolis (vol. I, p. 353, Fig. 20. This coin-portrait was formerly taken for Chrysippos the Stoic, and the head before us consequently received the same name. Both the one and the other, however, seem rather to pourtray Aratos, the founder of the astronomical epic (comp. Nos. 287, 479). The fact that the old man is wrapped up in his garment, as if chilly, may mean that the sculptor has chosen for his portrait the moment when the star-loving poet was pondering some astronomical problem in the cold middle of the night.

Visconti, Iconografia greca, I, T. XXIII a. 4, 5, p. 246. Baumeister, Denkmäler des klass. Alterthums, I. p. 395, Fig. 426. Comp. Braun, Ruinen und Museen, p. 704, No. 101. Schuster, Über die erhaltenen Portraits griech. Philosophen, p. 22, No. 12. Jahrbuch des Arch. Instituts, v (1890), Archäolog. Anzeiger, pp. 56–58. The writer of this last article believes (p. 57) that a fracture in the beard of this head indicates that a hand touched it. This opinion is, however, wrong, and there is no mark of the kind on the beard. It is true that a small splinter has been broken off at the lower end of the left moustache; but this is far too small to give any cause to believe that there was a hand here. — On the coins of Soli-Pompeiopolis, see under No. 479, where one of them is reproduced (Figs. 19. 20).

534 (628). **Caryatid.**

Found along with No. 721. The restorations include the front edge of the calathos, the nose, the lips, fragments of the hands and drapery, the feet with the border of the drapery resting on them, and the plinth.

Attempts have recently been made to connect this figure with an original by Scopas or Praxiteles. Comp. No. 721.

Guattani, Mon. ant. ined., 1788, Septembre, T. 1. Clarac, III, Pl. 442, No. 808. Comp. Beschreibung Roms, III, 2, p. 544.

Braun, Ruinen und Museen, p. 705, No. 105. *Friederichs-Wolters*, Bausteine, No. 1556. *Furtwaengler*, Masterpieces, p. 337, note 1.

S35 (633). Head of Caligula, with the toga drawn over it.

The nose and bust are modern.

The sly and malicious expression of the young emperor is admirably rendered.

Bernoulli, Römische Ikonographie, II, p. 305. *Mau*, Statua di Marcello nipote d'Augusto (Naples, 1890), p. 6.

On the top of a column, to the left, —

S36 (724). Statuette of Poseidon.

The right leg is modern; perhaps the right arm also, which, however, closely resembles the ancient portions both in the quality of the marble and in execution. The writer cannot understand how Benndorf and Schöne (Die antiken Bildwerke des lateranischen Museums, p. 183), supporting themselves by a passage in the Bull. dell' Inst. (1834; p. 106), can draw the conclusion that this statuette was found in Nettuno.

This statuette reproduces the same original as No. 667. The position of the extremities is, however, altered, while the bearing is stiffer and the expression shows a mixture of attention and excitement. The god seems to survey his domain with the feeling that his active intervention may very soon be necessary. The trident, moreover, is not held by the left hand, as in No. 667, but with the right, so that the attribute which symbolizes his power is ready for immediate use.

Overbeck, Kunstmythologie, III, p. 255, p. 265, No. 6, p. 279, No. 3, p. 280; Atlas, XI, 5, XII, 30.

S37 (725). Caryatid.

Found along with No. 721. The restorations include the front rim of the calathos, the nose, the chin, almost all the right arm with the drapery covering it, the left hand, several fragments of the drapery, and the margin of the plinth.

As this head seems akin to that of the Cnidian

Aphrodite, it has been supposed that its original was created by the Second Attic School. Comp. No. 721.

Clarac. III, Pl. 444, No. 814B. Comp. Beschreibung Roms, III, 2, p. 548. Friederichs-Wolters, Bausteine, No. 1557. Furtwaengler, Masterpieces, p. 387, note 1.

838 (733). Statue of Aphrodite.

The restorations include the neck, both arms, the left shoulder, part of the left breast, the posteriors, several fragments of the drapery, the front of the feet, and almost the whole plinth. The head (nose, lips, left lock of hair, and the top-knot modern) is ancient, but does not seem to belong to the body.

This statue has been inaccurately restored. It represented the well-known type of Aphrodite holding a shield in front of her, but deviated from the usual pattern in not supporting the shield on the left thigh. The left thigh shows no trace of contact with any object, such as would certainly have been left if the shield had rested on it.

Clarac, IV, Pl. 602, No. 1332A. Valentin, Die hohe Frau von Milo, T. IV, 10. Furtwaengler, Masterpieces, p. 384, note 5. Comp. Bernoulli, Aphrodite, p. 162, note 2.

To the right, —

839 (737). Head of Zeus.

The back part of the mass of hair to the right, the bust, and the lower part of the neck are modern.

The type recalls the Zeus of Otricoli No. 291, but both forms and expression are less placid. The eyes are smaller; the nose is slightly curved; the nostrils are open more widely; the arrangement of the hair and beard is less imposing.

Overbeck, Kunstmythologie, II, p. 77, No. 5; Atlas, I, 14.

840 (711. Statue of Heracles.

The restorations include the end of the nose, the nape and right side of the neck, the right arm and cup, the left hand. most of the club (middle ancient), the right leg from a little above the knee, the left foot (heel ancient), parts of the lion-skin, and almost all the plinth.

Heracles is represented in one of the happiest mo-
ments of his laborious life. The upright attitude of his
vigorous body shows that the hero feels himself in full
possession of his giant-strength, while the expression of
the handsome bearded face is one of mingled content and
proud self-consciousness. The right arm, as is proved
by the position of the shoulder, was raised. It is quite
possible that the restorer has rightly placed a cup in the
right hand, for this attribute accords well with the general
character of the figure. The forms are, on the whole,
those characteristic of Greek art from about the middle
of the fourth century B.C. until it was led into a new
course by the realism of Lysippos. Recent criticism has
connected the statue with a type of Praxiteles. That our
statue is a copy of a bronze original is indicated by the
interval between the lion-skin and the hero's body and
by the chased-metal appearance of the hair and beard.

Clarac, v, Pl. 804 B, No. 2007 A. *Furtwængler*, Masterpieces,
Fig. 145, pp. 340, 341. Comp. Beschreibung Roms, III, 2, p. 549.
Braun, Ruinen und Museen, p. 706, No. 108.

841 (744). **Archaic Portrait of a Greek.**

The end of the nose, part of the right herma, the
lower half of the right ear, and the shaft are modern.

To judge from the freshness and vigour of the execution, this head seems to be an original Greek work. The
treatment of the parted lips is particularly effective. The
mouth seems to inhale deep draughts of air, and thus expresses, in the most emphatic manner, the vigorous vital-
ity of the person represented. The features show some
resemblance to the portrait of Pericles No. 281, but the
style of the head is that of an earlier period. It has therefore been suggested that it is a portrait of Peisistratos,
since we know that when Pericles first entered public life
his strong likeness to that ruler struck those of the old
Athenians who had seen the tyrant in person. The short
hair, however, forbids this supposition; for a portrait of
Peisistratos would show the long, conventionally arranged

hair that was customary at Athens in the time of the
Tyrants and during the earlier part of the fifth century B.C.

Furtwaengler, Masterpieces, Fig. 73, pp. 175 et seq. (where
this type is ascribed to Myron). Comp. Bull. dell' Inst., 1851,
pp. 87, 88. *Braun*, Ruinen und Museen, p. 707, No. 110.

542 (749. Statue of Persephone.

The restorations include the forefinger, the thumb,
and the first joint of the middle finger of the right hand,
the left arm (except the inner half of the upper part),
the part of the hanging sleeve near the left elbow, and
the margin of the plinth.

The composition and style prove that this statue is
a reproduction of an Attic original of the best period
fifth century B.C.). It has been taken for Demeter, because the arrangement of the drapery is the same as that
of a figure in an Eleusinian relief, which has been identified with either Demeter or Persephone. The latter
name, however, seems the more suitable for the relief-
figure, and there is nothing inconsistent with it in the
figure before us. The forms and expression of the head,
the close-fitting cap (frequently used by ancient art for
divine as well as for mortal virgins), and the short curls
issuing from below it all indicate a youthful goddess.
The right hand may have held one of the attributes characteristic of Persephone, such as a bunch of flowers in
metal. To judge from the preserved portion of the upper
part of the arm, the lowered left hand may, as in the relief, have held a long torch, which leant against the left
shoulder. This was made, not of marble, but of some
other material such as gilded wood.

Clarac, v, Pl. 936 F, No. 2264. *Overbeck*, Kunstmythologie,
III, pp. 428, 416, p. 469, No. 20; Atlas, xiv, 11. Jahrbuch der
Kunstsammlungen des österr. Kaiserhauses, xii (Vienna. 1890),
p. 72, Fig. 2. *Brunn und Bruckmann*, Denkmäler griech. und
röm. Sculptur, No. 265. There is a replica of this type in the Capitoline Museum (No. 511) and another at Cherchel (Caesarea): *Waille*,
De Caesareae monumentis (Alger, 1891), Pl., No. 21, p. 88. — For
the bas-relief of Eleusis, see *Friederichs-Wolters*, Bausteine,
No. 1182. *Roscher*, Lexikon, II, pp. 1347-1350.

843 (757). **Statue of Dionysos.**

> The restorations include the right arm from a little below the shoulder, the whole of the left arm, the left knee with the leg above and below it, various fragments of the folds of the drapery, and nearly all the plinth. The head placed on the body is ancient (except the nose, under-lip, right cheek, and chin), but does not belong to it, and is much inferior in execution. Besides, the lock which falls on the right shoulder is entirely disconnected from the rest of the coiffure.

The god was represented as resting, with his right arm bent above his head; the left arm, supported on the stump, may have held a cantharos or a bunch of grapes. This statue was highly esteemed by Winckelmann, especially for the delicate moulding of the abdominal regions; but his praise seems exaggerated, now that we know so many better executed statues of Dionysos. The head belongs to a statue of the same god of very inferior workmanship, and is absolutely without expression. The hair, the garland, the inner corners of the eyes, and the mouth are worked in the rudest manner with the drill.

> *Gerhard*, Antike Bildwerke, T. 105, 1. Comp. *Winckelmann*, Geschichte der Kunst, v, 1, § 23; Monumenti ant. inediti, trattato preliminare, pp. LI, LII. Beschreibung Roms, III, 2, p. 550. *Gerhard*, Prodromus, p. 348.

Passage leading to the Galleria del Canopo.

To the right, —

844 (711). **Hovering Figure of a Girl.**

> Found in Hadrian's Villa, near Tivoli. The restorations, made by Cavaceppi, include both arms, the knee and lower part of the left leg, half of the right foot, several fragments of the drapery, and most of the plinth. The head is ancient but does not belong to the body; most of the diadem, the point of the nose, the curls falling behind the ears, and the nape and lower part of the neck are modern.

This statue represents a girl flying down to the earth, her garments inflated by the current of the wind and forming innumerable folds. It undoubtedly reproduces

6*

an important original. The difficult problem of representing a flying figure has been tackled with distinguished success; and the natural and lifelike impression is heightened by the way in which the supporting stump is concealed by the feet and drapery. The disposition of the folds is at once abundant and perspicuous. Among the numerous interpretations that have been offered of this statue, we need here particularize only those which see in it either Hera or Iris, the messenger of the gods. Or, perhaps, Cavaceppi was right in putting a torch in the right hand and thus characterizing the figure as Selene, descending on the sleeping Endymion ,comp. Nos. 152, 462).

Raffei, Osservazione sopra alcuni monumenti esistenti nella Villa Albani, Diss. vii, T. ii, pp. 125 et seq. *Clarac*, iii, Pl. 416, No. 719 A. Comp. Bull. dell' Inst., 1849, p.71; Ann., 1852, p. 230. *Braun*, Ruinen und Museen, p. 709, No. 112. *Overbeck*, Kunstmythologie, iii, p. 202, note 65.

845 (706). **Relief of Theseus and Æthra.**

Vulpius, the Jesuit, saw this relief in 1732 in a vigna at Ostia, and published it, from a very inaccurate drawing, in his work entitled 'Vetus Latium profanum' (Romæ, 1734; vol. vi, T. 15). When Winckelmann made an excursion to Ostia in 1763 he seems to have found the monument still in the same place (*Winckelmann*, Briefe an Bianconi, § 35, 26th March, 1763; Werke, vol. ii, Stuttgart, 1847, p. 214; *Fea*, Misc., i, p. clxxxvi, No. 3), and he also published it, in a more correct form, in the 'Mon. ant. ined.' (T. 96, ii, p. 130). — The restorations include the head (lower part ancient), left hand, and right arm of the first girl from the left; half the face and part of the back of the head of the next girl; almost the whole face, the right forearm (hand ancient), and right foot of Theseus; the head and right hand of the girl standing to the right of the rock; the front of the skull, the forehead, the eyes, the nose, and the lips of the matron beside her; the top of the skull, the forehead, the left arm from the shoulder to the wrist, the sword-hilt, and the left leg below mid-thigh of the adjacent youth; and the upper left corner of the background.

When Ægeus left Æthra in Troizene, with her unborn child, he hid his shoes and his sword under a rock, and forbade his mistress, if she should bear a son, to reveal his father's name to him until the youth was able to roll away the rock. Thereafter she was to send him to Athens, bearing the shoes and sword as tokens of identity. To the left we see Theseus, accomplishing, in the presence of two Troizene maidens, the feat required by his father. The strength he displays in the action is combined with the ease and grace which the exercises of the gymnasium developed in the young Athenians. The scene to the right is supposed by some to represent Ægeus telling Æthra, in the presence of two maidens, of the proof to be hereafter required of his son. Another view sees in it Theseus taking leave of his mother on his departure for Athens. The latter explanation seems the more probable on account of the strong likeness borne by the youth standing beside Æthra to the Theseus at the other end of the slab. The round object on which he places his foot is one of the rollers, frequently seen in Campanian mural paintings, which the ancients used to level roads, areas for games, and the like.

Zoega, I, 48. *Millin*, Galerie mythol., Pl. 128, 482*. *Hirt*, Götter und Heroen, T. 38, 325. *Guigniaut*, Rel. de l'ant., Pl. 196, 696. Comp. *Braun*, Ruinen und Museen, p. 710, No. 113. Arch. Zeitung, xxvii (1869), p. 107.

In the same small room are two statuettes of comic actors (Nos. 710, 713 of the Museum), in the room opposite are two more (Nos. 640, 643), and in the right front corner of the passage itself stands a fifth (No. 717). These figures served, perhaps, to decorate small theatres. They give us a good idea of the costumes of the New Attic Comedy, but cannot be connected with any definite characters in this branch of the drama, since they all bear modern heads and have otherwise been freely restored.

Clarac, v, Pl. 874 B, No. 2221 E (710); Pl. 874 A, No. 2222 B (713); No. 2222 C (640); Pl. 874 B, No. 2222 D (717). Comp. Beschreibung Roms, III, 2, p. 545. No. 8, pp. 546, 547.

In the small room to the left, —

546 (641. **Statue of Marsyas.**

Both legs, from mid-thigh downwards, and both arms, from the biceps to near the wrist, are modern. The ancient parts have also been more or less retouched by a modern hand.

On the type, comp. No. 576.

Overbeck, Kunstmythologie, IV, p. 476, No. 1; Atlas. XXVI. 25.

Galleria del Canopo.

847 (698). Bust of a Barbarian.

The front of the nose, parts of the ears, most of the bust, and the muzzle and claws of the panther-skin are modern.

This bust is the portrait of a Barbarian, whose woolly hair, broad, flat face, and thick lips show a strong infusion of negro blood. The panther-skin thrown over the left shoulder affords farther proof of his African origin. He may have come to Rome as an ambassador or as a hostage, and seized the opportunity to have his portrait taken. The style of the execution points to a pre-Hadrianic date.

Berichte der sächs. Gesellschaft der Wissenschaften, 1868, p. 136.

848 (696). Mosaic of the Deliverance of Hesione.

Found in 1760 at Atina, near Arpino, in the kingdom of Naples.

Telamon helps the liberated Hesione to descend from the rock on which she had been chained as a victim for the sea-monster. Heracles, who has slain the monster with his arrows, stands by with a self-conscious air, his right hand resting on his club and his left hand holding a bow and two arrows. In front of him the head of the monster, transfixed by an arrow, protrudes from the sea. The square object lying on the ground beside Hesione, with its top in the shape of a pediment, has been taken for a house on fire and supposed to refer to the future destruction of Troja by Heracles. The article, however, is really nothing more or less than a toilette-casket.

Similar objects are seen in Campanian mural paintings, not only in connection with Hesione, but also accompanying Andromeda in a similar situation. This explanation is confirmed by the mirror leaning against the rock behind Hesione, and by the bottle of ointment in front of her. All these objects used to be placed in the tombs of women and girls, and their presence in the mosaic indicates that Hesione, like Andromeda, was considered as good as dead when exposed to the monster.

Winckelmann, Mon. ant. ined., T. 66, ii, pp. 90-92. *Millin.* Gal. myth., Pl. 115, No. 443. *Hirt.* Götter und Heroen, T. xxx, 266. *Guigniaut*, Rel. de l'ant., Pl. 282, 663. Comp. Beschreibung Roms, iii, 2, p. 554. *Welcker*, Alte Denkmäler, ii, p. 302. *Braun*, Ruinen und Museen, p. 718, No. 124. — For the wall-paintings. see *Helbig*, Wandgemälde der vom Vesuv verschütteten Städte Campaniens, Nos. 1132 (Atlas, xiv), 1183, 1187. Comp. Ann. dell' Inst., 1872, pp. 116-120.

849 (852). Ibis in rosso antico.

The restorations include the head and serpent, the neck, the tail, the rock below the tail, the legs, and probably also the claws and the plinth.

The sculptor's choice of material has evidently been determined by his desire to represent the ibis in its natural colour.

Beschreibung Roms, iii, 2, p. 497, No. 19. *Braun*, Ruinen und Museen, p. 715, No. 118.

850 (864). Atlas bearing the Heavens.

The only ancient portions are the upper half of Atlas, the rectangle on his back (with representations of Phosphoros and Hesperos, the morning and the evening star), and the signs of the Zodiac immediately adjoining this square — viz. the Balance to the right and the Virgin (head, front half of the lower right arm, and the adjoining drapery modern to the left. Enough, however, remained to show that the heavens were not represented by a globe but as a disk encircled by the Zodiac. Phosphoros and Hesperos are represented as youths with torches in their hands and stars on their heads. Phosphoros rises with his torch erect, while Hesperos sinks with his torch inverted. The sign of the Balance is also represented by a young man, holding a pair of scales in his lowered right hand (right arm from a little above the elbow modern, but attribute antique). The centre of other, more fully preserved representations of the Zodiac is occupied either by Zeus on his throne or by Helios in his chariot. The restorer of this work has selected the first of these motives, and has placed within the disk a figure of Zeus, which is mostly antique but does not belong to this monument.

Guattani, Mon. ant. ined. per l'ann. 1786, Luglio, T. III, pp. 53-56. *Zoega*, II, 108. *Müller-Wieseler*, Denkmäler der alten Kunst, II, 64, 823. Comp. *Raoul-Rochette*, Mémoire sur les représentations figurées du personnage d'Atlas, pp. 67, 68. *Braun*, Ruinen und Museen, p. 712, No. 116. *Gerhard*, Gesammelte akademische Abhandlungen, I, p. 20, p. 43, No. 2. *Gaedechens*, Der marmorne Himmelsglobus zu Arolsen, p. 8, p. 35, No. 3.

851 (685). Quadrangular Base with a Procession of Gods.

This base had already been discovered in the 16th century, as a drawing of it occurs in the Codex Pighianus (Berichte der sächs. Gesellschaft der Wissenschaften, 1868, T. v, 4, p. 193, No. 77). The restorations include the face and right arm of Dionysos, the head and right arm of Hermes (two fingers and the caduceus ancient), and the whole of the figure behind Hermes except a part of the left forearm. The drawing of Pighius represents Hermes with a bearded head. The reliefs have been retouched by a modern hand in several places; thus, in the Pighius drawing, Dionysos wears a nebris over his short chiton and not a cuirass.

It is generally agreed that these reliefs refer to the marriage of Zeus and Hera. The morsel of drapery still seen in front of the left knee of Artemis is supposed to have belonged to a figure of Apollo, chanting the bridal song and heading the procession. Artemis followed as the conductress of the bride, holding two torches. The matronly figure behind Artemis, with a sceptre in her right hand, is taken for Leto Latona , Tethys, or Rhea.

Next come Zeus, with his thunderbolt and his bird-crowned sceptre; Hera, modestly bending her head and drawing her mantle over her head and left cheek in the archaic manner; Poseidon, with his trident; Demeter, with a sceptre and a bunch of wheat-ears and poppies; Dionysos, with the thyrsos; and Hermes, with the caduceus. The figure behind the last-named god, of whom only a part of the left forearm has been preserved, was probably Hestia (Vesta), who was generally coupled with Hermes in assemblages of this kind. The theory that the base represents the marriage of Zeus and Hera, is, however, by no means beyond cavil. If this indeed be his subject, the sculptor has not been happily inspired in separating the bridal pair by putting them on different faces of the base. Moreover, we do not know whether the missing fourth side was occupied by an inscription or by other members of the procession, or how much is lacking of the adjacent portions of the connecting sides. Under these circumstances, it seems prudent to confine ourselves to the general assertion that the subject is a procession of gods. The execution is weak, and the imitation of the archaic style is very affected.

Zoega, II, 101. *Welcker*, Alte Denkmäler. II. T. 1, pp. 14-26. *Overbeck*, Kunstmythologie, II, p. 22, No. 5, III, p. 174c (where the entire bibliography on this subject is collected), p. 4023; Atlas, I, 4, x, 29. Comp. *Hauser*, Die neu-attischen Reliefs, p. 62, No. 91, p. 171.

852 (678). **Boy with a Mask.**

> The lower part of the mask, the hand projecting from the mouth, the legs, the stump, and the plinth are modern.

A boy has hidden himself behind a colossal mask and thrusts his left hand through the opening for the mouth, in order to terrify a companion, who must be imagined as standing in front of him. Comp. No. 825.

Braun, Ruinen und Museen, p. 716, No. 119.

853 (676). **Colossal Head of Serapis,** in green basalt.

> The upper edge of the modius, fragments of the hair, the point of the nose, the part of the face from the mouth downwards, and the bust are modern.

The sculptor has aimed at producing the effect of a
work in bronze. This is seen especially in the falling
curls, which look as if cast and chased. The expression
is one of melancholy seriousness. Comp. No. 241.

Overbeck, Kunstmythologie. II, p. 310, 10; Atlas, III, 14.

854 (677). Fragment of a Relief.

This badly mutilated fragment formed part of a
roughly-executed relief, probably on the lid of a sarcophagus, which represented the education of Dionysos or
some other infant god. The warrior at the right end
probably belonged to a scene in which the Curetes were
represented as guarding the boy — a motive properly
confined to the myth of the infant Zeus but also transferred to that of Dionysos. To the left are two rustics
with beards, whipping a naked boy; they were assisted
by a third individual of whom the left foot alone has been
preserved. The suggestion that this represents the Titans,
in the act of tearing Zagreus-Dionysos limb from limb, is
untenable. An ancient artist would have represented that
scene in a much more tragic fashion, and would never
have made the Titans of so vulgar a type. It is much
more likely to be one of those genre-scenes which are so
often intercalated in representations referring to the up-
bringing of infant deities. Comp. No. 443.

Zoega, II, 81. Guigniaut, Reliefs de l'ant.. Pl. 148, 554b.
Müller-Wieseler. Denkmäler der alten Kunst, II, 35, 413. Comp.
Beschreibung Roms, III, 2, p. 497, No. 14. Braun, Ruinen und
Museen, p. 716, No. 121. Ann. dell' Inst., 1870, p. 101.

855 (668). Torso of a Youth.

To judge from the delicacy of the forms and from the
curls falling on the shoulders, this torso must have belonged to a statue of Dionysos. The style, simple and
majestic, but still somewhat severe, is that characteristic
of Attic art in the best period (fifth century B. C.. The
imperfect light makes it impossible to say whether it is
an Attic original or only an excellent copy.

856 (662). Statue of Artemis.

The restorations include the right arm of the goddess, her left forefinger, and the front of the right foot, the head, the fore-legs, and the lower half of the left hind-leg of the animal, and almost all the plinth. The head (nose modern) is ancient but does not belong to the statue.

The simple and severe style of this statue points to a Greek — indeed we may say an Attic — original of about the middle of the fifth century B. C. It has been, with great probability, identified with Artemis, a goddess to whom both the virginal forms and the attributes are appropriate. The right arm, extended to the side, doubtless rested on a spear or sceptre. The restoration of the animal resting on the left arm of the goddess as a fawn is vindicated by its slender body and by the right hind-foot, which is cloven. Its position on the hand of the goddess is explained by the fact that Artemis was regarded, not only as the huntress who destroyed game, but also as the protectress of woodland creatures. Moreover, the earlier and more conventional Greek art was fond of placing the sacred animals in the closest possible relations with the divinities to which they were consecrated (comp. No. 923). The ancient head placed on this statue is a reproduction of that of the Apollo Sauroctonos of Praxiteles (comp. No. 194).

Clarac, II, Pl. 678F, No. 1621B. *Gerhard*, Antike Bildwerke, T.12. *Roscher*, Lexikon, I, 1, p.562. Comp. *Winckelmann*, Mon. ant. ined., II, p. 84. Beschreibung Roms, III, 2, p. 551. *Gerhard*, Prodromus, pp. 179 et seq. *Stephani*, Compte-rendu pour 1863, p. 221, note 5. Bull. dell' Inst., 1868, p. 37. *Furtwaengler*, Master-pieces, p. 26.

857 (663). Mosaic representing an Assembly of Sages.
Found at Sarsina in Umbria.

Six savants, grouped in a semicircle, listen attentively to a lecture delivered by one of their colleagues standing to the right. The latter is making a demonstration with his stick on a globe, and is evidently a geographer or astronomer. The young man standing to the left is a physician, if we may judge by the serpent held in his right hand. The architrave above him bears four vessels resembling retorts. In the background is a sun-dial, placed on the top of a pillar.

Winckelmann, Mon. ant. ined., T. 185, II, p. 242. *Grivaud de la Vincelle*, Arts et métiers des anciens, Pl. VIII, 19. Comp. *De Laborde*, Descripción de un pavimento en mosayico desc. en Itálica (Paris, 1806), p. 90. Beschreibung Roms, III, 2, p. 551. Abhandlungen der sächs. Ges. der Wiss., V (1868), p. 301, note 160.

In the garden, below the Galleria del Canopo, —

558 (590). Colossal Female Figure.

Formerly at the Villa d'Este, in Tivoli. The certain restorations include the nose, lips, left hand, and right fingers of the woman, the horns and fore-legs of the ox, the front part of the plinth, with its waves, and a large piece of the back of it.

The fact that waves are plastically represented on the plinth has led to this figure being taken for Amphitrite. No part, however, of the waves can be unhesitatingly recognized as ancient. Besides, the ox on which the figure leans its left hand would be quite out of place in a representation of Amphitrite. This animal is much more a symbol of dry land and occurs on two reliefs of the goddess or personification of the earth; the statue before us may therefore be either the Earth or the patron-deity or personification of some country.

Winckelmann, Mon. ant. ined., II, p. 52. *Zoega*, II, p. 279. Beschreibung Roms, III, 2, p. 563. *Braun*, Ruinen und Museen, p. 720, No. 126. — For the two bas-reliefs: *Fröhner*, Notice de la sculpture antique du Louvre, No. 414.

In the apse of the terrace above the Caffè, —

559 (799). Chimæra.

The certain restorations include the lion's head and the goat's head, with most of their necks, the ears and jaws of the wolf's head, the two fore-legs of the lion, nearly all the tail, and the plinth.

According to the legend the chimæra had two heads, one like a lion and one like a goat; and sculptors have usually represented them one behind the other. The artist of the present work, however, in order to enhance the terrific aspect of the creature, has added a wolf's head, and has placed all three heads alongside of each other, like those of Cerberus.

Braun, Zwölf Basreliefs, Vignette above the text of plate 1: Bellerophon. Comp. Ruinen und Museen, p. 722, No. 129.

Museo Boncompagni.

(Formerly in the Villa Ludovisi).

The most recent catalogue of this collection is *L. C. Visconti's* 'Descrizione dei monumenti di scultura antica del Museo Ludovisi' (Roma, 1891). *Theodor Schreiber*, in his work entitled 'Die antiken Bildwerke der Villa Ludovisi' (Leipzig, 1880), has carefully collected all the bibliography relative to the contents of this museum down to 1880; and the present writer therefore refers to this work, in the same way as he did to Benndorf und Schöne's catalogue in the case of the Lateran (see vol. I, p. 465), using the abbreviation *Sch.*, followed by the number.

First Room.

By the entrance, —

860 (75). **Seated Figure of a Man.**

> The restorations include the left forearm with the scroll, the right arm below the drapery, the front of the right foot, the left foot with the part of the drapery just above it, and the front half of the plinth. In the head, which seems to be ancient but does not belong to the figure, the restorations are the end of the nose, parts of the ears and forehead, and the right half of the chin.

According to the inscription on the border of the mantle, which dates, to judge from the forms of the letters, from not earlier than the second century of the present era, this statue is a work of Zeno, son of Attinas, of Aphrodisias Caria . Like Aristeas, Papias Nos. 512, 513), and other artists of the same town, Zeno did not invent for himself the motive of his statue, but used an earlier work as a model. A seated figure in the Capitoline Museum (No. 499, which apparently dates from the republican era, resembles in its general lines the statue before us. The latter, to judge from the tilting of the seat, was intended to occupy an elevated position (comp. No. 303).

Sch., No. 16. *Loewy*, Inschriften griechischer Bildhauer, No. 365.

The herma in the right front corner of this room (No. 76 of the Museum) and four others in the following room (Nos. 46, 62, 56, 52) evidently belong to the same series, since they are wrought in the same variety of Pentelic marble and closely resemble each other in arrangement, dimensions, and style. The writer will, therefore, treat of them together, beginning with those of certain identification and finishing with those that are doubtful.

561 (Room II, No. 16). **Heracles.**

The god wears a beard and has his lion-skin drawn over his head. The right hand rests on his club, the left holds a cornucopia, the symbol of fertility.

562 (II, 62). **Theseus.**

The name assigned to this herma is justified by the traditional description of Theseus as a 'second Heracles'. The type resembles that of No. 561; but the face is beardless, and the body more slender. The right hand shoulders a club. The attribute in the left hand, of which the handle alone remains, was evidently the strigil, with which the ancients removed from their bodies the sand and oil of the palaestra (comp. No. 31).

563 (II, 56). **Pallas.**

The head and neck down to the beginning of the drapery, the right forearm, the left hand and wrist, and most of the helmet have been restored. Of the last, however, most of the crest (touching the upper part of the arm) is ancient.

The goddess wears a chiton, the upper fold (apoptygma) of which reaches to mid-thigh, and an aegis of archaic form, which covers the back down to the lower edge of the apoptygma. The chiton and apoptygma are girt above the hips with a belt of serpents, knotted in front. The left hand held a helmet. The attribute in the right hand was doubtless a spear, the shaft of which touched the body near the right shoulder, where a piece of the marble has been broken off. The execution is inferior to that of the other hermæ.

564 (I, 76). **Hermes.**

This identification seems vindicated both by the general form of the body and by the fact that several undoubted images of the god have been found in this attitude and with this arrangement of the drapery. The lower part of the slender body is covered by a himation, which is wrapped round the left arm and held in place by the left hand on the hip. The deep mortise in the right forearm seems to indicate that the right hand held some heavy attribute, requiring a substantial fastening. This was, undoubtedly, a caduceus of bronze.

565 (II, 52). **Dionysos.**

> The front half of the right forearm and both hands, with the globes, are restorations. The whole figure has been slightly retouched by a modern hand.

This figure, of the masculine sex of which there can be no question, is clad in a long chiton and over it an ample mantle with numerous folds. Among the gods a dress of this kind has always characterized the Bearded Bacchus; and the identification of the herma with this deity seems, to say the least, very probable. To judge from the remains of the ancient arms, the hands were placed near each other and seem to have both held the same object, perhaps a two-handled cantharos.

These five hermæ were long regarded as Attic originals, some authorities dating them from the end of the fifth century B.C., others from the first half of the fourth. It is only quite recently that some doubt has been thrown upon their originality, the latest research holding them for admirable copies, perhaps by an Attic sculptor, of types by different masters. If this view, however, be correct, the copyist has so neutralized the differences in style, that it would be difficult to name definitely the creators of the originals. The identification of No. 862 with Theseus has been challenged, and the name of Heracles suggested as a substitute. As, however, the five hermæ evidently form an ensemble and as No. 861 is undoubtedly a Heracles, it is clear that this hero would not be represented twice over in the same series. In any case the simple and imposing, and at the same time somewhat severe, style proves that the hermæ stand in close relation to Athenian art of the best period (fifth century B.C.). The transition from the human body to the shaft of the herma is accomplished in the most masterly manner. The shafts are of just the length that would have naturally been assigned to the legs in the art of the period. In order to appreciate the execution, it is desirable to pay particular attention to those parts that were least exposed to the weather and so have preserved their surface more or less intact. These parts are treated with a delicacy of feeling and of finish that are in every respect worthy of an Attic chisel. The Pallas alone (No. 863; Room II, No. 56) is somewhat less perfect in this regard. As we know from express statements that the ancients used to erect images of Heracles, Theseus, and Hermes in their gymnasia, it has been assumed that our hermæ adorned a gymnasium or some similar building. There is, however, good evidence that cycles of hermæ were also used in the decoration of sanctuaries.

Mon. dell' Inst., x, T. 56, T. 57, Nos. 2, 2a; Ann., 1878, pp. 210 et seq. — *Sch.*, Nos. 1, 3, 55, 60. 65. Comp. *Hartwig*, Herakles mit dem Füllhorn (Leipzig, 1833), p. 3, No. 1. pp. 49 et seq., p. 56. *Roscher*, Lexikon der griech. und röm. Mythologie, I, 1, p. 2159. Bayerische Sitzungsberichte, 1892, pp. 660-662. *Furtwaengler*, Masterpieces, pp. 299, 357.

866 (80). Head of a Sleeping Fury, from a Colossal Group.

This head is carved in Pentelic marble. The restorations include almost all the nose, the right half of the lower lip, the lock falling below the chin (upper end ancient), the breast, the shoulders and the ends of the locks touching them, and the whole of the oval background.

To judge from the conception, style, and technique, this beautiful head dates from an advanced stage of the Hellenistic period. The expression is serious and severe, while the protruding under-lip gives it an air of displeasure.

Fig 35.

The eyes are closed; but the gentle inclination of the head towards the left and the lips, parted as in regular and quiet breathing, prove that the head is that of a woman asleep, not of one dying or dead. It is not Medusa, as has hitherto been supposed, and differs materially from the authenticated types of the Gorgon. It also lacks the serpents and the wings, which invariably characterize the head of Medusa when represented by ancient art in profile. On the other hand the head agrees in all essential points with a type assigned in various monuments to the Furies. The hair, tangled by the wind, and the locks on the cheek, heavy with perspiration, indicate the ardour with which the Fury has been pursuing a criminal. She is sleeping for the nonce; but even in her sleep she retains her severity of expression and her wrath against the miscreant. The head seems to have belonged to a group of two sleeping Furies, of which we can form some idea by a painting on a vase of Magna Græcia (Fig. 35).

One of the Furies leans her head against her sister. A close examination of the head before us shows that the hair at the back, immediately above the modern background of the relief, is not treated like the rest. This part of the marble also shows no trace of corrosion. It may, then, be surmized that there was an 'amorce' here, which the modern restorer has removed, chiselling it away down to the level of the head and then carving the hair on the surface thus prepared. In all likelihood this amorce projected from the breast of the other Fury, on which the head before us reclined. The Hellenistic artist who created this colossal group of sleeping Furies may have been inspired, either by the opening scene of the Eumenides of Æschylos, or by two celebrated paintings, one of which depicted the same subject as the plastic group, the other the Furies sleeping at the grave of Agamemnon.

Mon. dell' Inst., VIII, 35; Ann., 1871, Tav. d'agg. ST, pp. 212 et seq. *Baumeister*, Denkmäler des klass. Alterthums, II, p. 911, Fig. 986. *Brunn und Bruckmann*, Denkm. griech. und röm. Sculptur, No. 1419. *Roscher*, Lexikon der griech. und röm. Mythologie, I, p. 1726. *Sch.*, No. 110. Comp. *Friederichs-Wolters*, Bausteine, No. 1419. *Six*, De Gorgone, p. 65. Verhandlungen der 37. Philologenversammlung in Dessau, pp. 72 et seq. (= *Brunn*, Griechische Götterideale, Pl. V, pp. 54–67). Journal of Hellenic Studies, XI (1890), pp. 197, 198. Rendiconti della reale Accademia dei Lincei, classe di scienze morali, vol. VI (1890), pp. 342–350. Römische Mittheilungen, VII (1892), pp. 106. 107.

867 (83). Statue of Antoninus Pius.

> The restorations include the lower half of the face, the right ear, some of the locks of hair, almost all the right arm, and the left forearm. The head has been broken off and replaced, but seems to be the original.

This statue shows the emperor in the act of addressing his troops. A military commander in this attitude is usually represented by Græco-Roman art in the armour he might actually have worn (comp. Nos. 5, 649 ; but Antoninus Pius is here depicted, in the Greek heroic fashion, as clad in a chlamys only (comp. No. 637). The armour is indicated by the accessories. A Corinthian helmet stands on the plinth; while on the stump, supporting the right leg, hangs a cuirass, apparently made of leather and furnished with lambrequins.

Sch., No. 87. *Bernoulli*, Römische Ikonographie, II, 2, p. 141, No. 3, p. 150.

By the first window (in the corner by the door), —

568 (74). Herma of an Athlete.

The powerful chest, fully inflated and with out-standing muscles, indicates that the young athlete was engaged in an exercise requiring violent exertion. The remains of the arms show that they were raised above the head and inclined to the left, so that the right arm was somewhat higher than the left. The head is also bent a little to the right, while the eyes look over the upper part of the right arm into the distance. The lips are parted in a slight smile. The hands must have been pretty close to each other. All these points make it probable that the athlete was swinging a disk with both hands, and looking at the same time at the spot he was about to aim at. In choosing the form of a herma to represent such an action as this, the sculptor has undoubtedly committed an artistic error; for the animated movement of the body forms a glaring contrast to the architectonic principle of the shaft. The transition from the body to the shaft seems also much less skilfully managed here than in Nos. 561-565. The style still shows traces of archaism, especially in the treatment of the hair and in the too high position of the ears. The head recalls that of Cladeos in the east pediment of the temple of Zeus at Olympia. The surface has been so much injured, that it is hard to tell whether we are in presence of an archaic original or merely of a good copy; but the latter supposition is the more probable. The back is in a fair state of preservation but does not show the freshness which usually characterizes genuine archaic works.

Mon. dell' Inst., x, T. 57, Nos. 1, 1a; Ann., 1878, pp. 216-221. Sch., No. 8. Comp. Römische Mittheilungen, II (1887), p. 106.

Second Room.

869 (54). Colossal Replica of the Aphrodite of Cnidos.

The head, the torso, the shoulders, the thighs, and the left knee are ancient, while the rest of the figure has been restored. The forms are somewhat heavy, and the surface has been freely smoothed by a modern hand. Comp. No. 316.

Sch., No. 97. Journal of Hellenic Studies, VIII (1887), p. 335J. *Furtwaengler*, Masterpieces, p. 366, note 3, No. 6.

For the Herma of Pallas, No. 56 of the Museum, see No. 863 of the present volume.

870 (57). Colossal Statue of Pallas.

> The restorations include the crest of the helmet, the point of the nose, part of the lower lip, both arms, the part of the edge of the aegis at the shoulders, the ends of the snake-girdle projecting from the knot, and various fragments of the folds of the drapery. The restorer has retouched the bridge of the nose; and in many cases where the restoration of the folds gave him trouble, particularly in the apoptygma, he has simply smoothed them out of existence.

This statue is one of the largest, and at the same time one of the most faithful, of all extant reproductions of the Athena Parthenos of Pheidias (comp. Nos. 598, 600, 898). Its effect, however, is sadly impaired by false restorations and by its free retouching and modification by a modern hand. The new crest of the helmet is too small. The end of the nose has been unskilfully restored and the bridge retouched. The apoptygma, or overhanging fold of the chiton, looks as if it were in rags, the restorer having chiselled away many of its folds, especially near its lower edge. The arms are too thick, and their attitude is inaccurate. The right hand was outstretched and held a small figure of Victory, while the left hand hung by the side and rested on the rim of the shield. The statue is most effective when viewed in profile from the right, as the folds on this side have been less tampered with, and the general impression is not marred except by the incorrect restoration of the arm. The sculptor seems to have followed his model not only in its main features but also in many points of detail. The helmet of the Athena Parthenos was adorned with winged animals; and it is still evident that the helmet of the figure before us bore some similar emblems, though the restorer has done his best to efface the traces of their existence. As is well known, the flesh-parts of the Athena Parthenos were made of ivory, while the rest of the figure was of gold, relieved at places by enamel. In the statue before us the treatment of the short curls on the cheeks, as well as of the longer ones falling on the shoulders, resembles the chasing of cast metal; while the angular folds of the drapery suggest the sharp edges produced in metal either in the casting or by repoussé work. The scales of the ægis, which Pheidias doubtless represented by enamelled plates of gold, were evidently indicated in the Boncompagni statue by painting. The sculptor has carved his name on the end of the drapery near the right foot; but, as the first two letters have disappeared, we cannot determine whether it should read Antiochos or Metiochos. The form of the letters points to the last century of the Republic or the first of the Empire. The sculptor informs us that he is an Athenian; he must have belonged to the number of those late-Attic artists who confined themselves to the production of more or less faithful copies of ancient masterpieces. The statue he has left us gives us at least an approximate idea of one of the most important creations of Hellenic art. In his Athena Parthenos Pheidias expressed, in the most majestic and exhaustive manner, the views of their patron deity held by the cultivated Athenians of the golden age of Pericles. While the helmet, the ægis, and the sturdy body proclaim the warlike virgin, who protects the city of Athens and increases its power, Athena appears at the same time as a goddess of peace, with youthful face and clear and calm eyes. Conscious of her might, she has placed her shield on the ground, and holds out to the worshipper in her temple the symbol of her power — Nike, who brings victory and safety.

Sch., No. 114. Abhandlungen der phil.-hist. Classe der sächs. Gesellschaft der Wissenschaften, VIII (1883), T. II B, 1, 2, pp. 556 et seq. *Brunn und Bruckmann*, Denkmäler, No. 253. Comp. *Loewy*, Inschriften griechischer Bildhauer, No. 342. Arch. Zeitung, XLI (1883), p. 207. Jahrbuch des Arch. Instituts, V (1890), pp. 101 et seq. For the head and the helmet of the Parthenos: Festschrift zum fünfzigjährigen Jubiläum des Vereins von Alterthumsfreunden im Rheinlande (Bonn, 1891), pp. 1 et seq. *Furtwaengler*, Masterpieces, pp. 107 et seq.

871 (59). Statue of Hermes.

> The restorations, which were made by Algardi, include the end of the nose and the right nostril, most of the brim of the hat, the wings on the hat (of the former presence of which no marks are traceable), the right arm (part next the shoulder ancient), the forefinger and half of the thumb of the left hand, the wallet, the feet, and the plinth.

The right arm and the attribute in the left hand have been wrongly restored. The movement of this arm lends an emotional trait to the statue, quite out of keeping with the general attitude of the figure and with the expression of the face. As is proved by the so-called statue of Germanicus in the Louvre, which is identical in motive with the figure before us, the right arm was raised towards the head, and the right hand, with the thumb and forefinger together, was placed near the temples. The left hand held, in lieu of a wallet, an inverted caduceus, of bronze, a fragment of which still exists inside the hand. Hermes was thus represented as the god of eloquence (λόγιος). He stands in a collected attitude, inclining his head, the features of which express thoughtful seriousness, towards his auditors. The gesture of his right hand was that of one demonstrating a point with logical accuracy. As he speaks, the drapery slips from his left arm. This detail is evidently intended to heighten the impression of absorption in his discourse. The sculptor, however, has failed to overcome the difficulty attending a plastic representation of an object in motion; for the drapery does not look as if it were slipping downwards, but as if it were artificially fixed to the arm. In its forms and proportions the head recalls the type of the early Peloponnesian school, such as is reproduced, for example, in the statue by Stephanos (No. 744). The body strikes us by the contrast between the powerful forms of the torso and thighs and the weak development of the lower part of the legs. We may date the creation of the original somewhere about the middle of the fifth century B. C. The hypothesis that it is a work of the Phocian Telephanes, a sculptor little known in ancient times, seems to the writer to lack satisfactory foundation.

Müller-Wieseler, Denkmäler der alten Kunst, II, T. 29, 318. *Rayet*, Monuments de l'art antique, II. Text of Pl. 70, p. 5. *Sch.*, No. 94. Comp. *Overbeck*, Geschichte der griech. Plastik, II⁴, p. 446, p. 456, note 4. *Friederichs-Wolters*, No. 1630. Aus der Anomia (Berlin, 1890), pp. 62, 69. Fünfzigstes Berliner Winckelmannsprogramm (1890), p. 152. *Furtwaengler*, Masterpieces, p. 57.

The herma of Theseus 'No. 62 of the Museum' is discussed under No. 862.

872 (66). Colossal Head of Hera.

> This head is probably identical with the colossal female head, which Cardinal Ludovico Ludovisi acquired from the Villa Cesi in 1622. The restorations include the end of the nose, part of the right nostril, and the lock of hair hanging on the right side of the neck (except a small piece near the upper end of it).

The way in which the lower edge of the neck is cut shows that this head was meant to be inserted in a colossal statue, and that, consequently, it was intended to be seen at a considerable height. Known as the Juno Ludovisi, it is one of the most famous of ancient monuments; and men like Herder, Winckelmann, Goethe, Schiller, and Wilhelm von Humboldt have eloquently described the deep impression it made on them. The question of the date of its original creation has lately been thoroughly thrashed out by numerous archæologists, but so far with-

out agreement. This difference of opinion is primarily
caused by the paucity of the land-marks handed down
to us by tradition concerning the evolution of the ideal
of Hera. In the next place, we have no adequate idea
of the effect the head would produce if put in position
on a colossal statue. Lastly, many of the finer points of
the face elude our analysis, because the surface has suffered seriously from corrosion and injudicious attempts
at cleaning. In any case the conception and style of the
head prove that its type was created at a later date than
that of Nos. 297 and 507. If the latter belongs to the
end of the fifth century B. C., then the original of the
Juno Ludovisi cannot date earlier than from an advanced
stage of the fourth century. We may also take for granted
that the Second Attic School had a prominent share in
the creation of this type; for the head before us shows
the deep hollow between the nose and the eyes that was
characteristic of the work of this school. The handling
of the flesh, so far as we can judge in the present state
of the surface, reveals a softness and a delicate feeling
for naturalism such as do not occur in Hellenic art before the time of Alexander the Great. If, therefore, we
credit the Second Attic School with the entire invention
of this type, it is of the younger, and not of the older,
generation of the school that we must think. The original was created in an epoch of varied and advanced cul-
ture, when the Hellenes, especially those of the upper
classes, invested the ideal of the wife with a milder character than that of the fifth century, and one more in
touch with the conception of the present day. Thus,
among all the celebrated types of Hera, that of the
Juno Ludovisi has appealed most strongly to the modern beholder. It is distinguished, not only by a perfect
physical form, but by that harmonious blending of dignity
and mildness, which, according to the conception of the
Greeks of the period, was appropriate for the consort of
Zeus. Comp. Nos. 50, 244, 297, and 507.

Starting from the premise that the knot of hair at

the nape of the neck and the knotted ribbons entwining the diadem never occur in heads of goddesses but do occur in numerous portraits of ladies of the Julian-Claudian dynasty, an authority has recently tried to prove that the Juno Ludovisi is an idealized portrait of a Roman empress or of some other member of the imperial family. Demeter, in a Pompeian mural painting, wears, however, this kind of headdress. Moreover, the degree of idealization assumed in this case is such as would annihilate every individual trait, and would seek in vain for an analogy elsewhere.

Müller-Wieseler, Denkmäler der alten Kunst, II, 4, 55. *Overbeck*, Kunstmythologie, III, pp. 63 et seq., pp. 83 et seq., No. 4, p. 199, note 53; Atlas, IX, 7, 8. *Baumeister*, Denkmäler des klass. Alterthums, III, p. 1352, Fig. 1505. *Roscher*, Lexikon der griech. und röm. Mythologie, I, pp. 2120, 2122, 2123. *Brunn*, Griechische Götterideale, pp. 9-14. *Furtwaengler*, Masterpieces, pp. 326 et seq. For other references, see *Sch.*, No. 104. — On the Pompeian wallpainting, see *Helbig*, Wandgemälde, No. 176.

S73 (67). Bronze Head of an Aged Roman.

Acquired from the Villa Cesi in 1622 by Cardinal Ludovisi. The bust is modern.

This highly lifelike head appears, both from the type of the physiognomy and from its style, to belong to the transition from the Republic to the Empire. It is the portrait of an elderly Roman, with well-marked features, a wrinkled visage, and an expression of mingled meditation and vexation. He must have been a man of some reputation, as at least one other ancient replica of his portrait is extant. The identification with the elder Scipio Africanus comp. No. 484) or with Julius Caesar is as baseless as the doubt that has been thrown on the genuine antiquity of the head.

Sch., No. 91. *Bernoulli*, Römische Ikonographie, I, p. 177, Fig. 26, p. 37, note 3, p. 157, pp. 165, 175, 176.

For the Herma of Heracles, bearing the number 46, and for the so-called Herma of Dionysos No. 52), see Nos. 861 and 865 of the present volume.

Third Room.

874 (38). Youth resting.

> The restorations include the left forearm, the thumb,
> forefinger, middle finger, and most of the ring-finger of
> the right hand, the sword (part between the right thumb
> and the left leg ancient), parts of the right side and of
> the right hip, the left foot, the right foot (except the
> heel), and a great part of the front margin of the plinth
> (to the right). The head (nose and most of the upper lip
> restored) is ancient, but is of a different kind of marble
> from the body and does not belong to it. In order to
> join the two fragments, the modern restorer has pared
> down the back and sides of the part of the neck belong-
> ing to the head. The parts thus retouched are recogniz-
> able by their white colour, contrasting with the brownish
> tone of the rest of the marble.

A vigorous youth sits in an easy attitude on the
ground. He has thrown his left leg over the right, and
crossed his arms in such a way that the left elbow rests
on the left knee, while the right hand, holding a sheathed
sword, rests on the left shin. The statue was destined
for a position below the level of the beholder; and if the
visitor will mount upon a chair he will escape the carelessly executed under-side of the left thigh and so get a
better impression of the perfection of modelling in the
rest of the figure. It may be supposed that this statue
and a companion-figure were placed in front of an entrance as ideal guardians. The proportions, especially
the slenderness of the trunk as compared with the limbs,
resemble those ascribed to Euphranor, one of the earlier
masters of the Second Attic School (comp. No. 188). The
treatment of the nude also accords with the practice of
the early days of this school, before it was influenced
by the realistic tendencies of Lysippos. The head, dating
at the earliest from the time of the Antonines, shows a
superficial resemblance to the type of Meleager discussed
under No. 133.

Sch., No. 118. Comp. Römische Mitth., IV (1889), p. 221,
No. 17.

875 (20). **Colossal Bust of Atys.**

The point of the bonnet, the nose, parts of the lips, the chin, and the pedestal are modern.

The identification of this bust is vindicated by full-length figures of Atys, with his attributes comp. No. 700). The shape of the bust is that of a man, but the face and neck show rounded feminine forms, while the coiffure is also that of a woman. The pensive and melancholy expression characteristic of the favourite of Cybele is heightened by the treatment of the mouth, which is open, as if to emit a gentle plaint. The Phrygian cap ends on both sides and behind in three broad ribbons, the ends of which, weighted with balls of lead, fall on the neck and shoulders.

Sch., No. 76.

876 (23). **Colossal Bust of Hygieia.**

The nose and the pedestal are modern.

The naming of this bust is based on the two serpents, placed opposite each other on the diadem (comp. No. 158). The expression, indicating a singular blending of benevolence and severity, is also characteristic of the goddess Hygieia. The left shoulder of the bust is higher than the right, an anomaly which may, perhaps, be explained by the assumption that it was modelled after a statue. The transition from the bust to the pedestal is masked by a garland of leaves, as in the bust of Antinoos,

No. 300. The execution is indifferent.

Sch., No. 107.

877 (25). **Colossal Statue of Apollo.**

The following restorations are quite evident: both arms, the cithara (except a small piece of the sounding-board, adjoining the drapery), most of the left breast, the left leg below the drapery, the lower end of the pedum, and parts of the rock, particularly in front of the right foot. The head is ancient, but has been freely retouched and belonged to another type of Apollo, in which the right hand was placed on the head.

The numerous restorations seem vindicated by the condition of the ancient parts and by better-preserved replicas of the same type. The cithara, however, seems to have been lower down, and thus the left arm of the god, if the hand rested on the bridge, must also have occupied a lower position. It is, however, possible that the left hand touched the strings. It also seems likely that the right arm did not occupy the unintelligible and theatrical attitude assigned to it by the restorer, but hung by the side, holding a plectrum. This type owes its special place among the types of Apollo to the idyllic spirit with which it is pervaded. The god sits in an easy attitude on a rock, over which his mantle is spread. The pedum leaning against the rock accentuates the pastoral character of the motive. We have, however, in this connection to think of the god, not in his capacity of protector of the flock (νόμιος), but as acting as shepherd for Admetos or Laomedon. The sculptor has undoubtedly made a mistake in reproducing the figure on a colossal scale, for it is obvious that more moderate dimensions would have been vastly more suitable to the idyllic-genre nature of the statue. The motive of the figure seems borrowed from a type of Apollo known to us from the reliefs of the Altar of the Twelve Gods at Athens.

Sch., No. 116. Overbeck, Kunstmythologie, II, p. 202, No. 2; Atlas, XXII, 38. Furtwaengler. Masterpieces, p. 337, note 2. For the Altar of the Twelve Gods, see Athen. Mittheilungen, IV (1879), T. xx, pp. 340-342.

878. Circular Base.

The restorations include the cornice and a piece of the upper part of the drum, with the upper part of one winged figure and the head of another.

Four short-skirted female figures stand on tiptoe on ornaments in the form of calices, placed among four interlacing vine-tendrils, which the girls grasp with both hands. In attitude and in costume these figures resemble dancing girls on other monuments (comp. Nos. 769, 816); and, in spite of their wings, they probably represent dancers and not Victories. A base in the Palazzo Doria is adorned with similar reliefs, and there the four winged maidens wear the coronets of reeds peculiar to dancing-girls (comp. No. 816). As the figures here are in the closest connection with the ornamental flourishes and thus belong, so to say, to a decorative sphere, the artist has felt at liberty to free himself from the usual trammels and to represent his dancing girls with the fanciful attraction of wings. The composition is full of fine feeling, but the execution is slight.

Sch., No. 79. *Hauser*, Die neu-attischen Reliefs, p. 97, No. 20a. — For the base in the Pal. Doria, see *Matz-Duhn*, Antike Bild-werke in Rom, III, No. 3678.

879 (30). Trunk of a Tree, with Bacchic Attributes.
The base is modern.

This knotty and gnarled stump, ascending in regular spirals, is entwined with tendrils of ivy and vine. The branches have been cut off close to the stem, and on one of them is placed a small patera filled with votive offerings. A little lower down is an ivy-crowned mask of Silenus, suspended by a string of pearls, while on an adjoining branch hangs a pair of cymbals. The lower part of the trunk is missing. The upper end is surrounded by a garland of leaves, opening in the form of a calyx; its section is rough-hewn, and in the centre is a mortise-joint intended for the reception of some object now wanting. Tree-trunks of this kind, of which several have come down to us, have generally been taken for the shafts of candelabra. Several examples, however, have been found in the Villa of Quintus Voconius Pollio, near Marino, in the upper end of which a pine-cone was inserted; and a similar stump in the Villa Borghese (No. 909) is surmounted by two pine-cones. These stumps seem then to be, not candelabrum-shafts, but plastic ornaments for a garden, like No. 310.

Sch., No. 18. The examples found in the Villa of Pollio are mentioned in one of the reports of the excavations (Notizie degli scavi, 1881, p. 84) simply as 'candelabri marmorei'. In the other report (Bull. della commissione arch. comunale di Roma, XII, 1884, p. 162 h) they are also described as candelabra, but it is expressly added that they were crowned with pine-cones.

550 (31). Colossal Bust of Demeter with diadem and veil.

The end of the nose and a piece of the neck below the right ear are modern.

The mild expression of this beautiful face culminates in the marvellously gentle look in the eyes, which are comparatively small; the lips are parted in a benevolent smile. These details are decidedly out of keeping with the current identification of this bust with Hera, and seem, from all points of view, much more characteristic of Demeter. The supposition that the bust represents Demeter finds confirmation in the statue, now in the collection of Mr. Karl Jacobsen of Copenhagen, which seems to be identical with the much-discussed example, formerly in the possession of the Marquis Rondanini. After a minute examination of the left hand of this statue, which holds a bunch of wheat-ears and poppies, the writer is convinced that it is antique, except the third and little fingers; the statue must therefore represent Demeter. The type of the head is in all essentials the same as that of the bust before us.

Overbeck, Kunstmythologie, III, p. 95, No. 15; Atlas, IX, 12. Sch., No. 78. Friederichs-Wolters, Bausteine, No. 1515. Roscher, Lexikon, I, pp. 2122, 2126; II, p. 1360. — For the Rondanini statue, see Müller-Wieseler, Denkmäler der alten Kunst, II, 8, 87. Roscher, Lexikon, II, pp. 1359-1361, Fig. 10. Comp. Overbeck, Kunstmythologie, III, pp. 110, 111.

551 (32). Young Satyr pouring wine.

The restorations include the raised right arm, with the adjoining part of the breast, the left forearm with the drinking-horn, the lower part of the right leg, and parts of the stump and of the rear-edge of the plinth. The right foot and the lowest part of the horn, touching the left thigh, are antique.

This figure must have been very popular in antiquity, as numerous replicas of it have come down to us. It represents a young Satyr of the highest type, whose animal nature is but slightly hinted at in his pointed ears and matted hair. The restorer has made a mistake in placing a bunch of grapes in the right hand; other replicas, in which the attribute has been preserved in whole or in part, show that it rather held a pitcher, from which the Satyr poured wine into the drinking-horn in the left hand. The easy attitude and the movement of the arms are incomparably graceful. There seems no doubt that the type stands in close relation to the art of Praxiteles, though it cannot be identified with any special Satyr handed down by tradition as the work of that master. The whole statue is very finely worked, and the sculptor has treated with an almost excessive care such accessories as the goatskin hung over the stump, the pedum leaning against it, and the syrinx hanging from one of the branches.

Sch., No. 71. Bull. della commissione arch. comunale, xx (1892), Pl. xi, xii, No. 1, pp. 237 et seq. Comp. *Kekulé*, Ueber den Kopf des praxitelischen Hermes, p. 31. *Friederichs-Wolters*, Bausteine, No. 1217. Arch. Zeitung, xliii (1855), pp 82-85. *Furtwaengler*, Masterpieces, pp. 310 et seq., 319.

882 (33). Colossal Archaic Head of a Goddess.

The front of the nose has been restored in antiquity.

The edge of the section of the neck is cut in such a way as shows the head was meant to be inserted in a statue. This statue seems to have been an acrolith — *i.e.* a figure in which the flesh was made of marble, while the parts covered by the drapery were made of wood, lined with sheets of metal. The vertical section of the neck is only 3-4½ centimètres in height. Its execution is careless, and below this section the marble forms a somewhat acute angle. This arrangement would be pointless, if the head were meant to be joined to a marble body. The lower part of the neck, not now visible, must have been pierced by a hole for the reception of the wooden peg attaching the head to the body.

In order to obtain an adequate idea of the effect of

this head, we must supply in imagination various accessories worked in metal. On the upper part of the forehead, just below the hair, are drilled sixteen small holes, most of which still contain bronze pegs. These evidently represent sixteen small locks of bronze, placed below the marble part of the hair. Two somewhat larger holes drilled in the hair, near the ears, must have served for the attachment of one or two curls falling on the neck on both sides. The ears are pierced, evidently for metal earrings; while two holes in the neck show it was encircled by two metal necklaces. It also seems that a metal drapery covered the top of the head. The front part of the coiffure, including the locks both of marble and bronze, is very carefully worked; while the locks falling from the skull are merely indicated by lines in the marble. This is easily explained by the assumption that the skull was covered by the drapery. This supposition is confirmed by two other facts. In front, on the upper part of the marble section of the hair, is cut a strip, the length of which corresponds almost exactly to the distance between the external angles of the eyes. Two holes, both on the right side, are also bored on the upper edge of the fillet encircling the head. We may assume that the sculptor cut away the strip of hair above the forehead in order to provide a suitable fastening for the front part of the mantle; and that the holes in the fillet contained metal hooks to fix the vertical folds of the drapery. The presence of these holes on the right side only might be explained by the hypothesis that the left hand drew a fold of the drapery across the left check, a not uncommon gesture in archaic art. In this case the metal drapery on the left side would be supported by the hand and there would be no occasion for hooks. A consideration of all these details leads us to the conclusion that the mantle was drawn over the head in the same way as in the representations of Penelope (so called; Nos. 92, 191) and of the young wife (?) on the support of the throne No. 592.

Authorities are agreed that the head before us is an archaic Greek original of the early part of the fifth century B. C., but they differ as to the school to which it should be assigned. It offers points of contact with works differing widely in origin, such as archaic types of Peloponnesian art, the head of the statue of a woman dedicated on the Acropolis of Athens by a certain Enthydicos, and the head of a goddess represented on some coins of Syracuse (Fig. 36).

It is difficult to give any precise name to the head before us. The art which produced it had still to struggle

Fig. 36.

with technical difficulties and consequently was not in a position to characterize diverse individualities with clearness. The head, moreover, has not yet been examined at the height at which it was meant to be seen. The suggestions offered oscillate between Hera, Artemis, and Aphrodite. The last suggestion seems the most probable; for the careful arrangement of the tresses and the rich ornaments accord best with the goddess of love. It is true that the protruding under-lip gives the head, in its present position, a certain air of ill-humour, but this expression is not visible in a plaster cast placed at a higher elevation. On the contrary, the mouth then seems to wear a sweet smile entirely appropriate to Aphrodite. Comp. No. 592.

Mon. dell' Inst., x, 1; Ann., 1874, pp. 38 et seq. *Baumeister*, Denkmäler des klass. Alterthums, I, p. 337, Fig. 362. *Brunn und Bruckmann*, Denkmäler griech. und röm. Sculptur. No. 223. *Sch.*, No. 23. Comp. Athenische Mittheilungen, VII (1882), p. 117, xv (1890), pp. 11, 13. Röm. Mittheilungen, VII (1892), pp. 62 et seq.

Fig. 36 reproduces, on double the actual scale, a didrachma of Syracuse in the possession of Signor Francesco Martinetti.

883 (37). **Ares reposing.**

Found between the Palazzo Santa Croce and the Palazzo Campitelli. The restorations include the nose of Ares (right nostril ancient), the right hand except the part touching the left knee, the ends of the thumb and index-finger of the left hand, the sword-hilt and part of the sheath, and the right foot (heel ancient); the head of the Eros, the left arm and quiver, the right forearm and bow, the right foot, and a piece of the lower part of the right leg. The restoration of the quiver was indicated by the nature of the fracture.

Ares sits at his ease on a rock, stretching out his right leg, while the left rests on his helmet, lying on the ground beside him. The hands are crossed on the left knee, the left hand holding the sheath of the undrawn sword. The head, slightly inclined towards the right shoulder, wears an expression of dreamy pensiveness. To indicate the cause of this unusual mood of the god of war, the sculptor has placed a small figure of Eros, sitting, as in ambush, behind the right leg of Ares. It seems doubtful whether the Eros held a bow in his right hand, as assumed by the modern restorer. Possibly he had no attribute in this hand, but gently touched the leg of Ares in order to apprize him of his presence. The head of Ares corresponds to a type created by the Second Attic School, while the body approaches the naturalism introduced into art by Lysippos. It has been supposed that the group before us may be a reproduction of a work placed in the temple of Concord at Rome — *viz.* the Ares of Piston, who seems to have flourished at the end of the fourth, or the beginning of the third, century B.C. But this hypothesis is one of those which can neither be demonstrated nor refuted. A more plausible theory is that it may go back to a later work of Scopas, such as the sitting Ares in the temple of Mars built at Rome by D. Junius Brutus Callœcus (Pliny, Nat. Hist., 36, 26). We cannot, of course, attribute to Scopas the teasing motive of the Eros and his conception under the form of a child. But it seems quite possible that the Eros is a detail added by the copyist. The melancholy expression of the god in this case would be explained, not by his being in love, but by his condemnation to temporary inactivity. The execution is mediocre and even, in such accessories as the greaves, positively formless.

Certain traces visible on the left side indicate that the group is imperfect in this direction. On the left shoulder of Ares are the remains of an elongated support, running aslant and widening towards its middle. In this support, at the height of the shoulder, a round hole is drilled in an oblique direction. Below the left shoulder is an incision, of rather more than a finger's breadth, running towards the support on the shoulder. Behind the end of the sword, just under the drapery, is the fragment of a square support; and on the rock below this is the trace of a fracture. The part of the mantle above this fracture seems to have been freely retouched by the modern restorer. Traces of a slighter retouching are also visible on the part of the rock below the fracture, and the corresponding part of the edge of the plinth has been cut smooth by a modern hand. One hypothesis is that a second Eros stood on the projection of the rock that has been broken off, laying his right hand on the left shoulder of Ares (comp. No. 893). But if this Eros ever existed, his position, from the nature of the case, must have been singularly forced and at a very unnatural angle. Besides, the 'amorce' on the shoulder of Ares seems much too large for the tiny hand of Eros. Another theory places Aphrodite to the left of Ares. The goddess, on this supposition, must have just approached and must be touching the left shoulder of her lover with some such object as the handle of her fan. In this case, however, it seems, to say the least of it, curious, that the god of war, instead of paying any attention to Aphrodite, is looking straight in front of him, as if he were alone. Besides, the harmonious play of the lines of the figure of Ares, from whatever position we regard it, would be seriously marred by the introduction of a second figure of coördinate importance. Still another supposition is that a spear, with its point downward, leaned against the left side of the god, and that the strap attached to it for hurling it through the air (ἀγκύλη) passed round his arm, just below the shoulder. It is quite possible that the incision below the left shoulder may have been occupied by a metal band. But the presence of a light object, such as the shaft of a spear, seems entirely inadequate to account for the marks on the left shoulder and for those on the rock below. The problem as to what originally occupied the place to the left of the figure must therefore be regarded as still unsolved.

Baumeister, Denkmäler des klass. Alterthums, I, p. 121, Fig. 126. *Sch.*, No. 63. Athenische Mittheilungen, vi (1881), p. 121. Jahrbuch des Arch. Instituts, iv (1889); Arch. Anzeiger, p. 41. Verhandlungen der 41. Versammlung deutscher Philologen in München (Leipzig, 1892), pp. 244, 245. *Roscher*, Lexikon, I, 1, pp. 490, 491. *Furtwaengler*, Masterpieces, p. 304.

In the middle of the room, —

884 (43). Colossal Group of a Gaul and his Wife.

The restorations in the figure of the man include the front half of the nose, the right arm with the sword-hilt, the detached part of the sword-blade, the left forearm down to the wrist, the index-finger of the left hand, the floating part of the drapery, and the support — the last vindicated by remains on the man's body. The restorations of the woman include the nose, the left arm except the piece next the shoulder, the lower part of the right forearm with the hand, four toes on the right foot, and parts of the drapery. Both figures have suffered much from ruthless scouring and partly also from retouching; this is especially noticeable on the front of the woman. On the quality of the marble, see No. 533.

His enemies are close on his heels, and the Gaul has just found time to give his wife a mortal blow below the left arm; now he inflicts death on himself by severing the great artery above his collar-bone. His left arm still supports his dying wife. His face, turned towards his pursuers, shows defiant satisfaction that he will not fall into their power alive.

The right arm of the Gaul and the left arm of his wife are wrongly restored. The upper part of the man's right arm was, to judge from the ancient part of the deltoid muscle, considerably farther from the face, and the hand grasped the sword in such a way that the thumb, and not the little finger, was uppermost. On the one hand it is evident that the arm could thus deal a much more effective blow; while on the other the face would not be so much concealed, and the spectator could see its profile by standing opposite the left leg — *i. e.* on the side next the woman. The left arm of the Gaul's wife was not so stiffly extended but hung limply downwards. This group probably formed the centre of a cycle of statues, the right corner of which was occupied by the so-called Dying Gladiator of the Capitol 'No. 533). Like that statue, the group seems to be a copy in marble, by a Pergamenian sculptor, of a Pergamenian bronze original of the time of Attalos I., which perhaps formed part of the triumphal monument erected by that monarch on the Acropolis of his capital. A bronze original is indicated by the detached pose of the woman's left arm, by the two supports uniting the bodies of the man and woman, and by the third support for the floating drapery at the man's back. The mantle is almost concealed behind the back and adds little to the artistic effect of the ensemble; and if the group had been originally intended for execution in marble, it would be hard to say why the sculptor had been at the pains to under-cut it in a way so foreign to the technique of his material. The supposition that the group was executed at a late period and on Roman soil is contradicted in this case, as in that of the Dying Gladiator, by the marble in which it is wrought and by the freshness of its touch. Moreover, the two ends of the woman's mantle do not actually meet at her neck, obviously because the sculptor felt that absolute accuracy was unnecessary in a spot concealed by the chin. A Roman copyist would certainly have considered this a defect and would have corrected it.

Sch., No. 92. *Baumeister*, Denkmäler des klass. Alterthums, II, p. 1237, No. 1410, p. 1238, p. 1241. *Von Sybel*, Weltgeschichte der Kunst, p. 342, Fig. 272. Revue archéologique, XII (1888), p. 273, Fig. 1, pp. 281 et seq. *Loewy*, Lysipp und seine Stellung in der griech. Plastik, p. 29, Fig. 14. Comp. *Bie*, Kampfgruppe und Kämpfertypen, pp. 127 et seq.

885 (42). Fragment of a Statue of a Hyksos, in granite.

The facial type, so different from that of the Hamitic races, and the arrangement of the hair and beard, prove that this statue represents a Hyksos — *i. e.* a member of the nation of shepherds, predominantly of Semitic origin, that invaded Egypt from Syria about the year 2000 B.C. and remained masters of the country till about the seventeenth century B.C. The colossal dimensions of the figure indicate royalty. The section of the lower part of the extant fragment is smoothly cut, and hence it would appear that the missing portion of the figure was carved out of a separate block of granite. This is the only perfectly authenticated monument of the time of the Hyksos to be found in any European museum.

Bull. della comm. arch. comunale di Roma, 1877, T. IX, pp. 104 et seq. *Sch.*, No. 99.

886 (41). Colossal Group of Dionysos and a Satyr.

Found, under Sixtus V., on the Quirinal, near the Quattro Fontane.

This poorly executed and freely restored group reproduces the same original as No. 110 in the Vatican, but differs from it, among other points, in the stronger accentuation of the animal nature of the Satyr. Its effect is marred by the maladroitness of the restorer, who has made the legs of Dionysos too short and his body leaning too far to the right.

Sch., No. 77. Comp. Museo italiano di antichità classica, III, pp. 786 et seq. (p. 787C). Comp. also our No. 110.

887 (39). Group by Menelaos.

The restorations include the end of the youth's nose, part of his skull and drapery, the right arm from the biceps downwards, half of the thumb, the forefinger, and part of the little finger of the left hand, and the front of the right foot; also the end of the woman's nose, the front of her skull, the bare part of her left arm, half the thumb, the forefinger, and the little finger of the right hand, and other insignificant fragments. The drapery of both figures has been ruthlessly scoured and parts of it have been retouched. The flesh parts have all been retouched and smoothed, the woman's head suffering especially from this cause. It is also obvious, at a glance, that the restored part of her skull is too high.

Menelaos, a pupil of Stephanos, whom the inscription on the stump names as the sculptor of this group, belonged to a school which began, so far as we know, with Pasiteles, the master of Stephanos comp. No. 744). As Pasiteles was a contemporary of Pompey, Menelaos must have flourished about the time of Tiberius — a supposition that is confirmed by the palæography of the inscription. From all that we know of the school of Pasiteles, it is highly improbable that Menelaos himself created the group before us. He must have imitated a more ancient work, perhaps some Attic sepulchral group of the middle of the fourth century B.C. Even a careless observer of the work will notice the vague, indefinite character of the action — a vagueness which is doubtless caused in part by the modifications made by Menelaos on his model. It would be difficult to say whether the youth and the woman are meeting or parting from one another. The body of the youth is inclined towards his companion, and this would lead us to infer that he is meeting her. On the other hand the fact that the right foot of the youth and both feet of the woman are turned outwards would suggest that they are in the act of leaving each other. This vagueness of action frustrates all attempts to connect the group with a definite mythical event. Those authorities who believe that a meeting is represented, suggest the recognition of Orestes by Electra or of Cresphontes (Æpytos) by Merope. The supporters of the opposite view call it the farewell of Telemachos and Penelope, of Theseus and Æthra, or of some similar

couple known to ancient poesy. The characterization of
both youth and woman is, however, so little individualized, that no compulsion exists to identify them with
definite mythological personages; and it seems questionable whether the group really pourtrays any mythical
scene. Its whole character seems rather to indicate that
it is an ideal motive, symbolizing in a general manner
the relation of mother and son. Herder seized the gist of
the group when he named it 'Die stillen Vertrauten', *i.e.*
'The Quiet Confidants'. The mother lovingly embraces
her son, who looks up to her with filial devotion. Both
are permeated by a gentle breath of melancholy, as if their
intercourse were haunted by painful reminiscenses or
premonitions. And all these details would be quite in
place if the group were intended for the adornment of a
tomb.

Sch., No. 69, p. 265, appendix to p. 92. *Baumeister*, Denk-
mäler des klass. Alterthums, II, p. 1193, Fig. 1393. *Brunn und
Bruckmann*, Denkmäler, No. 309. Comp. *Loewy*, Inschriften griech.
Bildhauer, No. 375. *Friederichs - Wolters*, Bausteine, No. 1560.
Furtwaengler, Sammlung Sabouroff, I, introduction, pp. 50, 51.

Corridor.

888. Roman Tombstone with a Modern Inscription.

The restorations on the principal face of the relief
include most of the two ram's heads, the heads and most
of the legs of the eagles, pieces of the wings of the eagle
to the left, and the head of the cock to the right, below
the Medusa. The reliefs have been freely retouched,
and the head of Medusa in particular has thus acquired
a very modern character.

The tasteful decorative ornamentation of this tombstone is animated by the addition of several figures. On
the front are a mask of Medusa and two birds, pecking
at the snakes which emerge from amid the hair of the
mask. Below the garland are two cocks fighting. On
the right lateral face is a garland, above which is a nest
of young birds, fed by the old ones. Below the garland
are two birds fighting for a lizard. On the left side are

a pitcher, two birds fighting for a lizard, and two others
(below) contending for a butterfly. The careful workmanship points to the first century of the Empire. The
cartouche above the mask of Medusa contains a Renais-
sance inscription, to the effect that a Cardinal Julius or
Julianus erected this stone to the Eucharist. This probably means that the cardinal had caused it to be used
as the base for a ciborium. As Cardinal Ludovico Ludovisi, the founder of this collection, received a number of
antiques from the Cesarini family, it is not unlikely that
the ecclesiastic named in the inscription was Cardinal
Giuliano Cesarini (created cardinal in 1493, died in 1510).

> *Sch.*, No. 105; comp. also p. 6 of Introduction to *Sch.*

889 (12). Draped Statue of a Woman.

> The head, the neck, and both forearms are modern.
> The statue is made of Parian marble.

This statue resembles the female types referred to
the early Peloponnesian school — some with certainty, like
those from the pediment of the temple of Zeus at Olympia; others with great probability, such as the statue
known as the Vesta Giustiniani and the so-called Dancing
Women of Herculaneum. Like these figures, the statue
before us is clad in a Doric chiton, with a long apoptygma or upper fold. The realistic representation of the
seam on the right side of this garment is interesting.
The hole drilled in the left shoulder served for the attachment of a metal fibula or brooch. The legs are so treated
that it is difficult to say on which the weight of the body
is thrown. Although executed in marble, the figure still
betrays the influence of the archaic bronze technique.
The drapery over the breast looks like a sheet of metal
in repoussé work; the folds of the chiton below the apoptygma, especially on the right side, resemble the sharp
edges of cast and chased metal. The general character
of the execution seems to put it beyond a doubt that the
statue is an archaic original. Thus, the singular crudity
with which the toes are treated would certainly have
been modified by a copyist.

Sch., No. 29. Comp. Röm. Mitth., ii (1887), pp. 55, 102. *Furt-waengler, Koerte und Milchhoefer*, Archäolog. Studien Brunn dargebracht (Berlin, 1893), p. 81, note 62.

890 (10). Colossal Sarcophagus, with Contest of Barbarians and Romans.

> Found in 1621 in the Vigna Bernusconi, outside the Porta S. Lorenzo. The reliefs on this sarcophagus are not so well preserved as is generally supposed. Many of the detached heads seem modern, as they differ both in the quality and the corrosion of the marble from the parts that are undoubtedly antique. The head of the general in the middle of the upper row is, however, obviously ancient.

The composition of the principal face makes a somewhat confused and disagreeable impression on account of its over-crowding. It represents a victory gained by the Romans over the Barbarians. The upper row depicts the decisive charge of the Roman cavalry, with the Roman general in the middle, raising his right arm and encouraging his troops. In the lower row are the Barbarians, most of them already *hors de combat* and only a few offering a feeble resistance. Among known portraits of Roman emperors that of Volusianus (d. 254 A.D.) most resembles the head of the general. The relief contains several details of interest for the military antiquarian, such as the dragon-standard behind the general. The design of most of the figures is somewhat clumsy, but the technical execution is very careful. When the sarcophagus was discovered, traces of gilding were apparent on the figure of the general and on the bridles of the horses.

Sch., No. 186.

891 (7). Sarcophagus, with Contest of Romans and Barbarians.

The upper row of reliefs on the principal face of the sarcophagus represents the victorious advance of the Romans, most of whom are mounted; below are the Barbarians, put to rout by this attack, some falling from their horses, others overthrown, man and horse. The Roman general gallops in the midst of his men. A Barbarian on foot, clad in a mantle, attacks him with a curved sword. Another Barbarian, also in the upper row, is quite nude and is evidently trying to escape. The gesture of his right hand is indistinct, and it is difficult to say whether he is pressing a short sword to his side or is trying to remove an arrow which has pierced his breast. Several of the figures have evidently been sculptured after pictorial models. This is true of the first Roman cavalier to the left, who is shown in a foreshortened front view, and of the second Barbarian from the right in the lower row, who falls from his horse, with his back towards the spectator. The reliefs of the chief face are bounded at each end by a Victory, bearing a palm-branch and setting her foot on a fettered Barbarian crouching below her.

Sch., No. 138.

892. **Part of a Throne (?).**

> Found in 1887 in that part of the grounds of the Villa Ludovisi now bounded by the Via Boncompagni, the Via Abbruzzi, and the Via Piemonte.

Like No. 882, this work was garnished with several accessories in metal or in separate pieces of marble. A hole is bored in each of the two upper ends of the marble; and there was probably a third hole in the central part that is now missing. These undoubtedly served for the attachment of ornaments. At the corners of the lower extremities are triangular cavities, which were probably occupied by metal or marble plates. Each of the three fields of the work is adorned with reliefs in an advanced archaic style, which reveal a fine artistic sense in composition and execution, though some of the details are somewhat carelessly designed. The principal relief has been interpreted as the birth of Aphrodite, who emerges from the sea, aided by two Horæ. The thin chiton allows all the forms of the body to be seen through it; and the Horæ modestly cover the lower part of the figure with a sheet. The reliefs in the side-pieces would refer to the cult of the goddess. That to the right represents a young woman, offering a sacrifice of incense. On the left side is a nude girl, playing on the double flute. This latter figure would be one of the 'hierodoulæ', or slaves attached to the temple of the goddess.

This interpretation, however, seems to the writer by no means beyond dispute. The function attributed to the Horæ seems to him to betray a modern and not an ancient spirit; while the sea, from which the goddess emerges, is indicated with anything but clearness. All analogies would lead us to expect that the artist would have represented it by a series of waves, either with or without fish. These difficulties would at once be disposed of if we accepted the recent suggestion that the reliefs of the principal side represented the approaching accouchement of a goddess or heroine. We should in this case regard the chief figure as kneeling, and we know, both from statements in books and from other works of art, that the women of old sometimes awaited the process of child-birth in this attitude. The two girls adjoining the chief figure would be ready to support her in her pangs and to hold out the swaddling-clothes for the reception of the infant. The figures on the two ends of the throne would be conceived of as trying to exercise a healthy influence on the obstetric event of the central scene, the one by offering incense, the other by playing the flute.

The right hand of the figure with the incense and the left hand of the musician show traces of an ancient restoration.

The style of these reliefs resembles the paintings on the red-figured Attic vases dating from the period immediately after the Persian wars. Certain details, such as the nude body of the flute-player and the cushions on which she and the incense-offerer sit, are treated in a realistic manner that can hardly be called archaic. The profiles also exhibit a strikingly individual treatment.

In speaking of the head No. 882, the writer pointed out that it undoubtedly belonged to an acrolithic statue of Aphrodite. Starting from this very reasonable assumption and interpreting the reliefs as illustrations of the myth and cult of this goddess, a recent authority has suggested that the work before us formed the back of the throne of the statue in question. He then goes on to surmize that the statue was that of the ancient temple of Aphrodite on Mt. Eryx, in Sicily, and that it had been brought to Rome at a later date and placed in the temple of *Venus Erycina*, which lay outside the Porta Collina, about 300 yards from the spot where this fragment of the throne was found. This theory, however, is confronted by several difficulties, which, indeed, did not escape its ingenious author. The provenience of the colossal head, No. 682, is unknown, and its marble is of a finer grain than that in which the reliefs before us are carved. Nothing, it is true, prevents us from attributing the execution of the two works to the same period; but the style of the reliefs is less archaic than that of the head. Thus, if the two formed parts of the same whole, we should have to assume that the sculptor of the statue remained faithful to the ancient traditions of his art, while his colleague who carved the work before us adopted some of the principles of a freer style.

Bull. della commissione arch. comunale, 1887, Pl. xv, xvi, pp. 267-274. *Lützow*, Zeitschrift für bildende Kunst, new series, I (1890), p. 153, Fig. 14 Denkmäler herausgegeben vom Arch. Institut, II (1891-92), T. 6, 7, p. 3. Röm. Mitth., VII (1892), Pl. II, pp. 32 et seq., where all the bibliography is collected (p. 32). Comp. Ἐφημερὶς ἀρχ., 1892, pp. 227-229.

Let into the adjacent wall, over the door, —

593. Alto-Relief of the Judgment of Paris.

Almost all the lower half and the whole of the right end of the relief have been restored in plaster. The line of fracture intersects the body of the fawn near the upper right corner, the right hand of the figure restored as a river-god, the right knee of the mountain-deity, the neck of the goat, the legs of Eros, the body and pedum of Paris, the left shoulder and head of the standing bull, and the thighs of Hermes; it then passes just below the cincture of Pallas and descends to the right of this goddess, in a nearly vertical line, to the lower edge of the slab. All below and to the right of this line is modern, and also a few minor fragments which are noticed in the text.

This carefully executed relief, which formed a mural decoration and not part of a sarcophagus, represents Hermes in the act of bringing before Paris the three goddesses of whose beauty he is to be judge. The central point of the composition is occupied by the figure of Paris, seated, in Phrygian dress, in the midst of his herds, and listening to the whispers in favour of Aphrodite of the Eros leaning against him. The young woman standing in front of him seems to be his wife Œnone. She has obviously just taken the syrinx, which she holds in her right hand, from her lips, and observes attentively the understanding between her husband and Eros. To the left of this central group are Aphrodite, already approaching Paris, and Hermes (front half of right forearm and point of caduceus restored), who leads the two other goddesses (Hera's right forearm and the top of her sceptre modern) towards the youthful judge. The figures in the background, to the right of the principal group, indicate the scene of action. The god of Mt. Ida sits beside a mighty oak, while a Nymph stands on the rock beside him, holding a pedum in her right hand; the fauna of the mountain is represented by a young roe-deer behind her. The figures farther to the right, including Artemis and Helios above and a river-god and a Naiad below, are entirely modern except the right hand of the river-god. The restorer has followed an engraving of Marcantonio Raimondi, made after a drawing of Raphael, which is itself a sketch of a sarcophagus-relief of the Judgment of Paris now in the Villa Medici.

Sch., No. 106. *Baumeister*, Denkmäler des klass. Alterthums, II, p. 1168, Fig. 1359. *Robert*, Die antiken Sarkophag-Reliefs, II, pp. 17, 18.

On the wall opposite the windows, —

891. **Colossal Tragic Mask,** in rosso antico.

Acquired in 1622, from the Villa Cesi.

This mask, crowned with bunches of grapes and vine-leaves, rests on a low basket, covered by a nebris. To judge from the holes in the pupils and the large opening between the lips, it served, like No. 734, for the circulation of heated air in a bathing establishment.

Sch., No. 46.

Villa Borghese.

Vestibule.

895-897. Three Fragments of large Reliefs.

One of these reliefs is let into the wall to the right, another into that to the left, while the third stands on the floor to the left, at the foot of the back-wall.

The reliefs to which these fragments belonged adorned an ancient arch, the remains of which were still standing in the Piazza Sciarra in the fifteenth century. According to a dedicatory inscription found there in 1641, this arch was erected by the Roman senate and people in the eleventh year of the reign of Claudius (51-52 A.D.), to commemorate that emperor's victories in Britain. It seems also to have been used to conduct the Aqua Virgo over the Via Lata. The figure in the centre of the relief to the left, clad in a cuirass, a cloak, and richly ornamented boots, is obviously the Emp. Claudius. Round him are grouped three officers, all, like the emperor himself, bare-headed. Higher up, arranged in two rows one above the other, are the helmeted heads of several Roman legionaries. The poles seen behind the heads in the upper row are probably the shafts of the military standards, borne over the shoulders of the soldiers. Among the figures in the relief on the opposite wall are two soldiers, each of whom holds a standard in his left hand. That held by the soldier to the left ends in an eagle, perched on a bundle of thunderbolts, and must therefore be the ensign of a legion. To the staff of the other standard are attached two medallions *(imagines clipeatae)*, the uppermost of which seems intended for Claudius, while the lower is supposed to be Narcissus, the freedman of that emperor. A third standard is preserved at the left edge of the relief, but its bearer is wanting. The hand in which it ends shows it to be the standard of a *manipulus* (or company), while the portrait fastened to the staff is doubtless that of Claudius. Behind the standard-bearers are seen the uncovered heads of two officers and the helmeted heads of three soldiers. Two of the latter, to judge from the thunderbolts on the check-pieces of their helmets, seem to belong to the 12th Legion *(Fulminatrix)*. The third fragment, lying on the ground, shows four heads with helmets and two without, a standard *(vexillum)*, and the insignificant remains of some other ensigns. Two planes are used in the reliefs, one quite low and the other considerably raised, while the sculptor of the reliefs on the Arch of Titus, about 30 years later, made use of three planes. The forms are marked by a certain severity. It should be noticed that the eyes of the heads shown in profile are all represented more or less in full front.

Abhandlungen der phil.-hist. Classe der sächs. Gesellschaft der Wissenschaften, vi (1872), T. i, pp. 271 et seq. Mon. dell' Inst., x, T. xxi, 1-3; Ann., 1875, pp. 42-48. — On the Arch of Claudius: Bull. della commissione archeologica comunale, vi (1878), pp. 15 et seq., p. 20.

In the left corner, —

89S. **Torso of Pallas.**

This torso belongs to a copy of the Athena Parthenos of Pheidias. The execution is careful, and almost as thorough on the back as on the front. The hollows between the great toe and its neighbour seem to have been occupied by the metal straps of the sandals. Comp. Nos. 598, 600, 870.

Abhandlungen der phil.-hist. Classe der sächs. Ges. der Wissenschaften, viii (1883), T. iv II, p. 527. Comp. Arch. Zeitung, xli (1883), p. 210.

Great Hall (Salone).

The **Fragments of a Large Mosaic** let into the floor of this room were discovered among the remains of an extensive ancient villa, brought to light in the course of excavations instituted by Prince Borghese in 1534 in the Tenuta di Torre Nuova, below the hill of Tusculum. The mosaic of which these fragments formed part adorned the floor of one of the colonnades surrounding the peristyle of the villa. It represented a great gladiatorial spectacle *(munus gladiatorium)*, combined with wild-beast hunts *(venationes)*, which had probably been given by the owner of the villa. The contestants, to judge from the fragments preserved, all belonged to barbaric races, and the names accompanying the figures are also those of barbarians or slaves. The execution is rude, but the mosaic is important for its realistic delineation of the armour and weapons of the combatants, their modes of attack and defence, their postures, and, in fact, all that interested the noble Roman patron of the ancient 'prize ring'. The characteristics of the figures recall those of the great mosaic from the Baths of Caracalla (No. 704), and the manner in which the movements both of the men and the animals are reproduced shows that the artist had, on the whole, a fairly accurate knowledge of the living organism. We may therefore conclude that the mosaic dates from the third century of the present era, and not, as commonly supposed, from the fourth. Unfortunately the restorer who arranged the fragments for the Villa Borghese was mainly concerned with the general decorative effect, and has thus, in more than one instance, combined fragments that had really nothing to do with each other.

The fragment in the middle of the room, near the entrance, gives a good idea of the diverse kinds of animals brought to Rome from all quarters of the globe for the 'venationes'. Thus, merely to mention those animals that are clearly recognizable, we see the lion and the ostrich of Africa side by side with the eland from the forests of

Germany. Their human antagonists (*bestiarii* wear short jerkins, adorned at various points with embroidery. Their shoulders are protected by disks of metal or leather, and the joints of the wrist, knee, and ankle are strengthened by leathern straps. One of the beast-fighters buries his lance in the breast of a lion springing to the attack, while another serves a charging bull in the same manner. Farther to the left is a third bestiarius, seizing a bull by the horns, while around him is a group of killed or wounded comrades.

Another episode in a 'venatio' is depicted in one of the scenes in the second row of the mosaics, farther from the entrance. Two panthers in the act of springing are transfixed by the whingers of their antagonists, while four panthers lie dead on the ground and two others crawl round the arena. The fragments representing two other men fighting with panthers, wrongly combined by the restorer with the mosaic to the left, below the Colossal Satyr (No. 900), obviously formed part of this representation.

The central part of the last-mentioned fragment shows the issue of a combat between a light-armed gladiator *retiarius*) named Alumnus, with a net, trident (*tridens*, *fuscina*', and short sword, and the heavily-armed Mazicinus (*secutor*', with his visored helmet. Alumnus, marked as the conqueror by the inscription VIC(tor), triumphantly holds aloft the bloody sword with which he has dealt the death-blow to his antagonist, while the corpse of the latter lies at his feet, covered by a large rectangular shield. The trident, which the retiarius has thrown on the ground as useless in the decisive hand-to-hand struggle, has been erroneously converted into a pole by the modern restorer. Of two other duels there remains in each case a single helmeted gladiator, one awaiting the onset of a retiarius, the other pursuing his fleeing opponent. Both are distinguished by the inscription VIC(tor). Callimorfus, represented in the upper part of the mosaic as lying, dangerously wounded, on the ground, belonged to a third group.

The man in the background, waving a flag or a whip, is either a trainer *(lanista)* or one of the *lorarii*, whose duty it was to egg on recalcitrant gladiators by blows with a whip.

Three pairs of gladiators are represented on the other fragment placed behind the central mosaic. The helmeted gladiator Bellerefons is just about to plunge his sword in the throat of Cupido, a retiarius lying on the ground before him. The Θ (theta) following the name of the latter is the initial of the words θάνατος (death) and signifies that Cupido must perish. Aurius, another retiarius, has been overcome by his antagonist Talamonius, who stands beside the corpse and seems to await some order. In the third group we see the retiarius Meleager, kneeling on his left knee and holding up his bloody sword. Apparently he is awaiting the decision of the spectators as to whether or not he is to despatch his foeman, who lies, severely wounded, behind him. In the background, above the wounded gladiator, appear a man and a horse, the latter probably intended for the removal of the fallen combatants from the arena. To the right is the figure of a heavily-armed gladiator named Pampineus.

The fragment to the right, at the end of the second row, represents three contests, in each of which the retiarius has got the upper hand. Licentiosus has struck down Purpureus with a blow of his trident and is now, having thrown down the trident, about to give the *coup de grâce* with his short sword. Entinus, another retiarius, plunges his sword in the back of the fleeing Baccibus. Astacius throws himself, with drawn sword, on the prostrate Astivus, whose fate is indicated by the theta attached to his name. Of a fourth group there remains only the figure of the retiarius Rodanus, also accompanied by the fatal theta. To the left, below, is a lanista or a lorarius; and there are two similar figures above, in the background.

Henzen, Explicatio musivi in Villa Burghesiana asservati, Romæ, 1845 (also in the Dissertazioni della pontef. Accademia romana, xɪɪ, pp. 73 et seq.). Comp. *Braun*, Ruinen und Museen, p. 521, No. 1. *De Rossi*. Bulletino di archeologia cristiana, v (1867), p. 87. Corpus inscr. lat., vɪ, 2, No. 10,206. — For a general account of the results of the researches into the matter of the Roman gladiators, see *P. J. Meier*, De gladiatura romana (Bonnæ, 1881).

The consideration of the sculptures begins with the side-wall to the left.

899 (xxxv). Colossal Head of Isis.

The restorations include the lotus, the eyebrows, the front of the nose, the under-lip, the lower part of the neck, and the lower half of the two locks falling on the neck.

The identification of this statue rests upon the trace of an attribute over the forehead, which can hardly have been anything else than a lotus-flower. If, therefore, the head be taken for that of Isis, which seems justified, it represents a type of that goddess very different from the colossal bust at the Vatican (No. 105). The Egyptian headdress has been given up, and sombre melancholy is replaced by majestic calm.

Nibby. T. 7, p. 40.

900 (xxxvɪ). Colossal Satyr.

Formerly at the Palazzo Cevoli (now Sacchetti), in the Via Giulia. The head, the right arm and pedum, the left arm and the part of the nebris enveloping it, the legs, the stump, and the plinth have all been restored.

This torso, which is represented in a state of violent movement, is admirably executed and full of life. The restoration has been made after bronze figures showing a similar movement of the body and seems substantially correct. The Satyr was sporting with a panther, either represented on the plinth or left to the imagination of the beholder, and playfully menaced the animal with the uplifted pedum.

Antiquarum statuarum urbis Romæ icones (Romæ, 1621), ɪɪ, Pl. 75. *Nibby*, T. 8, p. 41. *Clarac*, ɪv, Pl. 717, No. 1714. Comp. Beschreibung Roms, ɪɪɪ, 3. p. 325, No. 4. *Braun*, Ruinen und

Museen, p. 524, No. 2. Jahrbuch des Arch. Instituts, vi (1891), p. 170e, where the remainder of the bibliography is collected.

For the relief let into the pedestal of this statue, see No. 904.

901 (xxxix). Statue of a Man, with an Eagle on the plinth.

The restorations include the head (which bears the features of Tiberius), the right forearm, the left forearm with most of the drapery enveloping it and the sword, the lower part of the left leg, the right foot, and the plinth. The only ancient part of the eagle is the piece of the left wing touching the right leg of the statue.

No lengthy disproof of the current identification of this statue with Tiberius is necessary, since the head is obviously a modern addition. The eagle sculptured on the plinth would suggest that we have to do with a statue of Zeus. The arrangement of the himation, however, and the position of the arms differ from those in all well-authenticated statues of Zeus, whereas they are often met with in portrait-figures (comp., e.g., No. 637). The figure may therefore have after all represented a Roman emperor, assimilated in some degree with Zeus by the eagle on the plinth (comp. No. 305).

Nibby, p. 43, No. 7. *Bernoulli*, Römische Ikonographie, ii, 1, p. 148, No. 14.

902 (xl). Statue of Meleager.

The restorations include the head and neck, with the bare part of the chest, the right arm, the fingers of the left hand, part of the floating end of the chlamys, and most of the right leg. The point of the spear, the section of the shaft below the left hand, the front of the plinth, and the head, neck, and fore-paws of the dog are also modern.

This statue reproduces the same bronze original as that in the Vatican (No. 133). In the latter, however, the copyist's main concern was to reproduce his model with extreme fidelity, and hence he did not hesitate to mar the effect of his work by the addition of various unsightly supports. In the Borghese statue, on the other hand, the copyist has altered several details so as to admit of the execution of the work in marble without these disfiguring additions. Thus the left arm lies nearer the body, and the free end of the chlamys projects less from the arm and so needs no support. The general forms of the body are more compact. It is difficult to decide which of the two copies reproduces the original more closely in the bodily formation. In any case the effect of elastic strength, so admirably adapted for the vigorous huntsman and so emphatically expressed in the Vatican statue, has been considerably attenuated in the figure before us.

Nibby, p. 43, No. 8. Ann. dell' Inst., 1843, Tav. d'agg. I, pp. 258-260. Römische Mittheilungen, IV (1889), p. 220, No. 7. *Furtwaengler*, Masterpieces, p. 184, note 2.

903 (IXT.). Statue of Augustus.

> The head, which is certainly ancient and belonging to the figure, has been broken off and again attached to the body. The nose, parts of the drapery, the right forearm and cup, and the left hand and scroll are modern.

This statue represents Augustus, not Caligula as usually supposed. The fact that the toga is drawn over the back of the head shows that the emperor is represented in the act of offering a sacrifice (comp. No. 319. The restorer is accordingly justified in placing a cup in the right hand. The left hand was probably empty.

Nibby, T. 10, pp. 40-41. *Bernoulli*, Römische Ikonographie, II, 1, p. 32, No. 25.

Above the door in the back-wall, —

904 (VIII.). Slab of a Frieze with Bacchanalian Scenes.

The reliefs are admirably executed. To the left is a young Satyr, sitting on a rock covered with a nebris and playing the syrinx; an older and bearded companion approaches him, with a tympanon in his uplifted right hand. To the right a Satyr and a Bacchante are busy cleaning a statue of the bearded Dionysos, clad in a long chiton and a scanty cloak. The Satyr is pouring water from a pitcher into a basin; the Bacchante holds a sponge over the basin with her right hand and lays her left on the cheek of the statue. Of the Bacchic frieze to which this slab belonged, various other fragments have been preserved. These, as ancient drawings prove, have been combined by the modern restorer after the most arbitrary fashion. They are let into the bases of the Satyr No. 900 (XXXVI) and the Dionysos No. 907 (II.), and into one of the walls in the room to the left of the Salone, above the Pluto No. 942 (CCXXXIII).

No. 904 (VIIL) and the fragment in the other room have not yet been published. For the two others, see *Nibby*, T. 9, pp. 41, 51. Comp. *Braun*, Ruinen und Museen, p. 525, No. 3. The drawings will shortly be published by *M. Kern* (Röm. Mitth., v, 1890, p. 70).

905 (VI). Colossal Statue of a Satyr.

The traces of the previous existence of a tail on the back show that this statue represented a Satyr. The original motive cannot be determined, since the torso alone is ancient.

Nibby, p. 125, No. 4.

906 (IIL). Colossal Head of Hadrian.

Probably identical with an example formerly in the Palazzo Borghese.

Like No. 298, this head is one of the best idealized portraits of the Emperor Hadrian.

Nibby, T. 12, p. 49. Comp. *Winckelmann*, Geschichte der Kunst, XII, 1, § 21. *Visconti*, Museo Pio-Clem., VI, p. 195. *Bernoulli*, Römische Ikonographie, II, 2. p. 112, No. 37. p. 119.

907 (IL). Colossal Dionysos.

The torso alone is certainly antique, though, perhaps, the left thigh and part of the right are so also. It is therefore questionable whether the figure leant, as the restorer has represented it, with the left arm on a tree-stump. It is quite as likely that the god supported himself on the shoulder of a Satyr, as in Nos. 110 and 886.

Nibby, T. 11, p. 50.

On the relief inserted in the base of the statue, see No. 904.

908 (I.). Colossal Head of Antoninus Pius.
Formerly in the Palazzo Borghese.

This head has, unfortunately, been so freely worked over as to make the impression of a modern, rather than an ancient work.

Nibby, T. 12, p. 51. Comp. Visconti, Museo Pio-Clem., vi, p. 203. Bernoulli, Römische Ikonographie, ii, 2, p. 142. No. 21, p. 149.

First Room to the Right of the Salone.

909 (LXXII). Trunk of a Tree, in marble.

This stem, which like the similar No. 879, was doubtless used to decorate a garden, is entwined by acorn-bearing oak-branches and other foliage. On the top is a basket containing two pine-apples.

910 (LXXI). Relief of Artemis Courotrophos (?).

Found in 1760 in the Tenuta di Torre Nuova (see p. 131). The restorations include a triangular piece of the background (behind the neck of the seated figure), the ends of the noses of the two women, the right legs of the chair, the muzzle of the animal, and the lower part of the edge of the slab.

This relief apparently reproduces a Greek work of the close of the fifth, or the beginning of the fourth, century B.C., with details modified by Hellenistic or Roman art. It represents a young girl seated and in the act of receiving an infant from a woman standing in front of her. Below the seat couches a kid or a fawn. The seated figure has a narrow band descending from the right shoulder towards the left side. This band has been taken for the baldric of a quiver, and the virgin has therefore been supposed to be Artemis, in her capacity of protectress of children *(Courotrophos)*. The goddess would thus be receiving a newly-born child from its mother. If this hypothesis is correct, the original composition must have been a votive offering to Artemis Courotrophos, which later art converted into a decorative relief. The execution of the nude parts is elegant but lifeless, while the treatment of the folds is minute and restless. To judge from these characteristics, the relief cannot have been executed earlier than the time of Hadrian.

Winckelmann, Mon. ant. ined., II, T. 71, p. 96. *Visconti*, Illustrazioni dei monumenti scelti Borghesiani, II, 9, p. 27. *Nibby*, T. 18, p. 63. Ann. dell' Inst., 1830, Tav. d'agg. G, pp. 154-157. Comp. *Braun*, Ruinen und Museen, p. 530, No. 6. Römische Mittheilungen, VI (1891), pp. 177-182.

911, 912 (LXIX, LXV). Two Statuettes of Street Arabs.

At the close of the 18th century these two figures stood in the park of the villa (*Visconti*, Sculture del Palazzo della Villa Borghese detta Pinciana, II, Roma, 1796, p. 40), and they were afterwards transferred to the magazine in the basement of the villa. They were not placed in the gallery till 1889. The noses of both figures have been restored; also the left fist (below the cloak), the feet, and the plinth of No. LXIX, and the lowest part of the drapery hanging over the left arm of No. LXV.

That these boys belong to the lowest stratum of society is proved by the vulgar type of their faces, by the felt caps *(pileus)* characteristic of the lower orders, and by the clothing, consisting solely of a coarse cloak instead of the usual cloak and tunic. Both figures are probably copies of an excellent original of the Hellenistic period. Though executed merely from the decorative stand-point, the bold and roguish expression of the original is very cleverly indicated in these copies.

The best example of this type was formerly also in the Casino Borghese but was removed to Paris in 1806, when Napoleon I. acquired the sculptures then in the Casino (*Visconti*, Sculture del Palazzo della Villa Borghese, II, stanza VI, No. 2. *Clarac*, III, Pl. 334, No. 1165; *Panofka*, Asklepios und die Asklepiaden, in the Philolog. und histor. Abhandlungen der Berliner Akademie, 1845, T. VIII, 3, p. 323). The usual identification with the demon Telesphoros (see

No. 932) is contradicted by the vulgarity of the type and the effrontery of the expression.

913 (LXIV). Relief of Ajax and Cassandra.

The point of the nose and the left shoulder of Ajax, and the nose of Cassandra have been restored; also a strip of the left side of the upper part of the column behind Ajax.

This imposing composition shows Ajax in the act of tearing Cassandra from the statue of Pallas to which she clings as a suppliant. The contrast is very effective between the expressionless rigidity of the archaic statue and the violent movements of the hero and the virgin. The treatment of the drapery and of the flowing hair of Cassandra suggests a pictorial model; and this may very well have been the Cassandra of Theon, a painter whose pictures were marked, like the relief before us, by strong dramatic effect (comp. No. 348). The relief is best seen at a distance, as its workmanship is somewhat rude. It thus seems intended for a lofty situation, such as that of a frieze. It is difficult to decide whether the letters SA carved on the field of the relief are ancient or modern, and whether they formed part of the word CASSANDRA.

Nibby, T. 16, p. 61. *Gerhard*, Antike Bildwerke, T. 27; Prodromus, p. 272. *Overbeck*, Gallerie, T. 27, 5, pp. 651, No. 138. Comp. Beschreibung Roms, III, 3, p. 240, No. 12. *Braun*, Ruinen und Museen, p. 532, No. 7.

914 (LXI). Lateral Face of a Sarcophagus.

The restorations include the head of Eros and the end of the noses of the man and woman. The palm-branch is also almost wholly modern, the original attribute having apparently been a bow.

A drawing in the Berlin Collection of Engravings shows us that this slab formed the right side of the so-called Sarcophagus of Pasiphaë, formerly in the Villa Borghese and now in the Louvre. In front of a temple stand a bearded man, in full costume, raising his right hand in prayer, and an old woman holding a dish of fruit in her hands. The temple seems to be dedicated to a

marine deity, as a trumpet-blowing Triton is represented
in its pediment. In front of the columns is a statue of
Eros; but drawings executed when the relief was in a
better state of preservation show that there were originally two such figures. Since the principal representation on the sarcophagus refers to the myth of Pasiphaë, it has been plausibly supposed that this relief depicts Minos, the husband of Pasiphaë, in the act of
offering a bloodless sacrifice to Poseidon. The old woman may be his mother Europa. The scene may have
been suggested by 'The Cretans' of Euripides, a tragedy
in which Minos appears as the priest *(Myste)* of the Idæan
Zeus and as a vegetarian.

Nibby, T. 16, p. 59. *Robert*, Der Pasiphae-Sarkophag; Vierzehntes Hallisches Winckelmannsprogramm (Halle, 1890), T. I, II,
3, 3a, T. III, IV, 3a, p. 14, pp. 19 et seq.

915 (LVIII). Statue of Aphrodite.

The restorations include the head, the right hand
with the corner of the mantle held by it, the bare part
of the left forearm, patches of the drapery, the right foot
with the part of the chiton covering it, fragments of the
left foot, and the plinth.

This mediocre and badly-preserved statue gives but
a poor idea of the beautiful type it reproduces. Aphrodite is clad in a thin, semi-transparent chiton, through
which the forms of the young and lovely body are clearly
distinguished; the left breast is left bare. The right hand
is gracefully raised and draws over her shoulders, with a
charming gesture, the mantle, which hangs over the back,
leaving the front of the body uncovered. One end of it
is rolled round the left arm. The left hand probably
held an apple. In the better-executed replicas of this
figure the style shows a certain severity, such as we encounter in Attic works of the closing decades of the
fifth century B.C. It has therefore been suggested, with
considerable plausibility, that the original may have been
a celebrated statue of Aphrodite by Alcamenes, a pupil
of Pheidias.

Nibby, T. 15, p. 58. *Braun*, Vorschule, T. 73. For the rest of the bibliography, see *Bernoulli*, Aphrodite, p. 87, No. 3. Comp. Gazette archéologique, XII (1887), pp. 250 et seq., pp. 271 et seq. *Roscher*, Lexikon der griech. und röm. Mythologie, I, pp. 412, 413. Athenische Mittheilungen, XII (1887), p. 383, XIV (1889), pp. 199 et seq. Römische Mittheilungen, IV (1889), pp. 72, 73. Fünfzigstes Programm zum Winckelmannsfeste der archäolog. Gesellschaft zu Berlin (1890), pp. 118-121. Antike Denkmäler herausgegeben vom Arch. Institut, I, p. 45. *Overbeck*, Geschichte der griech. Plastik, I⁴, p. 377, p. 386, notes 7-12. Eranos Vindobonensis (Vienna, 1893), pp. 18-20. *Furtwaengler*, Masterpieces, p. 82.

Second Room.

916 (LXXVIII). Herma of Pan.

The end of the nose has been restored.

This herma reproduces the Peloponnesian type of Pan, already discussed under No. 389.

Nibby, T. 31, 1, p. 67. *Brunn und Bruckmann*, Denkmäler, No. 363. For other references, see *Friederichs - Wolters*, Bausteine, No. 521.

917 (LXXIX). Front, and (opposite) 918 (vc) Back of a Sarcophagus, with Reliefs of the Labours of Heracles.

The ornamentation of the sarcophagus represented a Corinthian colonnade, under each arch of which one of the labours of Heracles was depicted. That this scheme of decoration was also followed on the ends of the sarcophagus is proved by a foot preserved behind each of the corner-columns of the front, and evidently belonging in each case to a figure of Heracles. It is impossible to indicate the restorations, for the restorer has thoroughly worked over the ancient parts so as to efface the difference between them and his own additions. The labours on the front of the sarcophagus, which follow the usual order in reliefs of this kind, are the Nemean lion, the hydra, the boar, the hind, and the Stymphalian birds. The first three reliefs on the back of the sarcophagus show the conflicts of Heracles with the Cretan bull, Diomedes of Thrace, and the Queen of the Amazons. In the following two groups he appears as fighting with a dragon and a Centaur. In the regular order the contest with the Amazon is followed by the adventures with Geryon and Cerberus; hence it is likely that the dragon and Centaur groups are either modern or transferred hither from the original place on the end of the sarcophagus. The combat with the dragon is the more suspicious because it finds no analogy among the numerous other representations of the labours of Heracles. The plinth on both faces is adorned with hunting-scenes.

Nibby, T. 19, 20, pp. 68, 76. Comp. Ann. dell' Inst., 1864, pp. 315, 316.

On the front face of the sarcophagus No. 917 (LXXIX) has been placed, —

919 (LXXX). Cover of a Sarcophagus, representing the Amazons at Troy.

> The two corner-masks are for the most part ancient, but do not belong to the reliefs. That the cover has nothing to do with the sarcophagus on which it now stands is proved by its dimensions, by its subject, and by its style. The reliefs on the sarcophagus to which this cover belonged doubtless represented some subject that was cognate to the reliefs of the cover itself — such as, *e.g.*, Achilles and Penthesileia (comp. No. 144).

The scene on the left side represents the Amazons entering Troy during the mourning for Hector. To the left sits Andromache, gazing sadly at the little Astyanax in her lap. In front of her stand two mourning women, who may be either sisters-in-law or servants. A bowed-down old woman (Hecuba?) approaches Andromache from the rear, and, with raised right hand, seems to be making a communication to her. In all probability she is announcing the arrival of the Amazons, which is shown in the next scene to the right. Penthesileia, leading her war-horse by the bridle and accompanied by another Amazon, is received by Priam with out-stretched hand. Behind Priam stand five Trojans plunged in grief; four of them are bearded, while the beardless youth may, perhaps, be identified as Paris. The next group consists of two weeping women. One of these is seated, holding the sepulchral urn of Hector on her lap, while a youth in Phrygian dress seizes her chin with his left hand, as if to raise her down-sunk face. This woman is generally taken for Hecuba, the youth for her youngest son Polydoros. Another view sees in them a second representation of Andromache and Paris. The following scene, separated from this group by an archway, depicts seven Amazons arming themselves for the coming fray. The Amazon standing next the gateway, whose shield is being placed in position by a companion, seems to be Queen Penthesilcia.

Robert, Die antiken Sarkophag-Reliefs, II, T. XXIV, 59, p. 66.

920. Amazon riding over two Warriors.

[This group was removed from the gallery while this volume was in the press, and its place is now occupied by No. LXXXV of the gallery (No. 926 of the Handbook; see p. 148).]

> The certain restorations include the front part of the crest of the helmet, the end of the nose, the right hand with the battle-axe, and the left arm of the Amazon; the right ear, the free-hanging part of the bridle, and the tail of the horse; the right arm, the left foot, and the lower part of the left leg of the warrior prostrate under the horse; and the front of the crest, the left arm, and the lower part of the left leg (foot ancient) of the other warrior.

The Amazon has just ridden down the prostrate warrior below her steed and now aims a blow with her right hand at a second antagonist, who has sunk on one knee between the fore-legs of the horse. This latter warrior raised a buckler on his left arm to protect his head; and the Amazon also bore a shield on her left arm. A detailed examination of the style of this group is impossible, as the restorer has reworked the surface of the ancient parts and treated them with acids. Still, both in its general forms and in the dimensions of its figures, it recalls the well-known marble statuettes connected with the cycle presented to the Athenians by Attalos I. (comp.

No. 385). Some authorities therefore claim that the Borghese example is a copy of a group in that part of the Pergamenian gift which represented the contest between the Amazons and the Greeks. But this hypothesis is contradicted by the vulgar types of the faces of the warriors, and by the fell which covers the head of the one on the ground. It would have been impossible for a Greek sculptor to represent the Athenians fighting the Amazons of so ugly a type and with such a barbaric headdress.

Jahrbuch des Arch. Instituts, II (1887), T. 7, pp. 77–85. Comp. *Baumeister*, Denkmäler des klass. Alterthums, I, p. 1246. Revue archéologique, XIII (1889), p. 15. *Bie*, Kampfgruppe und Kämpfertypen, p. 128.

921 (IVc). **Cover of a Sarcophagus.**

The restorations include the two masks at the corners; the border of the relief adjoining the mask to the left; the right arm of the woman seated on the shoulder of the kneeling giant; the head and right arm (hand ancient) of the following, almost nude woman; the left forearm and lance of Pallas; the head and forearms of the maiden standing to the right of Zeus, with the casket she holds; the bust, head, and left arm of the woman advancing between two goddesses in the background, near the extreme right corner of the relief.

Of the numerous interpretations offered of the scene on this sarcophagus-lid, the latest and best sees in it a representation of the birth of Apollo and Artemis. In this case the three scenes composing the representation are explained as follows. To the left is Leto (Latona) wandering in search of a safe country for her accouchement. On the shoulder of a kneeling giant, who may typify the Ægean Sea, sits the Nymph of Delos, holding out both arms towards Leto and begging that her island may have the honour of being the birthplace of the celestial twins. To the extreme left Cythnos, the mountain-god of Delos, sits between two trees, one of which seems to be a laurel and the other an olive. Both these trees appear in the legend of the birth of Apollo and

Artemis; and the palm, which plays a more prominent rôle in the story, was probably pictured on the missing end of the slab. The scene on the right side is supposed to represent Iris, arriving in Olympos to beg Eileithyia, the goddess of childbirth, to hasten to the assistance of Leto in her pangs. The female figure to the left, with the upper part of her body nude, seems to be Aphrodite, while the fully-clothed and seated figure to the right, with the left forearm leaning on a basket, is probably Demeter — two goddesses who occupy an important place in the Delian myth. The short-coated figure hastening towards these goddesses from the right would be Iris; the other figure in the background, preparing for departure, would be Eileithyia. The central scene would depict Leto, presenting her children to their father Zeus, in the presence of Athena. The boy to the left of the enthroned Zeus is Apollo; the girl standing to the right is Artemis, who already wears the short chiton characteristic of this goddess.

Archäol. Zeitung, xxvii (1869), T. 16, 1-3, pp. 21 et seq., where the earlier references are cited (note 16). Comp. Hermes, xxii, pp. 460-463. Overbeck, Kunstmythologie, iv, pp. 368-370. Jahrbuch des Arch. Inst., v (1890), p. 220. note 6.

Third Room.

922 (cxx). **Colossal Head.**

The nose, most of the lips, the lower parts of the locks falling on the neck, and the bust are modern.

Although the neck shows feminine forms (which has led the restorer to make the bust that of a woman , the head, to judge from the arrangement of the hair and the fillet around it, seems to be really that of a man. It doubtless reproduces one of those types of late-Greek art in which an attempt was made to emphasize the tender delicacy of a youth by borrowing female forms (comp. Nos. 328, 135). The execution points to a late period of the Empire. The pupils of the eyes are indicated by an incised circle without a break, while the iris is denoted by an ellipse, open on the upper side.

923 (cxvii). **Statue of Apollo.**

The restorations include the right arm and sleeve,
the right foot, most of the plinth; the front part, wings,
and tail of the griffin (right fore-paw and a trace of
the left antique); the upper circle of the tripod, decorated with acroteria; the stag below (legs ancient);
the upper part of the lyre behind the stag; most of the
horizontal bands; the supports of the tripod (claw-feet
ancient); the head and tail of the serpent. The head,
which is joined to the body by a modern neck, is ancient
but does not belong to this statue; the nose, fragments
of the ears, the chin, and the locks adjoining the neck
have been restored.

The statue seems to be a copy of an ancient temple-
statue of Apollo, with modifications in the spirit of a
later art. It presents a certain kinship to No. 392. The
forms have, however, less stiffness, and the griffin appears
in a more intimate relation with the god, who presses it
to his side with his left arm. The original position of the
right arm and the attribute held in the right hand cannot now be determined. The execution is careful and
delicate.

Nibby, T. 32, p. 107. *Overbeck*, Kunstmythologie, iv, p. 177,
No. 1; Atlas, xxi, 28.

924 (cxv). **Statuette of a Boy playing with a Bird.**

Formerly in the collection of Giov. Batt. della Porta,
the sculptor (d. 1597; Röm. Mitth., viii, 1893, p. 244,
No. 42). The restorations include the left forearm and
the lower parts of the legs of the boy, the right wing and
tail of the bird, the stump, almost all the drapery hanging
over the stump, and the plinth.

This statuette reproduces an admirable original, probably created in the Hellenistic period (comp. Nos. 911,
912). The pleasure the urchin feels in his cruel sport is
expressed in his face with equal humour and truth to life.

Visconti, Illustrazioni dei monumenti scelti Borghesiani, ii, 29,
p. 67.

925 (cxiii). **Statuette of a Boy in Fetters.**

The restorations include the right hand (except fragments of the forefinger and thumb), the lower half of the

left forearm, with the hand and the corner of the drapery held by it, the right leg from the middle of the thigh downwards, the lower part of the left leg, the feet, the stump, and the plinth.

Ancient art delighted in representations of Cupid put in chains and condemned to hard labour as a punishment for his mischievous tricks; and it sometimes depicted ordinary children in the same condition. The statuette before us belongs to the latter category. The urchin stands crying, wiping the tears from his right eye with his right hand. One end of the chain hanging by his left leg is attached to a girdle round his waist, the other to a ring round his ankle. The left hand probably held some tool, such as a mattock or shovel, leaning on the ground.

Visconti, Illustrazioni dei mon. Borghesiani, II, 30, p. 67. Comp. Braun, Ruinen und Museen, p. 547, No. 19. Ann. dell' Inst., 1886, p. 85. Birt, De Amorum in arte antiqua simulacris (Marpurgi, 1892), pp. XXII, XXIX.

926 (LXXXV). **Head of Aphrodite (?)**, now in Room II (see p. 144).

The right eyebrow, the nose, part of the lower lip, and the bust have been restored.

This beautiful type was probably created in the last decades of the fifth century B.C. It is generally regarded as a portrait of Sappho on account of its alleged resemblance to the type of that poetess (No. 789). This resemblance, however, is limited to a certain analogy in style, while the forms and expressions of the two heads are quite different. The face of the type under review is longer and softer in expression than that of Sappho. The languishing look in the almond-shaped, half-closed eyes is more sharply accentuated. The narrow fillet, wound three times round the head, indicates a careful toilette, while the cap of Sappho makes the impression of a careless négligé. The curls protruding from below the headdress are arranged in a coquettish manner. All these details suit Aphrodite. Numerous replicas prove the popularity of the type before us. One archæologist

has recognized it as a copy of the Aphrodite by Pheidias
that stood in the Portico of Octavia (*Pliny*, Nat. Hist.,
36, 15). Comp. No. 930

On the type, see *Furtwaengler*, Masterpieces, pp. 66-68. To
the replicas mentioned on p. 66 (note 2) must be added an excellent example belonging to the Duke of Poggio-Nativo.

927 (cvii). Life by the Sea Shore, Marble Group for a Garden.

> The head of the man sitting on the rock, his right
> forearm, the front of the left forearm, both hands, and
> the shell they hold are modern. Of the two men stand-
> ing behind him nothing has been preserved except parts
> of the feet. The hoofs are the only ancient part of the
> uppermost goat, and several parts of the other goats are
> also restored.

This group, like No. 170, probably adorned one of
the small gardens usual in the peristyles of Roman
houses; and the opening near the middle of the front
served for a pipe, from which issued a jet of water. The
decoration shows that mixture of plastic and pictorial
elements, which, used by the Hellenistic artists in moder-
ation, became more and more extravagant in the Græco-
Roman period. The base of the rock forming the nucleus
of the group is washed by pictorially treated waves, on
which float two boats, each with two occupants. One of
the men in the boat to the left tries to transfix a fish
with a three-pronged spear. Above this boat sits a female figure, holding an oar in her right hand and leaning
her left hand on a sea-dragon. This is either Amphitrite, the goddess, or Thalatta, a personification of the
sea. Opposite to her, above the boat to the right, sits a
bearded river-god, holding a reed in his right hand and
supporting his left on an urn, from which a stream of fresh
water flows into the sea. On the rock sits a fisherman,
recognizable by his rod and basket of marine creatures.
The restorer depicts him as gazing at an open shell, but
it is, perhaps, more reasonable to suppose that the object of his regard is some jewel that he has fished up

from the deep. The figures approaching the fisherman from behind have been restored as fishermen also, but were more probably the shepherds in charge of the goats, seen scrambling over the rock. Shepherds and fishermen are often mentioned together in idyls and idyllic epigrams; and in this case it is natural to suppose that the former have descended from the hills to inspect the proceedings of their sea-shore cousin.

Gallery.

The sculptures in different kinds of coloured stone, which adorn this sumptuous hall, are works of the close of the 16th, or of the first half of the 17th century. The porphyry busts of the eleven earliest emperors are especially prominent. The ancient statues in the niches are not intrinsically interesting either in subject or execution, and they have, besides, been almost all freely restored. A glance may, however, be devoted to that ensconced in the niche in the south wall.

928 (clxi). **Girl with a Dolphin.**

> The restorations include the head and neck, the right forearm, the upper part of the dolphin, and parts of the feet.

This statue served as a fountain-figure, as appears from an opening for a water-pipe in the mouth of the dolphin on which the girl lays her right hand. The manner in which the forms of the body shine through the chiton, and the rich but artificial folds of the drapery indicate an original of the Hellenistic period. The current identification with Thetis is unwarranted. It is likely that the original figure bore the name of the Nymph whose waters fed the fountain it decorated.

Nibby, T. 23, p. 91. *Clarac*, iv, Pl. 693, No. 1296. Comp. Beschreibung Roms, iii, 3, p. 248, No. 39. Jahrbuch des Arch. Instituts, vii (1892), p. 90, No. 1b.

Room of the Hermaphrodite.

929 (CLXXXI). Head of a Woman in the archaic style.

> The end of the nose is modern. The bust is ancient but belongs to another head. According to the custodians, the head came from Anzio, and it is, therefore, probably identical with that found between Nettuno and Astura and described in the Bull. dell' Inst., 1834, p. 107.

This head makes the impression of an original work; and, as the line of the profile is very individual, it is usually assumed to be a portrait. It must not be forgotten, however, that the artists of the archaic period, even when creating ideal types, followed nature much more closely than was the case in a later and freer form of art. We have no data for assigning this head to any special school. Its distinguishing characteristics, besides the individual profile, are the elegant and complicated coiffure, the narrow, almond-shaped eyes, the simpering expression of the mouth, and the dimple in the lower lip.

> Berichte der sächs. Gesellschaft der Wissenschaften, 1878, p. 137.

930 (CLXXIV). Head of Aphrodite (?).

> Surface freely reworked. The point of the nose, the back of the head, and the cap covering it are modern. The bust is antique, but does not belong to this head.

This head reproduces the same type as No. 926, but in a somewhat freer fashion. The restorer has made a mistake in placing a cap on the head. Here, as in No. 926, the headdress consisted of a triple fillet.

> Nibby, T. 31, p. 105. Comp. Abhandlungen der sächs. Gesellschaft der Wissenschaften, VIII (1861), p. 722, note 66.

931 (CLXXII). Sleeping Hermaphrodite.

> The restorations, made by the sculptor Bergondi, include the head and neck, the right elbow, the left hand, the bare part of the left leg, the left foot, the heel and toes of the right foot, the part of the sheet touching these toes, other patches on the sheet, and the mattress.

To appreciate this figure properly, we must study better-preserved replicas, especially that formerly in the

Villa Borghese and now in the Louvre, and that found at Rome in building the Teatro Costanzi (No. 1065). The Hermaphrodite, as proved by the attitude and other indications, is represented as in the midst of a voluptuous dream. It is one of the most sensual creations of ancient art. In order to heighten the erotic effect, the feminine element has been made prominent in the bodily forms, and the soft and delicate flesh of the back has been treated with great refinement. To judge from these characteristics, the original cannot be dated earlier than the time of Alexander the Great. It has been assumed that this original was the famous Hermaphrodite mentioned by Pliny (Nat. Hist., 34, 80) as the work of Polycles, an artist who flourished in the third or second century B. C. This theory, however, is contradicted by the fact that the Hermaphrodite of Polycles was in bronze. The motive of the statue before us seems calculated for execution in marble, which allowed of a much softer rendering of the forms than was possible in bronze, and thus enabled the sculptor to give full expression to the voluptuous charm at which he aimed.

Visconti, Illustr. dei mon. scelti Borghesiani, I, T. 27. *Nibby*, T. 29, No. 99. Comp. Ann. dell' Inst., 1882, p. 250a. — For the replica in the Louvre: *Friederichs- Wolters*, Bausteine, No. 1481. — For the example in the Teatro Costanzi, see our No. 1065.

Corner Room.

932 cic . Asclepios and Telesphoros.

The restorations include the head of Telesphoros, and the nose, right arm, serpent-staff (lower end old), and left hand and cup of Asclepios. The surface of the marble has suffered from reworking.

The head of Asclepios shows a mild and slightly affected expression, a character peculiar to certain Attic types of the fourth century B. C. It is natural in this connection to think of Cephisodotos, son of Praxiteles, who was the sculptor of a statue of Asclepios in the Portico of Octavia at Rome (*Pliny*, Nat. Hist., 36, 24; comp.

Nos. 266, 662,. Beside the god stands Telesphoros, represented as usual as a boy wrapped in a thick cloak, provided with a hood. Telesphoros was formerly regarded as the demon of healing; but it has lately been argued that he personified the oracles of Asclepios, sent in the form of dreams to those who slept in his temple.

Beschreibung Roms, III. 3, p. 253, No. 15. *Braun*, Ruinen und Museen, p. 551, No. 24. — On the type of Asclepios: Athen. Mitth., xvII (1892), pp. 1 et seq. — For Telesphoros: Bull. de correspondance hellénique, xIV (1890), pp. 595–601; Athen. Mitth., xvII (1892), p. 241.

933 (cIxc). Woman carrying a Water-Vessel.

Perhaps from the Della Porta Collection (Röm. Mitth., vIII, 1893, p. 243, No. 20; comp. No. 924 of this Handbook). The restorations include the nose, the chin, both arms, the water-vessel, and the front of the right foot. The presence of the water-vessel in the original was vouched for by traces on the left knee.

This statue reproduces the same original as the Vatican statue No. 210, and doubtless also served as a fountain-figure. It has preserved its original head; and the difference of type offers another proof that the head and body of the Vatican statue have nothing to do with each other.

Nibby, T. 33, p. 111. Beschreibung Roms, III, 3, p. 252, No. 8.

934 (cxc). Three Women bearing a Vase.

This group is here mentioned simply because its forms depart in the most striking manner from those of ancient art and thus naturally astonish the spectator. This astonishment will vanish, however, when he learns that it is substantially a piece of modern patch-work. The three figures have been placed by the modern restorer on an ancient capital with foliage, turned upside down and manifestly destitute of all relation to them. The nucleus of the statues is ancient, but they have been freely worked over by a modern hand. This reworking accounts for the unpleasing individualistic type of each of the heads, one of which is that of a young girl, the second that of a middle-aged woman, and the third that of a wrinkled old hag. The restorer evidently meant them to typify the three periods of human life. The capital borne by the three figures, with its foliage, bearded masks, and pine-apple, is wholly modern.

Nibby, T. 36, p. 122, No. 1. Comp. Beschreibung Roms, III, 3, p. 252, No. 7.

935 (CLXXXIII). Statue of Pallas.

The restorations include the right arm with most of the sleeve, the left arm up to the biceps, the left hand with the part of the shield it touches, the front of the right thigh, the toes of the right foot with the corner of the plinth below them, a large part of the shield, and the head of the serpent. The head placed on the statue is antique but does not belong to the body.

Archæologists, starting from the assumption that this statue is connected with the Athena Parthenos of Pheidias, have concluded that the right arm was lowered and held in front of the body and perhaps bore a figure of Nike (comp. No. 870). This supposition is, however, erroneous. It is much more likely that the right arm was raised and supported on a lance, as in all analogous statues. An examination of the back of the ancient portion of the right sleeve will show that no other restoration is possible. Additional proofs that the right arm was raised are afforded by the direction followed by the folds of the chiton; by the fact that the right shoulder is somewhat higher than the left, and that the ægis seems to have slipped from the shoulder towards the neck; and, finally, by the position and angle of the support used by the sculptor to connect the right arm with the body. Recent attempts have been made to show that this figure is a reproduction of a statue of Athena in a group of Hephæstos and Athena by Alcamenes. The treatment of the drapery, however, points to late in the fourth century, not to the last decades of the fifth century B.C.

Berichte der sächs. Gesellschaft der Wissenschaften, 1861, T. I, II, pp. 1-17, 1866, T. I, 1-3, pp. 40-43. Eranos Vindobonensis (Vienna, 1893), p. 21. *Furtwaengler*, Masterpieces, p. 326, note 2. For other references, see Arch. Zeitung, VII (1867), pp. 25, 26.

936 (ccı). Statuette of a Dancing Bacchante.

> The restorations include the right arm, the thumb and forefinger of the left hand with the curved attribute held between them, the lower part of the drapery behind the legs, the feet, the stump, and the plinth. The head (nose modern) has been broken off and replaced, but is probably the original.

The graceful motive of this statuette resembles that of No. 793, though the position of the extremities has been reversed. It is easy to see that the left hand held some attribute of wood or bronze — probably a thyrsos; and this fact is an important help in the restoration of the lowered arm of No. 793.

Clarac, ıv, Pl. 775, No. 1934. Comp. *Braun,* Ruinen und Museen, p. 552, No. 26.

937 (ccııı). Statue of Paris (?).

> The restorations include the right hand and apple, the feet and lower part of the legs, the lower part of the drapery behind the left leg, the stump, and the plinth. The head, which has been broken off and replaced, is probably the original, but has suffered much from reworking.

The identification of this statue with Paris rests on the admission that the head is ancient and belonged to the body. The son of Priam would then be represented, as in the Vatican statue No. 382, at the moment when he is passing judgment on the beauty of the three goddesses. The mood in which he fulfils this task varies in the two conceptions. In the Vatican example Paris gazes dreamily before him, as if thinking of the reward offered by Aphrodite, while the head of the Borghese statue wears a critical and restless expression, as if the youth were uneasily conscious of the far-reaching consequences of his decision.

Beschreibung Roms, ııı, 3, p. 254, No. 4. *Braun,* Ruinen und Museen, p. 552, No. 25.

938 (ccxvı). Draped Female Statue.

> The upper part of the bust, the left hand and right forearm with the adjacent drapery, and two toes of the

right foot are modern. The head (locks hanging by the neck restored) is ancient, but it has been freely reworked and does not belong to this statue. It seems too small for the body, with which it is united by a modern bust reaching from the base of the neck nearly to the upper hem of the chiton.

This statue presents the same characteristics as No. 889, and seems, like it, to be an original work of the early Peloponnesian school. The archaic type of the head recalls that of No. 929.

Brunn und Bruckmann, Denkmäler, Nos. 261, 262. Beschreibung Roms, III, 3, p. 254, No. 14. Römische Mittheilungen, II (1887), p. 55.

Corner Room.

939 (ccxxvii). **Seated Figure, restored as Hermes.**

The right hand with the plectrum, the left arm and its drapery, and the lyre with the part of the mantle hanging over it are modern. The part of the drapery immediately below the lyre is, however, ancient, and the depression visible at the top of it proves that some attribute rested on the fold of drapery covering the seat. The head placed on the statue is ancient (except the petasos, nose, and chin), but does not belong to this statue. It is united with the body by a modern neck, and is of somewhat coarser workmanship.

Since the head is a modern addition, no elaborate refutation is necessary of the identification of this statue with Hermes, based on the presence of his invention, the lyre. The more recent identification with Apollo is equally arbitrary. It, too, rests on the assumption that the lyre is ancient, whereas the old part of the figure really leaves it quite uncertain as to whether the attribute in the left hand may not have been a scroll or something else entirely different from a lyre. Besides, the body seems too muscular for an Apollo created by the freer style of art.

Nibby, Monum. scelti della Villa Borghese, T. 38, p. 124. *Braun*, Vorschule, T. 95. Comp. *Overbeck*, Kunstmythologie, IV, p. 207, No. 12.

940 (ccxxxxi). **Group of Dionysos and a Maiden.**

> The restorations include the right hand of Dionysos
> (thumb and forefinger ancient), the right arm of the girl,
> part of her left hand, with the index and middle fingers,
> and the bird (except the tail). Both heads are ancient,
> but their relationship to the statues is questionable, since
> both are united with the bodies by modern necks. In the
> head of Dionysos placed on the male figure the restor-
> ations include the nose, the chin, fragments of the gar-
> land, and the long locks falling by the neck; the nose of
> the girl is also new.

To judge from the bodily forms, the seated figure is
really Dionysos, though it is uncertain whether the head
belongs to the same statue. Dionysos would then be
represented in friendly relationship with a little girl, who
stands beside him with her right arm on the god's lap,
while his left hand rests on her shoulder. In her left
hand the girl holds a pet bird. The group is unique of
its kind, and therefore difficult to explain. In the reliefs
on cinerary urns and sarcophagi (comp. No. 432) we
frequently meet with symbolic representations, in which
the deceased are shown as leading a happy existence in
the train of Dionysos. Possibly this group may have
been placed over a little girl's grave and intended to
pourtray the intimate relation between the deceased and
the god who radiates happiness. Why the sculptor has
placed the girl on a square base, like that of a statue,
remains inexplicable.

Nibby, T. 42, p. 136. Comp. Beschreibung Roms, III, 3, p. 257,
No. 20. *Braun*, Ruinen und Museen, p. 552, No. 27.

941 (ccxxxvii). **Seated Figure of a Man.**

> The restorations include the left shoulder and arm with
> their drapery, the right hand and scroll, the right foot, the
> front of the left foot, and the plinth. The head (nose
> restored) is ancient but does not belong to the statue,
> with which it is united by a modern neck. It differs
> from the body both in the quality of the marble and the
> style of the execution.

The general belief that the head before us is a portrait
of Periander is erroneous. It bears no resemblance to

the herma of the Corinthian statesman (No. 278', which is attested by an inscription, but rather recalls a portrait which has recently, with much plausibility, been identified with Thucydides. The statue to which the modern restorer has affixed the head is a figure resembling Zeus in attitude and arrangement of drapery, and seated in a chair ornamented with lions' claws 'in front) and griffins (on the sides'. The individualistic bodily forms and the somewhat withered flesh show that we have to do with a portrait. The left hand obviously leant on a sceptre. The assumption that a Roman is represented is met by two difficulties. In the first place the Græco-Roman artist, almost invariably (comp., however, No. 303), endued seated figures of this kind with ideal forms. In the second place the fine realistic treatment, which is visible in this statue in spite of reworking, can hardly find an adequate analogy in Græco-Roman art (comp. No. 221). It is thus not improbable that the work represents a Hellenistic ruler enthroned in the guise of Zeus.

Nibby, T. 40, p. 134. *Clarac.* v, Pl. 848, No. 2141. Comp. Beschreibung Roms, III, 3, p. 266, No. 15. *Braun*, Ruinen und Museen, p. 557, No. 32. — For the portrait of Thucydides, see No. 492.

942 (ccxxxiii). Statue of Pluto.

> The restorations include the right forearm and cup, the left forearm and sceptre, the front of the right foot with the piece of the plinth below it, and most of the back of the seat. The head placed on the trunk (nose and upper lip modern) certainly represents the same deity, but its relationship with the body is doubtful, as the neck is a modern addition.

In Pluto as in Poseidon (comp. Nos. 111, 667) we recognize a distinct family likeness to Zeus. The forms of Pluto's head, however, are less dignified; and the face wears a sad and pensive expression, which is intensified by the hair falling over the forehead. The ruler of Hades, moreover, wears a chiton as well as a cloak. Cerberus, seated beside his master, is represented with two dog's heads — one large and matted, the other smaller and resembling that of a greyhound. Round the body are coiled two serpents.

Nibby, T. 39, p. 127. *Braun*, Vorschule, T. 22. *Müller-Wieseler*, Denkmäler der alten Kunst, ii, 67, 853. *Baumeister*, Denkmäler des klass. Alterthums, i, p. 620. Fig. 690. *Roscher*, Lexikon, i, 2, p. 1803. Comp. Beschreibung Roms, iii, 3, p. 256, No. 8. *Braun*, Ruinen und Museen, p. 556, No. 31.

943 (ccxxxii). **Statue of a Satyr,** probably after Praxiteles.

> The restorations include the head, the neck, the right hand, the fingers of the left hand, the left foot, parts of the toes of the right foot (perhaps the whole foot), the stump, and the plinth.

For an account of this type, see No. 525. The execution is better than that of the Capitoline example.

Nibby, p. 126. Beschreibung Roms, iii, 3, p. 256, No. 7. *Furtwaengler*, Masterpieces, p. 310.

In the middle of the room, —

944 (ccxxv). **Statue of a Satyr.**

> Found in 1824 on Monte Calvo, near Rieti, in the Sabine district. The restorations, accomplished under the direction of Thorwaldsen, include the arms and cymbals, the lower part of the right leg (front of foot ancient), the tail, the lower part of the stump with the head and adjacent parts of the skin, and the back and edges of the plinth.

This statue has been inaccurately restored. Several replicas prove that the Satyr was playing the double flute, not clashing the cymbals. In no other way can be explained the puffed-out cheeks of the figure before us, or the treatment of the mouth, which clearly indicates that the end of a bronze or wooden flute penetrated each corner. The Satyr advances in solemn measure as he plays, turning his body on its axis and rising on his tiptoes. The infibulation noticeable in this figure is often seen in statues of athletes, actors, and flute-players; but we do not know whether its purpose was hygienic or æsthetic. That the original was a work in bronze is shown by the supports placed on the right leg, between the legs, and below the feet, which sadly interfere with the general sense of movement and can be explained only by the necessities of the marble-worker. The sharp edges of the nude parts and the conventional treatment of the hair on the body are additional proofs of this. The attitude of the Satyr and the treatment of his hair and beard suggest the artistic influence of Lysippos (comp. No. 31). On the other hand the imposing forms, with their touch of severity, recall the works of the great period of the fifth century B.C. The original of the figure before us would thus seem to have been created by an artist of the early Hellenistic period, whose handling of the nude was inspired by the art of the older schools.

Mon. dell' Inst., III, 59; Ann., 1843, pp. 266 et seq. *Müller-Wieseler*, Denkmäler der alten Kunst, II, 39, 463. Comp. Arch. Zeitung, XLIII (1885), p. 94. *Loewy*, Lysipp und seine Stellung in der griech. Plastik, p. 28. For other references, see *Friederichs-Wolters*, Bausteine, No. 1427.

Palazzo Spada.

The references to the sculptures in the Palazzo Spada have been carefully collected by *Matz* and *Von Duhn* in the 'Antike Bildwerke in Rom' (3 vols.: Leipzig, 1881-82). The writer contents himself with referring to this work, adding only what has appeared since its publication.

In the walls of the long room on the first floor, facing the court, are immured —

945-952. **Eight Reliefs.**

> These reliefs were discovered in 1620, in the course of a restoration of S. Agnese fuori le mura, undertaken by Cardinal Verallo. They had been employed as building material for the flight of steps at that church. Comp. *Bellori*, in *Fea*, Misc., I, p. ccι, No. 100; Arch. Zeitung, XXXVIII (1880), p. 150, note 32, p. 153. The restorations these reliefs have undergone are indicated in the Archæolog. Anzeiger (XXII, 1864, pp. 265*, 266*), in *Matz und Von Duhn* (work cited above, III, Nos. 3563-3570), and, with great exactness, in *Schreiber*, Die hellenistischen Reliefbilder (T. III-x).

These reliefs, perhaps with others now lost, belong to the same cycle and evidently served as the central ornaments of the wall-spaces of a room or colonnade. As the execution is much inferior to the beauty of the designs, they are probably copies, not original works. Their models seem to have been mainly decorative reliefs of the Hellenistic era. In accordance with a strongly marked tendency in the poesy of that period, most of the mythological personages are represented, not in dramatic situations, but in genre scenes, permeated either with a sentimental or with an idyllic spirit. The landscape background is treated with great detail and generally with much skill. Where mountains and rocks appear, they form, as it were, a frame round the figures, and in such a way that the effect of the latter is nowise infringed by the accessory details (comp., especially, No. 952). In three of the reliefs (Nos. 945, 948, 951) the background is occupied by a rustic fane, with its sacred tree — a very popular motive in both the poetry and the art of the Hellenistic period and later (comp. Nos. 713, 808).

Comp. Arch. Zeitung, xxxviii (1880), pp. 145 et seq. *Schreiber*, Die Wiener Brunnenreliefs aus Palazzo Grimani, esp. pp. 9-11.

To the left, —

945. **Paris and Eros.**

The restorations include the whole of the left end of the slab with the front part of the grazing cow, the right upper corner with the head of Paris and the upper part of Eros to a point a little below the wings, both arms and the left leg of Paris, the left arm of Eros, the head of the dog, the head of the recumbent ox (left horn ancient), and also the upper part of its right fore-leg, the right hind-leg, and the tail.

The upper part of this scene is taken from a larger composition, which we know from a relief in the Museo Boncompagni (No. 893). The sculptor, however, had not the skill to adapt his borrowed motive so as to make it occupy the whole of his background, for the left side of the slab is very inadequately filled by the rustic sanctuary with its attendant sacred tree. Paris is represented at the moment when he is about to pronounce judgment on the beauty of the three goddesses. He turns his head towards Eros, who stands on a rock behind the youth and urges him to give the meed of loveliness to Aphrodite. The restoration of the right arm of Paris as holding a flute is erroneous. Probably the arm was bent as in No. 893, and the empty hand placed lightly on the head. The sculptor has added the cattle of Paris in order to fill out the relief and make this slab correspond in size with its neighbours. .

Matz-Duhn, III, No. 3569. *Schreiber*, Die hellenistischen Reliefbilder, T. IX. Comp. Arch. Zeitung, XXXVIII (1880), p. 157.

Opposite, —

946. Dædalos and Pasiphaë.

> The whole of the left end of the slab has been restored,
> the line of fracture passing just behind the left fore-leg
> of the cow. The modern part thus includes the right leg
> of Pasiphaë and most of her right arm (front part of
> forearm ancient). Other restorations include the end of
> the nose, the chin, and the left hand of Pasiphaë; most
> of the head and the right fore-foot of the cow; the head
> of Dædalos (except the lower lip, the beard, and a frag-
> ment at the back of the head), his left shoulder, his left
> hand with the handle of the saw, and his left leg; small
> pieces of the legs of the chair, larger pieces of the build-
> ing in the background, and the whole of the lower edge
> of the slab.

In order to punish King Minos of Crete for his neglect
to fulfil a vow, Poseidon inspired his wife Pasiphaë with
an insensate love for a bull. At the queen's request
Dædalos made for her a wooden cow, concealed in which
she could gratify her unnatural passion. The relief shows
Dædalos conversing with Pasiphaë on the completion of
his work. He sits in the garb of an artizan on a low
stool, holding in his right hand the saw he has just been
using. With his head and right hand raised towards
Pasiphaë, he seems to be explaining the mechanism of
the wooden cow in front of him. On the other side of
the cow stands the unhappy queen, whose bowed head
and sad expression show a consciousness of the mon-
strous nature of her project.

Matz-Duhn, III, No. 3567. *Schreiber*, Die hellenistischen Reliefbilder, T. VIII. *Roscher*, Lexikon, I, 1, pp. 935, 937. Comp. *Robert*,
Der Pasiphae-Sarkophag, Vierzehntes Hallisches Winckelmannsprogramm, p. 19.

To the left, —

947. Death of Opheltes.

> Nearly the whole of the upper part of the right side
> of the slab is modern. The ancient parts include the right

shoulder and right half of the body of the soldier to the right; the part of the body of Opheltes encoiled by the serpent, his chest, and his face; the head and neck of the serpent and the coils round the boy's body; the right forearm, head, and front of the right foot of the soldier to the left; the nose and right forearm of Hypsipyle; and the whole of the lower edge of the slab, with most of the hydria.

Hypsipyle, daughter of Thoas, King of Lemnos, was sold to Lycurgos, King of Nemea, by the women of Lemnos, who could not forgive her for having spared her father in the conspiracy in which they had slain all the other men on the island. Lycurgos entrusted her with the care of his young son Opheltes. When the army of the Seven against Thebes arrived at Nemea, parched with thirst, Hypsipyle led them to a spring, and in doing so left her little charge for a time alone. During her absence Opheltes was slain by a serpent. The heroes killed the serpent, named the boy Archemoros. or 'forerunner in destiny', because they saw in his death a premonition of their own fate, and founded the Nemean Games in his honour. The vogue of this myth was mainly due to the tragedy of Euripides entitled 'Hypsipyle'. The relief represents the moment when the heroes discover the fate of Opheltes and are on the point of slaying his destroyer. The one, whom the tradition enables us to name Hippomedon, advances towards the serpent, holding out his buckler. The missing right arm has been properly restored as equipped with a lance. A second warrior, presumably Capaneus, is seen behind the rock in front of which the serpent rears itself on end. His right hand has also been restored as brandishing a spear, but it is more likely that it held a large stone, with which the hero was about to crush the snake. To the left flees the terror-stricken Hypsipyle, raising her hands and gazing back at the scene of horror behind her.

Matz-Duhn, III, No. 3568. *Baumeister*, Denkmäler des klass. Alterthums, I, p. 113, Fig. 49. *Schreiber*, Die hellenistischen Reliefbilder, T. VI.

Opposite, —

948. **Amphion and Zethos.**

> The restorations include the end of the nose in both youths; the left arm of Amphion, almost the whole of the drapery at his back, and the bridge of his lyre; both arms of Zethos (part of the right hand, laid on his head, ancient), most of his right thigh, part of the same leg below the knee, and the left foot; the right end of the slab and most of its lower edge.

In his tragedy of 'Antiope' Euripides had represented Amphion and Zethos, the sons of Zeus and Antiope, as types of two entirely distinct characters. Amphion appeared as a youth absorbed in intellectual interests and especially in music, while his brother found his chief delight in the chase and other bodily exercises. The tragedy opened with a dialogue in which each of the brothers defended his favourite pursuits with cleverness and passion. This scene, which enjoyed great popularity in antiquity and is often referred to by ancient authors, seems also to have been present in the mind of the sculptor of this relief. The conversation takes place in a milieu in which the hunter Zethos must have been at home, for in the background we see a rustic sanctuary of Artemis, with its appropriate oak-tree, while within the fane is a carefully executed archaistic statue of the huntress-goddess. Amphion stands in front of his brother, significantly supporting the lyre, the symbol of his view of life, on an adjacent pillar. Zethos sits opposite in a careless attitude and looks at his brother with an unequivocal air of ennui. His hound stands beside him and lifts his head towards Amphion as if in astonishment. The distinct individualities of the two brothers are pourtrayed with masterly skill. The simple and noble pose of Amphion forms a sharp contrast to the boorish ease of Zethos. The fine profile and deep skull of the one brother indicate intellectual capacity of no mean order, while the small and narrow head of the other is a sign of limited intelligence. The face of Amphion is framed in long locks, while the hair of Zethos is cut short after the manner of gymnastic-loving youths.

Matz-Duhn, III, No. 3565. *Schreiber*, Die hellenistischen Reliefbilder, T. III.

To the left, —

949. **Paris and Œnone.**

The whole left end of the relief is modern, including the whole figure of Paris except part of his left breast, the middle of his left forearm, his left leg, and his right foot. The other restorations include the head, the front half of the right forearm, and the left hand of Œnone; most of the right hand, the front half of the left forearm, the lower part of the knee and left leg with the drapery, and the lower part of the right leg of the river-god, and nearly the whole of the hydria.

The relief shows Paris and his wife Œnone at the moment when the former, seduced by the promises of Aphrodite, is about to embark on his fateful voyage to Greece. Œnone warns her husband against the dangers of the expedition, pointing with her left hand at the ship, which is seen in the background, ready to sail. In the arrangement of its oars and in certain details of its construction this vessel shows peculiarities usual in the Hellenistic period of the third century B.C. The same period is indicated by the pine-crowned standard of the commander, leaning against the elaborate ornament *(aphlaston, aplustre)* on the poop. The representation reproduces the same original as a relief in the 'Casino di Sora', or main building of the former Villa Ludovisi. The latter, however, obviously follows its model more faithfully than the relief now before us, and the relations between the two personages of the scene are represented with greater perspicuity. Œnone is more nobly conceived, while the nonchalant air of Paris shows clearly that his wife's warning will be in vain. In the relief in the Palazzo Spada the artist has added, below the principal actors, the recumbent figure of a river-god, presumably the Scamander, who lifts his head towards Paris and raises his arm, as if he, too, would dissuade the youth from his enterprize. In all probability this figure did not exist in the original composition, but was added by the sculptor of this relief to make it correspond in size with the other members of the series. It is absent from the Ludovisi example, it diverts attention from the principal group, and it is by no means skilfully adapted to the space it has to occupy.

Matz-Duhn, iii, No. 3570. Arch. Zeitung, xxxviii (1880), T. 13, No. 2, pp. 145 et seq. *Baumeister*, Denkmäler des klass. Alterthums, iii, p. 1635, Fig. 1696. *Schreiber*, Die hellenistischen Reliefbilder, T. x. Jahrbuch des Arch. Instituts, iv (1889), pp. 94, 95, Fig. 4. Comp. the Archäolog. Anzeiger of the same volume, 1889, pp. 140, 141. — For the bas-relief of the Villa Ludovisi: *Schreiber*, Die antiken Bildwerke der Villa Ludovisi, No. 149. Arch. Zeitung, xxxviii (1880), T. 13, No. 1, pp. 145 et seq.

Opposite is a plaster cast of the relief of Endymion in the Museum of the Capitol (No. 162).

To the left, —

950. **The Rape of the Palladium.**

> The restorations include part of the roof of the temple, the two outermost triglyphs, the apex of the pediment, and the front part of the left valve of the door; the nose of Odysseus and the front of his right forearm; the nose of Diomedes, most of his left shoulder, his left arm, almost the whole of his right hand with the sword, his left leg, and the lower part of his right leg; the object in the form of a base behind Diomedes; the lowest third of the first pilaster counted from the left; the whole of the lower edge of the slab.

After Odysseus and Diomedes had carried off the Palladium, on which hung the fate of Troy, from the Trojan temple of Athena, a quarrel arose between the two heroes, each of whom wished to monopolize the glory of the deed. The episode is variously narrated in the poems relating to the legend, and has consequently also received varying treatment in the plastic arts. In any case the relief before us represents the dispute between the two heroes. In the background we see a temple 'in antis', recognizable as a temple of Athena by the sculptures of its pediment (to the left a serpent, in the middle a shield with the head of Medusa, to the right a helmet). Odysseus crosses the threshold of the temple, gesticulating violently and turning his head towards Diomedes. The latter stands outside the building with his sword drawn, and looks menacingly at his approaching colleague. In all well-preserved representations of this scene the Palladium itself invariably appears; and there is little doubt that it was also figured on this relief and has been lost along with the left shoulder and left arm of Diomedes. It would appear that his left arm was extended downwards and a little forwards, the lower end of the image resting in the left hand while the head leant against his shoulder. The original motive must have been some such arrangement as this, as otherwise we should find traces of the former presence of the Palladium either on the body of Diomedes or on the background. The poem which inspired the sculptor of the relief must thus have followed the version of the story according to which Diomedes succeeded in first entering the temple and carrying off the image, while the subsequent quarrel was due to the objurgations of the disappointed Odysseus. The contrast between the individualities of the two heroes is admirably indicated. The face of the excited Odysseus shows the subtle and intellectual traits characteristic of him in ancient art comp. No. 121), while his body is represented as agile rather than muscular. His comparative size is explained, not only by his being nearer the background of the relief, but also by the fact that the sculptor meant to depict him as actually smaller than Diomedes. On the other hand, Diomedes possesses a comparatively small skull, the slight development of which indicates limited mental capacity; his frame is one of great size and vigour, and his attitude is pregnant with calm defiance.

Matz-Duhn, III, No. 3566. *Schreiber*, Die hellenistischen Relief-bilder, T. VII. Comp. particularly Ann. dell' Inst., 1858, pp. 238, 239. Arch. Zeitung, XVII (1859), pp. 93-95.

To the left, —

951. Wounded Adonis.

> The restorations include the whole of the right side
> of the slab with the rock, the fig-tree, and the left fore-
> leg of the hound to the right; most of the boar's head
> carved on the epistyle; the head of Adonis, part of his
> left breast, the left shoulder and arm (hand ancient),
> almost all the part of the chlamys hanging over his back,
> most of his left thigh and left foot; the head of the dog
> to the right (ears ancient); the head of the dog to the
> left (left ear ancient) and its left fore-leg; the left lower
> angle of the slab with the lower end and base of the
> pillar.

Adonis, tortured by the agony of his wound, leans
on his hunting-spear, which he has grasped just below
the point with his right hand and breast-high with his
left, in order to relieve the weight on his injured right
leg. The right foot just touches the ground with the ball.
The place of the wound is indicated by the double band-
age round the right calf. The hounds share the distress
of their master, one sadly hanging its head, the other
turning towards the wound. The temple in the background with its attendant plane-tree is shown, by the
boar's head nailed up in the epistyle, to be dedicated
to Artemis. The beholder is thus reminded of the goddess to whose wrath the death of Adonis is due.

Matz-Duhn, III, No. 3564. *Schreiber*, Die hellenistischen Reliefbilder, T. IV.

Opposite, —

952. Bellerophon watering Pegasus.

> A narrow strip at the left end of the slab (reaching
> down to about the shoulder of Bellerophon) and a broader
> piece at the right end (extending to about the level of
> Bellerophon's nose) are modern. Other restorations are
> the head of Bellerophon, his right forearm (fingers partly
> antique), his right leg (foot ancient), and the part of the
> chlamys hanging over his back; the right ear, most of
> the hoof of the right hind-leg, and the tail of Pegasus.

It has been supposed that this relief was inspired by
that version of the Bellerophon myth in which a spring

played a prominent part. It seems, however, more probable that the sculptor of the original simply meant to represent Bellerophon and his winged steed in a genre-scene. The contrast between the ideal form of Bellerophon and the realistic, not to say common, appearance of the horse is very striking. It would almost seem as if the artist had faithfully copied some particular underbred animal. The attitude given to the drinking horse shows close observation of nature; and the general arrangement of the composition may be called masterly. The group is framed on the left by a tree and on the right by a rock, while the vacant space above is admirably filled up with the wings of Pegasus.

Matz-Duhn, III, No. 3563. *Baumeister*, Denkmäler des klass. Alterthums, I, p. 300, Fig. 317. *Schreiber*, Die Wiener Brunnenreliefs aus Pal. Grimani, p. 9, Fig. 5; Die hellenistischen Reliefbilder, T. III. Comp. Athenische Mittheilungen, II (1877), p. 135.

In the adjoining Sala del Trono, —

953. Colossal Statue of Pompey the Great (so called).

> Found under Pope Julius III. (1550-55) in a cellar in the Via dei Leutari, near the Cancelleria (account of the discovery given by *Flaminio Vacca:* Berichte der sächs. Gesellschaft der Wissenschaften, 1881, p. 71, No. 57). The right arm, the fingers of the left hand (thumb ancient), and the sword-hilt are modern. The head is ancient but does not belong to the body.

The head that originally belonged to the statue was encircled by a garland or a tænia, for there are traces on the sword-belt near the left shoulder and on the cloak, behind the clasp, near the right shoulder, which show that a band, ending in a decorative motive in the form of an ivy-leaf, fell from the head on each shoulder. The right arm, to judge from the direction of the shoulder, was a little less elevated and more horizontal than the restorer has made it. In any case the movement of the arm betokens that the personage here represented was in the act of pacifying an audience, or imposing silence on it. The outstretched left hand holds a globe, which seems to have been surmounted by a figure of Victory, for a rectangular incision appears on the top of it. This would indicate that the statue was that of a ruler or warrior, whose dominion extended over a large part of the known world. The current appellation is due in the first instance to the fact that the statue was found near the Theatre of Pompey. It was assumed that this statue was identical with that in the neighbouring Curia Pompei, at the feet of which Cæsar was murdered. Augustus declared the Curia a *locus sceleratus* and caused it to be walled up. The statue was re-erected in front of the theatre, opposite the main door leading from the stage to the Hecatostylon (comp. vol. i, p. 314, tablet xvi, — a site which would be, roughly, behind the choir of the present church of S. Andrea della Valle. The distance from this point to the Via dei Leutari, in which the Spada statue was found, is about 330 yards, or rather too far to alone justify the usual identification. As soon as the belief that the statue represented Gnæus Pompeius Magnus gained ground, people began to find that the head placed on it resembled the portrait of Pompey the Great on the coins of his sons, Gnæus and Sextus. But any impartial judge will easily decide that this resemblance is wholly imaginary. The writer feels it utterly superfluous to waste more words on the point, since a head has recently been found which agrees in every respect with the coin-portrait and may be unreservedly recognized as a likeness of Pompey.

The head placed on the statue is a portrait of an unknown individual. That it is not the original belonging to the body is conclusively proved by the fact that the two neck-pieces do not harmonize, and also by the fact that the remains of ribbons near the shoulder show that the original head wore a wreath or a tænia, while the present head is devoid of any such headdress. The head also differs from the body in the quality of the marble. Though both are treated in a decorative style, the latter is well executed and the former poorly. The account of the discovery, which, however, seems somewhat apocryphal, tells us that the statue was discovered under the boundary line between the property of two adjacent owners, one of whom claimed the body and the other the head. If we may believe this, it would follow that the alien head had been placed on the body in ancient times. The statue before us would be an example of a custom, known to have prevailed both in the Hellenistic and the Roman imperial age, by which the head of a statue was sometimes removed to make way for the head of some other person whom the citizens of the period wished to honour by a public portrait.

Antiquarum statuarum urbis Romæ icones (Romæ, 1621), II, T. 74 (statue here treated as a portrait of Trajan). *Clarac*, v, Pl. 911, No. 2316. *Bernoulli*, Römische Ikonographie, I, T. VII, pp. 112 et seq., Fig. 15. *Baumeister*, Denkmäler des klass. Alterthums, III, p. 1384, Fig. 1532, p. 1385, Fig. 1533. For the rest of the bibliography, see *Matz-Duhn*, I, No. 1073, and *Bernoulli*, Röm. Ikonographie, I, p. 112, note 3. — The remarks of *Fea* on the remains of the bands or ribbons are entirely correct; see his Osservazioni intorno alla celebre statua detta di Pompeo lette il dì 10 settembre nell' Acc. romana d'archeologia (Roma, 1812), pp. 6, 7, and Notizia degli scavi nell' anfiteatro Flavio (Roma, 1813), pp. 31, 32. — On the undoubted portrait of Pompey, see Röm. Mittheilungen, I (1886), T. II, pp. 37-41. *Reinach*, Mithridate, Eupator, Pl. IV. Revue archéologique, xv (1890), Pl. VIII, pp. 339, 340. — On the custom, above referred to, of changing the heads of statues, see *Friedlaender*, Darstellungen aus der Sittengeschichte Roms, III, pp. 161-163. Comp. Bull. dell' Inst., 1885, pp. 95, 96. Berichte der sächs. Gesellschaft der Wissenschaften, 1891, pp. 102 et seq.

Picture Gallery.

951. So-called Statue of Aristotle.

This statue is probably identical with the headless 'Aristide assiso' described by *Aldroandi* (in *Mauro*, Le antichità di Roma, p. 256) as 'in casa di M. Francesco di Aspra, presso a S. Macuto' (Röm. Mittheilungen, v, 1890, p. 14, note 2). The restorations include the right forearm and elbow with a small piece of the upper arm, a considerable portion of the front of the himation, the left leg from the middle of the thigh downwards, and the drapery of the left leg. The head placed on the body is ancient (except the nose), but does not belong to it.

This statue represents a seated figure, leaning forward and plunged in meditation. The head is ancient, but does not belong to the body. The original head doubtless leant upon the right hand. On the plinth are inscribed the letters ΑΡΙΣΤΙΞ, followed by a blank space large enough for four other letters, and then by a mark (´) supposed to be the upper part of a final Σ. Until recently it has been supposed that the missing letters were those required to make the word ΑΡΙΣΤΟΤΕΛΗΣ; and the statue has therefore been taken for the great philosopher Aristotle. The square omicron, however, which this reading necessitates, is a late form, which does not harmonize with the character of the other letters, while the hiatus is not large enough for this and the other four letters. During the 16th century the inscription was read as ΑΡΙΣΤΕΙΔΗΣ; and this reading, which was also adopted by an archæologist of the 18th century, would satisfy the epigraphical conditions. The style of the statue and the palæography of the inscription point to the last century of the Roman Republic or, at latest, to the early years of the Empire; hence the inscription could not refer to Aristides the Sophist, who flourished in the time of the Antonines (comp. Nos. 468, 955), but to the more famous Athenian general and statesman. An ancient sculptor would, however, have certainly emphasized the military fame of Aristides, and would not have represented him in the attitude of a philosopher or scholar. All these difficulties vanish if we read the inscription as ΑΡΙΣΤΙΠΠΟΣ, and see in the figure a portrait-statue of the Cyrenian philosopher Aristippos, a disciple of the Socratic school, who declared pleasure the supreme good.

The most unpractised eye can see at a glance that the head does not belong to the body. The marble is different. No trace of the right hand can be seen on the right side of the head. To make the two neck-pieces fit each other, the restorer has smoothed the faces of the fracture, and has pared down the front of the part belonging to the body. In his treatment of the back he has been less careful, and the part of the neck belonging to the head projects about one-fifth of an inch over that attached to the body. The facial type, the arrangement of the hair, and the style of the execution prove that the head is a Roman portrait of the end of the Republic or the beginning of the Empire. The restorer obviously selected this head in the belief that the statue represented Aristotle, for, as a matter of fact, it reflects an existence devoted to serious thought and study and would be no unworthy presentment of the great Stagirite. If, however, we consider the definite details that we possess as to the appearance of Aristotle, we find that they do not agree with the head before us. According to tradition Aristotle was bald-headed and wore his beard trimmed, doubtless like those of his contemporary Demosthenes (comp. Nos. 30, 285) and his disciple Theophrastos (comp. No. 788). The question of what Roman this interesting head is the portrait must remain unsolved. There were several men at Rome during the transition period from the Republic to the Empire, whom we might justly conceive as bearing features like this. As an example, the erudite antiquary Marcus Terentius Varro may be mentioned.

Visconti, Iconografia greca, I, T. xxa, b, pp. 228 et seq. *Baumeister*, Denkmäler des klass. Alterthums, I, p. 129, Figs. 134, 135. For the rest of the bibliography, see *Matz-Duhn*, I, p. 343, No. 1174. Comp. Arch. Zeitung, xxxviii (1880), p. 107. Römische Mittheilungen, v (1890), pp. 12 et seq.

The Antiquities of the Vatican Library.

To the left of the entrance to the Musco Cristiano, —

955. Statue of the Sophist Ælius Aristides.

> According to the inscription on the base, this statue was found and placed in the Vatican Library under Pius IV. (1559-66). The restorations include the nose and fragments of the left ear and of the plinth.

The inscription chiselled on the plinth informs us that this statue represents Ælius Aristides (comp. No. 168), a sophist who enjoyed considerable reputation in the time of Marcus Aurelius. Aristides was born in 117 A.D. at Adrianopolis in Bithynia. He is called a Smyrniote in the inscription, owing to the fact that he had received from the grateful Smyrniotes the right of citizenship and the title of second founder of the city, in return for the successful eloquence with which he persuaded the Emp. Marcus Aurelius to bestow a large sum of money for the rebuilding of Smyrna after an earthquake. It is, indeed, quite possible that the statue may have been erected and the inscription composed by the Smyrniotes themselves.

> *Bellori*, Veterum illustrium philosophorum, poetarum, rhetorum et oratorum imagines (Romæ, 1635), T. 72. *Visconti*, Iconografia greca, I, T. xxxi, 4, 5, pp. 351-354. Comp. Beschreibung Roms, II, 2, pp. 329, 330. *Braun*, Ruinen und Museen, p. 838, No. 4.

Room of the Aldobrandini Nuptials.

On the upper part of the walls, —

956. Landscapes with Scenes from the Odyssey.

These pictures adorned a large room in an aristocratic ancient mansion discovered in 1848 in preparing the

foundations of a modern building in the Via Graziosa,
on the Esquiline. Along with other paintings now lost,
they formed a kind of frieze above the dado on the walls
of the room, which were made of *opus reticulatum*. This
frieze was symmetrically divided by red pillars, which,
however, are not the boundaries of distinct and separate
landscapes. On the contrary, the different parts of the
frieze as articulated by the pillars show a notable con-
tinuity both in design and in colour. The general effect
is that of a spacious panorama, seen from within a colonnade and gradually fading into the misty distance. The
perspective of the pillars shows that the representation
of Circe, now on the right wall of the chamber, formed
the original centre of the series. It was specially fitted
for this position through being the only scene with an
architectural background. The execution of this series
of mural decorations may be placed without hesitation
in the last century B. C. or, at latest, in the beginning
of the first century of the present era. This period is indicated by the construction of the walls adorned with
the paintings, by the palæography of the inscriptions
attached to the figures, and, finally, by the style of the
decoration — a style which was brought from the Hellenistic Orient to Italy at the beginning of the last century B. C. and gave place there to a new style in the first
century A. D. Like the decorative ensemble in which
we find them, the pictures themselves point to Hellenistic
originals. The Greeks of the Hellenistic period studied the
Homeric poems with the liveliest interest; and our artist
has consulted this taste by following the details of the
epic in the closest manner. The groups in his landscapes
are substantially accurate illustrations of the Odyssey.
A characteristic sample of his method is shown in the
first and second scenes of the Læstrygonians, where he
has added the herds of cows and sheep, which have no
direct connection with the subjects of the paintings but
are incidentally mentioned in the epic. The poet, wishing
to convey an idea of the light nights of the Hyperborean

country of the Læstrygonians, declared that one shepherd
might be conducting his flock to pasture at the same
time that another was leading his home. The fact that
the painter has taken note of this remark shows how
carefully he has followed the details of the epic. The
few instances in which his accessories are not borrowed
from the poem will be mentioned as they occur. In the
landscape the artist could act more freely, since the indications of this in the epic are very scant. Yet even
here we recognize an attempt to develop these hints in
harmony with the apparent intention of the poet. The
paintings in this Roman house were the work of a skilful
decorative painter. It is difficult to determine how faithfully they reproduce their originals and preserve their
quality. In any case they are the most important land-
scape-paintings of antiquity that have come down to us,
and the best fitted to give us at least an approximate
idea of what the Hellenistic painters accomplished in
this field. Examining the pictures from this point of
view, we find, in the first place, that the ancient painter
knew how to develop a landscape organically and arrange
it in a tasteful manner. The impressions that he tries
to reproduce with his pencil, he may have experienced
himself among the innumerable bays and rocks of the
islands in the Ægean Sea and along the coast of Asia
Minor. The linear perspective is generally correct.
It is, however, easy to see that the ancient painter
was usually guided by his personal sense of fitness and
that he did not have at his command the scientific rules
of the modern artist. As to the aërial perspective, these
decorative mural paintings afford no proper test of the
artistic skill of the period. In any case the first scene
of the underworld (see p. 180) shows considerable ability
in producing an effect by careful gradation of colours.
The accessory groups and figures are always most
skilfully adapted to the landscape in which they are
framed, and their colouring is subordinated to the
general effect.

On the bright nights of the country of the Læstrygonians, see *Müllenhof*, Deutsche Alterthumskunde, i, pp. 5-8. *Helbig*, Das homerische Epos aus den Denkmälern erläutert, 2nd edit., p. 20.

The series of the extant pictures begins with that on the left wall, to the right of the window.

First Picture of the Læstrygonians.

To the left is a bay in which lie the ships of Odysseus; above, in the leaden sky, are three winged gods of the winds blowing instruments like trumpets. The latter obviously refer to the preceding scene (now missing), which must have represented the storm that overtook the fleet of Odysseus on its departure from the island of Æolos. Farther to the right rises a steep and lofty rock, from which a narrow path descends, while a brook murmurs at its foot. The daughter of the King of the Læstrygonians, coming down this path with a pitcher in her hand to fetch water from the stream, meets the three Ithacan sailors whom Odysseus has sent to reconnoitre. As she belongs to a race of giants, she is represented as considerably larger than the Greeks. The gesture of her left arm indicates that she is answering the questions of the foremost of the Greeks, whose name (Antilochos) is inscribed beside him. Below is a boatman pushing his boat off the rocks — a realistic addition, intended, as the inscription (Ἀκταί) above his head betokens, to indicate the beach. Farther to the right, below the rock, lies a Nymph, with a pitcher and a reed. This is, doubtless, the Nymph of the above-mentioned brook; and her distance from it is probably due to the artist's desire not to overcrowd the space just above the stream. On a ledge of the rock reclines a mountain-god. On the margin of the brook stand two sheep, while higher up a herd of cattle follow their herdsmen.

Second Læstrygonian Scene.

The stream and the pastoral elements of the last scene re-appear in this one. The latter are reïnforced by a youthful Pan (comp. No. 389), seated on a mound and leaning on a shepherd's crook, and by a recumbent Nymph beside him. These figures, as indicated by the inscription (Νομαί), denote the pasturage. Farther to the right, on and under the rock, are seen the Læstrygonians, hastening to attack the Greeks. They are incited to this by their king Antiphates, who advances with his right arm raised, clad in a blue himation and bearing a sceptre in his left hand. Below, to the right, is a Læstrygonian, carrying a dead Greek on his back and dragging another along the ground by a rope bound round his legs. A little higher up is another Læstrygonian, wading through the water and seizing a Greek by the hair.

On the right wall, —

Third Læstrygonian Scene.

The Læstrygonians are shattering the vessels of the Greeks with huge blocks of rocks and trunks of trees. The mountains round the bay are drawn and grouped with great truth to nature and much æsthetic charm. The composition is full of animation.

Transition Scene.

The left side of the picture still refers to the adventures among the Læstrygonians. In the foreground a Læstrygonian raises a block of stone with both hands, to crush a Greek lying on the ground before him. In the background is the ship of Odysseus, making its escape with all sails set. To the right, separated by a narrow strait from the land of the Læstrygonians, rises the island of Circe, the mountains of which are lower and of softer outline than those of the previous pictures. The group of three female figures in the foreground personifies the coast Ἀκταί. The three figures in the background are probably Odysseus and two of his companions.

12*

Circe Scene.

To the left is the court of Circe. Odysseus has arrived to rescue his companions, who had been turned into swine by the enchantress, and is welcomed at the entrance by Circe, who opens the door for him. To the right is the interior of Circe's palace, where she throws herself at the feet of the hero, begging for mercy, after finding that he is proof against her spells. This scene deviates from the epic version of it, for Homer tells us that Odysseus, after the sorceress had touched him with her magic wand in vain, sprang to his feet and advanced to attack her with drawn sword.

The next scene, almost entirely obliterated, doubtless represented a later episode in the story of Circe. It is improbable that this scene, like the foregoing, had an architectural background; we may therefore surmize that it may possibly have represented the quarrel of Odysseus with Eurylochos, on his return to the shore to bring his companions to the house of Circe.

On the left wall, between the entrance-wall and the window, —

First Scene in Hades.

This is the most important painting in this series. To the left is the ship of Odysseus, approaching, under full sail, the rocky gate of Hades. Through this gate a broad and pale ray of light reaches the underworld, which, for the rest, is represented in a more sombre tone. The neighbourhood of the rock and the interior of Hades are overgrown with tall reeds. The front of Hades is bounded by a dark-green river, presumably the Acheron, with the river-god seated on its bank. The figure couched on the slope of the rocky hill over the gate of the infernal regions seems to be another river-god, perhaps the Cocytos. In the faintly lighted part of Hades we see two companions of Odysseus busied with the slaughtered ram, while the hero himself stands in front of them, listening to the predictions of Tiresias, who is clad as a priest. Behind the seer is a group of shades, mostly women; three of them are inscribed as Phædra, Ariadne, and Leda. On the slope above sits the disconsolate shade of Elpenor (also denoted by an inscription), who has lost his life on the island of Circe but is denied admission to Hades, because his body still lies unburned and unburied in the house of the enchantress.

Second Scene in Hades.

The next painting, in which the representation of the infernal regions is continued, is only one-half the width of those already described. The painter was prevented from extending it farther to the right by the presence of a door in the wall which it originally adorned; or the right half of the picture may have been destroyed by the insertion of a door at a later period. In the foreground are four Danaïdes, trying in vain to fill a vase with water (comp. No. 373). This episode is not mentioned in the Homeric account of the underworld, but is borrowed by the painter from later sources. It is uncertain whether the weeping female figure seated on the ground above this group is a fifth Danaïd or some other lost soul. To the right, below the projecting rock, lies the gigantic form of Tityos, whose flesh is torn by two vultures. On the rock is Sisyphos, laboriously urging his block of stone towards the summit. Above Sisyphos is a man hurrying forward, brandishing a club. If it were not that the scanty remains of the inscription denoted a different name, we should have no hesitation in identifying this figure with Orion, whom the epic describes as hunting in the lower regions.

The paintings are admirably published by *Woermann* in 'Die antiken Odysseelandschaften vom esquilinischen Hügel' (Munich, 1876). He has collected the earlier bibliography in this book (p. 2) and in 'Die Landschaft in der Kunst der alten Völker' (p. 322). — For the first scene in Hades, see *Woermann*, Die Malerei des Alterthums, p. 113, Fig. 29, and *Baumeister*, Denkmäler des klass. Alterthums, II, p. 858, Fig. 939. Comp. *Mau,* Geschichte der decorativen Wandmalerei in Pompeii, pp. 164, 165.

On the lower part of the walls, —

957. The Heroines of Tor Marancio.

These wall-paintings were found in 1816 in an ancient villa at the Tor Marancio, outside the Porta S. Sebastiano (comp. vol. I, p. 1). To judge from the defective orthography and the palæography of the inscriptions attached to them, they date from the third century of the Christian era. They form a gallery of mythical 'Fair Women', prominent for their crimes and misfortune in love, — a cycle which evidently received its definitive form in the Alexandrian period. They are rudely executed but presuppose excellent originals, the creation of which is doubtless also due to Alexandrian art. The names inscribed by the ancient painter have been preserved in all cases but one (No. 117, left wall. With the exception of Myrrha (No. 121, back-wall) all the heroines are represented at the moment where, driven by their passion, they are about to commit a terrible crime, but pause for an instant to consider the consequences of their act. The chief charm of the originals lay, no doubt, in the delicate individualisation of the different faces; this the mural painter has, naturally enough, entirely, or almost entirely, failed to reproduce. The most beautiful figures are those of Pasiphaë (No. 123, back-wall) and Scylla (No. 126, right wall. Pasiphaë stands beside the cow which Dædalos made to enable her to satisfy her unnatural passion for the bull sent by Poseidon. She is conceived in the same way as in the relief No. 946. Scylla was the daughter of Nisos, King of Megara, whose life and power depended on a purple or golden lock in the midst of his hair. When Minos besieged Megara, on his expedition against Athens, Scylla fell in love with him, severed the fatal lock from her father's head, and gave it to her lover. The result was that Megara was captured and Nisos slain. The painting shows Scylla, with the fatal

lock in her right hand, standing on the wall of Megara
and looking down at the camp of Minos with a look of
mingled love and melancholy. The other heroines whose
names are attached to the figures are Canace (No. 118,
left wall), Myrrha (No. 121, back-wall), and Phædra
(No. 127, right wall). Canace, daughter of Æolos, conceived an incestuous love for her brother Macareus, and
afterwards, filled with remorse, slew herself with a sword
sent to her by her father. The painter has chosen the
moment just before the suicide, where Canace, plunged
in sad thought, holds the sword near her head with her
right hand and rests her right elbow in her left hand. In
his design the artist has used a motive which was popular
in Attic art of the fifth century B.C. and may be seen in
one of the Peliades in the relief No. 635. Myrrha conceived a passion for her own father Cinyras and shared
his bed for twelve nights before he recognized her. Discovered at last, she was pursued by Cinyras with drawn
sword but was turned, on her prayer to the gods, into a
myrrh-tree. She is represented here in the act of flight,
the figure of her father being left to the beholder's imagination. Phædra is represented just before her self-
inflicted death, convulsively holding the cord with which
she is about to strangle herself. The figure of which the
name is missing (No. 117, left wall) seems to be Byblis,
who hanged herself on account of her unhallowed love
for her brother Caunos. The right hand and the disproportionately long arm are modern restorations; and
the original hand probably held some such attribute as a
rope or girdle.

Raoul-Rochette, Peintures antiques inédites, Pl. i-v, pp. 397-
401 (where the earlier bibliography is collected in note 1, p. 397,
and note 1, p. 398). *Biondi*, I monumenti Amaranziani, T. ii-vii.
— For Pasiphaë, see also *Braun*, Zwölf Basreliefs, Vignette of No. 5,
Dædalos and Pasiphaï. Comp. *O. Jahn*, Arch. Beiträge, pp. 245-
247. *Friedländer*, Über den Kunstsinn der Römer, p. 28, note 32.
Ann. dell' Inst., 1869, pp. 63-65. — For Scylla: Arch. Zeitung.
xxiv (1866), p. 198. — For Canace, see Arch. Zeitung, xli (1883),
p. 55. — On Phædra: ibid., pp. 41, 55. — On the supposed
Byblis: Rhein. Mus., xxv (1870), p. 156.

On the lower part of the right wall, —

958. **The Aldobrandini Nuptials,** a mural painting.

> Found under Clement VIII. (1592-1605) on the Es-
> quiline, behind S. Giuliano and near the Arch of Gal-
> lienus (*Bartoli*, in *Fea*, Miscellanea, I, p. ccxlix, No. 96).
> It passed through the hands of Cardinal Cintio Aldobran-
> dini, Camuccini the painter, and Vincenzo Nelli, 'mer-
> cante di campagna', and was sold by the last to Pope
> Pius VII. in 1818. The picture was twice carelessly
> restored, and thus the older engravings and the commen-
> taries founded on them contain many inaccuracies. It
> was not till 1815 that the painting was properly cleaned
> and freed from retouches.

The picture represents a wedding. The bride has
already retired to the bridal chamber *(thalamos)* and sits
on the nuptial couch, enveloped in a large white mantle
drawn over her forehead and modestly casting down her
eyes. The female figure beside her, with the myrtle wreath
and nude bust, is either Aphrodite, the goddess of love,
or Peitho, the goddess of persuasion (comp. No. 148),
urging the girl to yield herself to her bridegroom. The
latter, a strongly-built and bronzed young man, sits with
sparkling eyes at the threshold of the nuptial chamber
and awaits the signal that will allow him to enter. His
head is encircled by the chaplet of ivy and flowers he
wore at the bridal banquet. To the left of the central
group is a girl, with the upper part of her body nude,
who is pouring something from a phial into a shell-shaped
cup. This is probably one of the Graces (Charites), whose
function it was to besprinkle the bride with sweet-
smelling oil. At the left end of the picture are three
female figures preparing the bridal bath. A dignified
draped woman, with a fan in her left hand, apparently the
mother of the bride, is testing the temperature of the
water with her right hand. Beside her stand two girls,
probably servants, one of whom pours water into the bath
from a vase. A towel hangs from the base on which the
bath is placed. The right end of the painting depicts the
part of the festival which takes place in front of the

bride's house. Next to the bridegroom is a girl, holding an oval object (probably a cup) over a basin borne by a high pedestal. The action is not sufficiently definite to enable us to explain this figure or to say whether she is pouring water into the basin or ladling it out. The meaning of the other two figures is, however, clear. A friend of the bride sings the epithalamium, accompanying herself with a lyre, while her companion listens attentively to the music.

Obviously this fresco, along with others, formed a kind of frieze. The execution does not rise above the level of a handicraft; but the work before us is superior in its delicate and harmonious gradation of colouring to the average of the extant mural paintings of the first century of the Empire. The composition is rather that of a relief than of a picture, and exercises a peculiar charm through its simplicity, clearness, and grace. We recognize in it a reflection of the fine feeling of restraint that obtained in the works of the best Greek period. While the Roman painters generally sought their models in Hellenistic art, the artist of the Aldobrandini Nuptials seems to have imitated an original of the time of Alexander the Great.

S. Bartoli, Admiranda, T. 58, 59. *Boettiger und Meyer,* Die aldobrandinische Hochzeit, Dresden, 1810. *Pistolesi,* iii, 37. *Müller-Wieseler,* Denkmäler der alten Kunst, i, 43, 205. *Woermann,* Die Malerei des Alterthums, p. 112, Fig. 28. *Von Sybel,* Weltgeschichte der Kunst, p. 364. *Baumeister,* Denkmäler des klass. Alterthums, ii, p. 872, Fig. 946 (comp. p. 696). Comp. *Winckelmann,* Gesch. der Kunst, vii, 3, § 7. *Braun,* Ruinen und Museen, p. 839, No. 5. *Reinach,* Esquisses archéologiques, pp. 212-214. The Arch. Zeitung (xxxii, 1875; pp. 80-92) contains a detailed criticism of the earlier publications.

So-called Museo Profano of the Vatican Library.

To the left of the entrance,

959. Bronze Head of Septimius Severus.

On the rear-wall, —

960. Bronze Head of Augustus.
The nose is restored.

This head is one of the finest extant portraits of Augustus. The way in which the neck is cut shows that it was inserted in a draped or armed statue. The type resembles that of No. 5; but the emperor is more idealized and the face is longer. The artist has made the eyebrows run into each other, a physiognomical peculiarity of Augustus which is mentioned by Suetonius Divus Augustus, 79). This peculiarity is not seen in any marble portrait of the emperor, because the marble sculptors of the period generally abstained from any plastic representation of the eyebrows.

Ann. dell' Inst., 1863, Tav. d'agg. P, pp. 437, 449. *Bernoulli*, Röm. Ikonographie, ii, 1, T. iv, p. 31, No. 19, pp. 55, 57.

961. Bronze Head of Nero.

This head is a portrait of Nero between the ages of twenty-five and thirty. As in several coin-portraits of the emperor at this age, the cheeks are covered with a short beard.

Bernoulli, Röm. Ikonographie, ii, 1, T. xxiv, p. 392, No. 6, p. 402.

On the left wall, above, —

962. Mosaic Landscape, with Animals.

> Found by Alessandro Furietti in October, 1738, in Hadrian's Villa at Tivoli, and transferred to the Vatican Library in 1767, under Clement XIII.

A lion approaches a brook, to quench his thirst. A wild boar wallows in a marsh near the brook, while an elephant stands under a rocky arch to the right. In the background run a stag and a hind, apparently scared from the brook by the advent of the lion.

Foggini, Museo Cap., iv, p. 183, vignette at p. 397. *Penna*, Viaggio pittorico della Villa Adriana, iii, 61. Comp. *Braun*, Ruinen und Museen, p. 837, No. 2.

On the same wall, a little farther on, —

963. **Mosaic of Garlands.**

> Found in the same villa as No. 962, and at the same time.

Three garlands of leaves and fruit hang from a blue ribbon, which also encircles them lower down. On each of the garlands a bird is perched; and two butterflies sit on two stalks of wheat below.

Foggini. Museo Cap., IV, p. 183. *Penna,* III, 62.

Museo delle Terme.

Court or Cloisters.

The description begins with the sculptures arranged along the wall to the left.

964 (1). Statue of a Young Roman.

The restorations include the lower half of the face, parts of the fingers of the right hand, the left forearm with the part of the sword beside it, the sword-hilt (except the middle of the cross-piece), and the toes of the right foot. The left hand is ancient, except the forefinger and morsels of the other fingers.

The young man is represented in the Greek fashion, with nothing on but a himation enveloping the lower part of his body and falling over his left forearm. He holds a sword in his left hand. The raised right hand rested on a spear. The current identification of this statue with Tiberius is untenable.

965 (3). Statue of a Roman Lady.

In 1880, in the course of the works carried on to improve the bed of the Tiber, an ancient grave, inscribed as that of Gaius Sulpicius Platorinus and Sulpicia Platorina, was discovered not far from the Ponte Sisto, and close to the Aurelian Wall. The two statues, Nos. 964 (1) and 965 (3), were found lying on the ground in the middle of the cella of this tomb. It is thus probable that they represent the owners of the tomb, Sulpicius Platorinus and Sulpicia Platorina. The architecture and decoration of the tomb, the style of the statues, the cut of the man's hair, and the coiffure of the lady, all point to the time of the Julian emperors. The execution of both statues is mediocre.

Notizie degli scavi, 1880, pp. 132, 133 (female statue figured in T. v, No. 1).

966 (5). Statue of Ariadne (?).

Found in 1866 on the Palatine (Bull. dell' Inst., 1866, p. 162).

This figure reproduces the same original as a better-preserved statue in the Dresden Museum, which is generally recognized as Ariadne looking piteously after the retreating Theseus, though this explanation is open to question. The missing parts of the statue before us should be restored as in the Dresden example. The head was slightly raised and inclined to the left, while the right forearm was lifted towards the head. To judge from the character of the fracture, the left hand may have held some attribute.

Matz-Duhn, Antike Bildwerke in Rom, i, No. 835. Römische Mittheilungen, viii (1893), p. 96, No. 3. For the Dresden statue: *Friederichs-Wolters*, Bausteine, No. 1576.

967(9). Torso of the Statuette of a Youth.

Formerly on the Palatine.

The statuette, to which this torso belongs, is a small, well-made replica of a type generally named after an example in Munich, which has been interpreted, with apparent correctness, as Diomedes holding the Palladium (comp. No. 950). Recent critics refer it to Silanion (comp. No. 265) or, with more plausibility, to Cresilas (comp. No. 251).

Sitzungsberichte der philosoph.-philol. und histor. Classe der bayerischen Academie, 1892, pp. 651 et seq. *Furtwaengler*, Masterpieces of Greek Sculpture, pp. 146 et seq.

968 (11). Statue of a Youth.

The restorations include nearly the whole of the back of the head, the neck (except the nape), the nose, the right foot with the adjoining parts of the stump and plinth, and the upper part of the left foot.

The body of this insignificant statue was found in the Tablinum of the Villa of Quintus Voconius Pollio, situated below Marino, while the head was found at a distance of several yards from it. Head and body, however, seem to belong to each other, as their execution is similar and the fractures at the back fitted into each other exactly. The face recalls a special type of Apollo.

Bull. della commissione arch. comunale, 1884, T. xvii-xix, No. 11, p. 158, p. 215, No. 11. Comp. Notizie degli scavi, 1884, pp. 107, 159. Röm. Mitth., vii (1892), p. 337.

969 (13). Headless Statue of Heracles.

Found in the Villa of Voconius Pollio. The right foot, the front of the left foot, and nearly the whole plinth are modern.

The motive of this statue recalls that of the colossal bronze figure in the Vatican (No. 299); but the body is more slender. The character of the execution, particularly the deep under-cutting of the lion-skin, seem to indicate a bronze original.

Bull. della comm. arch. comunale, 1884, p. 158. Notizie degli scavi, 1884, p. 107. Röm. Mitth., vii, p. 337.

970 (14). Head of a Hellenistic Poet.

Formerly in the Museo Kircheriano. The nose is modern.

This type is discussed under No. 469.

971 (16). Statuette of Narcissus (?).

Found during the construction of the Teatro Nazionale.

This statuette represents a youth, who has just ceased walking, with his right leg advanced and his left behind. The forward bend of the body and the downward glance of the eye prove that his attention has been arrested by some object below him; and his interest was farther emphasized by the lively gestures of the arms.

The right arm was extended straight to the side, the left arm was doubtless bent. The mantle is composed of a quadrangular piece of cloth, which seems to have been slit halfway up the back. The part to the left of the slit was obviously wrapped round the left arm, and its hanging ends touched the left thigh at the two points where traces are still visible. The similar mark below the left shoulder was probably caused by some such attribute as a pedum, held in the left hand. The head of the statuette is clearly of a Hellenistic type. This fact, combined with the general motive of the figure, naturally suggests that the statuette represents Narcissus, reaching the fateful fountain and suddenly seeing his reflection in the water (comp. No. 206.

972 (17). **Statue of Apollo.**

> Found in the Villa of Voconius Pollio (Notizie degli scavi, 1884, p. 107). A piece of the skull is modern.

The quiet and collected attitude, coupled with the dreamy expression of the face, seems to indicate that the god is meditating over a musical motive. The missing cithara doubtless occupied the hollow visible in the mantle hung over the tripod. The remains of the left arm show that it was extended, probably resting on the cithara. Various suppositions are, however, possible in regard to the exact position of the hand. It may have rested on the bridge of the lyre, or grasped one of its horns, or lightly touched the strings. The right arm, extended in a downward direction, probably held the plectrum. So far as the very mediocre execution allows us to judge, the statue seems to go back to an original created about the middle of the fourth century B.C. The style of the hair and of the folds of the drapery, and also the detached treatment of the tripod-stand and of the serpent twined round it indicate that this original was in bronze.

> Bull. della comm. arch. comunale, 1884, T. XVII-XIX. No. 10, p. 158, p. 215, No. 10. *Overbeck*, Kunstmythologie. IV, p. 192, No. 7. Röm. Mitth., VII (1892), p. 337.

973 (19). **Head of an Athlete.**

Found in the Piazza Nicosia.

The outstretched neck and keen look of this carefully executed head suggest that it belonged to the statue of a wrestler, watching for a favourable moment to grapple with an antagonist standing in front of him (comp. Nos. 573-575). The face resembles Attic types of the fourth century B.C., which seem to have been determined by the Argive art of the fifth century and in their turn to have influenced the development of the Lysippian type.

Röm. Mitth., vi (1891), p. 304, No. 2. *Furtwaengler*, Masterpieces, p. 296, note 6.

974 (23). **Statue of Hera.**

Found in the Stadium of the Palatine in 1878.

This statue is closely related to the Hera Barberini (No. 301), and differs from it mainly in the concession made by the sculptor to Hellenistic taste in his treatment of the drapery and in the skilful way in which he has imitated the character of a work in metal. This is especially evident in the boldness with which the folds of the mantle on the left side of the body are represented.

Matz-Duhn, i, No. 583. Notizie degli scavi, 1879, T. i, 2, p. 40 (comp. 1878, p. 93). *Furtwaengler*, Masterpieces, p. 84, note 2.

975 (27). **Head of Hermes.**

Formerly on the Palatine. The nose, lips, and chin are modern.

This is a replica of the type represented in the Vatican statue, No. 145.

Probably identical with the head in *Matz-Duhn*, i, No. 1676.

976 (32). **Fragment of a Statue of a Boy-Satyr with a Flute.**

Found in 1884 in an old well on the Via Labicana, near the Torre Pignatara.

Although only the upper part of this figure has been preserved, it is of interest from the fact that a fragment of the flute is still attached to the chin (comp. No. 19).

Notizie degli scavi, 1884, p. 224a.

977 (35). Statue of an Athlete putting on a Wreath.

Found in the Via Ostiensis. The lowest portion of the left leg and the part of the plinth below it have been restored.

So far as the mediocre execution allows us to judge, this statue reproduces an original from the end of the fifth century B.C. Its restoration is vindicated by other works of art which represent athletes in the act of placing a wreath on their head with the right hand and holding a palm-branch in the left. The protuberance on the right shoulder has obviously been left by the end of the ribbon *(lemniscus)*, with which the wreath of a victorious athlete was adorned. It has recently been denied by one archæologist that the ancient statues of victorious athletes ever held palm-branches in their hands. The fact, however, has been proved by a statue found near Formiæ, and now in the Glyptothek of Mr. Jacobsen at Copenhagen. This statue shows the same motive as that of Stephanos (No. 744), although in a freer style of execution, and may be safely regarded as a reproduction of a Peloponnesian bronze original dating from the third decade of the fifth century B.C. The lowered right hand holds a palm-branch, shown in low relief against the right arm.

On the motive, see *Furtwaeng'er, Koerte und Milchhoefer,* Archæolog. Studien Brunn dargebracht (Berlin, 1893), pp. 62 et seq. The same restoration has been proposed for another statue in Römische Mittheilungen, vi (1891), p. 304, No. 3.

978 (36). Portrait-Head of a Roman.

Found in the course of the works for regulating the Tiber.

The style points to the republican era. The execution is full of life.

979 (40). **Head of Geta.**

> Formerly in the Museo Kircheriano. The nose, the lower lip, and most of the chin are modern. The bust is ancient but probably does not belong to this head.

The emperor is here represented at a relatively advanced age.

Rear Wall, —

980 (1). **Boy Dionysos,** the fragment of a group.

> Found on the Palatine in 1864.

The boy is recognizable as Dionysos by the ivy-wreath encircling his head. He is sitting upon a hand, which, to judge from the delicate treatment of the flesh, probably belonged to a female figure. If so, the fragment is doubtless part of a group representing the infant Dionysos in charge of a Nymph. The little fellow looked up to his nurse with a happy smile, raising his right arm and extending his left in front of him. As the childish forms of the body are treated in a thoroughly realistic way, the date of the original cannot be earlier than the time of Alexander the Great.

> *Matz-Duhn,* I, No. 355. Röm. Mitth., VIII (1893), p. 258.

981 (2). **Head of Julia Domna** (d. 217 A.D.).

> Formerly on the Palatine. Most of the nose is modern.

982 (3). **Slab of Frieze from the Mausoleum of Hadrian.**

> Found on Oct. 22nd, 1892, on the right bank of the Tiber, in the moat constructed round the Castel S. Angelo under Urban VIII.

The relief, the execution of which is evidently intended for distant effect, shows the head of a bull, adorned with ribbons and with a garland attached to each of its horns, of which that on the left horn is almost intact. The garlands obviously connected a series of heads like the one before us. The space over the garland is occupied by two shields, the lower of an oval form, while the

upper resembles the pelta, so often assigned to Amazons.
As the slab was found close to the Mausoleum of Hadrian
(the present Castel S. Angelo) and as we know from old
drawings that bulls' heads and garlands were used in the
decoration of this mausoleum, there can be no doubt as
to the provenience of the fragment. It appears to have
belonged to the frieze on the base of the statue of the
emperor placed on the top of the mausoleum. This lofty
situation would account for the unusually high relief.

Notizie degli scavi, 1892, p. 426, Fig. 10. Röm. Mittb., VIII
(1893), p. 324. The author is unable to find any trace of the
modern retouching of the background of the relief mentioned in the
first of these references.

953 (4). **Head of Meleager.**

Formerly on the Palatine. The front of the nose,
the under-lip, and part of the chin are modern.

The head is of the same type as the Vatican statue,
No. 133. Its execution is better than that of the latter,
but is considerably inferior to that of the splendid head
of Meleager in the Villa Medici.

Römische Mittheilungen, IV (1889), p. 220, No. 14.

954 (10). **Head of Pallas.**

Formerly in the Museo Kircheriano. The points of
the visor, the nose, and morsels of the lips are modern.

The head agrees with the type which is best represented by the Pallas Giustiniani (No. 51), but shows somewhat severer forms and a less individualized expression.

Furtwaengler, Masterpieces, p. 359, note 4 b.

955 (12). **Helmeted Head of a Youth.**

The front of the nose is modern.

This head seems to reproduce a Greek original, or,
to speak more definitely, an Attic original of about the
middle of the fourth century B.C. The keen expression of
the vigorously formed face indicates a youthful hero. The
leathern cap under the helmet finds analogy in heads of
Pallas on Corinthian coins, chiefly of the fourth century.

On the coins of Corinth, see *Poole*, Catalogue of Greek Coins in the British Museum, section Corinth, Pl. 2, No. 21, Pl. 3 et seq.

956 (13). Statue of Hermes.

Formerly on the Palatine.

Although the surface has been seriously injured by damp, this statue still gives an adequate idea of the merits of the type it reproduces. The god stands in a charming mobile attitude, which at once recalls the manner of Lysippos. The missing right arm seems to have held a caduceus. The bodily forms and the handling of the hair betray many clear reminiscences of the art of the fifth century B.C. The way in which the hair clings to the skull and ends in fine points suggests the style of Polycleitos. The head, on the other hand, is of a distinctly Attic type, and its forms point to the first half of the fourth century. The theory has been advanced that the original of this statue was an early work of Scopas. From the little we know of this artist, it seems quite possible that he may have adopted several of the formal elements of the Polycleitian school. while following in the main an Ionic-Attic tendency.

Matz-Duhn, I, No. 1046. *Furtwaengler*, Masterpieces, pp. 300 et seq., p. 301, Fig. 129.

957 (16). Head of a Woman with a veil.

Found in 1878 in the Stadium on the Palatine. The front of the nose and fragments of the upper lip are modern.

This head reproduces the same type as two other heads, of which one is in Berlin and one in Paris. The name of Aspasia has been suggested for the original of this type, and recent criticism has placed it in relation with the art of Calamis. The style points to somewhere about the middle of the fifth century B. C., while the wire-like hair and the deep under-cutting of the pendant part of the veil indicate a bronze original. The assumption that this type is a portrait rests mainly on the individual arrangement of the hair. We know, however,

that archaic art often took cognizance of prevailing fash-
ions, even in the creation of ideal types; and it seems
not impossible that a few sporadic instances of this tendency may have maintained themselves during the immediately following period of transition, to which the
original of the head before us belonged. The execution
of this example is mediocre. The pupils are slightly incised.

Röm. Mitth., viii (1893), p. 95, No. 1. — On the Berlin head:
Beschreibung der antiken Skulpturen des Berliner Museums,
No. 605. — On the Paris head: *Clarac*, vi, Pl. 1082, No. 393. Comp.
Furtwaengler, Masterpieces, p. 81.

988 (17). **Statuette of a Girl** (fountain-figure).

> Found in 1889 in the Prati di Castello, among the
> ruins of an extensive ancient building, not far from the
> iron bridge.

The girl is enveloped in an ample mantle, with
numerous folds, which is drawn over the back of her
head and also covers her arms. The pitcher by the left
foot indicates that this is a fountain-figure. The charming motive seems to belong to early Hellenistic art. The
skilful manner in which the creator of the original indicated the forms of the body beneath the many folds of
the drapery is still clearly discernible even in this decorative reproduction. The statuette retains numerous
traces of its original colouring. Thus it is obvious that the
general colour of the chiton was blue, while the borders
both of chiton and mantle were dark-red. Traces of
yellow are visible on the shoes and on the pitcher.

Notizie degli scavi, 1889, pp. 188, 189.

989 (18). **Head of a Hellenistic Warrior.**

> Found in the Tiber.

It is still obvious that the helmet had the shape of a
Phrygian bonnet, though the upper part, carved of a
separate block, is now missing. A helmet of an Oriental
form like this would be strangely out of place on the
head of a Roman, but is quite a natural equipment of a

Hellenistic warrior, since we know that Alexander the Great and the Diadochi frequently used the arms and armour of the East. The sharply-cut features and the emphatic expression also tally with the supposition of a Hellenistic origin.

990 (20). Idealistic Portrait of a Barbarian (?).

> Found in a Cloaca on the Esquiline, not far from the Columbarium of the freedmen and slaves of the Gens Statilia. The nose, the part of the forehead above it, and a small piece at the upper end of the right moustache are modern.

To judge from the individualized lines of the profile, this head is a portrait and not an ideal type. The character of the features, the helmet in the shape of a pileus, and the long hair falling on the neck, all indicate a barbarian of Asia Minor rather than a Hellene. The rendering, particularly that of the hair and beard, would suggest a Greek original of the fourth century B. C. The execution, however, is so poor, that it is impossible to deliver any very certain verdict on this point. The marble retains traces of its original painting.

Brizio, Pitture e sepolcri scoperti sull' Esquilino, T. 3, No. 10, pp. 122, 134.

991 (21). Helmeted Portrait-Head.

> Found at the same time and place as No. 990 (20). The part of the helmet covering the left part of the skull, and the hair on the forehead below this, are modern.

The attempt to declare this an ideal head is refuted by the individual character shown in the fulness of the face and in the singular arrangement of the beard. The closely-cropped hair of the latter covers not only the cheeks and chin, but also the upper part of the neck. It therefore seems more probable that we have before us a more or less idealized portrait. The execution points to about the middle of the third century A. D. It is careful, but introduces too many subsidiary details and hence makes a somewhat over-minute and unquiet effect.

We know of two personages of the above-mentioned period, *viz.* the emperors Balbinus and Gallienus, who wore their beard in this fashion.

Brizio, Pitture e sepolcri scoperti sull' Esquilino, T. 3, No. 12, pp. 122, 134.

992 (24). **Head of Sophocles.**

Found in the course of the works for regulating the Tiber. The nose and the lips are modern.

Recent attempts have been made, with some appearance of success, to identify two portraits of Sophocles, which are of earlier date than the type represented by the statue in the Lateran (No. 662). The first of these portraits may very well have been made during the lifetime of the poet; the second seems to have been executed, with the help of the first, in the early decades of the fourth century B. C. Both types are more realistic than the Lateran statue, which evidently presents the poet in a highly idealized aspect. The head before us is a reproduction of the later of the two portraits referred to.

On the two portraits of Sophocles, see Jahrbuch des Arch. Instituts, v (1890), pp. 160-162.

993 (28). **Bust of a Roman.**

Found during the works for the regulation of the Tiber.

To judge from the style, the mode of execution, and the form of the bust, this portrait certainly represents a man who lived towards the end of the Republic or at the beginning of the Empire. The person represented is marked by a positively terrific ugliness.

994 (30). **Portrait-Bust of a Bearded Man.**

Found in the Tiber. The front of the nose and the right shoulder are modern.

The style of this bust would indicate that it was executed in the time of Hadrian. Apart from the somewhat greater youthfulness, it shows a striking likeness to the portraits representing that emperor in the prime of life (comp. No. 295 ; and it may thus very possibly be a portrait of Hadrian in the early years of his reign.

995 (36). Portrait of a Greek Philosopher.

> Found during the construction of the Monument to Victor Emmanuel. The nose is modern.

The way in which the neck is cut shows that this important head was intended for insertion in a statue. The most striking features are the high and narrow skull and the long beard. It makes the impression rather of a freely treated head than of an iconic portrait. The very mediocre execution points to a period not earlier than the beginning of the third century of the Christian era. The head is possibly that of Pythagoras. A full-length portrait of this philosopher is given on a contorniate coin or medal. The features of this portrait are too small to recognize, but the shape of the skull and the arrangement of the beard are not unlike those of the marble head before us. A long beard is also mentioned by Martial as one of the characteristics of Pythagoras.

> On the contorniate, see *Sabatier*, Description des médaillons contorniates, Pl. xv, 1, p. 96. Comp. Martial. Epigr. ix, 48. Jahrbuch des Arch. Instituts, i (1886), p. 78.

996 (37). Relief of the Façade of a Temple.

> Brought to the Museum from the studio of the sculptor Viti, behind the Basilica of Constantine. For its former vicissitudes, see *Matz-Duhn*, iii, p. 35.

This relief, the style of which points to the second century of the present era, depicts the front of a temple of the Romano-Corinthian order. Though little more than the left half of the relief has been preserved, it is enough to show us that the temple had ten columns on its front. The groups in the pediment refer to the legends of the founding of Rome. In the centre reclines Rhea Silvia, upon whom Mars descends from the right. To the left are the Wolf and the Twins, whom two shepherds approach with obvious signs of astonishment. In the left angle lie a sheep and a ram. In front of the temple, on the missing lower part of the slab, was represented a sacrifice or a procession. The presence of lictors is proved by two fasces, represented in very low relief in the portico, one between the first and second column from the left, the other between the fourth and fifth. The temple seems to be that of Venus and Roma, begun under Hadrian and finished under Antoninus Pius, which we know to have had ten columns on its front. It is imaged on coins of Antoninus Pius, where its façade appears similar to the relief now under our notice. Other coins of the same emperor represent the two chief groups in the pediment in a manner that corresponds perfectly to those in the relief.

Raoul-Rochette, Monuments inédits, Pl. vIII, 1, p. 35. *Canina*, Architettura antica, sezione III, T. xxxIII, 1. For other references, see *Matz-Duhn*, III, No. 3519.

997 (41). Mosaic of a Nile Scene.

Found on the Aventine, near S. Saba, in 1858, in the Vigna Maccarani, now Torlonia. Preserved at first in the Museo Kircheriano.

We have reason to believe that under the rule of the Ptolemies a school of landscape-painting sprang up in Egypt, which took the Nile and its environs for its main subject, introducing Pygmies for the accessory figures. This branch of art also made its way into Italy and Rome, along with the numerous other novelties which the West received from the cosmopolitan city of Alexandria. The interest which it awoke in Latium may have been specially due to the fact that Egypt, that ancient land of wonders and mystery, became a favourite travelling-resort for Romans of the cultivated classes after its incorporation with the Roman empire through the victories of Octavian. Thus, from the beginning of the imperial period onwards, we frequently meet in Roman houses wall-paintings and mosaic floors representing Nile landscapes.

In the left background of the mosaic before us is a wall, over which rise a palm-tree and two lofty square towers. These perhaps indicate a villa surrounded with walls, for we know that in the time of the emperors towers were often erected in the grounds of villas for the sake of the view they commanded. To the right lies a pavilion in the Egypto-Hellenistic style, surrounded by palms. In front of these two structures flows the Nile, with reeds, stalks of papyrus, and lotus-flowers rising from its waters. A hippopotamus is advancing to attack a small boat containing two Pygmy-women, while two Pygmy-men are hastening to the rescue from above, brandishing their spears. Another Pygmy, also with a spear in his right hand, is seen below the hippopotamus. Instead of shields, the three Pygmies use the tops of clay amphorae, through which they have thrust their left arms. To the right, below, is another hippopotamus, opposite which, to the left, is a crocodile, with wide-open jaws, apparently ready for the fray. Above the hippopotamus is a Pygmy, holding two yellow sticks in each hand — a figure the relation of which to the others is not obvious. Numerous birds are flying in the air above. The frame of the picture is divided into compartments, filled with groups of scenic masks and birds. This motive also seems due to Alexandrian art.

Gazette archéologique, VI (1880), Pl. 25, pp. 170, 171. Bull. dell' Inst., 1870, p. 80. *De Ruggiero*, Catalogo del Museo Kircheriano, I, p. 265, No. 1. Röm. Mitth., VII (1892), p. 337. — On the Egyptian landscape-painting: *Helbig*, Untersuchungen über die campanische Wandmalerei, pp. 101, 302, 303; *Lumbroso*, L'Egitto al tempo dei Greci e dei Romani, pp. 11 et seq. — On the Roman travels in Egypt: *Friedlaender*, Darstellungen aus der Sittenge-schichte Roms, II⁵, pp. 92, 93, 124 et seq. — On the towers in Roman villas: *Helbig*, Op. cit., p. 107. — On masks and birds in Alexan-drian art: Abhandlungen der philol.-hist. Classe der sächs. Ges. der Wissenschaften, XIV (1894), pp. 449-452, 466, 467.

Right Wall, —

99S (7). Head of Emperor Balbinus (?; d. 238 A. D.).

Found in the Tiber. The nose, the middle of the moustache, and the neck have been restored. The bust is ancient but does not belong to this head.

As the profile is imperfect, we cannot be positive of this identification. It has, however, a measure of probability, for the head corresponds in its main lines to the coin-portraits of Balbinus, while the style and the peculiar arrangement of the beard point to the time of this emperor.

999 (17). Head of one of the Successors of Alexander the Great (?).

Found in the Tiber works.

The face, marked by a certain plumpness, appears too individual for a purely ideal type, and is probably an idealized portrait. The two holes bored in the front of the head, near the fillet, may have served for the insertion of small horns of metal, and it is thus possible that the head may represent one of the Diadochi in the guise of the 'New Dionysos' (comp. Nos. 221, 249). The style and the character of the physiognomy seem to suit the time of Alexander the Great or that immediately following it.

1000 (25). Head of a Roman.

Found in the Tiber. A fragment on the left side of the forehead, the upper part of the left eye, and almost the whole of the nose are modern.

In its main forms this head resembles the so-called portrait of the younger Brutus (No. 522).

1001 (29). Sarcophagus with the Story of Medea.

This sarcophagus is mentioned as having been in Rome towards the close of the sixteenth century. On this point, and on its other vicissitudes, see *Robert*, Die antiken Sarkophag-Reliefs, II, p. 215.

To the left we see the children of Jason and Medea bearing to Glauce or Creusa the fateful gifts which caused her death. The scene is treated in the same way as on the fragment in the Vatican (No. 325). At the left end, however, is added the figure of Jason, who has evidently brought the boys to his bride. The next scene to the right pourtrays the fatal effects of the gifts. The bride is springing, in a frenzy of agony, from the platform on which stands the bridal bed. Her father Creon looks at her in despair, clutching his hair with his right hand and stretching out his left arm. Behind him stand two guards, one of whom is in an attitude entirely devoid of sympathy with what is passing before him. The other is raising his chlamys with his left hand, perhaps to blot out the terrible spectacle from his sight. A helmet lies on the ground in front of him. The following scene depicts Medea preparing for the murder of her children. The figures in this group are much mutilated, but can be reconstituted from another better-preserved relief. Medea holds a drawn sword in her right hand, and the scabbard in her left. The boys before her have no idea of their impending fate but are disputing carelessly over a ball. The one in front, in order to escape from his brother, springs over one of the rollers, which the ancients used to level the ground comp. No. S 15), while he holds out the ball in front of him, grasped with both hands. The other boy lays both hands on his brother's shoulders in order to stop him. At the right end of the relief we see Medea about to take flight in her dragon-chariot. She has thrown one of the murdered boys over her shoulder, while the other corpse, of which only the legs are visible, lies in the chariot. In front of the dragons lies a personification of the earth (Gæa, Tellus , raising her right hand with a gesture of woe. The left end of the sarcophagus bears two figures, representing Jason pouring a libation on a burning altar in the presence of a priest's boy (camillus; comp. No. 607), who holds a tray of sacrificial offerings. This group is borrowed in the most unintelligent way from a scene on another sarcophagus, representing the marriage of Jason with Glauce or Creusa. The relief on the right end of the sarcophagus represents two youths conversing. No satisfactory explanation has yet been found of this scene, though the suggestion has been thrown out that it may be an episode in the legend of the Argonauts.

Robert, Die antiken Sarkophag-Reliefs, II. T. LXV, 201, 201b, pp. 215, 216.

1002 (31). Slab of a Frieze with Cupids holding Garlands.

Found in the Tiber works.

The relief represents two Amoretti, of which parts only have been preserved, supporting a garland of leaves, wheat-ears, and fruit. The other slabs of the frieze doubtless contained similar representations.

1003 (32). Head of Nero.

Found in the Tiber. The end of the nose, a large piece on the left side of the skull, and the left ear have been restored.

1004 (33, 3S, 40). Three Fragments of a large Frieze.

Found in the Tiber works.

The original motive can be clearly made out by a comparison of the three fragments. The central part of each slab was occupied by a burning thymiaterion (incense-burner), and on each side was a figure of Nike, with one knee on the back of a fallen bull and holding it by the neck or one of the horns (comp. No. 729).

1005 (37). Head of Apollo.

The front of the nose, almost all the lower lip, the chin, and the neck are modern.

1006 (11). Head of Dionysos.

The front of the nose and part of the lower lip are modern.

These two heads, both executed in a decorative fashion, were found during the work of regulating the Tiber. They belonged to a pair of statues used as architectonic supporting members in some building. Each of the heads retains a piece of the support on which the overlying

architrave rested. Apollo is characterized as a Citharœdos by the type of the face. by the arrangement of the
hair, and by the laurel-wreath adorned in front with a
medallion (comp. Nos. 220, 267). The head of Dionysos
is encircled horizontally by a wide fillet, above which the
hair stands erect. The type is much more finely represented than in this example by a magnificent colossal
head in the Museum of Leyden, which seems to come
from Asia Minor and is obviously a creation of Hellenistic art. The expression is vigorous and seems permeated
by that crude sentiment characteristic of Pergamenian
sculpture. As the Leyden head has a circular incision
in the skull which may have served to receive a support,
it is not unlikely that the statue to which it belonged
may also have played the part of a Telamon.

On the Leyden head: Mon. dell' Inst., II, 41, 1; Ann., 1837,
pp. 151-153. *Müller-Wieseler*, Denkmäler der alten Kunst, II,
31, 345. Comp. *Furtwaengler*, Die Sammlung Sabouroff, section on
Sculptures, text to T. XXIII.

1007-1013 (16, 18, 22, 24, 30, 34, 38). Seven Portrait-Hermæ of Charioteers.

> Found outside the Porta Portese, not far from the
> railway-station of Trastevere. All seven lay side by side
> on a base adorned with shells.

These seven hermæ are by different sculptors, but
their style and the cut of the hair show that they all
date from the same period — that of the Julian emperors.
Four of them (Nos. 22, 24, 34, 38) are undoubtedly portraits of the drivers of chariots in circus races (*agitatores
circenses*), as is proved by the arrangement of leathern
thongs they wear over their tunic (comp. Nos. 331, 1098).
As the seven hermæ evidently all belonged to the same
series, it is natural to conclude that the other three Nos. 16,
18, 30) are also portraits of circus-drivers, though they
lack the leathern guards. A survey of the heads shows
us what a variety of types belonged to this class of charioteers, so highly esteemed by the Romans. Thus No. 22
is evidently the portrait of a full-blooded Italian. It

possesses the Philistine features so often seen upon
Roman tombs of this period and also the large and ugly
ears characteristic of the early Romans (comp. No. 610).
No. 18, the best-executed of all the hermæ, offers the
strongest possible contrast to No. 22. The fine features
suggest that this young man was a scion of a race refined
by ancient civilisation and that he may have migrated to
Rome from the Hellenistic Orient. The manner in which
his hair is arranged over his head in parallel lines, evidently manipulated with the curling-tongs *(calamistrum)*,
points him out as a regular dandy. The expression of
No. 24 is one of extremely limited intelligence, while
that of No. 38 approaches brutality.

Notizie degli scavi, 1889, p. 246, Nos. 21-27. Röm. Mitth.,
vi (1891), pp. 237, 238; vii (1892), p. 331. — On the curled hair:
Marquardt-Mau, Das Privatleben der Römer, p. 147, note 7, p. 601,
p. 605, note 7.

1014 (25). **Head of Ares.**

Found in the Tiber works. The restorations include
the frontal bones, the eyelids, most of the nose, the
lips, and a piece of the chin.

This head belonged to a replica of a type of Ares,
which is best known through a statue at Paris. Recent
critics identify this type with that of the statue of the god
executed by Alcamenes for the temple of Ares at Athens.

Römische Mittheilungen, vi (1891), p. 239. — On the type:
Furtwaengler, Masterpieces, pp. 89 et seq.

1015 (29). **Portrait-Head of a Man.**

Formerly on the Palatine. Nose restored.

The British Museum possesses a colossal statue of
Maussollos (usually, but incorrectly, written Mausolus),
King of Caria (d. 350 B.C.), which belonged to the
Mausoleum (Maussolleum) erected to his memory at Hali-
carnassos by his widow Artemisia. The plastic adornment
of this monument was entrusted to Scopas and several
other younger masters of the Second Attic School. The
head before us shows a striking resemblance to that of

Maussollos, both in its style and in the arrangement of the hair, and doubtless represents a contemporary of the Carian monarch. The stylistic resemblance would probably be still more noticeable had not the head in the Museo delle Terme suffered seriously from reworking.

On the statue of Maussollos, see *Overbeck*, Geschichte der griech. Plastik, II[4], p. 101, Fig. 169; bibliography, p. 111, notes 16-20.

1016 (35). Portrait-Head of a Roman Matron.

Formerly on the Palatine. The nose and parts of the lips have been restored.

The matron appears with her mantle drawn over the back of her head. The features differ considerably from those we are used to see in portraits of Roman ladies, and rather resemble a type occasionally found among elderly Englishwomen. The style and coiffure point to the time of the Antonines.

1017 (39). Colossal Head of a Roman.

Formerly on the Palatine. The nose, the right ear, and the lower lip are modern.

The way in which the neck-piece is cut shows that this head was intended for insertion in a statue. The colossal dimensions and the fact that other examples of this portrait have come down to us indicate that it represents a man of importance. The singular character of the face is due mainly to the penetrating glance and to the sarcastic expression of the lips. The style and the cut of the hair point to the beginning of the Empire.

Rooms on the Ground Floor.

Central Room.

1018 (8). Head of Sabina, wife of Hadrian.

Found during the construction of the Monument of Victor Emmanuel. The front of the nose is modern.

1019 (7). Head of Antoninus Pius.

Found at Formiæ, the modern Formia (formerly Mola di Gaeta). Acquired from Eliseo Borghi, the art-dealer. The point of the nose is modern.

The execution is admirable. The head is one of the best extant portraits of Antoninus Pius.

1020 (6). Colossal Head of Clodius Albinus (?; d. 197 A. D.).

Formerly on the Palatine.

The style and the arrangement of the hair and beard indicate the transition from the second to the third century A. D. The head recalls the portraits of Clodius Albinus (comp. No. 184 ; but the latter show a thicker nose and a somewhat shorter beard.

1021 (5). Head of Livia (?).

Formerly on the Palatine.

Two undoubted marble portraits of Livia are known : — one a head in the Jacobsen Collection at Copenhagen, which shows the empress at the age of forty, and the other a statue in the Naples Museum, where she appears as well on in the fifties. The head No. 1021 shows a distinct resemblance to both these portraits. The chin and lower cheek-bones are certainly somewhat less massive; but it is very possible that this difference may be due to want of skill in the carver of the head before us. If this head be, indeed, a portrait of Livia, it occupies a position midway between the two hitherto known. It represents the empress as older than the Jacobsen head, which it resembles in coiffure, but as younger than the Naples statue. The execution is very indifferent; and the surface has suffered from cleansing by acids.

Probably identical with *Matz-Duhn*, i, No. 2043. Comp. *Bernoulli*, Röm. Ikonographie, ii, 1, p. 185, No. 15, p. 378. — On the Jacobsen head, see Röm. Mitth., ii (1887), T. i, pp. 3-13. — On the Naples statue, see Röm. Mitth., vii (1893), pp. 228, 229.

1022 (4). Statue of Dionysos.

Found in 1881 in the north part of Hadrian's Villa near Tivoli (Notizie degli scavi, 1881, pp. 105, 106). The restorations include the front of the nose, a piece of the chin, the free-hanging paws of the nebris, the thumb, index-finger, and parts of the other fingers of the left hand, the lower part of the left leg, the stump (except the upper end adjoining the thigh), the piece of the plinth below the left leg and the stump.

That this is a statue of Dionysos is proved by the nebris hanging over the breast and by the formation of the body, which, though of powerful scantling, is marked throughout by softness of surface, while the treatment of the neck and back is almost feminine in its delicacy. In the right hand, now wanting, the god probably held a large two-handled goblet *(cantharos)*, the presence of which is doubtless indicated by the traces on the right thigh. The style of execution points to the time of Hadrian. The five small 'copy-points' left on the head, among other indications, show that the work was not quite finished. The fact that the original was a bronze figure may be assumed from the under-cutting of the nebris and from the chasing-like treatment of the hair both of the nebris and of the god himself. The assumption of a bronze original also explains why the sculptor differs, in his treatment of the eyes, from the practice usually followed by his contemporaries in marble figures of ideal types. The iris is denoted by a well-marked circular incision, and the pupils by a deep round hole; and it is obvious that this is an attempt to reproduce as nearly as possible the effect of the different materials used in the eyes of a bronze statue (comp. No. 1055). When viewed from the right side, the flow of the lines in the marble work before us is seriously marred by the tree-stump adjoining the right leg; but the bronze original was, of course, free from this defect. The attitude resembles that of the Doryphoros (No. 58), while the type of the features and the arrangement of the hair also recall the manner of Polycleitos; there is therefore no doubt that our statue is connected with the art of that master. It has even been argued that this type of Dionysos was created by Polycleitos himself or by one of his pupils. The morbidezza with which the nude is handled in our statue finds, however, no analogy either in the known works of Polycleitos or in those of the schools of art of the same or the immediately subsequent period. If we examine the Amazon of Polycleitos (comp. No. 32), which lends itself better than the Doryphoros for a comparison with the Dionysos before us, it is evident that the difference between the severe style of the one and the delicate forms of the other cannot be accounted for by a less interval than that of an entire generation of artists. In any case the manner in which the right leg of the Dionysos is modelled finds its first prototype in the work of an advanced period of the fourth century B. C. The same period is indicated by the way in which the Polycleitian attitude has been developed. All these considerations lead to the conclusion that the original of this figure of Dionysos was the work of a Peloponnesian sculptor who carried on the traditions of Polycleitos and flourished about the middle of the fourth century B. C. It may, perhaps, be a little later than the youthful Pan created by the same school (comp. No. 359). As the transition from the distinctly virile forms to the more feminine parts of the body is very imperfectly managed, we may assume that this type was one of the first attempts to heighten the charm of the statues of youthful gods by a mingling of female forms. Recent authorities have tried to place this type in relation with Euphranor, a sculptor who flourished about B. C. 375-330 and who, as a native of Corinth, belonged to the Peloponnesian school in its wider sense.

Mon. dell' Inst., xi, 51, 51a; Ann., 1883, pp. 136 et seq. Comp. Arch. Zeitung, xl (1882), p. 178. *Friederichs-Wolters*, Bausteine, No. 520. *Furtwaengler*, Sammlung Sabouroff, i, text to T. viii-xi.. *Roscher*, Lexikon der griech. und röm. Mythologie, i, p. 1137, p. 1138, Fig. 17. Museo italiano di antichità classica, iii, pp. 761, 777-779, and p. 783 (where the type is referred to Myron). Römische Mittheilungen, vi (1891), pp. 238, 239. *Furtwaengler*, Masterpieces, pp. 350 et seq.

1023 (2). Head of Nero.

Formerly on the Palatine. The restorations include most of the back of the head, the front of the nose, a large piece on the right side of the neck, and morsels on the ears and chin.

This head is the best portrait of Nero in marble in Rome.

Matz-Duhn, I, No. 1829. *Bernoulli*, Röm. Ikonographie, II, 1, p. 393, No. 7, p. 397, Fig. 57, pp. 402, 403.

1024 (1). Colossal Head of Caligula.

Formerly on the Palatine. The restorations include the front of the nose, fragments of the lips, and the parts of the mantle near the cheeks and neck.

This head, with the toga drawn over the back of it, agrees so closely in all essentials with undoubted portraits of Caligula, that there can be no question as to its identity. The emperor appears here as an older man than in those other portraits; but this seems due to the sharper cutting of the lower eyelids and the stronger development of the chin. The sculptor was forced to emphasize those details in order to ensure them their proper effect at the height for which the head was intended. Seen at this height, the head would probably seem almost identical with the ordinary portraits of Caligula.

Matz-Duhn, I, No. 1830 (where, however, the head is wrongly identified with the younger Drusus). Comp. *Bernoulli*, Römische Ikonographie, II, 1, p. 170, No. 10.

Room to the Left.

1025 (2). Head of a Dying Persian.

Found on the Palatine about 1867.

As the rough surface of the back of the head shows it must have been attached to a plinth, we have to assume that the figure to which it belonged was in a recumbent posture. As a matter of fact, the head makes a much better impression when placed as the artist intended. The type of features and the tiara prove that a Persian is represented. The process of dying is indicated in a masterly manner. The eyes are half-closed and the muscles of the forehead are convulsively contracted; the open mouth seems to be expiring its last breath. The face, however, still shows the after-effect of the angry defiance felt by the man in the fatal combat. In execution and style, especially in the treatment of the hair, the head shows a strong resemblance to the Pergamenian types of Barbarians (comp. Nos. 533, 884), and thus stands apparently in close relation to the earlier art of Pergamum.

Bull. dell' Inst., 1867, p. 140; Ann., 1871, p. 238, note 31. *Matz-Duhn*, I, p. 349, No. 1190.

1026 (3). Colossal Head of Aphrodite.

Found in the Tiber.

The soft smile and the languishing expression of the almond-shaped, half-closed eyes indicate that this head represents Aphrodite. As the features betray a close kinship with those of the Venus of Cnidos (comp. No. 316), we may attribute the creation of the original either to Praxiteles or to some closely related artist. The head was encircled by a fillet of metal, narrow behind and gradually widening towards the forehead. This fillet was inserted in the holes visible in the tress of hair falling down on the back of the head, and the narrow part rested on the small groove cut in the hair. As in the Venus of Arles the ends of the fillet fell on the shoulders, covering the spaces behind the ears, left unfinished by the sculptor. Two holes on each side of the throat obviously served for the attachment of curls worked separately.

1027 (1). Headless Female Statue.

Found on the Palatine, above the church of S. Anastasia (Bull. dell' Inst., 1862, p. 233).

This well-executed figure seems derived from the type of Aphrodite discussed under No. 915. Both style and motive are similar. The figure before us also drew its mantle up over the shoulder with one hand, but apparently, unlike the Aphrodite, held no attribute in the other hand. On the contrary, the line of fracture

visible on the mantle behind the right leg indicates that
she held a corner of it in her right hand, at about the
height of the middle of the thigh. The girl was thus
represented in the act of arranging her mantle. Moreover two marks, one on the left shoulder, the other on the
right shoulder-blade, prove that this figure was furnished
with curls falling on the shoulders, a motive which we
do not encounter in any replica of this type of Aphrodite.

Bernoulli, Aphrodite, p. 86, No. 2. *Matz-Duhn*, I, p. 189, No. 717.
Furtwaengler, Masterpieces, p. 84, note 2.

1028 (5). Colossal Statue of Apollo.

The ancient portions of this statue were found, at
different times, in the Tiber, between the Ponte Palatino
and the Bagni di Donna Olimpia (Notizie degli scavi,
1891, pp. 287, 288). The right leg below the knee, a
portion of the lowest part of the left leg, the lowest
third of the stump, and the plinth are modern.

Although the execution is poor, it is easy to see
that this statue reproduces a highly important original.
The weight of the body rests on the left leg, while the
right is bent at the knee and extends a little to the
side. The trace above the right knee proves that the
right arm, stretched downward, held an attribute. It
has been supposed that this was a bow; but such a
long and thin object, judging from analogies, would have
been worked separately and inserted in the right hand,
without leaving any trace on the leg. The existence of
this trace, therefore, suggests that the attribute must have
been something of greater bulk, such as a branch of laurel
bound with ribbons (comp. No. 160). The face, following
the direction of the raised arm, is turned a little to the left
and affords by its mild and genial expression a charming
contrast to the imposing figure. The style, in which
a few archaic elements are still perceptible, points to
the time immediately before the golden age of Greek art.
The statue offers various points of contact with undoubtedly Pheidian types. Like the Olympian Zeus of Pheidias
(comp. No. 291) and like the Athena Parthenos (comp.

No. 870) it has curls falling on the shoulders, like the Athena Parthenos the form of the face is nearly circular, while its gentle and genial expression is shared by both these statues. The head in particular, apart from the fact that it seems somewhat earlier in style, betrays a close kinship with that of the Athena Lemnia, a work executed by Pheidias about 450 B.C., of which several reproductions are now known to have come down to us. The supposition that the original of our statue was a youthful work of Pheidias does not, therefore, seem overbold. In this connection we think of the bronze group, attributed by Pausanias to Pheidias, which the Athenians erected at Delphi as a tithe of the booty won at Marathon. The group represented Miltiades, the victor of Marathon, between Athena and Apollo, while five heroes stood on either side of these central figures. It is believed that the Apollo stretched out his left hand, either empty or with a garland, towards Miltiades; and as the Roman statue allows a restoration of that kind, it has been assumed that its original was the Apollo of the Delphic group. This 'combination', however, ingenious as it is, is confronted by difficulties. In the first place the statement of Pausanias, that this group was executed by Pheidias, is not beyond suspicion. In the next place it seems unlikely that such a series of statues, or any one of such a series, would have been copied for the Roman market.

Notizie degli scavi, 1891, pp. 287, 288, 337. Röm. Mitth., VI (1891), T. x-xii, pp. 303, 304, 377-379. *Overbeck*, Geschichte der griech. Plastik, I⁴, p. 347, Fig. 91. *Furtwaengler*, Masterpieces, pp. 79 et seq., 197 et seq.

1029 (6). **Headless Statue of Pallas.**

> Found in 1886, on the destruction of the church of S. Salvatore a Ponte Rotto. The marble is Parian.

This seems to be an original Greek work of about the middle of the fifth century B.C. Both in conception and style it is closely akin to the sculptures of the temple of Zeus at Olympia, but its execution enters much more into details. The goddess is represented as wearing

a scale-covered ægis, which is fastened at her right
shoulder and extends obliquely across her body. The
missing parts, viz. the head, the right arm, and the left
hand, were carved in separate pieces of marble. On the
sections of the right shoulder and the left forearm are
visible the holes and part of a peg, which served to fasten
on the right arm and the left hand. The smaller holes
on the edge of the ægis were probably used for attaching
serpents, also carved separately. The right arm hung
downwards and probably rested on a shield; the left hand,
stretched in front, may have held a helmet.

Notizie degli scavi, 1886, p. 123. Röm. Mitth., vi (1891),
p. 229. *Furtwaengler*, Masterpieces, p. 16, p. 23, note 8.

1030 (7). Colossal Female Head.
Formerly on the Palatine.

Although its surface has suffered from fire, this head
shows all the characteristics of an original Greek work.
Like No. 1029, it is closely related to the pediment
sculptures of the Olympian temple of Zeus. The hair,
parted in the middle, frames the forehead in a wavy line
and is gathered behind in a kind of 'chignon', which projects a long way from the base of the skull and is supported by a broad ribbon encircling the head. As a similar
coiffure has been recognized in figures of the Muses on
a red-figured Attic vase, which seems to have been made
about the middle of the fifth century B.C., it has been
suggested that the head before us is that of a Muse.

Röm. Mitth., vii (1892), pp. 337, 338. — On the Attic vase:
Gerhard, Auserlesene Vasenbilder, iv, 305.

1031 (8). Head of a Hellenistic Poet.
Formerly on the Palatine. The front of the nose is modern.

This head reproduces the same type as No. 469, but
is here crowned by an ivy-wreath, an attribute that en-
titles us to regard this frequently-recurring portrait
'Nos. 469, 710, 970' as that of a poet.

Ann. dell' Inst., 1873, Tav. d'agg. E, pp. 98-106. *Comparetti e De Petra*, La villa ercolanese dei Pisoni, T. iv, 1, 2, pp. 36-38. Comp. *Bernoulli*, Röm. Ikonographie, i, p. 278. For farther references, see *Matz-Duhn*, i, No. 1770.

Room to the Right.

All the sculptures in this room, except the bust of Caracalla (No. 1032), were found in the Atrium Vestæ, on the N. slope of the Palatine, or in its immediate vicinity. The portraits of the Vestals, which were all found in the Atrium itself, must necessarily be discussed in connection with each other. In the meantime, however, the writer leaves the head in relief (No. 11) unnoticed, as it demands a different point of view, and confines himself to the sculptures in the round.

None of the inscribed bases discovered in the House of the Vestals bear the name of an ordinary Virgo Vestalis; all are dedicated to the Virgo Vestalis Maxima. We may therefore assume that the portrait-statues found in the same place also represent Head Vestals, though we are not in a position to connect the different examples with special bases[1]. All represent more or less hard-favoured and soured old maids from 30 to 50 years of age. The various *nuances* of their expressions find ample analogies in those of Italian nuns belonging to a strict order. Of the examples in this room one only (No. 2) can be placed as undoubtedly belonging to the time before Hadrian; though the head No. 5, which is too much damaged for a positive opinion, may date from the same period. The first was probably executed in the time of the Flavian emperors, Nerva, or Trajan — a supposition that is not only forced upon us by the style, but is also supported by the headdress. The fillet encircling the head is so arranged that when viewed from in front it presents the appearance of an upright triangle; and this arrangement might very possibly be occasioned by the fashion of

---

[1] Comp. *Jordan*, Der Tempel der Vesta und das Haus der Vestalinnen, p. 47.

wearing the hair piled high over the forehead as was
usual under the Flavian emperors. The style of all the
other examples points to the reigns of Septimius Severus
or Caracalla.

Each of the statues of the Vestals is furnished with a
fillet, evidently made of wool, which is wound six times
round the head (occasionally only four, as in No. 11, or
five times, as in No. 7), while the loose ends fall on the
shoulders. In this fillet we have obviously to recognize
the 'Infula'[1], which was from time immemorial the emblem
of sacred objects as well as of the Vestals and other
sacerdotal individuals. It has lately been suggested that
this sixfold fillet is connected with the six plaits of hair
(sex crines), traditionally prescribed for brides and for
Vestals, which, in the course of time, had come to be
represented by a corresponding arrangement of the headgear[2]. If, however, this fillet represented the *sex crines*
only, then there is nothing to represent the infula, which
was a constant attribute of sacerdotal individuals down
to the decline of the classical period and which the Vestals
could not be without. With the materials at our disposal,
it is not in our power to decide whether the Vestals
retained their original coiffure down to the imperial
period. The six tresses cannot be distinguished on the
preserved portraits; but this, of course, may be due to
the fact that they are concealed by the convolutions of
the fillet.

When sacrificing, the Vestals wore the 'Suffibulum',
a square white veil, which covered the back of the head
like a hood and fell on the shoulders. In front it was
fastened by a fibula. In the statue numbered 7 we see
this garment worn in exactly the traditional arrangement[3].

The head in relief (No. 11) differs from the works

---

[1] For references on the Infula, see *Marquardt-Wissowa*, Römische
Staatsverwaltung, III, p. 180, note 3. Comp. *Jordan*, Der Tempel der Vesta,
p. 49.

[2] *Jordan*, in the 'Aufsätze Ernst Curtius gewidmet', pp. 218 et seq.;
Der Tempel der Vesta, pp. 47 et seq.

[3] *Jordan*, Der Tempel der Vesta, pp. 54. 55. Comp. Röm. Mittheil., IX
(1894), pp. 130, 131.

hitherto discussed in the fact that it does not exhibit the
features of an elderly woman but those of a young and
beautiful one. The relief to which the head belonged
evidently represented the Vestals engaged in a sacrificial
rite; and the sculptor has judged it better to depict the
Virgins by ideal types instead of by portraits. The style
of this fragment refers it to the last decades of the second
or the beginning of the third century. The fillet encircles
the head in four convolutions.

1032 (13). **Bust of Caracalla.**
Found on the Esquiline, in building the Finance
Office. The nose is modern.

This bust represents the familiar and apparently
officially recognized portrait of the emperor (comp.
No. 226), but shows somewhat less careful execution than
the examples in the Vatican No. 226, and the Capitol
(vol. I, p. 346, No. 53).
De Ruggiero, Guida del Museo Kircheriano (Roma, 1879),
p. 1, No. 5.

1033 (12). **Head of Gallienus.**
The execution appears unusually careful for the period
from which this head dates.

1034 (11). **Head of a Vestal in alto-relief.**
See the introductory remarks at pp. 218, 219.

1035 (10). **Bust of Geta as a Youth.**
The point of the nose is modern.
Bernoulli, Röm. Ikonographie, II, 2, p. 201, No. 3, pp. 202, 203.

1036 (9). **Head of an Elderly Vestal.**
See p. 217.

1037 (8). **Bust of a Vestal Virgin.**
This bust is one of those that go back to an earlier
date than that of the Emp. Hadrian (see p. 217).

1038 (7). **Upper Part of the Statue of a Vestal Virgin.**
This face shows a very discontented expression. The

suffibulum or veil hangs over the back of the head. See
p. 218.

Jordan, in the 'Histor. und philol. Aufsätze Ernst Curtius gewidmet', vignette at p. 211; Der Tempel der Vesta, T. IX, 10, pp. 44, 45, 54.

1039 (6). Head of Faustina the Younger.

Bernoulli, Röm. Ikonographie, II, 2, p. 194, No. 6.

1040 (5). Head of an Elderly Vestal.

The expression shows a curious mixture of resignation
and ill-temper.

1041 (2). Head of an Elderly Vestal.

This is one of the earliest examples of the portraits
of Vestals exhibited in this room. The expression shows
a high degree of stupidity. See p. 217.

Notizie degli scavi, 1883, T. XVIII, 2, p. 461. *Jordan*, Der Tempel der Vesta, T. X, 11, pp. 44, 47.

1042 (1). Bust of Marcus Aurelius at a somewhat advanced age.

The nose is modern. The bust is ancient but can
hardly belong to the head.

Bernoulli, Röm. Ikonographie, II, 2, p. 168, No. 29.

Upper Floor.

One of the chief attractions of this section is afforded
by the mural paintings and stucco-reliefs from an ancient
building discovered in 1878 in or near the garden of the
Villa Farnesina. As these are scattered throughout
several rooms, it seems advisable to give the necessary
introductory remarks on them at this place, to which reference may be made from the special numbers. The
building in which both reliefs and paintings were discovered combined the characters of an aristocratic town
mansion with those of a villa (see Plan in the Notizie
degli scavi, 1880, Tav. IV, pp. 127, 138, 139). The
mural paintings Nos. 1062, 1067-1074, 1080-1083,

1085-1087, 1091, belong to the so-called second decorative style (comp. No. 956), but exhibit this partly in that modification of it which paved the way for the so-called 'candelabrum style', a special variety of the third decorative manner[1]. The date of their execution may therefore be placed in the beginning of the imperial period. The same remark applies to the stucco-reliefs, which adorned the vaulted ceilings of three bed-chambers (Nos. 1015, 1016, 1057-1060). In respect of execution these mural and ceiling decorations are much above the average of the similar works found in Pompeii and the other towns of Campania that were buried by eruptions of Mt. Vesuvius. The stucco-reliefs in particular are among the most beautiful decorative ensembles of Græco-Roman art that have come down to us. The tastefully arranged decoration is marked at once by richness and perspicuity. The execution is fresh and full of life. It never loses itself in petty details, but contents itself with reproducing the essential features by light strokes of the modelling tool. If certain motives on the same ceiling are more sharply accentuated than others, this is certainly not due to want of skill or care on the part of the artist, but seems to have been purposely done on account of the difference of light. Both the decorative ornaments and the figures required to be more emphasized on those parts of the ceiling which were most faintly illuminated, if they were to produce the desired effect. The words ϹΕΛΕΥΚΟϹ ΕΠΟΕΙ, inscribed on one of the painted walls (No. 1051), prove that Seleucos, a Greek decorator established in Rome, was employed in the artistic embellishment of this house[2].

Room I.

[The numbers of the rooms appear above the doors, on the inside.]

---

[1] Comp. *Mau*, Geschichte der decorativen Wandmalerei in Pompeji, pp. 245 et seq.

[2] Notizie degli scavi, 1880, p. 139, No. 4

In the middle, —

1043. Fragment of a Group.

This fragment, consisting of the torso of a girl and the powerfully formed left hand of a man, grasping her left side, obviously represents a scene of abduction. It is clear that the girl is resisting and is twisting her body so as to escape, if possible, from the grasp of her captor. The right arm was raised, the left stretched to the side. As this fragment forms only a very insignificant part of the group, it seems dangerous to assign definite names to the individuals represented. It might, for instance, belong to a group of Pluto and Persephone, or of Orcithyia and Boreas, or of a Greek maiden and a Centaur. The style, and especially the realistic treatment of the man's hand, points to the early Hellenistic period. The execution is so admirable, that there seems no reason to take it for other than an original Greek work.

Röm. Mitth., vi (1891), p. 240.

1044. Human Skeleton in Mosaic.

Found in the excavations carried on by Count M. Tyskiewicz in 1866 in the grounds of the Camaldolensians of S. Gregorio, to the W. of the Via Appia. The mosaic formed the floor of a small tomb constructed of opus reticulatum (masonry resembling the meshes of a net). Formerly in the Museo Kircheriano.

In later antiquity human skeletons were not unfrequently pictorially represented, as a reminder of the fleeting nature of human existence; and the rudely executed work before us belongs to this category. It represents a recumbent skeleton, leaning on its left elbow and pointing with its right hand to the inscription ΓΝѠΘΙ ϹΑΥΤΟΝ ('know thyself') — an inscription meant to indicate that the permanent part of man is nothing but a skeleton. The fact that the ears are still attached to the skull, and that the arms and legs are partly covered with flesh and sinews shows that the mosaicist had never seen a real skeleton but had only an inexact idea of what it was like from other similar representations.

Bull. dell' Inst., 1866, p. 164. Archæol. Zeitung, xxiv (1866), p. 184*. *Treu*, De ossium humanorum larvarumque apud antiquos imaginibus (Berolini, 1874), p. 18, No. 51 (comp. Jahrbuch, iv, 1889; Arch. Anzeiger, p. 106). *De Ruggiero*, Catalogo del Museo Kircheriano, i, p. 272, No. 15. *Ersilia Caetani-Lovatelli*, Thanatos (Roma, 1888), pp. 49 et seq. (= Atti dell' Acc. dei Lincei, classe delle scienze morali, series iv, vol. iii, 1887, pp. 43 et seq.).

Room II.

1045 (3). Stucco Reliefs.

These reliefs adorned the ceiling of one of the bedrooms (No. 4 on the Plan in the Notizie degli scavi, 1880, T. iv) in the old Roman house excavated in the garden of the Villa Farnesina (see p. 220). The walls of the same room were embellished with the mural paintings Nos. 1080-1083.

Three framed scenes in relief are inserted in the ornamental scheme. The central scene is a landscape in the Hellenistic-Egyptian style. To the left is a group of women offering a bloodless sacrifice to a phallic herma. The scene to the right represents a Bacchante who is lighting an altar-fire by means of two torches, while a Satyr standing behind her plays on the double flute. In front of the Bacchante stands Silenus, apparently in a somewhat drunken condition, holding out a thyrsos in his left hand and leaning his right elbow on a square base. Above the latter rises the upper part of a veiled woman, whose mantle is drawn over the back of her head.

Monumenti inedit., pubbl. dall' Instituto di corr. archeologica, supplemento (Berlin, 1880-1891), T. 34 (below). *Lessing und Mau*, Wand- und Deckenschmuck eines röm. Hauses aus der Zeit des Augustus, T. 14 (foot).

1046 (10). Stucco Reliefs.

These reliefs come from the same room as No. 1045.

The reliefs inserted in the decorative scheme are as follows. The central scene represents a Hellenistic-Egyptian landscape, and that to the left women sacrificing; but of both these compositions only small fragments are left. The better-preserved scene to the right seems to refer to the dedication of a picture in the form of a triptych. A woman stands beside a square base on which lie ribbons and garlands, and holds aloft with both hands the picture, the covers of which are open. She is obviously showing the picture painted on the tablet to the two women before her, one sitting, one standing, both of whom are looking at it attentively.

Monumento inediti, supplemento, T. 34 (above). *Lessing und Mau*, T. 14 (top).

1017 (7). Female Bust.

Found in the tomb of Sulpicius Platorinus and Sulpicia Platorina (comp. the remarks on Nos. 964, 965).

This delicately modelled bust of a young woman of about 22 years of age perhaps represents a certain Minatia Polla, whose inscribed cinerary urn (No. 8 of the Museum) was found in the same tomb. The coiffure, the style, and the extremely narrow bust point to the first days of the Empire. The manner in which the lower side is treated is frequently seen in portrait-busts dating from about the end of the Republic or the beginning of the Empire. The bust slopes from the back to the front, while its section is smoothed and shows no trace of a mortise, which would have been necessary if the bust had been meant to be fastened, as is generally the case, to a stone pedestal. Moreover, no stone pedestal has ever been found in any of the tombs which contained busts hewn in this manner. It would thus appear that such busts as these were inserted in wooden bases which have decayed in the course of time and left no trace of their existence.

Notizie degli scavi, 1880, T. v, 2, p. 133. *Rayet*, Monuments de l'art antique, II, livraison II, Pl. II. Comp. *Bernoulli*, Röm. Ikonographie, II, 1, p. 186, note 21.

The cinerary urns exhibited in this room were also found in the tomb of Platorinus and Platorina. The square one near the entrance-wall (No. 1 of the Museum)[1]

---

[1] Notizie degli scavi, 1880, T. v, 3, p. 131 (vi. nicchia).

and the two cylindrical ones (Nos. 4, 5)[1] in the middle of the room are especially worthy of attention. All three are elaborately decorated, chiefly with bull's heads, united by garlands of fruit and flowers, and standing out from the background in very high relief. The existence of such a baroque scheme of decoration as this in works of the Augustan era cannot but appear strange to the student of art. On a closer investigation, however, it will appear that this style is a natural and direct development of a decorative tendency in vogue immediately before this epoch, the strongest manifestation of which is met in late-Etruscan cinerary urns and architectural ornaments.

Room III.

1048-1050 (1, 4, 7). **Three Female Hermæ in nero antico.**

Formerly on the Palatine.

Each of these hermæ shows the upper part of a girl in a Doric chiton, holding a corner of her mantle with one hand in the characteristic archaic manner (comp. Nos. 593, 766). The square incisions on the top of the heads prove that each of them carried some object on her head. This may have been a basket, in which case the hermæ must have served as Canephoræ (comp. Nos. 725, 726). To judge from analogous figures in Græco-Roman wall-paintings, it is, however, by no means impossible that the supports attached to the heads bore an architrave. Either restoration enables us to dispose easily and naturally of the arms not occupied with the drapery. The right arm of one herma is bent and the right hand, with its fingers outspread, is raised towards the head. The missing left arms of the other two hermæ doubtless occupied a similar position. This motion of the arms is evidently meant to indicate that the figures were ready to support the objects on their heads if they should lose their balance. The execution points to the time of the Roman

---

[1] Notizie degli scavi, 1880, T. v, 3, p. 131 (II. IV. nicchia).

15

Empire. It gives us the impression that the sculptor used
Greek bronze types of the fifth century B.C. as his models
but altered and attenuated them to suit the prevailing
taste of his own period. The missing eyes were executed
in some other material and inserted in the sockets.

Matz-Duhn, I, No. 851.

In the middle of the room, —

1051 (6). Bronze Statue of a Pugilist.

> Found in 1884 in building the theatre on the Via
> Nazionale. The point of the left thumb, a piece of the
> right thigh, and the rocky seat are modern.

This statue is a realistic portrait of a resting pugilist,
perhaps dedicated by the man himself in commemoration
of his victories. The well-individualized conception of
the person represented and the delicate sense of realism
point rather to the Hellenistic era than to the time of
the Roman emperors. The pugilist sits with his body
leaning forward, his arms resting on his thighs, and his
head somewhat raised and turned to the right. The face
is stupid and brutal in expression and shows many traces
of its owner's profession. The ears have been flattened
by numerous blows. To judge from the relative position
of the lips, his upper front teeth have been knocked out.
These mutilations may be of long standing, but other
marks indicate a recently fought battle. Two scars or
scratches are represented on each ear, and two drops of
blood, treated in low relief, ooze from each of the scars
on the right ear, while a similar drop is visible below
the upper scar on the left ear. The orbit of the left eye
is quite normal, but the right is so swollen that eyelid
and cheek melt into each other without any precise line
of demarcation. The assumption that this is the result
of a recent blow is strengthened by the fact that there
are a number of scratches under the left eye, though in
this case without drops of blood. That the interior of
the nose is supposed to be swollen and full of coagulated
blood is apparent from the open mouth and the protrusion

of the lower jaw. It is evident that the man can bring little or no air to his lungs by the nostrils but has to breathe through his open mouth. The partly staring and partly matted condition of the hair of the moustache is the natural result of a soaking in blood, which has afterwards coagulated.

The apparatus *(caestus)* which pugilists wore to protect their arms and make their blows more effective is represented on this statue with great distinctness. Each of the forearms is covered with a gauntlet, which leaves the upper joints of the fingers free. Over the finger-joints the glove is strengthened with three thick leathern bands connected by metal hooks or clasps. To these clasps small metal balls are attached, — the whole forming a most effective weapon for a knock-down blow. To prevent the leathern bands from hurting the hand, the glove below them is padded. A network of straps keeps the bands in place and at the same time protects the forearm. These straps prevent the free movement of the wrist; hence our pugilist cannot let his hands hang naturally but has to hold them stiffly in front of him. A long and deep incision on the right shoulder and a similar one on the right forearm seem to be flaws in the casting. They were probably filled up with strips of bronze, which have disappeared (comp. No. 611). On the infibulation, comp. No. 911.

Antike Denkmäler herausgegeben vom Arch. Institut, ɪ (1886), T. 4. *Lanciani*, Ancient Rome, plate before the frontispiece, p. 306. *Murray*, Handbook of Greek Archæology, p. 304, Fig. 99, p. 306. *Brunn und Bruckmann*, Denkmäler griech. und röm. Skulptur, No. 248. Comp. Notizie degli scavi, 1885, p. 223. Jahrbuch des Arch. Instituts, ɪɪ (1887), p. 192; vɪɪɪ (1893), p. 57, note 4. Kölnische Zeitung, July 3rd, 1887, No. 182. Römische Mittheilungen, ɪv (1889), pp. 175 et seq. Abhandlungen des archäol.-epigr. Seminars zu Wien, vɪɪɪ (1890), p. 41.

1052. Bronze Statue of a Man leaning on a Spear or Staff.

Found in 1884 near No. 1051 and almost at the same time. The restorations include the front of the left forefinger and the right middle finger, the staff, part of the left thigh (just above the knee), and the plinth.

The execution of this statue is unequal. While the head has been worked with great care and precision, the forms of the body are somewhat indeterminate. It represents a vigorous man of about thirty years of age. His left hand grasps, high up, a spear, pole, or sceptre, while his right rests on the small of his back. The weight of the body is borne by the right leg; the left leg is drawn back in a somewhat affected and unnatural manner. The cheeks, chin, and upper lip are covered with a beard engraved on the metal. To judge from the conception, the style, and the type of face (the last recalling the coin-portraits of Philip V. of Macedon, B.C. 221-179), the statue is a portrait of a person of the Hellenistic era. The strongly developed muscles of the chest and back indicate that it is an athlete, whom the artist has chosen to represent in repose. The left arm probably rested on a spear, and it was doubtless in spear-throwing that the athlete specially excelled. Between the thorax and the navel is an inscription, engraved on the metal after the casting. Like that on No. 615, this mentions the place in which the statue was erected: L.VI = *loco sexto.* The following part of the inscription has not yet been satisfactorily explained. On the right thigh are punctured the three interlacing letters MAR.

Antike Denkmäler herausgegeben vom Arch. Institut, I (1886), T. 5. *Lanciani,* Ancient Rome, plate to p. 303. *Murray,* Handbook of Greek Archæology, p. 305, Fig. 100, p. 306. Comp. Notizie degli scavi, 1885, p. 42. Kölnische Zeitung, July 3rd, 1887, No. 182. Jahrbuch des Arch. Inst., VI (1891); Arch. Anzeiger, p. 69. Röm. Mittheilungen, VI (1891), p. 238. *Furtwaengler,* Masterpieces, p. 364, note 2.

Room IV.

1053 (1). **Bronze Head of Tiberius.**
Found in the Tiber in 1884.

The thin, compressed lips, which were characteristic

of this emperor, are very strikingly reproduced in this head. Comp. No. 86.

> Notizie degli scavi, 1884, p. 305 (where the head is erroneously identified with Augustus).

1054 (2). **Statue of a Youth, in basalt.**

> Found on the Palatine (Bull. dell' Iust., 1869, p. 67).

The fracture visible between the left shoulder and the left breast, with one of its edges rising above the flesh, has been supposed to indicate the former presence of a spear, held in the youth's left hand. The fracture, however, seems too wide for so narrow an object as a spear, and could be better accounted for by the assumption of a support, connecting the outstretched left arm with the body. The support attached to the upper part of the right thigh cannot have served any other end than to steady the pendent right arm. The head is encircled, not by a branch, as one archæologist says, but by a hoop or ring. The style of the execution points to the early days of the Empire. The colour of the dark basalt of which the statue consists resembles that of a bronze statue after long exposure to the air; and the sculptor has evidently tried to imitate the characteristics of a bronze work. This attempt is particularly evident in his treatment of the locks of hair, which look as if they had been cast and chased. The head resembles a type (best represented in a beautiful bronze at Munich), which some authorities connect with the art of Polycleitos and others with that represented by the pediment sculptures of the temple of Zeus at Olympia, while a quite recent judge sees in it a mingling of Polycleitian and other (possibly Attic) elements.

> *Matz-Duhn*, I, No. 981. *Furtwaengler*, Masterpieces, p. 291. note 6 (where the Munich head is also discussed).

1055 (3). **Bronze Statue of Dionysos.**

> This statue was found in the Tiber on Sept. 20th, 1885, between the Farnesina and the Ponte Garibaldi. It is practically free from modern additions. The thyrsos

was found in fragments, but was restored with the aid
of a few insignificant insertions.

Dionysos stands erect, holding in his left hand a thyrsos, the shaft of which is covered with scale-like ornamentation. The position of the fingers shows that the
lowered right hand must also have held some attribute,
which seems to have been a two-handled vase *(cantharos)*.
Though the statue reproduces a Hellenic type of Dionysos in the free style, it shows, nevertheless, a singular
constraint in the treatment of the nude. It is manifest
that the artist who modelled it possessed but a limited
knowledge of the human body, and that he consequently
felt a certain timidity in the reproduction of its forms.
This attitude offers a most decided contrast to the routine
practised in the imperial period, even by mere stone-cut-
ters. So far as our knowledge goes, this statue finds its
nearest analogies in the terracotta figurine and reliefs
which were made in Campania in the third century B.C.
and afterwards imitated in other Italic manufactories.
The question thus arises whether this bronze may not be
a work of the third or second century B.C. produced either
in Campania or at Rome under Campanian influence.
The statue affords us an instructive lesson in the way
in which the ancient workers in metal introduced variety
of colour on the bronze ground of the statue. The ray-
like ornaments of the diadem are alternately of silver
and copper; the eyes are of white marble; the pupils,
now missing, were doubtless formed of some darker
material; the lips are covered with red copper; the nip-
ples, which are worked separately, are of the same metal.
On the outside of the lower part of the left leg is the
impression of a coin which had been stamped on the
clay or wax model; its diameter (0.022 mètre) corresponds rather to a Greek didrachma than to a Roman
aureus or denarius. This detail also suggests Campania,
for the ceramic artists of that district often used impressions of Greek didrachmæ as ornamental motives or as
trade-marks.

Lanciani, Ancient Rome, heliotype opposite p. 308. Comp. Notizie degli scavi, 1885, pp. 342, 343. Römische Mittheilungen, vi (1891), p. 238.

1056 (7). **Colossal Votive Hand in bronze.**

Found in the Tiber, near the Marmorata, in 1886.

This hand is recognized as that of a woman by its delicacy and by the bracelet round the wrist. It had evidently been dedicated by a Roman lady to a god of healing in return for her recovery from some injury to her hand. It is not improbable that the serpentine form of the bracelet and the ring bears special reference to the serpent as the symbol of the gods of healing. The stand on which the hand lies is provided with holes and pegs for attaching it to the wall of the temple.

Monumenti antichi pubblicati per cura dei Lincei, i, pp. 170-186.

Room V.

On the side-walls, —

1057, 1058. **Reliefs in Stucco.**

These reliefs adorned the sleeping-chamber marked No. 5 in the plan of the old Roman house discovered in the Farnesina garden (comp. p. 220). The mural paintings Nos. 1070-1074 belonged to the same chamber.

1057 (to the right, provisionally marked E).

The central scene in relief has been taken for an idyllic genre-scene, with two beardless young shepherds playing morra *(digites micare)*, and an older man, with a sword, acting as umpire of the game. None of the figures, however, are bucolic in character. Moreover, it must appear strange that the players turn their backs to the umpire and so make it impossible for him to see how many fingers they hold out. It is much more probable that a mythical scene is represented. The youth seated to the right is talking earnestly to the one standing in front of him, who seems to be preferring some request and is accompanied by his elderly armour-bearer. The

attendants in the Museo delle Terme explain the scene
as Phaëthon begging Helios to allow him to guide the
chariot of the sun for a day. Against this explanation,
which the Museum attendants must have received from
an archæologist, the only obvious objection is that the
traditional story of Phaëthon makes no mention of an
armour-bearer. On the other hand the movement and
expression of the two youths seem admirably adapted to
the theory that the standing figure represents the im-
portunate Phaëthon, the seated figure the unwilling
Helios. On the front of the head of the latter figure,
below the lofty stephané, is a pointed object which may
very well be the remains of a coronet of rays. And finally,
the scene on No. 1058 may also be explained with reference to the myth of Phaëthon.

Of the landscapes to the right and left of the principal scene, the latter only has been preserved. Each of
these landscapes was enclosed between two porticos or
colonnades, the only one of which still remaining to any
extent is that limiting the landscape to the left on its
right side. The chief architrave is borne by a bearded
figure, on whose outstretched right hand sits a bird.
The presence of a bearded Androsphinx on the architrave is another proof of Alexandrian influence.

Mon. dell' Inst., supplemento, T. 33 = *Lessing und Mau*, Wand-
und Deckenschmuck eines römischen Hauses, T. 12. On the central scene, see Gazette archéologique, x (1885), Pl. 10, pp. 87 et seq.

1058 (to the left).

It is possible to make out, with some difficulty, that
the central scene represents three women, harnessing
two horses to a chariot — perhaps the Horæ preparing
the chariot of the sun for Phaëthon (see above). To the
left and right are landscapes, opening, like those of
No. 1057, between two colonnades. The main architrave of the colonnade to the left is supported by a Hermes, holding out his caduceus. The architrave in the
other scene is borne by draped female figures, the better-

preserved of which holds two wheat-ears in her lowered left hand.

Mon. dell' Inst., supplemento, T. 22 = *Lessing und Mau*, T. 13.

1059, 1060. Stucco Reliefs.

From another bedroom (No. 2 on the Plan) in the same house. The walls of the room were adorned with the paintings Nos. 1067-1069.

1059 (to the right; provisionally marked B).

In the middle is a landscape with a rustic fane and its sacred tree (comp. Nos. 743, 508). In front of the temple are two women about to offer a sacrifice. The scene to the right of the landscape represents the Bacchic thiasos. The figures represented include a Bacchante, crouching to play with a panther; Silenus, looking down at this group; a drunken Satyr lying on the ground; and remains of a Bacchante who grasps the chin of the Satyr with her left hand, while he lays his left hand on her arm. The scene to the left of the landscape is sadly mutilated but seems to represent the preparations for some Bacchanalian ceremony. In the hands of the female figure, of which the lower part has been preserved on the left side of the scene, we can distinctly recognize the swinging basket (λίχνον, *vannus*), which played so important a rôle in the mystic cult (comp. No. 1108).

Mon. dell' Inst., supplemento, T. 35 = *Lessing und Mau*, T. 15 (top).

1060 (to the left).

The central scene is again a landscape. That to the left appears to represent an initiation into the Bacchic mysteries. The neophyte, who is represented as veiled and on a smaller scale than the other figures (comp. No. 1108), is led up to Silenus by a draped woman of dignified exterior. Silenus is about to lift a veil of some kind, but the part of the relief below this veil is lost. Whatever the lost objects were, their uncovering

doubtless formed part of the initiation. Behind the conductress of the neophyte advances a Bacchante, holding
a tympanon in her lowered left hand. A low base in
front of this last figure sustains a mystic cist. Behind
Silenus are a pillar and a (sacred ?) tree. The goat's head
at the foot of the pillar suggests the sacrifice accompanying the ceremony.

In the middle of the scene to the right of the central
scene we see a seated Satyr, bending down a branch of a
tall vine growing near him. To his left is another Satyr,
pouring wine from a wineskin into a cratera. In the
small nude figure standing to the right of the first-mentioned Satyr, with a thyrsos in its hand, we have, perhaps, to recognize a just-initiated neophyte, who is now
permitted to take part in the functions of the thiasos.
The scene is closed on the left by a Bacchante, apparently holding a cup in her right hand.

Mon. dell' Inst., supplemento, T. 35 = *Lessing und Mau*,
T. 15 (foot).

In the middle of the room, —

1061. Marble Cratera, with representation of Herons and Serpents.

Found in Hadrian's Villa, near Tivoli.

On one side of the vase are two herons, each with a
snake in its claws, while a third heron poses as a calm
spectator of the scene. The snake to the left (of the beholder) was in the act, when seized by the heron, of
swallowing some smaller creature, part of which still
protrudes from its mouth. The sculptor, however, has
reproduced this so indistinctly that we cannot tell whether
it is a locust or a small bird. The reliefs on the other
side of the cratera depict two herons struggling for a
lizard and a third heron fighting with a serpent. The
representations of the two sides are separated from each
other by goat's-head masks. The ornamentation of this
cratera seems to have been determined by the toreutic

of Alexandria, which busied itself by preference with the outdoor life of birds and beasts.

Notizie degli scavi, 1881, p. 138. — On the birds of the Alexandrian toreutic, see Abhandlungen der philol.-hist. Classe der sächs. Gesellschaft der Wissenschaften, xix (1894), pp. 466, 467.

Room VI.

1062 (1, 5, 7, 8, 9). Fragments of a Mural Decoration.

These fragments came from an oblong room (No. 3 on the Plan) in the house of the Farnesina garden (see above, p. 220).

The ground-colour of the walls is black. Of the decoration particular attention is due to the frieze, which consists of a series of court-scenes of Hellenistic, or as we may more definitely say, of Alexandrian origin. The fields below the frieze were occupied by landscapes, which are now almost obliterated. These were sketchily thrown upon the black background, with the use of but few colours (red, grey, and yellow).

Mon. dell' Inst., xi, 44; Ann., 1882, pp. 301-308 = Lessing und Mau, T. 9. — On the frieze: Mon. dell' Inst., xi, 45-48; Ann., 1882, pp. 309-314.

1063. Statue of a Youth.

Found in the Villa of Nero at Subiaco.

The execution of this statue shows such delicacy of refinement that we are warranted in taking it for an original Greek work. In style it recalls the so-called Ilioneus in the Munich Glyptothek, and, like that work, it probably dates from the time of Alexander the Great or the very beginning of the Hellenistic period. It represents a youth kneeling lightly on the left knee and stretching out both arms in front of him. The right arm is more elevated than the left; the fore-part of the latter was joined to the right thigh by a support, the mark left by which is visible near the knee. These indications would suggest that the youth is defending himself from a danger that threatens him from above. At the same time and place a left hand was found, holding an object in the form of a leathern thong. It cannot, however, have belonged to this statue, as its execution is neither so delicate nor so fresh.

Antike Denkmäler herausgegeben vom Arch. Institut, I, T. 56. *Brunn und Bruckmann*, Denkmäler griech. und röm. Sculptur, No. 249. Comp. Notizie degli scavi, 1884, pp. 426, 427. Röm. Mittheilungen, VI (1891), p. 238. Gazette des beaux arts, 1891, pp. 470-478. — For the statue of Ilioneus, see *Brunn*, Beschreibung der Glyptothek, No. 142.

First Room beyond Room VI.

1064. Head of a Woman.

Found in 1893 in the Stadium of the Palatine.

There is no obstacle to the view that this admirably executed head is an original Greek work of about the middle of the fourth century B.C. It is encircled by a head-cloth, which leaves a narrow band of hair exposed about two-thirds of the way up the skull. The expression is one of meditative seriousness. The gaze of the large eyes is directed downwards, and the eyeballs are almost concealed by the strongly-marked lids. It would thus seem that the statue to which the head belonged was that of some one reading or writing. This idea might suggest a Muse, all the more as we find undoubted figures of Muses with a similar headdress (comp. No. 1030). We may also think of a poetess, for we know that Naucydes made a statue of Erinna about the end of the fifth or the beginning of the fourth century B.C., while Silanion created types of Corinna and Sappho during the first half of the latter century. Our head shows a certain resemblance to the supposed type of Sappho seen in No. 789, which also shows the same head-wrap, though in a somewhat different arrangement. It has, however, none of the dreamy and yearning expression so emphasized in No. 789 — an expression necessary to our ideal of Sappho. The identification of the head as that of this poetess seems, therefore, impracticable.

Notizie degli scavi, 1893, p. 162a. Röm. Mittheilungen, VIII (1893), p. 96, No. 6.

Second Room beyond Room VI.

1065. Sleeping Hermaphrodite.

> This statue was found in 1879 in the peristyle of a large ancient residence, in digging the foundations for the Teatro Costanzi. This house, to judge from its construction, dated from the time of the Antonines, and seems at one time to have belonged to Gaius Julius Avitus, husband of Julia Maesa and grandfather of Heliogabalus.

This statue reproduces the same original as that in the Villa Borghese (No. 931), but is far better preserved. The head differs from that of other replicas of this type, and seems to be determined by an ideal Apollo of a late period.

Mon. dell' Inst., xi, 43; Ann., 1882, pp. 245 et seq.

Room VII.

1066 (1). Head of Asclepios.

> Formerly on the Palatine. The restorations include the left eye, part of the forehead and chin, the front of the nose, and the moustache, with a piece of the upper lip.

This type, marked by its mild dignity, is certainly earlier than that discussed under No. 932. It seems to have been created in the transition period from the fifth to the fourth century B.C.

Matz-Duhn, I, No. 64. *Roscher*, Lexikon der griech. und röm. Mythologie, I, 1, p. 637. *Furtwaengler*, Masterpieces, p. 89, note 6.

The mural paintings in this room were found in the house of the Farnesina garden (see above, p. 220), in the sleeping-chamber marked No. 2 on the Plan in the Notizie degli scavi (1880; T. iv). Several of the paintings in this room differ strikingly from the Graeco-Roman mural paintings hitherto known to us. The style of mural decoration in which separate scenes in fresco were placed in the middle of the compartments or in other parts of the general scheme arose in the Hellenistic era and was an imitation of the custom of hanging actual easel

or panel pictures on the decorated walls. In harmony
with this origin we generally find that the figures and
groups in these frescoes reveal both in style and execution
the taste of the Hellenistic period. In opposition to
this rule, however, the paintings now under discussion
point to an earlier period. The subjects are arranged as
in a relief and are treated more like coloured drawings
than as paintings. They resemble the figures on the
Attic lecythi with a white ground, and probably illustrate
the same phase of painting. We may assume that the
painter who designed the decoration of these two chambers had in view a room in which an amateur of art had
collected examples of ancient as well as of contemporary masters. Each of the two chambers contained one
large ancient picture and several smaller ones. We
shall encounter this mingling of Hellenistic and earlier
compositions in two other bed-chambers of the same
house, the decoration of which has been preserved for us
in the mural paintings in Rooms VIII and IX.

1067 (3).

The principal scene represents the rearing of the infant Dionysos. In the foreground is a seated Bacchante,
with her thyrsos by her side, engaged in placing a garland on the head of the young god. Two well-dressed
women, more in the background, look on at the operation,
one holding a thyrsos in her right hand, the other a fan
in her left. In the background are a gate, with a recumbent statue of a Satyr, and a wall. These would suggest
that the scene takes place before the peribolos of a Bacchic sanctuary. From the architrave of the gate hangs a
light-violet curtain, which is drawn back towards the
wall but would obviously close the gateway if allowed
to fall vertically. The art of Alexandria, as is well known,
was especially addicted to curtains of this kind and used
them with great effect. The general style of this painting
is that of the Hellenistic period, as familiar to us in other
Græco-Roman mural paintings. Two smaller pictures,

however, which occupy the centres of the red pannels and are treated in the style of the scenes on the lecythi with a white ground (see p. 238), betoken originals of the transition period from the fifth to the fourth century B.C. The picture to the left represents a woman seated on a stool, touching with her left hand the strings of a harp-like instrument and stretching her right hand towards a girl standing in front of her. The latter seems to be handing her some small animal like a squirrel. In the picture to the right we see another seated woman, with a plectrum in her right hand and her left hand on the strings of a cithara. In front of her stands a girl, holding out a spray of blossoms with her right hand.

For the mural decoration as a whole, see Mon. dell' Inst., xii, 18; Ann., 1885, pp. 304 et seq. *Lessing und Mau*, T. 8. — On the large central scene: Mon. dell' Inst., xii, 20; Ann., 1885, pp. 310, 311. — The two smaller works: Mon. dell' Inst., xii, 22, Nos. 4, 5; Ann., 1888, p. 313.

1068 (10).

In this mural decoration our attention is called to the one figure of Zeus Ammon, used as a Telamon — a figure which once more points to the Hellenism of Egypt.

Mon. dell' Inst., xii, 25 (to the right); Ann., 1885, p. 304. *Lessing und Mau*, T. 2.

1069 (12).

The principal scene here is treated like those of the white-ground lecythi. In its grace and delicacy it recalls a style of art current in Attica just before and also during the golden era. Aphrodite is represented sitting on an elaborately decorated throne, with a flower in her right hand. Her figure suggests that it may have been copied from a chryselephantine statue. Behind her stands a girlish form, perhaps Peitho, placing a fine veil over the lofty *polos*, which surmounts the head of the goddess. Eros stands in front of his mother and holds the sceptre ready for her. Four smaller scenes which embellish the frieze to the right and left of the main picture are in the usual Hellenistic style. The two immediately adjacent to the upper parts of the columns enclosing the principal picture are concerned with the doings of scenic artists. To the left is an ivy-crowned poet or actor, seated in a chair and laying his left hand on a mask resting on his knee. Before him stand two women, one of whom is looking fixedly at the mask. The man has, perhaps, won a prize at some dramatic representation, and the mask may refer to the comedy or the rôle that secured him this honour. The corresponding scene to the right shows a tragic actor delivering a recitation. Behind him are a poet or prompter, reading the text, and a woman accompanying the recitation with the cithara. The two small pictures adjoining these just described show a pair of lovers at different stages of their wooing. In the scene to the left the lovers are seated on a couch, surrounded by three slave-women, one of whom is pouring wine or water from an amphora into a bowl. The other scene shows the lovers alone and in a more confidential relation[1]. In both these pictures the artist has represented the lids, with which panel paintings were frequently furnished.

The general scheme of decoration: Mon. dell' Inst., xii, 19; Ann., 1885, pp. 304 et seq. *Lessing und Mau*, T. 7. — The large picture with Aphrodite: Mon. dell' Inst., xii, 21; Ann., 1885, pp. 311, 312. — On the supposed Peitho: Röm. Mitth., vii (1892), p. 60. — The smaller pictures: Mon. dell' Inst., xii, T. 8, Nos. 4, 5, T. 22, Nos. 2, 3; Ann., 1884, p. 309, 1885, pp. 312, 313.

Room VIII.

The mural decorations in this room come from a bedchamber of the house in the Farnesina garden (p. 220', marked No. 5 on the Plan.

1070 (2).

The central scene, a landscape, is so much damaged that no description of it can be attempted. The two

---

[1] This scene is now lost, as the stucco on which it was painted has crumbled away.

smaller pictures to the right and left are again furnished
with their (painted) shutters (comp. No. 1069). That
to the right shows a stout elderly woman, seated in a
chair, holding a goblet in her right hand, and turning
her head towards a beautiful young woman standing
beside her and talking earnestly. On the other side of
the old woman stands a slave-girl, behind whom is a
table with a small cratera on it. The corresponding scene
to the left represents a young man and a young woman
seated on a couch and kissing each other, the latter
holding a cup in her left hand. In front of the bed
stands a table with drinking-vessels. The female figure
looks as if she might be the same person as the beautiful
young woman in the companion picture. If this is correct, the first picture may be explained as a young woman
applying to a go-between for aid in some love-affair. She
treats the old lady to wine and explains the object of her
desires. The second picture shows the successful outcome
of the old woman's intervention. Situations of this kind
frequently occur in the Mimiambi of Herondas (comp.
No. 518) and other Alexandrian writings.

The whole decoration: Mon. dell' Inst., xii, 23; Ann., 1885,
pp. 313 et seq. *Lessing und Mau*, T. 3. — The small pictures: Mon.
dell' Inst., xii, T. 27, Nos. 2, 5; Ann., 1885, p. 316.

1071 (5).

Both the larger central scene (a landscape) and the
smaller side-pictures are so mutilated as to defy description.

Mon. dell' Inst., xii, 24; Ann., 1885, pp. 313 et seq. *Lessing
und Mau*, T. 4.

1072 (6).

This figure is from one of the walls in the same bedchamber as the other mural decorations in this room,
where it formed the central point of one of the large
white fields. The original arrangement will be understood by a reference to No. 1073. A girl is seen sitting

on a chair, and daintily drawing forward her mantle with
her right hand. In point of drawing and style it calls
for the same remarks as the principal scene in No. 1069.

Mon. dell' Inst., xii, T. 26, No. 6; Ann., 1885, p. 316. — In its
design the figure recalls a figure of Cassandra (or Manto) in a mural
painting from Herculaneum (*Helbig*, Wandgewälde, No. 203), but
its style is more severe.

1073 (8).

Much faded. In the middle of each of the white
panels is a standing female figure, the style of which
corresponds to those in No. 1072.

Mon. dell' Inst., xii, 25 (to the left); Ann. dell' Inst.. 1885,
pp. 313 et seq. *Lessing und Mau*, T. 2.

1074 (9).

A seated girl pours oil out of a bulky bottle (an *Aryballos*) into a slender lecythos. In design, drawing, and
style this figure resembles those on Nos. 1072, 1073.

Gazette archéologique, viii (1883), Pl. 16, p. 100. Mon. dell'
Inst., xii, T. 26, No. 5; Ann. dell' Inst., 1885, p. 316.

1075 (10). Roman Portrait-Head of the Republican Period.

Found in the Tiber. The cut below the left corner
of the mouth was caused by the dredging machine.

The extant portraits of the republican era prove that
the ancient Romans, of a date which has yet to be definitely settled by farther investigation, were in the habit
of shaving, not only their face, but also the entire skull.
This custom is best known to us from the so-called bust
of the Elder Scipio in the Capitoline Museum (No. 484),
and thus it has been customary to identify with Scipio
all similar portraits that show any resemblance to the
Capitoline example and that have a scar on the head or
face. The head before us is shaven, and there is something
like a scar above the forehead; and thus the Roman
ciceroni see in it a portrait of the victor of Zama. It is,
however, obvious that during the prevalence of the custom

referred to, there must have been many noble Romans who were wounded in the head. The head in the Museo delle Terme and the bust in the Capitol cannot possibly represent the same individual. Not only do they differ from each other in the shape of the skull and in the features, but the wounds are on different parts of the head. The identification of the Capitoline bust with Scipio may have some justification, but there are absolutely no grounds for such an identification in the case of the head before us. The latter wears an ill-humoured and philistine expression, and shows no trace of intelligence, ability, or power of idealization — qualities which we should expect in a portrait of Scipio and which are distinctly visible in the Capitoline bust. Besides, we know that the Elder Scipio died at the age of 52, while the head in this museum is that of a much older man.

The glass-case in the middle of this room contains smaller antiquities mainly found in the Tiber. The following four objects may be noticed (Nos. 1076-1079).

In the upper part of the case, —

1076. **Bronze Figure of Aphrodite.**

The goddess is represented nude and in the act of wringing the water from her tresses. Like many similar ones, this type seems to be derived from the famous painting by Apelles of Aphrodite rising from the sea.

On the types derived from the picture of Apelles, see *Stephani*, Compte-rendu pour 1870 et 1871, pp. 78 et seq. Comp. Athen. Mittheilungen, I (1876), pp. 50 et seq.

1077. **Bronze Figure of a Lar**.

The right hand (now wanting) held a rhyton, the outstretched left hand a cup. Comp. No. 551. The execution is good but dry.

In the lower part of the case, —

1078. **Bronze Sistrum.**

Instruments like this played a prominent part in the

worship of Isis (comp. No. 146). The fact that so many rattles of this kind, as well as other objects connected with the Egyptian cults, have been found in the Tiber, may be explained by the edicts published by the Roman government from time to time against the practice of these cults within the city, one result of which was that the apparatus used in them was simply thrown into the river. Josephus, indeed, relates (Jewish Antiquities, XVIII, 3, 4) that in consequence of an edict of Tiberius this fate befell an image of the goddess Isis, — probably the image in the main sanctuary of the goddess (near S. Maria sopra Minerva), which formed the focus of the cult.

1079. Bronze Helmet.

Found in 1891 below the Ponte Sisto.

This helmet seems too heavy for use in actual warfare, and was probably made either as a votive offering or for placing on a statue. On each side is a flower, emerging from a scheme of foliage, and provided with a deep hole for the insertion of a plume. The horizontal tubes on the lower edge of the cap were doubtless used for fastening the check-guards.

Notizie degli scavi, 1891, p. 287.

Room IX.

The mural decorations and fragments of decorations in this room were found in the bedchamber marked No. 4 in the Plan of the house in the Farnesina garden (Notizie degli scavi, 1880, T. IV).

1080 (1).

The pictures on this section of wall are all in the Hellenistic style. To the left, above, on a dark-violet ground, is a girl seated on a bench beside a herma, drawing her mantle over her shoulder with her right hand, and looking downwards in a reverie. A scene farther to the right represents a young man and woman probably

a hetæra), sitting upon a bed and kissing each other; in
the background is a servant preparing something to drink.
On a table at the foot of the bed stand a cantharos and a
tall cylindrical vessel, while beside the table is a youthful
slave, apparently holding a small ladle *(simpulum)* in his
right hand. A female slave, who has drawn her cloak
over her head on account of the chilliness of the night,
approaches the table with another cylindrical vessel.

On the paintings, see Mon. dell' Inst., XII, T. 7a, No. 3, T. 8,
No. 3; Ann. dell' Inst., 1884, p. 321.

1081 (2).

The central scene, which is sadly faded, represents a
young woman, seated on a chair and carrying on a lively
conversation with a half-grown girl, standing on tiptoe
in front of her. A roe-deer is grazing in the foreground.
The style recalls that of the Attic lecythi, with a white
ground, of about the transition from the fifth to the fourth
century B.C. On the other hand the scenes in the upper
part of the decoration show the usual Hellenistic style.
On each side of the central scene, adjoining the upper
parts of the columns enclosing it, is painted, on a dark-
violet ground, a girl standing in front of a herma and
playing with a hare. The pictures to the right and left
of these figures each represent a pair of lovers. In that
to the left we recognize a young couple in the first night
of their wedded life. The girl, modestly looking towards
the ground, resembles the bride in the Aldobrandine
Nuptials (No. 958). The woman in the corresponding
scene to the right seems to be a hetæra. The lovers lie
on a bed and kiss each other in the presence of two
slaves. The name of the artist Seleukos is engraved on
the column to the left of the last scene (see p. 221).

On the general scheme of decoration, see Mon. dell' Inst., XII,
5a; Ann. dell' Inst., 1884, pp. 309 et seq. *Lessing und Mau*, T. 5. —
On the central scene: Mon. dell' Inst., XII, T. 6, No. 1; Ann., 1884,
p. 319. —On the smaller scenes: Mon. dell' Inst., XII, T. 7a, Nos. 1,
2, T. 8, Nos. 1, 2; Ann., 1884, pp. 321, 322.

1082 (3).

The central scene, almost entirely obliterated, represents three beautiful women, apparently preparing to offer a sacrifice to the image of a female deity.

On the general scheme of decoration: Mon. dell' Inst., xii, 17; Ann., 1885, p. 302. *Lessing und Mau*, T. 6. — On the main scene: Mon. dell' Inst., xii, T. 6, No. 1; Ann., 1884, p. 319.

1083 (4).

In this fragment we recognize a standing figure of Zeus, marked by a strikingly melancholy expression. The god holds a thunderbolt in his right hand, and a sceptre in his left. The writer cannot explain the round object with which the sceptre is crowned.

Gazette archéologique, viii (1883), Pl. 15, p. 99. Mon. dell' Inst., xii, T. 7, No. 5; Ann., 1884, p. 320.

Room X.

1084 (1). Head of a Sleeping Maiden.

> Found in the Villa of Nero at Subiaco, in the same room as No. 1051.

The statue of which this admirably executed head was part belonged to the category of plastic representations styled by ancient critics ἀναπαυόμεναι, or the 'resting'. On the right side of the head is a depression, which seems to be of ancient origin and can be best explained by the supposition that something has been chiselled away here. This may have been the girl's hand, which she had placed on her head in a manner frequently encountered in ancient representations of resting figures. The deep breathing of the fair sleeper is indicated naturally and charmingly in the treatment of the half-opened mouth. The expression shows a slight trace of melancholy. As there are no determinative attributes, we have to give up the idea of a definite identification; but the fillet seems to indicate a mythical personage rather than a genre-figure. The suggestion that it is a copy of the dying Jocasta of Silanion (comp. No. 276) is untenable; it is quite obvious that we have to do with sleep, not death. Besides, the forms of Jocasta would be fuller and more matronly. The style points to an original of about the middle of the fourth century B. C.

Notizie degli scavi, 1884, p. 427. Jahrbuch des Arch. Instituts, v (1890). p. 167. note 77. — On the ἀναπαυόμεναι, see Rheinisches Museum, xxv (1870), pp. 153-155.

The wall-paintings Nos. 1085-1087 were found in the house of the Farnesina garden, in the Crypto-Porticus marked No. 1 on the Plan.

1085 (12).

The framed pictures are entirely obliterated. The Sphinx and the Androsphinx, couched opposite each other under the projecting vestibules, again point to Alexandria, where the various phases of Græco-Roman decoration were developed.

Mon. dell' Inst., xii, 28; Ann., 1835, pp. 316 et seq. *Lessing und Mau*, T. i.

Among the smaller paintings, attention may be paid to the two that are best preserved.

1086 (15).

A priestess, clad in a Doric chiton, advances slowly, holding the colossal key of a temple with both hands. In front of her moves a half-grown girl, holding a branch in her right hand, while her left steadies a flat dish of fruit and herbs on her head.

Mon. dell' Inst., xii, T. 34, No. 3; Ann., 1885, p. 318.

1087 (16).

This scene seems to have to do with the preparation of a sacrifice at a rustic fane. A bearded man, clad in chiton, cloak, and shoes, advances bearing a large sack on his back and also a square chest hanging from a strap over his left shoulder. His right hand rests on a staff, and he looks round at a girl following him, who supports a round box on her head with her left hand. To judge from the rude features and his general bearing, the man must be a peasant.

Mon. dell' Inst., xii, T. 34, No. 1; Ann., 1885, p. 318.

The two paintings, Nos. 1086 and 1087, and a number of others which may be passed over on account of their bad preservation, are very inferior in execution to the rest of the decorative scheme of which they form a part. Obviously they were inserted at a later period, when the pictures which originally occupied their spaces had been defaced.

Room XI.

1088. Fine Bust of Antoninus Pius.

Found in the Stadium of the Palatine. The end of the nose is modern.

Notizie degli scavi, 1893, p. 163b.

1089. Statuette of a Woman, in grey marble (bigio).

Found in the Tiber, near the Ponte Cestio.

A fully draped woman, with her hair hanging over her back, sits on a richly decorated chair and supports herself on her left arm. The right arm rested on the lap, while the hand drew the mantle over the right shoulder. The execution, which imitates the technique of bronze, is delicate but dry.

Römische Mittheilungen, vi (1891), p. 239. Notizie degli scavi, 1892, p. 267e; the statuette is here described as of white marble, obviously because the writer attributed the grey colour to the Tiber mud.

1090. Bust of Faustina the Elder.

Found on the Appian Way.

1091. Mural Decoration.

This was found in the semicircular corridor marked No. 6 in the Plan (Notizie degli scavi, 1880, T. iv) of the house in the Farnesina garden (comp. above, p. 220).

The frieze is adorned with landscapes alternating with groups of scenic masks, to which other objects connected with the stage or the cult of Dionysos are occasionally added. The groups of masks betoken the influence of Alexandrian art.

Mon. dell' Inst., xII, 5; Ann., 1884, p. 307. *Lessing und Mau*, T. 11. — On masks in the art of Alexandria: Abhandlungen der philol.-hist. Classe der sächsischen Gesellschaft der Wissenschaften, xiv (1894), pp. 449-452.

Room XII.

1092 (1). **Head of Socrates**.

Found in 1892, in digging the foundations for the monument to Victor Emmanuel. The front of the nose, two spots on the forehead above the eyes, and the left eyelid are modern.

This head reproduces the same type as that in the Capitol (No. 164), but the execution is better.

Notizie degli scavi, 1892, p. 345, No. 6.

1093 (2). **Slab with Fragments of Mosaic**.

The mosaics inserted in this slab were found in the villa excavated at Tusculum in 1741. The theory that they formed part of the floor of which the mosaic No. 320 was the centre lacks sufficient evidence. Formerly in the Museo Kircheriano.

The fragments include four scenic masks and three hovering figures of Victory. The Nike in the middle holds her fluttering mantle with both hands; the central part of the mantle seems to be a modern restoration. The second Nike holds a tropæon, the third an oar, indicative of a naval victory.

Canina, Descrizione dell' antico Tuscolo, T. 45, p. 158. Comp. *Visconti*, Museo Pio-Clem., vii, pp. 231, 232, note. *De Ruggiero*, Catalogo del Museo Kircheriano, i, p. 268, Nos. 4-10.

Nearly all the other mosaics in this room came from an ancient villa on the Via Cassia, between the 16th and 17th milestones, which was excavated in 1873. When the mosaics described below come from elsewhere, it is

expressly so stated. The ancient name of *Praetorium Fusci*
has been handed down as applied to part of the buildings
above referred to. The villa seems to have belonged to
Pescennius Niger, son of Annius Fuscus, and to have
passed into the hands of the Emp. Septimius Severus by
confiscation. We have direct testimony that Caracalla
built in this district, and the same seems to be true of
his brother Geta[1]. The mosaics found in the villa are
generally known as the Mosaics of Baccano, from the
Statio ad Baccanus or *Vaccanas* (the modern Baccano),
which lies on the Via Cassia, at the 21st milestone.
Their style points to the reign of Septimius Severus or
his immediate successors, while the rude attempts at
restoration visible in most of the pieces obviously date
from the later period of the decadence. The mosaics were
placed in the Museo Kircheriano before they were brought
to the Museo delle Terme.

1091 (Slab 2).

The mosaic in the upper part of the slab, to the right,
represents, apparently, a mythical scene, which the writer
does not venture to interpret. On the ground, in front
of the rocky background, sits a gigantic nude figure, resembling Hellenistic types of Polyphemos. His bearded
head is enwreathed in foliage and the skin of an animal
is wrapped round his right arm. By his left side hangs a
syrinx, attached to a band passing over his right shoulder.
In front of him stands a youth in Phrygian dress, laying
his left hand on a basis or altar, adorned with a red
ribbon. The giant's face is turned towards the youth and
his left arm outstretched, while the latter seems to listen
attentively to the animated harangue of his huge neighbour.

---

[1] *De Rossi*, Bull. di archeologia cristiana, 2nd series, vi (1875),
pp. 148-150. In the excavation of the villa a leaden pipe (now missing)
was found, the inscription on which was read as C. SEPTIMI GETA
(*Lanciani*, I commentarii di Frontino intorno le acque e gli acquedotti,
p. 259, No. 3XI). The suggestion is obvious that probably we should read
P. (Publius) for C., and refer the inscription to the brother of Caracalla.

Bull. dell' Inst., 1873, p. 132. *De Ruggiero*, Catalogo del Museo Kircheriano, I, p. 276, No. 22.

The mosaic in the upper part of the slab, to the left, represents the Rape of Ganymede. Comp. No. 400.

Bull. dell' Inst., 1873, p. 131. *De Ruggiero*, p. 274, No. 17.

The mosaic to the right, below, is a bucolic scene. A shepherd, clad in a nebris, sits on a rock and is about to clean the tubes of his syrinx with a small stick. On the ground beside him lie a pedum and a yellow satchel (of leather?). In front of him stands a goat. In the background, to the right, are a small temple and its sacred tree (comp. Nos. 743, 808). To the left, on an elevation above the goat, is a second shepherd, extending his left arm and gazing out of the picture.

Bull. dell' Inst., 1873, p. 134. *De Ruggiero*, p. 276, No. 22.

The mosaic to the left, below, shows the blinded Polyphemos sitting on a rock at the entrance of his cavern and examining with both hands the fleece of the ram, below whose belly Odysseus is concealed. The hero, who wears the pileus, is represented as of very small proportions in comparison with the gigantic Cyclops.

Bull. dell' Inst., 1873, p. 132. *De Ruggiero*, p. 277, No. 23.

1094a (Slab 5).

To the right, above, is the figure of a Muse, which has been rudely restored in ancient times and is now much mutilated. It belonged to the same cycle as the Muse on Slab 6, whose attributes are distinctly recognizable.

Bull. dell' Inst., 1873, p. 130. *De Ruggiero*, p. 280, No. 31.

To the left, above, is a youthful female form, scantily draped in a fluttering mantle and wearing a stephané on her head. Her right hand rests on the beak of a bird in front of her. The suggestion has been made that this is Leda and the swan; but the bird, to judge from its shape, its colour, and the absence of webbed feet, is not a swan but an eagle. It would thus seem that the mosaic depicts Hebe, with the eagle of Zeus.

Bull. dell' Inst., 1873, p. 131. *De Ruggiero*, p. 279, No. 29.

Below, to the right, is the punishment of Marsyas. To the left is Marsyas hanging by the arms from a tree, in the manner familiar to us in plastic representations (comp. Nos. 576, 846). A slave is busy fastening his feet to the tree. On the ground lies the double flute of the victim. To the right sits Apollo, holding the cithara in his left hand and looking before him with calm indifference. In front of the god kneels the young Olympos, with a Phrygian cap on his head, beseeching Apollo to spare his master. To the right of Apollo stands Artemis, armed with bow and quiver and wearing the dentated crown, which is so often assigned to her in the mural paintings of Campania. Behind the god is a female figure, presumably Nike, holding out a wreath towards Apollo.

Bull. dell' Inst., 1873, p. 128. *De Ruggiero*, p. 276, No. 21.

Below, to the left, is a bearded man, of brown complexion, wearing a chaplet of reeds and sitting on the ground. His right hand supports a cornucopia filled with herbs and fruit, among which figs and pomegranates are recognizable. His left hand holds an olive-branch (?). The legs are covered with a green mantle. The crown of reeds and the attitude betoken a river-god, for whom the cornucopia is also a suitable attribute (comp. vol. I, No. 47 and p. 291).

Bull. dell' Inst., 1873, p. 135. *De Ruggiero*, p. 280, No. 33.

1095 (Slab 6).

Above, to the right, is a figure of a Muse, already freely restored in antiquity. To this restoration is apparently to be ascribed the indistinct form of the attribute in the left hand, which looks most like a diptych. As Clio is elsewhere distinctly recognizable in this cycle of Muses, we may assume that the present figure is Calliope (comp. vol. I, p. 191).

Bull. dell' Inst., 1873, p. 130. *De Ruggiero*, p. 275, No. 19.

Above, to the left, is the Muse of tragedy, supporting a tragic mask with her left hand. The letter E, visible to the right of the head, is evidently the last of the name Melpomene.

De Ruggiero, p. 279, No. 30.

Below, to the right, is Polyhymnia, identified by an inscription.

Bull. dell' Inst., 1873, p. 130. *De Ruggiero*, p. 275, No. 18.

Below, to the left, is Clio, identified by the incorrect inscription CLION. She holds a diptych in the left hand and a stylus in the right. Comp. No. 274.

Bull. dell' Inst., 1873, p. 130. *De Ruggiero*, p. 275, No. 20.

1096 (Slab 7).

Above, to the right, is an Eros, riding on a sea-goat and holding a palm-branch in his right hand. Below is a dolphin.

Bull. dell' Inst., 1873, p. 134. *De Ruggiero*, p. 280, No. 32.

Above, to the left, is a combat between the Bacchic thiasos and the Indians. This mosaic is not one of the Baccano series, but was found in the villa, excavated at Tusculum in 1741, from which Nos. 320 and 1093 also came. As it has been freely restored by a modern hand, it is difficult to determine its original content. We see a reed-crowned Satyr brandishing a pedum against a warrior clad in the skin of some animal, while a Bacchante, armed with some object apparently misunderstood by the restorer, attacks a youth sitting on the ground. The latter seems to be wounded. The Indians are not fully armed, as usual in representations of this kind, but wear the most primitive equipments, such as the skin of the first-mentioned warrior. Their lack of characteristic weapons is probably to be ascribed to the defective condition of the mosaic.

Ann. dell' Inst., 1879, Tav. d'agg. G, pp. 66-79. *De Ruggiero*, p. 270, No. 11.

1097 (8). Head of a Youth.

Found in the Tiber.

Since the expression of this head betokens both terror and physical anguish, we may naturally enough assume that it belongs to one of the companions of Odysseus in the grip of Scylla, and that it formed part of a group like that indicated in the fragment in the Vatican, No. 66.

1098 (Slab 9). Four Mosaics of the Factiones Circenses.

The passionate interest that the Romans of the Empire took in the Circus races was largely due to the organisation of the parties of the circus. These parties were distinguished by the colours which prevailed in the dress of the charioteers and in the adornment of the chariot. Disregarding those that were merely temporary, we find four such parties under the emperors: the Reds *(factio russata)*, the Whites *(f. albata)*, the Greens *(f. prasina)*, and the Blues *(f. veneta)*. Our mosaics represent each of these parties by the figure of a charioteer, holding a horse by the bridle with one hand and wielding a whip with the other. The horses are probably the *sinistri funales* — *i.e.* the left (or near) outside horses of the *quadriga*, which had the most dangerous position, next to the *metae* (comp. Nos. 337–339). The charioteers wear tunics of the colour of the factio to which they respectively belong. All four wear a long-sleeved knitted under-garment beneath their tunics. The thorax is protected by the arrangement seen in the statue at the Vatican (No. 334) and in the hermæ Nos. 1007–1013 in this museum. The representative of the *factio russata* also wears the straps round the thighs we have already seen in the Vatican statue; the charioteer of the *factio albata* wears greaves over his short hose. The helmet-like caps are coloured blue or grey, which seems to indicate that they are of steel, not, as often, of leather.

Ersilia-Caetani-Lovatelli, Antichi monumenti illustrati, T. xiii, xiiibis, pp. 143–163 (also in the Atti dell' Accademia dei Lincei, serie terza, Memorie della classe delle scienze morali, vol. VII, 1881, pp. 149-156).

1099 (10). **Portrait-Head of a Hellenistic Ruler.**

It is obvious that this head is a portrait, though both the features and the arrangement of the hair strongly recall certain types of Satyrs. The style points to the Hellenistic period; the fillet indicates a ruler. The reason that induced a Hellenistic ruler to have his portrait executed in the guise of a Satyr must have been of a highly original character. Perhaps he stood in some relation of dependance on one of the great sovereigns, who played the rôle of the 'New Dionysos' (comp. No. 221); and the vassal may have tried, with well-calculated flattery, to indicate his subordinate part by assuming the modest rôle of a member of the thiasos standing in close relation to Dionysos.

1100 (Slab 11, below). **Mosaic of a Wrestling Match between Eros and Pan.**

The contest is practically decided in favour of Eros. The winged boy has seized his opponent by one of his horns and is about to throw him to the earth, while the wrathful Pan rolls his eyes till little is seen of them but the white. Adjacent stand Silenus and a Satyr, the latter raising his right arm as if to enjoin the combatants to cease their struggle.

Bull. dell' Inst., 1873, p. 132. *De Ruggiero*, p. 281, No. 35.

1101 (Slab 12). **Mosaic Bust of a Woman.**

The forms are full and voluptuous; the head is crowned with a garland of leaves and violets and other flowers. As the former environment of this bust is unknown, it is difficult to offer any explanation of it. It may possibly have belonged to a series representing the seasons, in which it may have personified spring.

Bull. dell' Inst., 1873, pp. 134, 135. *De Ruggiero*, p. 281, No. 34.

Room XIII.

Among the mural paintings in this room, those of the greatest general interest are the series marked with No. 1 in white, while the individual pictures also bear the small bronze numbers (19, 21, 22, and 26) by which they were formerly catalogued in the Museo Kircheriano. These paintings were found in a Columbarium excavated in 1875 on the Esquiline, near the Columbarium built for the dependants of the Statilii[1], where they formed a frieze running above the uppermost row of the niches that contained the urns. The construction of the Columbarium indicates the end of the Republic or the beginning of the Empire, and we may attribute the paintings to the same period. The subjects refer to the founding of the three cities of Lavinium, Alba Longa, and Rome, which tradition connects so closely with each other. The version of the story on which they are based is one that was popular with the Roman public at the era above indicated, and which shows no trace of the influence of Virgil's Æneid. It is easy to see that the representation avoids the miraculous whenever it can. The episode of Rhea Silvia and Mars (bronze number 26), forming, as it does, the starting-point of the legend, could not be omitted; but it is, to say the least, significant that the painter has avoided a representation of the she-wolf and the twins, though this had become, as it were, the popular emblem of Rome. It would thus seem that the version of the legend on which the paintings were based had been determined by a rationalistic view of history.

The painter has drawn no sharp lines of demarcation between the individual scenes, but has placed them side by side without external signs of separation. This method was fore-shadowed in the treatment of the accessory groups in Hellenistic landscapes (comp. No. 956), but does not seem to have been followed in figure-paintings or in reliefs until the Roman period, where we meet it

[1] See Plan in *Brizio*, Pitture e sepoleri scoperti nell' Esquilino, T. I d, and in Corpus inscr. lat., VI, 2, p. 982L.

in the paintings before us and in the reliefs of cochlear (or spiral-banded) columns and sarcophagi.

These mural paintings have suffered considerably, partly at least in ancient days. In the third century of the present era, when the practice of interment had got the upper hand of cremation, the Columbarium was transformed into a burial-place for unburned bodies. At the same time a restoration of its mural decoration was begun, though never finished. In this restoration the paintings on the east wall (No. 20) and the adjoining scenes on the north and south walls (Nos. 19, 21) were sadly injured. Incisions, intended for the attachment of a new fresco-ground, were made in them with the chisel. When the Columbarium was discovered in 1875, it was found that the fresco-ground had fallen off, both at the beginning and at the end of the series of pictures. Other pieces have since become detached. Further, for the first 10 or 15 years after the opening of the Columbarium many of the scenes were accompanied by inscriptions in black paint, giving short explanations of the subjects represented. Now, nothing can be deciphered of these inscriptions except a few isolated letters. Finally, the outlines and colours of the figures have greatly faded throughout the whole frieze. Those, therefore, who wish to make a thorough investigation of the paintings must have recourse to the drawings made of them soon after the opening of the Columbarium, when they were still in comparatively good preservation. In regard to the defaced originals, the writer must content himself with the briefest characterization and a statement of what he believes to be the most probable interpretation of their subjects. In doing so he follows, not the present arrangement of the pictures in the museum, but the chronological order they occupied in the Columbarium.

1102 (22). **Paintings on the West Wall.**

To the right, when the scene was better preserved, could be seen a group of workmen, occupied in rearing

a city-wall with blocks of hewn stone. This doubtless
referred to the foundation of Lavinium. The following
painting, which extended to the adjacent part of the
S. wall, seems to have been the representation of a battle
between the united Latins and Trojans and the Rutulians.
The allies appear as the civilized warriors, equipped with
helmet, armour, and oval shields, while the Rutulians
fight more or less in a state of nudity and bear oblong
wooden (?) shields.

Brizio, Pitture e sepolcri scoperti nell' Esquilino, T. 2, parete
ovest, pp. 11, 15 et seq. Mon. dell' Inst., x, 60, parete I; Ann.,
1878, pp. 240, 241.

1103 (21). Paintings on the South Wall.

The main episode of the battle is represented at the
beginning of the wall. Æneas has just slain Turnus,
who lies at his feet (now almost undistinguishable).
Victoria advances towards the conqueror, with a palm-
branch in her left hand and holding out a wreath to him
with her right. To the extreme right of the battle sits a
bearded river-god, holding a reed in his left hand — a
figure which indicates that the battle represented is that of
the river Numicius. The group behind the river-god personifies the conclusion of peace. Two warriors extend their
right hands to each other, one recognizable as a leader
of the allies by his oval shield, while the other is marked
out by his oblong shield as a leader of the opposite
party. The next scene represents the erection of another
city-wall. The assumption that this refers to Alba Longa
is probable enough in itself and receives confirmation
from the fact that the word *Alba* occurred in the inscription formerly legible under the painting. With a kind
of prolepsis not uncommon in ancient art the painter
has represented the goddess of the nascent city seated
on a block of stone before its rising walls and adorned
with a mural crown. The scene that closes the series of
paintings on the left side of the south wall offers great
difficulties of interpretation. The chief personages are

two young women, seated and carrying on what seems a
melancholy conversation with a young man standing in
front of them. A third female figure, corresponding in
all respects to the just-mentioned goddess of Alba Longa,
extends her right hand to the nearer of the seated women,
as if to solicit her attention. One supposition is that the
young man is Ascanius, ceding the city of Lavinium to
Lavinia, his father's widow, after the foundation of Alba
Longa. In this case Lavinia would be the seated figure
to the right, whom the goddess of Lavinium is inviting
to the city she represents. The other seated figure, the
upper part of whose body is nude, is explained as the
Nymph Egeria.

Brizio, T. 2, parete sud, pp. 12, 16-18. Mon. dell' Inst., x,
60, parete II a b; Ann., 1878, pp. 241 et seq.

1104 (20). Paintings on the East Wall.

The paintings on this wall have suffered to such an
extent that their subjects can be recognized either with
great difficulty or not at all. The first scene has been
explained as Rhea Silvia, compelled by her uncle, King
Amulius of Alba Longa, to become a vestal virgin. If
this be correct, the seated man supporting his left hand
on a sceptre would be Amulius, while the standing figure
beside him would be Numitor, trying to induce his
brother to revoke the harsh decree. The seated and
mourning girl immediately behind Numitor must be
Rhea Silvia. The matronly figure laying her right hand
on Rhea Silvia's shoulder would be the wife of Amulius,
persuading the girl to submit to her fate. The other
girls are simply companions of Rhea Silvia. The meaning of the next scene is clear. Mars surprises Rhea Silvia as she is fetching water, while Victoria flies down
to his aid. To the right are two peasants, fleeing in
terror at the sight of the god. Behind Mars sits a river-
god, with a reed in his left hand; while behind him in
turn stands a local goddess, holding a cornucopia in her
left hand and pointing with her right at Rhea Silvia and

Mars. The third scene has been explained, with some plausibility, as Amulius, in the presence of Numitor, pronouncing sentence on the erring vestal.

Brizio, T. 2, parete est, pp. 12, 13, 18-20. Mon. dell' Inst.. x, 60a, parete III; Ann., 1878, pp. 260 et seq.

1105 (19). Paintings on the North Wall.

So little was left of the first scene that nothing could be made of it even on the discovery of the Columbarium. The second scene represents the exposure of Romulus and Remus in the Tiber. On the bank sits the river-god, holding an oar in his right hand. The next scene refers to the life led by the twins with the shepherds after their rescue. The last part of the frieze, now missing, undoubtedly represented the closing scene of this series of mythological events, — *viz.* the foundation of Rome.

Brizio, T. 2, parete nord, pp. 13, 14, 21 et seq. Mon. dell' Inst., x, 60a, parete IV; Ann., 1878, pp. 275-278.

1106 (S). Mural Painting of Fortuna.

Found on the Aventine, in the same excavation as the mosaic No. 997. Formerly in the Museo Kircheriano.

The goddess is seated on a throne, holding a cornu-copia in her left hand and a rudder in her right. Her head is surrounded by a whitish nimbus (comp. No. 698). Among the contents of the cornucopia are ears of corn, two pomegranates, and a pine-cone.

De Ruggiero, Guida del Museo Kircheriano, p. 115, No. 8.

1107. Mural Painting.

Found in Ostia. Formerly in the Museo Kircheriano.

A youth is seated in a chair, with his sword by his side, and resting his left hand on a spear. He holds out his right hand towards an undistinguishable brown object (resembling a long ringlet?) held out by a girl standing in front of him. The scene may possibly represent

Scylla, handing to Minos the lock of hair cut from the head of her father Nisos (comp. No. 957).

De Ruggiero, Guida del Museo Kircheriano, p. 121, No. 23.

1108 (red number 12). **Cinerary Urn, with scenes from the Eleusinian Mysteries.**

> All that is known of the provenience of this urn is that it was found in a tomb on the Esquiline, not far from the Columbarium built for the freedmen and slaves of the Statilii.

One of the three groups on this urn depicts a young man, clad in a lion-skin and about to place a sucking-pig in an enclosure adorned with garlands (*puteal;* comp. Nos. 439, 685). A priest pours some liquid out of a vessel, either on the head of the pig or into the opening of the puteal. The two objects which the young man holds in his left hand are probably round loaves of bread. The left hand of the priest supports a dish containing three poppy-heads. The following group obviously represents some symbolical action usual in the initiation into the mysteries. The novice sits in a chair covered with a lion's hide; his face is veiled and he holds a torch in his left hand. A woman, standing behind him, holds over his head the basket (λίκνον), or symbol of purification (comp. No. 1059). The ram's horn visible between his feet perhaps refers to the sacrifice made by the Daduchos, one of the priests of Eleusis. The third group shows Demeter and Kora (Persephone), the two great goddesses of Eleusis, the former seated and the latter standing behind her. Each of them holds a large torch, Demeter also a bunch of ears of corn. In front of the older goddess is a youth clad in a long fringed chiton, a nebris, and a cloak, resting his left hand on a club and caressing with his right a serpent uprearing itself on Demeter's lap. Archæologists have tried to connect the three scenes with each other by the assumption that they represent the three grades of initiation into the Eleusinian mysteries. The first two scenes would depict the inferior grades, while the third embodies the highest grade, in which the initiate is honoured by the sight of the dread goddesses themselves. On this assumption, however, we should expect the face of the initiate, where not concealed, to show the same type in each scene. This, however, is not the case. The countenance of the young man with the pig is of an individual character, while that of the youth standing before the Eleusinian goddesses is of a decidedly ideal type. The lion-skin in the first scene and the club in the third have led some authorities to the conclusion that the person represented is Heracles, of whose initiation into the Eleusinian mysteries various myths were current. But the head of neither figure is at all suitable for this hero, not to speak of the discrepancy in showing Heracles first in a lion-skin and then in a nebris.

It would also appear that the reliefs before us refer, not to the genuine and original Eleusinian mysteries, but to those of Alexandria. One of the suburbs of Alexandria was named Eleusis, and the Attic festival and its ceremonies were celebrated here with great pomp. On the urn Demeter wears a vertical plume of wheat-ears over her forehead. No similar feature is known to occur in any purely Hellenic representation of the goddess, whereas she is shown with just such an adornment in goldsmith's work found on Egyptian soil. The supposition that this attribute was invented in Alexandria is confirmed by the fact that it sometimes occurs in representations of Isis; for we may assume that most, if not all, of the Hellenistic types of the Egyptian goddess were of Alexandrian origin. The fringe on the chiton of the youth caressing the snake is frequently encountered in figures of Egyptian priests and priestesses of the Hellenistic era. The individual features of the young man with the pig also correspond to a well-known tendency of Alexandrian art. And, lastly, the scale-ornamentation of the lid of the urn occurs in Hellenistic, and especially in Alexandrian decoration.

Ersilia Caetani - Lovatelli, in Bull. della commissione arch. comunale, vii (1879), T. ii, iii, pp. 5 et seq., and in the Antichi monumenti illustrati, T. ii, iii, pp. 25 et seq. Comp. *Preller-Robert*, Griechische Mythologie, i, pp. 790, 791, note 5. — On the Eleusinian Mysteries at Alexandria, see Verhandlungen der 40. Philologenversammlung in Görlitz (1889), pp. 310 et seq. — On Egyptian goldsmith's work, see Abhandlungen der philol.-hist. Classe der sächsischen Gesellschaft der Wissenschaften, xiv (1894), p. 307, Fig. 39.

The Etruscan Museum in the Vatican.

(Museo Gregoriano Etrusco.)

The Museo Etrusco, founded in 1836 by Pope Gregory XVI., was originally intended as the depository for the numerous antiquities discovered since 1828 in Western Etruria, while at the same time the collection of similar articles previously in the Vatican was incorporated with the new museum. Subsequent discoveries made from time to time in Rome and Latium were added, and Pius IX. also placed here his various acquisitions. A few years ago the entire collection was re-arranged on a new system under the superintendence of Sig. C. L. Visconti (d. 1894). In the following description we begin with the vestibule, then enter the rooms to the right containing the funeral urns and terracottas, beyond which is the collection of vases, and finally return through the rooms with the bronzes.

Museo Etrusco-Gregoriano, Rome, 1842, 2 vols. (the first edition, privately circulated, is distinguished below by the prefix 'A'). Comp. Arch. Zeitung, xxxvii (1879), pp. 34 et seq. *(Klügmann)*. A detailed scientific catalogue of the Museum is in preparation.

Vestibule.

Three Terracotta Sarcophagi, with figures on the covers.

Of the recumbent figures of the deceased resting upon the lids the two male figures lie supine and asleep, one

(No. 12) with his right arm under his head, while the richly adorned female figure (No. 15) is supported by a cushion in a half-sitting posture. All the motives are conceived in a thoroughly realistic spirit; the details of the movement are in many points accurately observed, and an attempt at portraiture is made in the heads. But there is a striking contrast between this realism and the absolute want of skill and appreciation that are conspicuous in the erroneous proportions of the long, lank bodies. These sarcophagi probably date from the first or second century B. C.

Found in 1834 near Toscanella. Mus. Gregor., I, T. xcii (A I, T. xlix). Comp. *Braun*, Ruinen und Museen, p. 831. *Martha*, L'art étrusque, pp. 347 et seq.

13, 17. Two Horses' Heads.

These heads, carved in nenfro or volcanic tufa, were placed at the entrance of a tomb at Vulci, and probably therefore had some funereal significance.

Mus. Gregor., I, T. xcvii (A II, T. ci), 2.

Room II.

The numerous Cinerary Urns of alabaster and travertine exhibited here were for the most part discovered at Volterra and Chiusi in Northern Etruria. Their material and execution amply prove them to be products of native industry, dating chiefly from the second and third centuries B.C. (comp. p. 289). The covers of these square urns usually bear figures of the deceased, in an easy recumbent position, with cups, wreaths, fruit, fans, or similar attributes in their hands. No. 56, an alabaster urn in good preservation, has on its lid a man and wife in loving union.

The front of each urn is adorned with crudely executed reliefs, often coloured. These usually borrow their subjects from Greek mythology in its later developments, as modified by the dramatic poets; but the Greek

motive appears in an Etruscan garb, frequently disguised
by misapprehension or ugly distortion, and rendered obscure by the addition of figures from the Etruscan demonology. Representations of life and death according
to purely Etruscan conceptions are not infrequent. The
following urns are of special interest from the subjects
of their reliefs: No. 44 (and 67). "The last journey" (the
deceased on horseback, conducted by a spirit). — No. 56.
Death of Oinomaos in the chariot-race with Pelops. —
No. 60. Recognition of Paris. (Exposed as an infant by
Hecuba and reared by shepherds, Paris comes as a young
man to Troy, where funereal games are being celebrated in his honour, as he was believed to be dead;
taking part in the contests, he defeats all his brothers,
who in their jealous anger attack him with their weapons
and force him to take refuge at the altar of Zeus, until he
is recognized by his sister Cassandra.) — No. 61. Helen
and Paris embark with their suite for Troy. — No. 86.
Actæon torn to pieces by his hounds. — At the window,
repellant in the crudity of its execution, Iphigencia
at Aulis.

The most important specimens (formerly in the Appartamenti
Borgia; comp. Beschreibung Roms, II, 2, p. 25) are figured in Mus.
Gregor., I. T. xciv et seq. (A 2, T. cii et seq.), and in *Brunn und
Koerte*, I rilievi delle urne etrusche, I, Rome, 1870, II, 1, 1890.
Comp. *Schlie*, Darstellungen des Troischen Sagenkreises auf Etrusk.
Aschenkisten.

On the shelves are numerous terracotta and nenfro
portrait-heads, most of which were originally intended
to occupy some such position. The majority come from
tombs, but some were probably placed as votive offerings
in temples. The national types of the ancient Etruscans
are well illustrated by these heads. They are of different
dates and very unequal execution; but nearly all show a
lively appreciation of individual peculiarities, which are
so realistically reproduced that many of the faces seem
like modern portraits.

Room III.

105, 108, 111, 115, 118. **Primitive Italian Urns in the form of Huts.**

These curious vessels of blackish clay were found in the early-Italian necropolis between Albano and Marino, and were used as cinerary urns. In shape they are imitations of the earliest Italian abodes, simple huts *(tuguria)* with mud-walls and straw roofs held together by wooden beams crossing each other at the roof-tree and projecting above it (comp. No. 111). The compluvium, or opening in the roof, a distinctive feature of later dwellings, had not yet been evolved; light entered and smoke escaped by the wide doorway, which could be closed by a door fastened with a bolt (No. 105). The great antiquity of these vessels, which date from the beginning of the so-called First Iron Age (circa eighth century B.C.), is farther vouched for by the engraved ornamentation, which reproduces various motives of a primitive geometric style of decoration. They closely resemble the 'House Urns' found in Germany and Denmark, which also were used to preserve the ashes collected after the burning of a body. And on Greek soil also the custom of shaping tombs and cinerary urns — the abodes of the dead — on the model of the abodes of the living, may be traced back to the remotest antiquity.

A. Visconti, Lettera a Carnevali sopra alcuni vasi rinvenuti nelle vicinanze di Alba Longa, Rome, 1817. *Abeken*, Mittelitalien, p. 360. *Helbig*, Italiker in der Po-Ebene, pp. 50 et seq., 82, 95 (with bibliography of earlier works). Sitzungsberichte der Berliner Akademie, 1883, p. 1008 *(Virchow)*. Bonner Studien, p. 24 *(Von Duhn)*. Monum. ant. pubbl. per cura della reale Accademia dei Lincei, I (1890), pp. 210 et seq. *(Orsi)*.

106. **Marble Cinerary Urn.**

The front is carved in relief as a bed, upon which the figure of a beardless man on the cover is supposed to be lying. The bed is richly adorned with female figures ending in serpents as feet, and with a frieze of small boyish figures chasing birds (swans?) on the side. Between the legs of the bed is an Etruscan inscription.

Comp. *Dennis*, Cities and Cemeteries of Etruria, II³. p. 456.

110. Broken Pillar with an Inscription.

This stone is of great philological importance, for on each side is a short sentence in Celtic and Latin. On the better-preserved side the inscription runs: *Coi]sis Drutei f(ilius) frater eius minimus locavit et statuit. Ateknati Trutikni karnitu artuas Koisis Trutiknos*, i.e. 'Coisis, son of Drutos, has erected the tombstone *(artuas)* of Ategnatos, son of Drutos'.

From Todi. — *Pauli*, Altitalische Forschungen, I, pp. 12, 84 et seq. Corpus inscriptionum latinarum, XI, No. 4687, where earlier references are mentioned.

112. Colossal Head of Medusa.

This head is made of nenfro, or volcanic tufa, which is found at Corneto and other places in Etruria.

Mus. Gregor., I, T. xcvii (A II, T. ci), 3.

Tombstone in the shape of a Circular Temple.

This cylindrical tombstone, of nenfro, bears a relief of Ionic columns supporting an architrave with the following Etruscan inscription (now much defaced): *[Eca] suthi Thanchvilus Masnial*, i.e. 'this is the tomb of Tanchvil (Tanaquil) Masnia'.

Mus. Gregor., I, T. cv (A II, I, cv), 3. *Canina*, Etruria marittima, II, T. 109, 182. Comp. *Fabretti*, Corpus inscriptionum italicarum, No. 2602. *Corssen*, Sprache der Etrusker, I, p. 592. *Pauli*, Etrusk. Studien, III, p. 25.

Room IV.

In the centre, conspicuous by its size and excellent preservation, is a **Terracotta Statue of Hermes**, of elegant design and smooth finish, dating possibly from the late republican era. Part of the head, the cap, and the right arm with the caduceus are restorations.

Found in 1835 near Tivoli, at the same time, it is said, as Nos. 211 and 234. Mus. Gregor., A I, T. II.

The terracotta plaques, of which numerous specimens are here exhibited, were originally arranged in continuous series so as to form a kind of frieze upon walls. This style of decoration was borrowed by the Romans from the Greeks in Campania, and from the end of the republican period onwards was very common both in tombs and in country-houses. The tablets were manufactured in large quantities from moulds, and afforded an inexpensive and popular substitute for the marble and metal wall-incrustation, which had once more come into vogue in the Hellenistic period. The reliefs with which they are embellished borrow their subjects partly from the ornamental patterns of the highly developed decorative art of the fourth and third centuries, partly from the great pictorial compositions of the classic age.

154-157. Terracotta Frieze in high-relief.

From a rich garland two heads, each between a graceful pair of Cupids, project in high-relief. One is the head of a woman with vine-leaves and grapes in her hair (perhaps Ariadne?); the other, on which traces of painting may still be discerned, is the head of a youth. The delicate grace and freedom of the ornamentation refer the origin of the frieze to the early Hellenistic period.

Martha, L'art étrusque, p. 282. Comp. *Dennis*, Cities and Cemeteries of Etruria, II³, p. 456.

Terracotta Plaque : Scene from the Rape of the Leucippidæ.

One of the daughters of Leucippos is being carried off by a youth, whom the pileus and the star near his head identify as one of the Dioscuri, while a companion of the maiden is fleeing in consternation for aid.

Mus. Gregor., A I, T. xli, 5. *Campana*, Due sepolcri, T. viii B, and Antichi opere in plastica, T. 55. Archäol. Zeit., x, 1852, T. 40, 3, p. 489. Comp. *Benndorf*, Heroon von Gjölbaschi-Trysa, p. 165.

Terracotta Plaque: Heracles overcoming the Cretan Bull.

This tablet belongs to a series (preserved in many reproductions), representing the Labours of Heracles. Two other plaques in this room (Heracles and the Lernean hydra; Heracles and the Nemean lion) belong to the same series.

According to *Braun* (Ruinen und Museen, p. 831) these tablets were found amidst the ruins of Roma Vecchia, but according to *Abeken* (Mittelitalien, p. 3674) they were discovered along with No. 223 during Canova's excavations on the Via Appia (comp. Corp. Inscrip. lat., VI, 4, No. 26, 426). Mus. Gregor., A I, T. xli, 10. *Campana*, Antiche opere in plastica, T. xxii et seq. Comp. Arch. Zeit., IV, 1846, p. lxxii *(Gerhard)*.

168. Stucco Relief: Jupiter, Neptune, and Pluto.

Jupiter, as a long-haired youth, with sceptre and thunderbolt, is enthroned in the middle, his feet on the terrestrial globe. On his right sits the bearded Neptune; on his left, Pluto with his club, his head resting on his hand as though in sleep. There are some striking peculiarities, both in the general composition and in the treatment of the drapery, that have awakened suspicion as to the antique origin of this relief. Comp. No. 265.

Found in 1816 along with No. 265 in the Vigna Moroni, outside the Porta S. Sebastiano, in a tomb ascribed to the second century of our era (from the coffered decoration of the roof); afterwards in the Appartamenti Borgia. *Guattani*, Memorie enciclopediche, V, T. I, p. 49 (IV, pp. 33 et seq.). *Pistolesi*, Il Vaticano descritto, III, T. 36c, p. 103. Comp. Beschreibung Roms, II, 2, p. 9. *Overbeck*, Griech. Kunstmythologie, II, p. 566, note 70; III, p. 403, note 33.

On the principal wall of this room are a considerable number of Etruscan portrait-heads, and also a few interesting polychrome heads used for architectonic purposes (edging-tiles, antefixæ, acroteria). The manufacture of these latter, both by Greek artists (Damophilos and Gorgasos are named by tradition) and in Etruria in imitation of Greek models, received a great impetus at the end of the sixth century, which lasted until the second century B.C. (Comp. vol. I, p. 448).

Among the more interesting specimens, the following may be mentioned: No. 170 (above, to the left), Archaic Head of Silenus, with red face and black beard; 194 (above, to the right), Female head in a similar style; 246. Polychrome female head, in a style not yet free of archaic influences; fore-part of a very antique winged horse (on the floor), with the wing-feathers painted alternately red, white, and blue 'this perhaps adorned the angle of a pediment'.

197. Terracotta Plaque: Isis and Sphinxes.

Isis, with a lotus-blossom in her hair and the sistrum and offerings in her hands, rises from an acanthus-flower, between a bearded Sphinx and a female Sphinx. Egyptian motives of this kind were first used in this fanciful, decorative manner by the Greek sculptors of Alexandria, and were afterwards repeated a thousand times over in the art-industry of imperial Rome.

Mus. Gregor., A I, T. xl, 5. Comp. *Campana*, Opere in plastica, T. 113.

203. Terracotta Statue of a Seated Boy.

The child is represented with graceful realism. Clad in a cap and a shirt girt up in a roll round his waist, he places his right hand upon a bird. This statue was probably a votive offering, like the bronze figures of children, Nos. 283, 329, in Room IX (pp. 385, 393).

From Cervetri. — Mus. Gregor., A I, T. xlxii.

209. Terracotta Plaque: Bacchanalian Design.

A cantharos stands here between two panthers rampant, behind each of which a thyrsos is added to fill up the space. Above are traces of a Latin inscription, which included the maker's name.

Mus. Gregor., A I, T. xl, 6. Comp. *Benndorf und Schoene*, Bildwerke des lateran. Museums. pp. 387, 561. Corpus inscrip. latin., xv, No. 2556 (comp. Nos. 2539 et seq.).

211, 234, 266. Fragments of Terracotta Statues.

The free design and careful execution of the drapery
of these lifesize female statues point to some excellent
models of the third or fourth century. There are traces
of painting on the drapery.

Found in 1835 during the tunnelling of Monte Catillo near
Tivoli, and, it is alleged, at the same time as the statue of Hermes. —
Mus. Gregor., A I, T. l. Comp. *Braun*, Ruinen und Museen Roms,
p. 831. Museo italiano di antichità class., I, p. 937 *(Milani)*.

215. Painted Terracotta Sarcophagus: Adonis.

This sarcophagus represents in detail a bed richly
furnished with cushions and coverings. Upon it lies
supine the figure of a youth, in chlamys and hunting-
boots, with a wound in his left thigh. On the dais
beside him is his dog. The figure is Adonis, mortally
wounded by the boar. The youth for whom the sarcophagus was designed may have resembled the favourite
of Aphrodite in his early death, or in his love of hunting, his beauty, or the manner of his death. The work,
which is in good preservation, reproduces the skilfully
designed motive with intelligence and vivacity. The
strong Etruscan bent towards realism, here united with
Greek forms, asserts itself also in the painting. The flesh
parts are ruddy brown, the garments and mattress pink,
and the coverings blue.

Found at Toscanella in 1834. — Mus. Gregor., I, T. cxiii (A I,
T. xlvi), 1. *Daremberg-Saglio*, Dictionnaire des antiquités, I, p. 73.
Comp. *Braun*, Ruinen und Museen, p. 831.

223. Terracotta Plaque: Perseus with a Colossal Head of Medusa.

Found on the Via Appia along with the reliefs of the Labours
of Heracles (see above, p. 270). — Mus. Gregor., A I, T. xII, 8.
Comp. *Combe*, Ancient Terracottas in the British Museum, T. xI,
25. *Campana*, Opere in plastica, T. 56.

On the floor, —

265. Stucco Relief: Venus and Adonis.

This is the exact counterpart of No. 168. Beside
Adonis is a small Cupid busied in binding up the wound

in the youth's left thigh; to the left is Venus, her back towards the spectator.

Place of discovery, see under No. 168. — *Visconti-Guattani*, Museo Chiaramonti, T. a, III, 9, pp. 277, 350. *Guattani*, Memorie encicloped., v, T. 2. *Pistolesi*, Il Vaticano descritto, III, T. 36 A, p. 97. Comp. Beschreibung Roms, II, 2, p. 9.

Above the doors to the Third and Fifth Rooms are several terracotta *Feet*, votive gifts from convalescent invalids. On the window-wall are several noteworthy terracotta simatiles, with finely characterized ornament-ation in relief: fore-quarters of griffins and lions ending in wreaths of flowers; Arimaspi with ewer and goblet giving drink to seated griffins; Amazons in combat with gigantic griffins pressing hard upon them.

D'Agincourt, Recueil de sculpture antique en terre cuite, T. XI, 1-4. Mus. Gregor., A. 1, T. xl, 7-9. *Campana*, Opere in plastica, T. 78 et seq. Comp. Beschreibung Roms, II, 2, p. 19. Ann. dell' Inst., 1871, pp. 144 et seq. *(Roulez)*. *Klügmann*, Amazonen in Litteratur und Kunst, p. 55.

By the window-wall, —

Terracotta Plaque : Pelops and Hippodameia.

According to one version of the story, Oinomaos used to send his daughter Hippodameia herself with her successive wooers in their chariots while they were racing against him, by way of distracting their attention from the business in hand. This plaque represents Pelops, in Phrygian costume, and Hippodameia, in bridal veil, in a galloping four-horse chariot; a motive that may very possibly have been borrowed from some larger compo-sition based on the above version of the legend.

Winckelmann, Monumenti inediti, T. 117. Comp. *Friederichs-Wolters*, Berliner Gipsabgüsse, No. 1957. There are replicas of this motive in the Palazzo dei Conservatori (comp. vol. I, p. 449) and inthe Museo Kircheriano (Room I, No. 417).

To the left of the entrance, —

Terracotta Plaque: Egyptian House.

On this fragment we see, to the right, a round house with a stork (or ibis) standing on the roof, and, to the

left, a semi-nude female figure stretched on a couch.
The fragment is part of a larger representation of a Nile
landscape, which is extant in several replicas (*e.g.* in the
Museo Kircheriano; comp. p. 417).

D'Agincourt, Recueil de sculpture, T. 9, 2 (Beschreibung
Roms, II, 2, p. 19, 8). *Schreiber*, Kulturhistor. Bilderatlas, T. IIII, 9.
Comp. bibliography given under No. 40 on p. 417.

Rooms V-VIII.
Collection of Vases.

By far the greater number of the vases exhibited in
Rooms V-VIII were found in the tombs of Western Etruria
(Cære and Vulci), though, with very few exceptions, they
are not of native manufacture, but have been imported from
Greek cities in Asia Minor, Greece proper, or Southern
Italy. They owe their preservation to the pious custom
of furnishing the abodes of the dead with terracotta vessels, as well as with other domestic articles used by the
living. Thus all the varieties of vases in ordinary domestic use are represented in this collection from the
tombs: the roomy, wide-mouthed *Amphora* or jar, with
two vertical handles, used for storing wine and oil; the
so-called water-vessel (*Hydria*), with two small horizontal handles and a larger vertical one to carry it by;
the wide-mouthed bowl for mixing wine and water
(*Crater*); the *Oinochoé*, with its cylindrical or clover-leaf
shaped mouth, for pouring wine; the flat cup (*Kylix*) for
quaffing wine; the wide bowl (*Scyphos*); the two-handled
goblet (*Cantharos*); and the so-called ointment-flasks,
for pouring oil in drops, such as the slender narrow-
necked *Lekythos*, the long wineskin-shaped *Alabastron*,
and the small globular *Aryballos*. All these main shapes
are represented by many varieties; and it is both interesting and instructive to observe how the ancient
artists were constantly striving to accommodate the traditional types, with a full appreciation of their practical
uses, to the gradually developing sense of beauty, both

in the general harmony of the lines as well as in the carefully calculated relations of the separate details. A lively appreciation of the tectonic character of the vase as a whole is moreover apparent both in the choice and in the skilfully planned distribution of the ornament, the development of which in the course of centuries may be here traced step by step. At the same time the mechanical part of the potter's work was gradually brought to such a pitch of delicacy and precision as has never again been attained, much less surpassed.

The chief interest, however, which these vases possess for us, centres in the paintings that adorn them. From these we have drawn a well-nigh inexhaustible treasure of elucidations of the myths, the manners and customs, and the philosophy of life of the ancient Greeks. In many cases they are the solitary witnesses on points about which the scanty literary remains of the past leave us in absolute darkness. No less important is their testimony for the history of art. To them we owe a faithful conception of the pictorial art (especially as regards drawing and composition) of precisely those times from which no great painting has come down to us. They illustrate the gradual dawn, growth, and decay that mark the successive stages of development in an industrial art of the first importance; and these details, in virtue of their typical significance for the history of other kinds of monuments, throw the most valuable light upon the whole question of the general development of art.

The collection in the Museo Gregoriano illustrates only a small section, albeit the most important, of the history of ceramic art that stretches back to the hoariest antiquity. It contains but few specimens of the earliest vases imported from Greece, or of the native varieties in black clay (bucchero). The vases in the shape of wine-skins, with light-coloured ground (Nos. 1-3; Room VIII), decorated with animal-friezes and with rosettes, rows of disks, and similar designs, usually very delicately executed, date from the eighth and seventh centuries B.C.;

some have been brought from Corinth, others from manufactories under the influence of Corinth and Rhodes. Large importations of vases from Corinth were made in the seventh and sixth centuries, and from this source date the numerous small ointment-flasks (comp. p. 337), a few larger vases with Corinthian inscriptions (Nos. 6, 7), beautiful store-vases (Nos. 11, 19) with vertical handles *(vaso a colonette; celebe)*, and the *Deinos* or mixing-bowl without foot or handles (No. 34). The earlier Corinthian vases may be recognized by their reddish-yellow clay (often impure), on which the figures are painted in blackish-brown or other dull glaze. Details of the design are represented by scratched (or engraved) lines, in imitation of work upon metal plates, the figures in silhouette being not unlike figures cut out of such plates; some portions are picked out with red pigment in the later specimens, sometimes with white). An Oriental influence is clearly traceable in the ornamentation; the characteristic animal-friezes frequently include lions, panthers (heads shown full-face), Sphinxes, so-called Sirens (birds with human heads), and other fantastic forms; while the other spaces of the available surface are filled with conventional flowers (rosettes) and parts of flowers. The chivalric tastes of the age expresses itself in representations of duels, rows of riders, processions in chariots, hunting-scenes, etc., while larger mythological scenes are not wanting.

Ancient Etruria maintained an active trade not only with Corinth, but also with the Ionic cities of Asia Minor and with their colonies in Italy; and evidences of this intercourse may be traced in the bronzes of native Etruscan manufacture (Room IX) as well as in several imported terracotta vases (Nos. 51, 228, 245). The Cyrenian style also, in which the influence of Asiatic Greece unites with that of Corinth, is represented in one important example No. 275. But the great bulk of the vases found in Etruria come from the potteries of Athens, which before the middle of the sixth century had driven all competitors from the field by their wonderful act-

ivity, their admirable material, and the uniform excellence
of their finished products. Syracuse and the other Greek
cities in Sicily were the chief intermediaries between
Athens and the markets on the W. coast of Italy.

In the earlier varieties of these Athenian vases, the
lingering influence of Ionian and Peloponnesian models
may frequently be detected. This is especially true in
the case of the so-called Corinthian-Attic or Tyrrhenian
amphoræ (Nos. 5, 6), dating from the 4-6th decades of
the sixth century. This class of vase received its current
name at a period before the inscriptions were deciphered;
but the names which are inscribed on some of the specimens are ample evidence of the Athenian origin of the
entire class. These slender vessels are, like the Corinthian vases, decorated with friezes of animals below
the principal paintings. But while the clay and glaze of
the Corinthian vases are still of a dull tone, the products
of the Athenian potters, who had developed an individual style, are distinguished by the uniformly baked
terracotta, coloured a light red by the use of some pigment, and by the deep black glaze, prepared by a process no longer fully understood. The figures and ornamentation, painted black, like shadow-pictures, are thrown
into farther relief enlivened by means of incised lines,
and by red and white paint (in many cases now completely destroyed) used in a perfectly conventional system,
the flesh-parts of women (faces, feet, hands) being white,
the beards of the men, garments, etc., being red. Various
other details of the design are also influenced by conven-
tion; thus the eyes of men are large and round, those of
women are narrow and almond-shaped.

The vase-forms handed down by tradition were altered
by the Athenian potters in their own way. In the earlier
period the amphora was the favourite kind of vase among
the workers in the black-coloured or 'black-figured' style,
at least so far as their Etruscan market was concerned.
Two chief classes of these amphoræ may be distinguished,
viz. the unglazed and the glazed. Vases of the former

class (Room V) are usually slender and bold in outline,
the neck rising abruptly from the body and adorned with
a chain of lotus-flowers placed back to back (conventionalized almost beyond recognition) and double-pal-
mettes. Elaborate schemes of foliage (with palmettes and
one or more lotus-flowers) below the handles separate the
pictures on the front and back of the vase, beneath which
runs a continuous chain of lotus-flowers, and in many
cases also a simple meander-pattern. From the foot of
the vase radiate a number of pointed leaves, amidst which
the body of the vase rests as though in a cup or basket,
an effect found also in Corinthian and Tyrrhenian amphoræ. The paintings on the Athenian amphoræ frequently reveal an already developed power and a free
feeling of motion, which impart to the black silhouettes
the effect of a hampering garment. The great majority
date back to the latter half of the sixth century B.C.,
though a few belong to the former half of the fifth century.

The amphoræ of the second class (Room VI), often
of great size, are almost entirely covered with a shining
black glaze in imitation of metallic vessels, the only
parts left in light clay-colour being a portion on the foot
for the cup of radiating leaves, and a square panel on
each side of the body for the paintings and their ornamental borders. The neck is usually united with the
body by means of a gradually curving line. The paintings on these vases are, as a rule, executed with a minute
and often exaggerated care, but almost without exception
betray a certain severity and stiffness that seem to indicate a deliberate retention of the older mechanical traditions. A gradual development can be traced only in
certain details of secondary importance. These vases
were freely sold in Etruria in the sixth century (after
about 570 B.C.), but by the end of the same century they
had almost entirely disappeared. A kind of intermediate
position between these two classes of amphoræ is occupied by the Panathenæan amphoræ (named after a festival, see p. 302), which have borrowed their shape from

one, their mode of decoration from the other. Other
variations are also found; *e.g.* the peculiar vases of Nicosthenes (p. 293, No. 10a; p. 333).

A similar diversity of shape and decoration may also
be observed among the hydriæ, ewers, and lecythi of the
same dates. The 'black-figure' technique maintains its
ground in the perfunctory paintings of the lecythi until
a late period. The forms given to the shallow cups at
this period are especially varied (R. VIII). Some are
heavy and thick, with clumsy supports, others are light
and elegant, with slender handles and tall feet; some
have paintings in the interior, others have none. The
exterior decorations are equally diverse; sometimes the
black glaze covers the entire vase with the exception of
a narrow strip for a frieze of figures or of a square panel
for a painting (No. 263); sometimes the vase is left almost wholly unglazed, and is adorned with isolated
figures, a drinking-motto (Nos. 211, 266), or the signature of the artist between elegant palmettes (Nos. 217,
249, 251). A peculiar variety is that known as *Tazze a
occhioni* ('eye-cups') on which the pictorial decoration is
framed by large, ornamentally treated eyes (Nos. 258,
261, 270, 273); a method of decoration springing, on
the one hand, from the very primitive tendency to form
or adorn vessels in the shape of human faces, and on the
other, from the common ascription of power to the eye
to avert all evil, especially the 'malocchio.' In all these
hesitating and tentative efforts of the vase-painter there
distinctly appears the restless attempt to adapt the ornamentation to the shape of the vessel, while comparatively little importance is attached to the subject or content of the pictorial design.

The subjects in vogue with the artists of the black-
figured vases may be most conveniently studied on the
large amphoræ; and it is at once apparent that these
artists were dependent for their intellectual material
upon painting as enlisted in the service of religion to
adorn votive tablets and sacred vessels. Thus subjects

from the myths of the gods preponderate; the solemn assemblies of the gods, their processions on foot and in chariots, and their common warfare against the giants constantly reappear. Athena, however, is more prominent than the other gods, for the Athenian potters, who lived under her protection, especially delighted to do her honour; and she is represented again and again driving her four-horse chariot against the giants or aiding her favourites in their dire contests. The only other god that appears as often is Dionysos, with his dancing and musical retinue of Mænads and bearded, horse-tailed Sileni; and for vessels meant as the receptacles of wine, pictures of this kind must have seemed peculiarly appropriate. Heracles is the most frequently commemorated among the heroes. The cult of Heracles must have been extraordinarily popular in Attica during the sixth century; certain pictorial presentments of his various adventures became recognized as typical; and he himself always appears as the impetuous hero, clad in a lion's skin girt close to his body and drawn over his head, and armed with bow and quiver and with sword or club. Of the feats of Theseus, the overthrow of the Cretan Minotaur alone is at all common on these vases. Many scenes are borrowed from the cycle of myths that clustered round the tale of Troy, though with but scanty respect to the epic accounts of the war. These myths were doubtless well known to the people at large from the recitations of the rhapsodists, from popular songs, and from the teaching in the schools. Representations of scenes from the Iliad and Odyssey of Homer are, on the other hand, comparatively rare. In many cases it is impossible to decide, owing to the absence of characteristic details, whether the artist had in his eye, in these pictures of warriors arming, the setting out and return of warriors, duels over the bodies of the fallen, the bringing of the dead warrior from the battle-field, and the like, some particular event celebrated in the myth or only a generally typical occurrence of a warrior's life. Apart from these warlike subjects, genre scenes from ordinary human life figure but little in the paintings on the black-figured vases. Pictures of gymnastic exercises were retained by the traditions as to the decoration of the Panathenæan vases, and scenes at fountains were suggested by the destined use of the hydriæ; but other genre scenes are of merely isolated occurrence. The number of types, with which these thousands of paintings have been composed, is surprisingly small. Motives, once established, were eternally repeated or merely slightly altered to adapt them for the most diverse purposes. Groups of figures, once they had become familiar, were adjusted to the varying spaces at the disposal of the artist, by excision or addition, sometimes in the most superficial manner. The inter-relations of the various figures were expressed in a conventional language of gestures, which may possibly convey a wealth of meaning to the inhabitants of southern climes, even in those cases where its unintelligibility or ambiguity leaves us in a mist of doubt. The art of writing was, of course, not universally known in these times; and the use of written characters on these vases varies with the education and the taste of the artist. Letters, either singly or in meaningless conjunction (even at a much later date), were placed in the otherwise empty intervals on the surface of the vase, sometimes with a decorative intent, sometimes in a purely arbitrary manner, either to convey the effect of an inscription or simply to gratify the artist's naïve delight in making marks. The ancient Athenians, it is true, were fond of writing upon doors and walls, frequently thus commemorating their favourites; and these 'lovers' inscriptions' or 'pet names' were also placed upon vases, though not often upon the black-figured vases of the earliest period. The painters and potters did not sign their vases until the latter half of this period (550-500 B.C.; comp. the signatures on Nos. 10a, 78, 251, 258). They had, indeed, little temptation to do so; for individual characteristics seldom appear in the vases of this style, and when they do, they generally take the shape not so much of creative originality as of technical excellence, or of peculiarities in drawing, superficial deviations from the type, or other personal whims. Generally speaking, the paintings suffer from a kind of monotonous uniformity: and it is impossible to overlook the fact that the ancient pictorial formulæ, repeated and reused a thousand times, gradually fell into rigidity, so that the necessity for some fresh reviving and liberating force became imperatively felt. And as a matter of fact in the last thirty years of the sixth century a new tendency forced its way to the front, fostered by the impulse given to all branches of art, which was a consequence of the relations with the Greeks of the Oriental Archipelago under the influence of the Pisistratidæ.

In the domain of ceramic art this revolution found its first external expression in a change of technique. Henceforth the practice of an older art was followed in leaving the figures alone in the light colour of the terracotta ground; the coating of black glaze, covering the entire surface of the vase, stops only at the outlines of the drawing. In this manner the light-coloured figures stand out vividly from the dark background; and it becomes possible for the artist to use his pen or brush in elaborating the drawing within the contours of the figures, by means of lines in black or brown *i.e.* thinned glaze. Along with this new variety, usually known as 'red-figured vases', arose a new style of decoration. New problems are placed before the vase-painter, and a new conception of his material comes into force; a living impulse operates on all sides; and free room is granted to the individuality of the artist. Figures of men are now by preference represented nude, and the artist deals with the details of muscles and bones with ever-growing success. The difficulties presented by the drapery in figures of women are grappled with in various ways, though they are not successfully overcome until a late period. Innumerable changes are rung upon the motives for figures in repose and figures in action. The rigid types of the black-figured compositions are fairly thrown overboard; and everything is in a constant flux.

Side by side with this revolution, another significant revolution takes place in the choice of pictorial subjects, giving evidence of the altered aims and philosophy of life that obtained in the age of Cleisthenes. The once popular material gradually disappears altogether, or appears with a new face. The gods are no longer represented in dignified conclave but are grouped in genre scenes of banquet and carousal; and their relations with the daughters of men appear more frequently than their combats with the giants. Apollo now disputes with Athena the palm of popularity, while Dionysos falls more and more into the background, though, on the other hand, his retinue continues to be rendered with undiminished zest. The solemnly dancing Sileni are now replaced by wanton, active, and excitable creatures, playing a thousand wine-inspired pranks, and continually pursuing the Mænads, their light-footed companions. In the cycle of heroic compositions, the old types of the Labours of Heracles lose their position, and other adventures from the chequered career of the hero gain a new pictorial vogue. But the first place is now occupied by Theseus, brought into popularity by the patriotic movement of the age of Cleisthenes, and exalted into a national hero by the enthusiasm evoked by the Persian Wars. The Attic ideal of youthful valour is mirrored in his single combats: and he is now represented as leader of the Athenians in the contests against the Amazons and the Centaurs, in scenes that yield opportunity for an inexhaustible variety of charming groups. Thus Attic myths, or myths edited in the Attic spirit, advance more and more into the foreground, side by side with the ancient subjects from the Trojan cycle of myths.

Scenes from human life are, however, now far in the majority. Besides the tumultuous Bacchic thiasos, we have also scenes from the 'Comos', processions of Attic youth, warmed by wine, advancing in a vivacious dancing-mea-

sure to the sound of flutes and the clash of cymbals.
Carousals are presented to us, with all their jests and
merriments, their episodes and consequences, not unfrequently with a freedom beyond the strictly becoming.
The life of youths in the school and the palæstra suggest
an ever fresh series of designs; youthful nude forms are
represented sometimes in gymnastic exercises of the most
varied kinds, sometimes preparing for these, holding
disci, halteres (weights used in leaping), scrapers, etc.
Warlike scenes are much rarer; and representations of
the actual combat yield to scenes of preparation for it,
the arming, the departure, or the return of the warrior.
Occasionally the family of the young hoplite is grouped
about him, or his mother or wife welcomes him back or
hands him the stirrup-cup. Other pleasant scenes are also
frequent, such as men conversing with beautiful boys, or
young men wooing the maidens of their choice. The
pious reverence for the gods shown in sacrifices and
libations, the peaceful contests at the festivals in their
honour, and the rewarding of the victors are the subject
of other representations. The artists of this animated
period, in their youthful joy in creation, thus embrace
all aspects of life in their designs; nothing human is
alien to them.

The heightened sense of beauty and the self-conscious
skill of the potter manifest themselves also in the altered
shapes of the vases. Amphoræ are now made more slender, their details are more delicately finished, and the
handles are generally carried higher, sometimes like a
plaited braid and sometimes like a ribbon. Specially
attractive is a series of vases dating from the first thirty
years of the fifth century, which are decorated on each side
with a single delicately conceived and carefully executed
figure (Nos. 82-86, 223). In these, both sides of the vase
receive equal attention, but it soon became customary to
neglect the side which was to be concealed from view
when the amphora was in its destined position, and to
paint on it merely supernumerary 'draped figures', of no

particular significance. Of the very numerous varieties
of store-vases, the favourites are now the wineskin-
shaped *Amphora* or *Pelike* (Nos. 135, 136, 183, 188, and
70; the last being in the late black-figured style), and the
so-called *Stamnos* or *Olla* (Nos. 110-116, 129, 132). The
amphora 'a colonette' also occurs in a modified form
(Nos. 122, 123, 128). Mixing-vases attain a new development; and besides the beautiful calyx-shaped *Crater*
(*Vaso a calice*; No. 103) occurs later the bell-shaped
Oxybaphon (*Vaso a campana*; Nos. 178, 180). The *Hydriae*
(in the corridor) are distinguished by their full curves,
their skilfully arranged paintings, and their wonderfully
delicate bands of ornamentation. At this period, however,
by far the most beautiful vases are the *Kylices* or flat
cups. The foot and the cup are now combined in a homogeneous whole, of which the graceful handles form a
harmonious part; while the most suitable place has now
been found for the pictorial decoration. The vases with
black figures in the interior and figures of the ground-
colour on the exterior (between eyes; comp. Nos. 239,
254) belong to a brief transition stage. The red-figured
style soon made its way also to these interior paintings,
which were treated with increased care, and not unfrequently form the only ornament on the otherwise
wholly black vase. More usually, however, paintings
also occur round the entire exterior, generally divided
into two portions by means of elegant palmette-orna-
ments below the handles. It is on these vases that we
can best trace the astonishing progress made in the art
of drawing, and obtain a glimpse of that vivid and pul-
sating life and restless yearning, whence, at the close of
the Persian Wars, Attic art, fructified by new foreign
elements, emerges in its striking maturity and dazzling
perfection. The increased self-appreciation of the vase-
painters and potters, who at this time occupied no insignificant position among the merchants of Athens, is apparent in the growing frequency of signed vases (comp.
No. 226); and these signatures, along with the 'lovers'

inscriptions', form, as it were, a documentary basis for determining the chronology, and for distinguishing the relations of family or of school, among the guilds of vase-painters and potters.

The Museo Gregoriano contains a large number of choice specimens dating from the period of the most eminent kylix-painters. At the same time, it contains no specimens bearing the actual signature of the maker, with the exception of two by Pamphaios Nos. 256, 258, which are still affected by the traditions of the earlier style. All the same, however, the unmistakable style of many of the paintings allows them to be attributed with certainty to artists whose names are known to us from other sources. No. 230 may be recognized as one of the later works of Epictetos, whose name is connected with the beginnings of the red-figured style; and No. 222 is a closely related specimen, though no more definite judgment can be pronounced owing to the extensive restoration it has undergone. Nos. 209 and 246 may be taken as examples of Chelis and Cachrylion, two artists of about the same period. Allied to these and to each other are Hieron, Euphronios, Duris, and Brygos, whose artistic activity falls about 500-160 B.C. No. 196 is certainly by Hieron; probably also No. 218. No. 51 may be accepted as a specimen of the later style of the studio of Euphronios, to whom also the Jason vase has been ascribed (comp. p. 336). Brygos is the artist of No. 227, and probably also of Nos. 225 and 174. No. 232 is a specimen of Duris, and No. 156 of some closely-related artist; while Nos. 149, 159, and 151 date from the studio of Duris or some slightly later master. The tendencies created by this school underwent farther development at a later period; and their types only gradually vanished (comp. Nos. 112, 117).

In the middle decades of the fifth century, vase-painting received a new impetus, under the stimulus of the higher branches of art. The lasting influence of the paintings of Polygnotos and Micon distinctly reveals itself not only in obvious improvements in drawing and in innumerable new single motives (Nos. 162, 169) and groups (Nos. 115, 128), but also in the method of the general arrangement (Nos. 99, 103) and in the choice of subject. Many vase-painters, indeed, attempt to enter the lists with their great models, by using tints like water-colours (comp. No. 103). But at the same time we feel that the chasm betwixt art and handicraft is ever widening, and that the narrow limits at the command of the vase-painter cannot offer room enough for the enhanced powers of expression enjoyed by the higher art. Yet the easel-painting of the succeeding period, which far transcended all previous achievements in its sensuous beauty, its dramatic life, and its fidelity to its models, also cast an afterglow over the Attic vases of the fifth and fourth century; though few of these vases found their way to Italy and none are to be seen in the Museo Gregoriano.

With the political and material decline of Athens, the Attic potteries lost their power of large production. The export-trade dwindled away; and the Greek cities of Lower Italy were compelled to meet their own requirements in the shape of pottery with the products of native factories, which had previously developed but a very modest activity. The Museo Gregoriano contains few specimens from any of these new factories except those of Apulia, which are represented by some choice vases found at various spots in Southern Italy and originally included in the collection of Cardinal Gualtieri and other earlier collections. In the older examples of this variety, their close connection with Attic productions, whose shape and decoration they copy and develop, is clearly seen. But in the course of time a leaning towards showiness of effect gradually becomes apparent in the increasing size of the vases and in their over-elaborated ornamentation. The amphoræ, made with unduly elongated bodies, long necks, and tall feet, are ornamented with several bands of pictures, and the necks and the spaces beneath the handles are covered with luxuriant wreaths

of flowers or foliage (Room VIII. The large and corpulent "volute amphoræ", which reproduce in terracotta
the forms of the developed bronze technique, are specially
characteristic. Their tall handles usually end at the bottom in swans' necks, while at the top appear coloured
Gorgons' heads or masks, treated plastically and surrounded by elaborate volutes.

That these vases were intended for funereal purposes,
is obvious from the paintings on their exterior. Nearly
all of them have on one side a tomb in the form of a
stele or of a recess-like *heroön* (generally supported by
columns), round which are grouped men and women,
sitting, standing, or walking, and holding cups, fillets,
wreaths, mirrors, or other funeral offerings in their hands.
Bacchanalian scenes also occur repeatedly, as well as
genre scenes with young men and women, Victories and
Cupids (toilet-scenes). Where representations from the
myths appear, they are almost always modified in accordance with the versions rendered popular by the dramas
of Euripides and his successors. The influence of the
theatre, passionately favoured in Magna Græcia, betrays
itself in numerous details of dress and in the theatrical
grouping of the figures. Scenes from the comic plays of
the *Phlyakes*, faithfully reproducing the costumes, are
not wanting (No. 121. In the pictorial decoration of the
older and better Apulian vases a faint trace of the Attic
spirit may still be discerned, but even in the third century the lightly-won inheritance vanishes entirely in the
hands of the degenerate successors. The old freedom of
style degenerates into slovenliness, the former precision
and boldness into negligent superficiality. Thus the
Apulian vase-industry gradually expired at the beginning
of the second century, its extinction doubtless accelerated
by the altered requirements of the cult of the dead.

Little or no attention need be paid to the perfunctory
daubs that are found, chiefly on kylices, among the products of the Etruscan potteries; but we may note in
passing the peculiarly dry and angular drawings that

attempt, with more zeal than success, to copy Greek models. These drawings, which date probably from about the beginning of the third century, show an obvious relationship with the Etruscan mirror-engravings, and, to an eye accustomed to Greek painting, produce an almost un-antique effect (pp. 32S et seq.). Finally, there grew up, on the same soil as the late-Campanian painting, a group, limited both in numbers and in duration, consisting of small shallow vases with painted Cupids. As the Latin inscriptions upon them indicate, these were introduced into commerce by a factory in Latium in the latter half of the third century (p. 306).

The production of terracotta vases with raised ornamentation, which had flourished at various points in the Hellenic world since the Alexandrian epoch, found a second home in Italy. In the latter half of the third century the Campanian town of Cales became a centre for the production of a peculiar variety of black glazed saucers or platters, without handles or feet *(Patera; Phiale)*. At a later period the potteries of Arretium enjoyed a high reputation for their shining red vases, decorated with reliefs, which were sold all over the Empire down to the later imperial epoch, as a cheap and satisfactory substitute for metal-ware. These, therefore, appear as the last representatives of a once flourishing art-handicraft, at a time when the noblest products of the art had for centuries lain forgotten along with the dead for whose use they were made, to be summoned to a new life by the spade of the treasure-seeker and the explorer.

Room V.

Corinthian and Early Attic Vases.

5. Corinthian-Attic Amphora: Heracles and Nessos.

For the shape and style of decoration of this vase, comp. p. 277. In the upper band is Heracles rescuing Dejaneira, his wife, from Nessos the Centaur, who threatens her with violence. The hero brandishes his sword against the Centaur, who has seized Dejaneira with both hands, and is carrying her off on his back, but is now suddenly arrested in his career. The presence of Athena, patron-goddess of Heracles, and of Hermes, the messenger of Zeus, place the issue of the combat beyond doubt. To the right stand the aged Oineus, father of Dejaneira, and his wife (in a robe ornamented with figures), both evincing their interest by animated gestures. The man and woman farther to the right were added to fill up the space. At the back are four Centaurs hastening to the assistance of their comrade. — Beneath the principal painting are three bands of animals, in which panthers and Sphinxes occur along with rams, mules, and cocks.

From Vulci. — Mus. Gregor., ii, T. xxviii (A ii, T. xxxii), 2. Comp. *Roscher*, Lexikon der Mythologie, i, p. 2191 *(Furtwaengler)*. Jahrbuch des archäolog. Instituts, v, p. 253 *(Holwerda)*.

6. Corinthian Ewer: Ajax and Hector.

In its coating of black glaze, interrupted only by the space for the painting, this shapely vase shows the influence of Attic potters, which made itself felt even in Corinth about the middle of the sixth century. The battle-groups in the principal paintings repeat well-known types from earlier vases. To the left two heavy-armed warriors stand opposite each other in an attitude of attack, to the right a warrior dashes with levelled lance against a foe, who has fallen on one knee in his flight but makes a last effort to defend himself; an ally, brandishing his spear, approaches to the aid of the last. The names Aivas, Hektor, and Aineas are written in Corinthian letters beside these three figures. The Iliad mentions no scene exactly corresponding with this; but the painter, seeking to invest a trite pictorial composition with fresh interest by the addition of heroic names, was probably influenced in his choice of the latter by some vague recollection of the passage Iliad, xiv, 402 et seq.) describing the combat between Ajax and Hector, in which the latter, disabled by a stone, fell into dire extremity and was rescued only by the intervention of Æneas and other Trojan heroes.

From Cære. — Mus. Gregor., II, T. 1 (A II, T. IX), 3. Monumenti dell' Instit. archeol., II, T. 38a. Comp. Jahrbücher für class. Philologie, XI, Supplement, p. 540 *(Luckenbach)*. Rhein. Museum, 37, p. 344 *(P. J. Meier)*. *Dumont-Chaplain*, Les céramiques de la Grèce, p. 250. *A. Schneider*, Der troische Sagenkreis, pp. 20 et seq.

7. Corinthian Hydria: Boar-Hunt.

This clumsy vase, which dates perhaps as early as the seventh century, has little in common with the elegant hydriæ of a later period, except its three handles, and even these are differently arranged. The body of the vase is adorned with an animated hunting-scene, the separate figures in which are distinguished by names in Corinthian lettering. In the centre, Dion thrusts his lance through the neck of a boar, which falls upon its knees; one dog, injured by the boar, cowers on the ground, another has sprung on the back of the quarry, while a third seizes it from behind. A second hunter, named Vion (corresponding to the Attic form Ion), pierces the boar from behind with his lance, while three others (two of them also named Vion and one named Polyphamos) hasten to aid. To the right of Dion a bearded man (Charon) has taken to flight, but turns his head to see the issue of the fight; while, on this side also, Polystratos and a rider, whose horse bears the name Korax, approach to lend their assistance.

From Cære. — Mus. Gregor., II, T. XVII (A I:, T. XXIII), 2. Comp. Annali dell' Instituto archeol., 1836, p. 310 *(Abeken)*. *Dumont-Chaplain*, Les céramiques de la Grèce, p. 250, 3. *Kuhn*, Zeitschrift für vergleich. Sprachwissenschaft, XXIX (1887), p. 161 *(Kretzschmer)*.

S. Corinthian-Attic Amphora: Achilles and Memnon.

On the front is the duel between Achilles and the Ethiopian prince Memnon, in presence of their divine mothers, Thetis and Eos, a combat highly celebrated in the post-Homeric epos *(Æthiopis)*. Achilles is in the act of dealing the death-blow, which Memnon vainly tries to evade by flight. The goddesses stand stiff and motionless on either side, wrapped in their mantles; and beyond each of them the space is filled in by the addition of a bearded man, with uplifted arm. The reverse of the vase is occupied by two Sphinxes arranged symmetrically between two lions; while below is a band of lions, boars, rams, and water-fowl.

Mus. Gregor., II, T. xxviii (A II, T. xxxi), 1. Comp. *A. Schneider*, Der troische Sagenkreis, p. 144. *Baumeister*, Denkmäler des klass. Alterthums, III, p. 1972 *(Von Rohden)*.

9. Early-Attic Amphora.

This unusually slender vase is a specimen of a peculiar variation from the usual amphora type. The body is unglazed and its lower part is decorated with narrow black stripes, a reversion to a very archaic method of ornamentation. Beneath the handles are heraldic animal-groups (panthers devouring a deer), such as are common in the art of Asiatic Greece. The pictorial bands contain seated, running, and standing men grouped with bearded figures with wings, but not apparently representing any particular scene (perhaps messengers of Hermes?). We seem to have here a purely decorative combination of separate figures. The style is dry and wanting in life and betrays a certain affectation in the unflexible movements and stiff draperies. In spite of these remarkable characteristics, which are partly to be explained by Oriental Greek influence, this vase probably dates from an Attic pottery of about the middle of the sixth century. It is closely related to the variety of amphora represented by No. 10. Both the neck and body of the latter bear figures of equally stiff drawing, grouped more with reference to appearance than to meaning; and its lower part is glazed black.

Mus. Gregor., II, T. xxxv (A II, T. li), 2. Comp. Röm. Mittheilungen, II, p. 184 *(Dümmler)*. — For No. 10, Mus. Gregor., II, T. xxx (A. II, T. xliv). Comp. *Jahn*, Vasensammlung zu München, p. clxxi. *Urlichs*, Beiträge zur Kunstgeschichte, p. 21. — For the Attic origin of this variety, comp. the potsherd painted by Euphiletos, Ephemeris archaiol., 1888, T. 12, 2.

10a. Amphora by Nicosthenes.

The inscription upon this vase shows it to have been made by Nicosthenes, apparently one of the most industrious potters at Athens between 540 and 510 B. C. Nearly ninety vases bearing his signature are preserved in modern museums, and more than fifty of these are amphoræ of the same shape as this one. The broad ribbon-like handles and the shape of the body, the separate stripes of which seem to be held together by rings in relief, point clearly to some model in primitive bronzework. The paintings are interesting merely as decorations. On each side, between conventionalized eyes, stands a fully-armed warrior beside his horse, while his hound, seated in front of him, looks upwards at a bird flying on the left. On one handle is a nude dancing youth, on the other a female dancer with *crotala* (castanets) in her hands.

Comp. Deutsche Litteraturzeitung, 1887, p. 980 *(Studniczka).* — For Nicosthenes, see Archäol. Zeit., 1881, pp. 34 et seq. *(Loeschcke).* *Klein*, Vasen mit Meistersignaturen², p. 51. Römische Mittheilungen, V, pp. 327 et seq.

11. Corinthian Amphora 'a colonette'.

This heavy and corpulent vase, with its carefully executed painting, is an excellent specimen of the Corinthian style (comp. p. 276). The battle-scenes, in the principal band on the obverse, the horsemen, on the reverse, and the monochrone frieze of animals below, in no wise rise above the ordinary typical representations of such subjects. The disks on the branch-like handle each bear a painted cock. No. 19 closely resembles this vase in shape and decoration.

Mus. Gregor., II, T. XXIII (A II, T. XXVIII), 1 and 2. For No. 19, comp. *Rayet-Collignon*, Histoire de la céramique grecque, p. 73.

12. Attic Amphora: Athena in the Battle with the Giants.

The free drawings on this vase show that it belongs to the later black-figured style; as to its shape and decoration, see p. 278. On the front is a quadriga in which stands Athena, armed with helmet, aegis, and lance, while beside her is Heracles, of whom only the head, with the lion's skin, and club resting on his shoulder are seen. A fully armed giant gives way before the chariot. On the back appears Athena between two combatants. The inscription 'Nikostratos is beautiful' is a specimen of the so-called 'lovers' inscriptions' which are frequently found upon vases and generally refer to some aristocratic Athenian youth whose personal beauty, distinguished manners, or gymnastic or warlike prowess had excited the sympathy and admiration of the susceptible Athenian demos (comp. p. 281).

Mus. Gregor., II, T. xli (A II, T. lv), 1. Comp. *Mayer*, Giganten und Titanen, pp. 304 et seq. *Klein*. Vasen mit Lieblingsinschriften (Denkschriften der Wiener Akademie der Wissenschaften, XXXIX. 1890), pp. 18, 66.

13. Amphora: Triptolemos.

Triptolemos, seated in a chariot of the simplest construction, is about to obey the behest of Demeter and convey the knowledge of cereals throughout the world, beginning from Eleusis. He here appears as a bearded man, with ears of corn in both hands and a sceptre on his arm. He turns to the left toward Kore-Persephone, who holds up a flower in greeting, while, like Demeter, who stands on the right, she also has a sceptre. On the reverse appears Dionysos, with two dancing Sileni and a Maenad, beside a goat, the animal usually sacrificed to the god.

Mus. Gregor., II, T. xl (A II, T. lv), 3. Comp. *Overbeck*, Griech. Kunstmythol., III, 4, p. 531, T. xv, 6.

25. Amphora: Heracles playing the cithara, Europa.

Heracles, in characteristic armour (comp. p. 280). here appears in Apollo's rôle of citharoedos. To the left is Dionysos with ivy twig and goblet, and to the right is Athena, with a small panther beside her. — On the reverse is shown Europa, seated on the bull into which

Zeus has metamorphosed himself in order to convey her beyond the sea (comp. No. 29).

Mus. Gregor., II, T. xl (A II, T. lvi), 1, No. 29; II, T. xli (A. II, T. lv), 3. Comp. Commentationes in honorem Mommseni, pp. 262 et seq. (Klügmann). Overbeck, Griech. Kunstmythol., II, p. 426.

27. Amphora: Heracles and Pholos.

During his expedition to Arcadia Heracles is hospitably entertained by Pholos the Centaur. Attracted by the fragrance of the wine, which rises from the large cask sunk into the ground, the other Centaurs approach in order to claim a share, but are dispersed by the doughty blows of the hero's club. One Centaur has fallen to the ground and raises his right hand in an appeal for quarter, while another, vainly endeavouring to escape the hero's violence, leaps over the cask, with raised arms and crying aloud. On the reverse is a scene from the battle of the Centaurs and Lapithæ. One of the latter, in retreat, thrusts his lance towards a Centaur that threatens to crush him with a huge stone; while another Centaur, on the other side, dashes up with another massive rock in his arms.

Mus. Gregor., II, T. xxx (A II, T. xli), 2. Comp. Bonner Studien, p. 252 (Loeschcke).

31. Amphora: Achilles and Memnon, Heracles and the Cretan Bull.

An arrangement representing two warriors about to engage, frequently recurring in archaic art, has here been used by the artist to depict the famous duel between Achilles and Memnon (comp. No. 5), while he has merely inscribed the names of the heroes beside the figures, without adding a single characteristic or individualizing detail. On the reverse the capture of the Cretan bull is represented. Heracles (here without the lion's hide) has cast a rope round the hind-legs of the bull, and, bracing his left leg against its head, is pulling on the rope, so as to cause the animal to fall.

Mus. Gregor., II, T. xxxviii (A II, T. xxxix), 1. Comp. *Over-beck*, Gallerie heroischer Bildwerke, p. 514.

34. Corinthian Vase on a tall stand (in the centre of the room).

This vase without feet (so-called *Deinos*), which resembles the Corinthian-Attic vases in point of decoration, is adorned with four pictorial bands. In the top band, on one side, is a contest over the body of a fallen warrior, in which numerous hoplites, archers, and horsemen take part; and on the other side is the Hunt of the Calydonian Boar, a favourite theme in primitive Corinthian art. The huge boar, attacked by two hounds, has borne one of the huntsmen dead to the ground; six others, armed with lances, and an archer hasten up on the left, while on the right approach a spearman, an archer, and the courageous Arcadian huntress, Atalanta. The separate huntsmen, whose leader is Meleager, are not differentiated by the artist. Beneath the principal band are three others containing animals: swans, goats, rams, boars, so-called Sirens, panthers, and lions. The lid is also decorated with a frieze of animals. The tall stand, with its numerous bulges, is shaped on the model of bronze works used for a similar purpose (comp. p. 413). It is decorated throughout its whole height with paintings, the lower part having a frieze of animals.

From Cære. — Mus. Gregor., II, T. xc (A II, T. vii). Comp. *Kekulé*, De fabula Meleagrea, p. 38.

The glass-case by the window contains a selection of Roman lamps, some of them decorated with figures in relief.

Room VI.
Black-Figured Amphoræ and Hydriæ.

36. Amphora: Battle of the Giants.

On the clay-coloured panel on the front is represented the battle of the gods and giants. Zeus, holding the reins in both hands, is on the point of mounting his four-horse chariot; Heracles, standing beside him in the same car, has placed one foot over the front of the chariot upon the pole, so as to secure a firm position in using his bow. Close by is Athena with brandished lance, and in front of her is Ares. Beside the chariot a dying giant has fallen to the ground, while two others, in full armour, advance impetuously to the attack. Battle-scenes of the usual kind appear on the reverse.

Mus. Gregor., II, T. I (A II, T. lii), 1. Comp. *Mayer*, Giganten und Titanen, pp. 293 et seq.

37. Amphora: Heracles and the Erymanthian Boar.

Heracles, at the bidding of Eurystheus, has pursued the Erymanthian Boar, and is here shown bringing his quarry home alive and apparently about to deposit it in the large *pithos* or store-vase, half sunk in the earth, from which project the bearded head of Eurystheus and his interceding arm. The craven king, fearing both the hero and the formidable boar, had sought refuge in the pithos. On each side is a woman, looking on in astonishment. In the original composition these were probably characterized respectively as Athena, encouraging her protegé, and Calliphœbe, the alarmed mother of Eurystheus. On the reverse is a painting representing two warriors being greeted in their father's house.

Mus. Gregor., II, T. li (A II, T. liv), 2. Comp. *Klein*. Euphronios[2], pp. 57 et seq. *Roscher*, Lexikon der Mythologie. I, p. 2201 *(Furtwaengler)*.

39. Amphora: Heracles and Geryon.

After various successful labours Heracles penetrated to the extreme western island of Erytheia, in order to steal the great herd of cattle owned by the triple-bodied Geryon. The combat which he had to wage with the monster is depicted on the front of this vase. Encouraged by the assistance of Athena, Heracles has already mortally wounded the herdsman Eurytion (identified by his garment of skins and his wallet), and now, with uplifted club, approaches Geryon. Of the monster's three complete bodies, joined at the middle, two, in full hoplite armour, still rear themselves to the fight, but the third has collapsed from its wounds. Beside Geryon is his two-headed dog Orthros, own brother, according to Hesiod, of Cerberus and the Chimæra; the tail of this animal is in the form of a serpent. On the reverse is a battle in which hoplites and a four-horse chariot are engaged.

Mus. Gregor., II, T. xlviii (A II, T. xlii), 1. Comp. *Klein*, Euphronios[2], pp. 58 et seq., 77 et seq.

43. Amphora: Lamentation for the Dead, Helen and Menelaos.

In a grove of plane-trees and laurels a woman is standing, her right hand raised in grief, her left tearing her hair, while on a couch of twigs before her lies the nude corpse of a bearded man. The weapons of the deceased lean against the plane-trees on the left, among the branches of which a bird is perched. The mourner has been identified as Eos, goddess of the dawn, bewailing her son Memnon, slain by Achilles (comp. No. 8). A later tradition describes the dew as the tears shed by the goddess every morning for the departed. — In the painting on the reverse, Menelaos appears, approaching the recaptured Helen with drawn sword, after the fall of Troy, with a warrior in flight on one side and a youth, idly looking on, on the other. Helen raises her veil in the usual manner, a gesture containing perhaps a hint of the effect of her beauty, the sight of which caused Menelaos to let his sword sink.

Mus. Gregor., II, T. xlix (A II, T. xlvii), 2. Comp. *Overbeck*, Gallerie heroischer Bildwerke, pp. 635, 628. *A. Schneider*. Der troische Sagenkreis. p. 182.

44. Amphora: Apollo and Heracles.

A very popular myth (the original significance of which is not fully explained) relates that Heracles and Apollo once came to blows for the possession of a tripod, described in the common version as the Delphic tripod.

The scene before us depicts the strife at its earliest stage; each disputant has seized a ring of the tripod standing on the ground between them, and their weapons are not yet raised. — On the reverse is a quadriga with a charioteer in the usual costume; possibly Iolaos, the hench- man of Heracles, awaiting the issue of the dispute.

☞ Mus. Gregor., II, T. xxxi (A II, *T. li), 1. Comp. *Welcker*, Alte Denkmäler. III, p. 272. *Overbeck*, Kunstmythologie, IV, p. 397. -- For the myth, comp. *Roscher*, Lexikon der Mythologie, I, pp. 2189 et seq.(*Furtwaengler*). *Von Wilamowitz*, Euripides' Herakles, I, p.265.

45. Amphora: Heracles and the Nemean Lion.

The first labour of Heracles, the slaying of the Ne- mean lion, is one of the most popular subjects with vase-painters. The painting on the obverse of this vase shows the earlier type of this fight. Heracles seizes the lion by the throat as it springs upon him and plunges his sword between its jaws. Athena and Iolaos, the faith- ful companion of Heracles, watch the struggle. On the reverse is a bearded man arming himself and surrounded by his family.

Mus. Gregor., II, T. xlvii (A II, T. xlv), 2. Comp. Athen. Mittheil. des Instit., XII. p. 123. *Roscher*, Lexikon der Mythologie, I, p. 2196 (*Furtwaengler*).

49. Small Amphora: Heracles and a Triton.

Heracles bestrides the back of a Triton, whom he is strangling with both hands. Like similar marine monsters, the Triton is represented with a human trunk, ending below in a scaly fish's body. The dolphin above sym- bolizes the sea, the place of combat. To the left stands Poseidon with a tall trident, and to the right is a Nereid fleeing in alarm. The design is repeated on the reverse of the vase, except that a second Nereid takes the place of Poseidon.

Mus. Gregor., II, T. xliv (A II, T. xliii), 2. Comp. Annali dell' Instituto archeol., 1882, pp. 73 et seq. (*Petersen*).

51. Hydria (of Ionic-Italic workmanship?).

This singular vase has been attributed to some pottery in Lower Italy, which worked after the models of the

Oriental Greek vases of the sixth century (comp. No. 228),
not, however, without exaggerating and degrading their
peculiarities. On the shoulder of the vase is painted a
hare-hunt; the disproportionately large hare is pursued by
a dog and two tiny men. Beneath the dog is a hedgehog.
The body of the vase is adorned with six maidens, clad
in sleeved Ionian chitons, running rapidly towards the
right. The care with which the details of the bodies and
garments are engraved does not compensate the disagreeable impression produced by the exaggerated activity of the figures.

Comp. Römische Mitthell. des deutschen archæol. Instit., III,
p. 177 (Dümmler).

52. Hydria: Athenian Knights.

The shoulder of this vase bears scenes from the palæstra. On the left two pairs of pugilists are boxing to
the music of a flute-player, and an athlete seated on the
ground is apparently bandaging his leg. On the right is
an athlothete or umpire, with his long staff, watching
three youths running towards the right with swinging
arms. The principal painting displays two bearded horsemen, in the armour of Athenian knights, upon proudly
pacing horses. The inscriptions ('Beautiful is Olympio-
doros', 'Beautiful is Leagros') leave no doubt that these
are the names of the persons the painter meant to depict.
This Leagros is certainly to be identified with the stra-
tegos of that name who fell in 467 B.C., and is commemorated upon many other vases, so that the hydria
before us, which represents him as already full-bearded,
probably dates from the first decade of the fifth century.
The horses also have their names inscribed beside them,
viz. 'Thrasos' and 'Arete' or 'Courage' and 'Valour'.

Mus. Gregor., II, T. VIII (A II, T. XIV), 2. Comp. Jahrbuch
des deutschen archæol. Instituts, II, p. 163 (Studniczka). Klein,
Vasen mit Lieblingsnamen, pp. 16, 39.

53. Hydria: Fountain-Scene.

On the shoulder of the vase is the combat of Heracles with the Nemean lion (comp. No. 45), in the later

arrangement, which appeared at the close of the sixth century. The hero has thrown himself upon the lion, and strangles it with his left hand, while the beast seeks vainly to free itself from its opponent, upon whose head he has set his talons. To the left is Iolaos with the quadriga; and Athena is also present. — The principal painting represents a fountain, from which the water issues through four openings shaped like lions' and asses' heads. Two men and two women, filling their hydriæ at the fountain, carry twigs in their hands as though celebrating some religious ceremony. Similar fountain-scenes are very frequently used for the decoration of hydriæ or water-vessels. Comp. Nos. 60 and 64; also p. 281.

Mus. Gregor., II, T. x (A II, T. xIII), 2. Comp. No. 45, p. 299. — For Nos. 60 and 64: II, T. IX, 2, and T. XI, 2 (A II, T. XII, 1, and T. xvii, 2).

56. Hydria: Peleus and Thetis.

Thetis, the godlike daughter of Nereus, was forced, by the decree of Zeus, to marry Peleus, but did not surrender herself to the mortal without an effort. Gifted, like other marine divinities, with the power of changing her shape, she attempted to terrify Peleus by assuming all kinds of forms and thus to escape from him, until he finally overcame her after a desperate struggle. This changeful combat is the subject of the principal painting on this vase. The metamorphoses of the goddess are naïvely indicated by a lion's head placed beside her own, and by the front part of a snake beneath her hands. On each side is a fleeing Nereid.

Comp. on the general subject Overbeck's Galleric heroischer Bildwerke, pp. 128 et seq. Jahrbuch des deutschen archæol. Instit., I, p. 200 (B. Graef).

70. Amphora in the form of a wine-skin (askos): Oil-selling (to the right of the door to the corridor).

The paintings on this vase, which belongs to the later period of the black-figured style, depict scenes from the

life of an oil-dealer in a thoroughly original manner. On
the front, the oil-dealer, seated in a chair beside an olive-
tree, is transferring oil from an amphora to a small lecythos by means of a funnel-shaped siphon, apparently
in order to submit a sample to the man seated opposite
him on a folding-stool. The latter is doubtless the custom-
er; and a dog, probably the guardian of the oil-garden,
is inquisitively regarding the stranger, who seems to be
teasing him with his stick. The thoughts of the oil-seller
are revealed by the words inscribed in a curve beside
him: 'O Father Zeus, would that I were rich!' The scene
on the reverse is different, and the key to the situation
is again afforded by the words inscribed beside the man
standing on the left and supposed to be spoken by him:
'the vase is full, in fact running over'. The youth on a
folding-stool opposite him reckons on his fingers and
appears not quite satisfied with the quantity measured
to him. Here also a dog plays a part in the dispute,
and looks up, barking, at the reckoner.

Mus. Gregor., II, T. lxl (A II, T. lxv), 1. Monumenti dell' Instit.
archeol., II, T. 44b; Baumeister, Denkmäler des klass. Altertums, II,
p. 1047. Comp. Ritschl, Opuscula, I, p. 788. Sitzungsberichte der
sächsischen Gesellschaft der Wissenschaften, 1867, p. 89, T. III, 3
(O. Jahn). Robert, Bild und Lied, p. 81. Jahrbuch des deutschen
archæol. Instit., VIII, p. 180 (Pernice).

71-75. Panathenaic Amphoræ.

An inscription on the front of No. 71 expressly states
that these vases were among the prizes won at Athens;
and the paintings upon them prove that they were connected with the great contests (agones) of the Panathenæa.
The victors in these famous contests were rewarded with
considerable quantities of the celebrated Attic olive oil,
which they were permitted to export free of duty. These
vases were apparently used originally to contain this oil,
and their uniform shape and decoration, sometimes also
an express inscription, vouched for the origin of the contents. We possess a long series of such amphorae (of

different sizes), ranging from the first half of the sixth to
the end of the fourth century, all adhering in a conventional or archaistic manner to the black-figured style. All
the specimens before us, with the exception of No. 75,
seem to date from the sixth century. Each shows, in front,
a fully armed figure of Athena as champion, advancing
towards the left, between two columns, on each of which
is a cock. On the reverse of No. 71 are two exercises of
the pentathlon or quintuple contest: an athlete is about
to hurl the discus, in presence of an umpire, another is
on the point of launching his spear *(akontion)*, which he
holds by the thong. On Nos. 72 and 75 we see foot-races
(with four and five competitors respectively); and Nos. 73
and 74 each display a quadriga at the galop.

Mus. Gregor., ii, T. xliii (A ii, T. xxxv), 1 and 2, T. xlii
(A ii, T. xxxiv), 1-3. Monum. dell' Instit., i, T. 22. Comp. Annali
1830, p. 218. Compte-rendu de la commission archéolog. de St.
Pétersbourg, 1876, pp. 7 et seq. *(Stephani)*. *Urlichs*, Beiträge zur
Kunstgeschichte, pp. 33 et seq. *Hauser*, Neu-attische Reliefs,
pp. 159 et seq.

76. Amphora: Heracles in the Underworld.

The final labour imposed upon Heracles led him into
Hades, whence he had to drag Cerberus to the light of day,
without using any of his usual weapons. The painting
on this vase shows him approaching the palace of the
underworld accompanied by Athena, and raising his left
hand either to greet or to appease the infernal deities.
Within the house, on the right, which is indicated by a
Doric column and a portion of the pediment, is seated
Persephone, wearing a headdress resembling a calathos,
while Hades, depicted as an aged king, seems to debate
with her concerning the request of Heracles. The huge
Cerberus turns one of his heads, gnashing his teeth, towards the undismayed hero, while the other glances backwards at his mistress. On the reverse is a Bacchic procession.

Mus. Gregor., ii, T. lii (A ii, T. xlvi), 2.

In the middle of the room, —

77. Amphora: Slain Warrior brought home.

A warrior bears on his back the fully-armed corpse of a comrade, followed by another hoplite and by an archer, clad and armed like a Scythian (leathern cap with flaps, garment with sleeves and trousers, quiver on the left side, and pointed axe on his shoulder). A woman in keen excitement precedes the procession to convey the sad tidings to an old man on the left, who raises his right hand in grief. The letters on the pictorial panel are introduced in meaningless combination merely as ornaments to fill up space. The scene has been referred to the post-Homeric epos, which relates that Ajax bore the body of Achilles from the battle-field to the Greek camp, where it was received by Phœnix, the aged tutor of Achilles, and by Briseïs. It is very possible that a picture of this subject was known to the painter of the amphora, and has been added to by him, so that the composition has assumed the character of a general, typical delineation from the warlike life. — On the reverse appears Dionysos in his chariot, accompanied by two Mænads and Silenus playing on the cithara.

Mus. Gregor., II, T. 1 (AII, T. lii). 2. *Gerhard*, Auserlesene Vasenbilder, III, T. 211 et seq., 3 and 4. Comp. *Overbeck*, Gallerie heroischer Bildwerke, pp. 548, 550.

78. Amphora by Exekias.

Inscriptions round the mouth and on one side of this vase indicate that it was made and painted by Exekias, an Athenian vase-painter of about 550-530 (or 520) B.C. This splendid amphora admirably illustrates the peculiar characteristics of its artist. Carefully considered compositions are here executed with a high degree of technical ability; innumerable refinements lend a fresh charm to old and familiar motives; details are reproduced with a minute accuracy that seems almost inexhaustible; while the ornaments on the draperies and weapons are engraved with amazing elaboration. This vase thus marks the

zenith of the black-figured style, but at the same time
also the limit of its development, beyond which it could
not avoid falling a victim to feeble affectation and lifeless
formalism. The painting of Ajax and Achilles dicing
(the names are inscribed) is especially unexcelled for its
finish of execution. The two heroes, seated opposite each
other, lean forward in keen attention towards the cubical
block between them, on which each has placed a hand.
'Three' cries Ajax; 'four' says Achilles. Although no
dice are actually visible, there is no doubt that the game
which so keenly interests the heroes during one of the
idle hours of their long life in camp is a kind of back-
gammon, which, according to the Cyprian poems, was
invented by Palamedes. The players wear elaborately
ornamented mantles over their armour, and behind them
are their magnificent shields. That of Ajax is adorned
with a Gorgon's head and serpents; that of Achilles with
a head of Silenus in relief, between a panther and a
serpent.

On the other side of the vase the painter has delin-
eated the return of the Dioscuri to their ancestral house,
with all the charming and ingenious clearness of which
the matured archaic art was capable. Polydeuces stoops
to caress his faithful dog, which joyfully springs to meet
its returning master. In front of him stands Leda, who
holds palm-branch and flowers in greeting towards her
son Castor, who turns towards her. Castor has just committed Cyllaros, his noble steed, to his father Tyndareos,
who lays his hand caressingly on the animal's head. A
boy (on a disproportionately small scale) bringing a chair
with two cushions and an anointing-flask indicates that
the wearied heroes will presently find rest and the refresh-
ment of a bath. The names of the figures (except the
servant) and of the horse are inscribed beside them; while
on both sides also is the 'lovers' inscription' 'Beautiful
is Onetorides'.

Mus. Gregor., II, T. liii. Monumenti dell' Instituto archeol., II,
T. 22. Wiener Vorlegeblätter, 1888, T. vi, 1. Comp. *Klein*, Vasen

mit Meistersignaturen[2], p. 39, 4. *Rayet-Collignon*, Histoire de la céramique grecque, p. 121.

Table-Case in front of the First Window.

This case contains a variety of small terracotta figures; a mosaic of the Gorgon's head, repulsive in drawing but interesting in technique; two small vases shaped like eagles' heads, distinguished by careful modelling and delicate ornamentation; and also three goblet-shaped vases in red clay, resembling the pottery of Arretium (comp. p. 289). The exteriors of these last are decorated with delicate raised ornamentation, which finds its archetype in the metal goblets of the Hellenistic period and in the so-called Samian pottery (comp. p. 335). One of the vases shows heraldic groups of goats facing each other, amidst a rich foliage decoration; on the upper rim of another is a frieze of Cupids racing in two-horse chariots.

For the eagles' heads: Mus. Gregor., II, T. xciii (A II, T. III). — For the Arretine vases: II, T. CI (A I, T. xxxv). Comp. *Marquardt und Mau*, Privatleben der Römer, II, p. 660.

Table-Case in front of the Second Window.

In this case are a number of animals' heads in black terracotta, which served as handles or ornaments on very archaic vases. It also contains an ointment-flask in the form of a running hare, executed in colours. The visitor should also notice three ROMANO-CAMPANIAN CUPS, the decoration of which is added in white and yellow (partly also red) pigment above the black glaze (comp. p. 289). One of these cups has no painting in the interior and is much damaged. One of the others is decorated inside with the winged figure of a curly-haired boy playing the double-flute, beneath the inscription '*Keri pocolom*' (i. e. 'this cup belongs to Cerus'). This cup, therefore, was dedicated to the old Italic deity, whose name (analogous to that of the goddess Ceres) was derived from his creative activity (*creare*). The interior of the remaining vase is occupied by a similar figure of Eros, holding a cup and branch, with the inscription '*Lavernai pocolom*', indicating that it also was dedicated to a deity, *viz.* Laverna, the old Italic goddess of gain. These two vases are farther ornamented with four small stamped rosettes, placed without reference to the painting, which is of later date.

For the hare: Mus. Gregor., II, T. XCIII. — For the vases (from Vulci and Orte): Mus. Gregor., II, T. lxxxviii (A II, T. III). Comp. Corpus inscriptionum latin., I, 46, 47. Compte-rendu de la commission archéolog. de St. Pétersbourg, 1874, p. 63 *(Stephani)*. Annali dell' Instit. archeol., 1884, pp. 1 et seq., 357 et seq. *(Foerster)*. — For Cerus, comp. *Roscher*, Lexikon der Mythologie I, p. 867 *(Wissowa)*.

Corridor VII.
Red-figured Vases.

80. Amphora: Theseus and the Minotaur, Eos and Cephalos.

Theseus has seized the Cretan Minotaur by the neck, as it seeks to flee, and prepares to strike it with his sword. The building of the Labyrinth is concisely indicated by a lofty column with Doric capital. To the left is Ariadne, holding a fillet ready to adorn the victorious hero; and to the right is King Minos, raising his right hand in astonishment.

On the reverse of the vase appears Eos, the winged goddess of dawn, following the youthful Cephalos, her beloved, in order to adorn him with a fillet, as a pledge of her love. The youth, in the garb of a hunter, raises his hand, as though in alarm to ward off the goddess. The bald-headed man to the left is perhaps Dioneus, father of Cephalos, extending his right hand to protect his son. Beside him is a dog, looking up attentively at his master, the young hunter.

From Nola. — Mus. Gregor., II, T. lvii (A II, T. lxi), 1. *Gerhard*, Auserlesene Vasenbilder, III, T. 160, pp. 36 et seq.

81. Amphora: Poseidon in the Battle of the Giants.

Poseidon, the earth-shaker, carries a huge mass of earth (the island of Nisyros according to tradition) on which all kinds of animals and plants are seen, in order to hurl it upon his opponent, against whom he thrusts at the same time with his trident. The young giant falls mortally wounded, unable to offer any farther resistance. — On the reverse are a warrior in complete armour and an archer in Scythian costume, standing opposite a youth not yet fully armed, with chlamys and bow slung round him.

Mus. Gregor., II, T. lvi (A II, T. lx), 1. *Overbeck*, Griech. Kunstmythologie, III, p. 331, T. XII, 25.

84. Amphora: Achilles.

This magnificent vase is decorated on each side by a single figure left in the original colour of the terracotta ground (comp. p. 284). On the front is an armed youth, in a dignified attitude, grasping a tall spear in his left hand and described as 'Achilles' by the accompanying inscription. The cuirass-like jerkin, the details on which are most carefully executed, has a Gorgon's head in the centre; beneath it appears the fine, short chiton. Calm dignity is predominant in the expression of the noble head, which is drawn with admirable delicacy. The whole artistic conception and execution vividly recall the most successful vase-paintings that issued from the studio of Euphronios in his later period (comp. p. 286). The painter might well challenge by the name he has inscribed a comparison with the ideal hero of the Homeric poems. In the domain of the pictorial arts he has here created an ideal youthful warrior, which one is almost tempted to place side by side with the ideals of the gods created by the plastic art of the fifth century. — The other side of the vase, which is much bruised and faded, presents the painting of a woman, with the ungirt Doric peplos, carrying a ewer and cup in her hands. This figure, which is of equally charming but simpler execution than the Achilles, has evidently an intended relation to the latter. It represents Briseïs, the lovely daughter of the priest (or king) of Lyrnessos, who fell to the hero as part of his booty. Taking upon herself the office of a wife, she advances to offer her lord a refreshing draught.

Mus. Gregor., II, T. lviii (A II, T. lxii), 3. *Gerhard*, Auserlesene Vasenbilder, III, T. 184. Journal of Hellenic Studies, I, T. vi. Comp. *Klein*, Euphronios[2], p. 245. *Winter*, Jüngere attische Vasen, pp. 20, 28.

89. Apulian Amphora with volute-handles: Funeral Scenes.

This vase, which is distinguished by the richness and careful execution of its ornamentation, dates from the most flourishing period of vase-painting in Lower Italy. On the neck appears the youthful Dionysos driving in a chariot drawn by griffins, preceded by a Satyr with a torch, and followed by a dancing Mœnad, bearing thyrsos and tympanon (tambourine). The centre of the principal painting is occupied by a magnificent sepulchral monument resembling a temple, with Ionic columns and pediment; on a lofty pedestal stands a group of figures, painted white and therefore intended to represent marble. As is occasionally the case on Attic monuments of this kind, one of the distinguished exploits of the deceased is here represented: a warrior, holding his horse by the bridle, pierces with his lance the back of a fleeing youth; the latter bends backward in agony and lays his hand on the mortal wound, while his spears escape from his grasp and the left arm bearing the shield hangs powerless. The outside of the tomb is surrounded by six figures in three rows, testifying by their gifts their respect for the deceased, thus exalted to the rank of a hero. — On the reverse is a simpler tomb, adorned merely with a single wreath of conventional flowers, and also surrounded by six figures.

From Ruvo; afterwards in the Vatican Library. — *Pistolesi*, Il Vaticano descritto, III, T. 93. *Passeri*, Pict. in vasculis, III, T. 270 et seq.

90. Amphora, with plaited handles: Victorious Citharœdos.

The principal painting on this vase, which belongs to the second half of the fifth century, introduces us to a musical competition. A garlanded citharœdos, in solemn festal attire, stands upon a low bema or platform, with a large cithara, from which hangs an ornamental covering, in his left hand, while his lowered right hand holds the plectrum or rod with which the strings are struck. He has just concluded the performance which has won him the prize; and two figures of Nike fly towards him, themselves bringing the sacrificial vessels from which he is to offer a libation in thank-offering to the gods. The slender column behind the bema is a concise indication of the festival hall in which the performance takes place. — On the reverse three figures enveloped in mantles are painted in a careless style.

Mus. Gregor., II, T. lx (A II, T. lxiv), 3.

91. Amphora, with plaited handles: Death of Orpheus.

Orpheus, the renowned bard of Thrace, who could tame wild beasts and move rocks by the magic of his art, was put to death by Thracian women, for whose hostility very various reasons are given by the legends. The tragic end of the singer is the subject of the painting before us. A woman, with uplifted axe, rushes towards the retreating Orpheus, who holds his tortoise-shell lyre in his right hand, and raises the left in intercession, to ward off the murderers. On the reverse another woman, lance in hand, hurries to the scene of action. Behind her stands a man in the Thracian national costume; over his chiton he wears a heavy mantle *(zeira)*, fastened at the neck; and on his head is a fox-skin cap *(alopeke)*.

Mus. Gregor., II, T. lx (A II, T. lxiv), 1. *Gerhard*, Trinkschalen und Gefässe, T. J. Comp. Archæolog. Zeitung, 1868, p. 3 *(Heydemann)*. Ann. dell'Instit.,1871, p. 126 *(Flasch)*. Journal of Hellenic Studies, 1888, pp. 143 et seq. *(Harrison)*. For the costume, see Fünfzigstes Berliner Winckelmannsprogramm, 1890, p. 159 *(Furtwaengler)*.

92. Amphora: Contest for the Tripod.

Heracles has seized the tripod and with his club menaces Apollo, who has overtaken him. Apollo, with long

hair and quite unarmed, is less violent than his rough
opponent, and lays his right hand on the shoulder of the
latter, while he grasps with his left at one of the handle-
rings of the tripod. Athena, with sloping lance, steps
between them, and raises her right hand in protest, as
though shocked by the vehemence of Heracles. — On
the reverse is a scene from the 'Comos' (comp. p. 283).
A youth, bearing a pointed amphora and cup, saunters
along, with his arm round the neck of a girl who is performing vigorously on her flute. Behind them follow a
youth, playing on the lyre, and a maiden, carrying a
double-flute in her left hand, and apparently accompanying her companion's music with her voice. These
admirable drawings date from about 490-470 B. C.

Mus. Gregor., II, T. liv (A II, T. lviii), 1. *Gerhard*, Auserlesene
Vasenbilder, II, T. 126. Comp. *Welcker*, Alte Denkmäler, III, p. 284.
Overbeck, Griech. Kunstmythologie, IV, p. 402, T. xxiv, 8.

93. Amphora: Heracles and Athena.

The friendly relations which existed between Athena
and Heracles are here visibly portrayed in a most naïve
manner. The hero places his right hand, with outspread
fingers, in the hand of his patron-goddess; and between
them is inscribed the friendly word *'chaire'* or 'hail'.
Iolaos, the trusty comrade of Heracles, is present at the
interview, holding the hero's helmet. — On the reverse
is another admirable 'Comos' scene, delicately executed.
A bearded man, singing and playing the cithara, advances
between two dancing youths, one of whom holds crotala
or castanets. The style and technique refer this vase to
the earlier group of red-figured amphoræ, the principal
representative of which is Euthymides. The contours of
the hair, *e.g.*, are still indicated by incised wavy lines in
the style of the 'black-figured' art.

Mus. Gregor., II, T. liv (A II, T. lviii), 2.

97. Hydria: Apollo's Voyage.

According to the religious myth Apollo spent the
winter among the distant and mythical race of the

Hyperboreans, on the extreme limits of the earth; but at the beginning of spring, yielding to the songs of his worshippers, he returned to his shrines in Greece. Then nature awoke to joyful life; as a beautiful hymn of Alcæus expresses it, "the sacred rock-spring (*i. e.* Castalia) then gushes forth again in silver-bright waves; nightingale, swallow, and grasshopper chant the praises of the god". The vase before us shows us a scene from this voyage of Apollo, which in its living freshness and delicate grace deserves a place among the most charming creations of the great vase-painters. It dates from about 480 B. C. The youthfully-formed god, with short, light-brown hair, and clad in a rich Ionic festal garb, with bow and quiver on his back, is seated, lyre in hand, on a huge winged tripod which floats across the sea. In the water, which is indicated by shading in lighter colour, are fishes and a polyp; while around the tripod dolphins are playing.

Mus. Gregor., II, T. xv (A II, T. xxi), 1. Monumenti dell' Instituto archeolog., I, T.46. *Lenormant-De-Witte*, Élite céramographique, II, T. 6. *Baumeister*, Denkmäler des klass. Alterthums, I, p. 102. Comp. *Flasch*, Polychromie auf Vasenbildern, p. 21. *Overbeck*, Griech. Kunstmythologie, IV, p. 360, T. xx, 12. *Roscher*, Lexikon der Mythologie, I, pp. 2806 et seq. *(Crusius)*, p. 2839 *(M. Mayer)*.

99. **Hydria: Thamyris.**

It is related in the Iliad that the Thracian singer Thamyris was cruelly punished by the Muses, with whom he had presumed to compete. Whether the painting before us represents the prelude to this event, or the victory won by Thamyris in the Delphic competition, is doubtful. Thamyris, clad in a rich Thracian costume and sweeping the strings of his lyre, is here seated upon a rock, in a hilly region indicated by white lines. In front of him, with one foot on a rock, stands an old woman (Pythia or the mother of the singer?), extending a twig towards him as the singer's meed of victory. The two garlanded female figures, to the left, who are obviously affected by the song, are Muses, one of whom is named Choronica or 'Victor of the choir'. The three whitish objects, like daggers, above, to the right, are plants. The adjacent inscription 'Euaion is beautiful' has nothing to do with the picture. The entire composition, in its mode of grouping and its harmonious conception of the subject, reveals the influence of paintings in the mode of Polygnotos (comp. p. 286), and probably dates from about the middle of the fifth century.

Mus. Gregor., II, T. XIII (A II, T. XIX), 2. Monumenti dell' Instit., II, T. 23. Annali dell' Instit., 1835, p. 231 *(Panofka)*; 1867, pp. 363 et seq.*(Heydemann)*. Römische Mittheilungen des archæol. Instituts, III, p. 252 *(Jatta)*. *Klein*, Vasen mit Lieblingsinschriften, p. 69, 1.

101. Hydria: Rape of Oreithyia.

Boreas, god of the North Wind, seized Oreithyia, daughter of Erechtheus, King of Attica, as she was playing with her companions on the banks of the Ilissos, and bore her through the air to his Thracian home. The bearded and winged god is here depicted tempestuously pursuing the terrified maiden, who flees, a garland in either hand, towards an altar, marked as a shrine of Apollo by the adjacent laurel-tree. On the other side appears the amazed and horrified companion of the fugitive.

Gerhard. Auserlesene Vasenbilder, III, T. 152, 1, p. 12. Wiener Vorlegeblätter für archäol. Uebungen, II, T. 9, 2. Comp. *Welcker*, Alte Denkmäler, III, pp. 144 et seq., 186. Ann. dell' Instit., 1870, p. 225 *(Heydemann)*.

102. Hydria: Poseidon and Æthra.

The love of Poseidon for Æthra, daughter of Pittheus of Troizen, who bore him Theseus, is frequently commemorated in Attic legends. The present vase, like No. 101, shows us the pursuit of the loved one. Poseidon, with carefully arranged hair and holding the trident in his right hand, reaches with the left towards Æthra (indicated by her name), who tries to flee and raises her right hand to ward off the god. In her left hand she carries a large basket for work or flowers.

Mus. Gregor., ii, T. xiv (A ii, T. xx), 1. *Gerhard*, Auserles. Vasenbilder, i, T. 12. *Lenormant-De-Witte*, Élite céramographique, iii, T. 6. *Overbeck*, Griech. Kunstmythologie, iii, p. 237, T. xiii, 2.

103. Polychrome Crater: Childhood of Dionysos.

This remarkable vase, which in many respects is unique, is perhaps the most valuable specimen in the entire collection. The pictorial composition, with its numerous figures, is executed partly in mere outlines, partly in polychrome painting, upon a coating of pipe-clay; and in its arrangement and execution reflects the high stage of development reached by Athenian painting in the central decades of the fifth century, under the influence of Polygnotos and his contemporaries. Using but few colours, the painter has achieved an admirable result by well-calculated touches and delicate graduation of his shading. The outlines are tenderly and gracefully drawn, and the whole is suffused with a magical charm that converts into an enhanced beauty the very limitations in expression and the stiffness of the execution. The subject of representation is the entrusting of the infant Dionysos to Silenus and the Nymphs of Nysa who were chosen as his nurses. Hermes walks cautiously in advance, attentively regarding the infant enveloped in a cloth, as he places it in the outstretched right hand of the aged Silenus. The entire body of Silenus is covered with shaggy white hair (colour restored by a modern hand), in the style of the Papposilenus of the theatres; he is seated on an ivy-covered rock, holding in his left hand a thyrsos crowned with ivy-leaves. The head of the child, which inquisitively inspects its new guardian, is represented like that of a grown person; for Greek art did not learn till a late period how to reproduce children's faces in conformity with nature. A Nymph behind Silenus, clad in chlamys and nebris, leans forward in sympathetic interest. On the other side is a corresponding Nymph, seated on a high rock and holding an ivy-branch in her left hand. — On the reverse of the vase is a triplet of graceful maidens, who may be either Nymphs or Muses, for there was no very sharp distinction drawn between these, either in the popular religious conceptions or in the art of the earlier period. But in view of the subject of the painting on the obverse, the former designation is doubtless to be chosen here. The Nymph seated in the middle plays upon the lyre; opposite her is a companion holding her lyre in her lowered right hand; while the third Nymph, wholly enveloped in her mantle, seems to be preparing to dance.

From Vulci. — Mus. Gregor., II, T. xxvi (A II, T. xxxi). 1. Comp. *Flasch*, Polychromie der Vasen, p. 59. *Rayet-Collignon*, Histoire de la céramique grecque, p. 223. *Heydemann*, Dionysos' Geburt und Kindheit, p. 24.

104. Hydria: Zeus and Ganymede.

A well-known story relates that Ganymede, son of Tros, and fairest of mortal men, was carried to heaven by an eagle to become the cup-bearer of the gods. According to the older legends, Zeus himself carried off the beautiful boy, who had excited his love; and this is the version adopted in the painting before us. The ruler of the gods, with his sceptre in his left hand, pursues Ganymede with arms outstretched in longing. The latter grasps his childish hoop and stick in his right hand, while in his left arm, half-concealed under his himation, he holds a cock, an appropriate gift to an ephebos, probably presented by Zeus.

Passeri, II, T. 156. Mus. Gregor., II, T. xiv (A II, T. xx), 2. *Lenormant-De-Witte*, Élite céramograph., I, T. 18. *Overbeck*, Griech. Kunstmythologie, II, pp. 515 et seq., T. 8. Ann. dell' Instit., 1876, p. 50 *(Koerte)*. Röm. Mitthell. des arch. Instit., II, p. 240 *(Von Duhn)*.

106. Hydria: Death of Hector.

The shoulder-painting on this vase closely corresponds in composition and style with the vase-paintings of Duris (comp. No. 232, p. 346); and the mode in which it represents the celebrated combat between Hector and Achilles is most instructive as to the relations between the epos and its artistic illustration. The combat here, which in all its separate details deviates from the description in the 22nd book of the Iliad, is witnessed not

only by Athena, who stands beside Achilles to encourage
him, but also by Apollo, who is placed beside Hector.
Apollo is on the point of quitting the scene of battle,
just as in the epos the defeated warrior is abandoned by
his protecting god; but as he goes he threatens Achilles
with an arrow in his raised right hand — the arrow which,
impelled by the hand of Paris, is a little later to slay the
son of Peleus at the Skæan Gate. The painting thus endeavours to render briefly the spirit and general idea of
the epos, without seeking to illustrate its actual words.

Mus. Gregor., ii, T. xii (A ii. T. xviii), 2. *Gerhard*, Auserlesene
Vasenbilder, iii, T. 202, 1 and 2. Comp. Sitzungsberichte der Münchener Akademie, 1868, p. 76 *(Brunn)*. Jahrbücher für Philologie,
supplementary vol. xi, pp. 515 et seq. *(Luckenbach)*. Archæol. Zeit.,
xl (1882). p. 21 *(P. J. Meier)*.

113. So-called Stamnos: Zeus and Ægina.

Zeus here appears once more in pursuit of a maiden,
with whom he has fallen in love; his object on this occasion being, as the inscribed name informs us, Ægina, daughter of Asopos, King of Phliasia. The god has surprized her
in the midst of her sisters, who flee to the right and left.
The painting on the reverse shows us the terrified maidens
bringing the alarming news to their aged father Asopos.
In the pictures of Peleus wrestling with Thetis, the Nereids
who flee to their father are usually represented in a similar fashion.

Mus. Gregor., ii, T. xx (A ii, T. xxvi), 1. *Braun*, Antike
Marmorwerke, i, T. 6. *Overbeck*, Griech. Kunstmythologie, ii, p. 400.

115. Stamnos: Battle of the Amazons.

The earlier art preferred to depict the Amazons in
their battle against Heracles as heavy-armed infantry; but
Micon in his picture in the great stoa of the market-place
at Athens of the Amazons fighting against the Athenians,
painted about 460 B.C., presented the Ionian view by
painting the former as bold horsewomen. This composition definitely influenced all subsequent representations of the myth; and the group before us, of a mounted

Amazon (perhaps the queen?) in Scythian dress charging two youths with her lance, is also borrowed from it.
One of the youths, perhaps to be identified as Theseus, is
entirely nude and armed with sword, shield, and helmet;
the other is clad as a subordinate with chlamys, boots,
and hat, and raises a stone in his right hand. Comp.
Vases Nos. 128, 131. — On the reverse appears a man in
Thracian costume, between two women; a subject pointing also to the northern regions in which the Amazons
were said to have their home.

Mus. Gregor., II, T. xviii (A II, T. xxiii). 1. *Gerhard*, Auserlesene
Vasenbilder, III. T. 164. *Benndorf*. Heroon von Gjölbaschi-Trysa.
p. 142, Fig. 134. Comp. *Klügmann*, Die Amazonen in Litteratur
und Kunst, p. 46. Fünfzigstes Berliner Winckelmannsprogramm.
p. 157 *(Furtwaengler)*. — For Nos. 128 and 131: Mus. Gregor., II,
T. xxiv (A II, T. xxxix). 2. and II, T. xx (A II. T. xxvi), 2.

117. Apulian Amphora with volute - handles: Orestes at Delphi.

The painting on the front of the neck shows Artemis
in a chariot drawn by two deer. The subject of the
chief painting on the body of the vase is the matricide
Orestes, who seeks shelter in the temple at Delphi from
the pursuit of the Furies and kneels upon the altar, beside
which sprouts a laurel-twig. Apollo, leaning against the
pillar to the right, seems to be addressing words of com-
fort to the fugitive. Above, to the left, stands Athena,
by whose influence the final acquittal of Orestes at Athens
was obtained. A Nike, bearing a palm-leaf fan and looking
towards the goddess, sits above Orestes, thus indicating
the future acquittal by the help of Athena. To the right,
at the top, is one of the Furies (clad like Artemis in a
hunting-dress) turning her head in mingled wrath and
terror towards Athena. The grouping of the figures clearly
conveys the conception of the legend that had become
dominant through the drama of Æschylos. — The reverse
is decorated on the neck with a half-length of Helios and
on the body with a Bacchic scene.

From Naples; afterwards in the Vatican Library. —*Visconti*, Atti
dell' accademia Romana di archeologia, II, pp. 601 et seq. *Raoul-*

Rochette, Monuments inédits, T. 38. *Overbeck*, Gallerie heroischer Bildwerke, T. xxix, 8, p. 711. Archæolog. Zeit., xviii, 1860, T. 137, 4, pp. 54 et seq. Comp. Arch. Zeit., xlii, 1884, p. 285 *(Wernicke)*.

118. Crater from Lower Italy: Europa.

The artist has here adopted the version of the legend that makes Zeus send a bull to carry off Europa. The princess caresses the head of the animal with both hands, while a companion takes to flight with gestures of amazement. Above the bull hovers a Cupid, with a mirror and ladder, the symbols of love. To the right is Aphrodite, with mirror and jewel-case; to the left, Zeus in person, with a long sceptre and a vase.

From the collection of Cardinal Gualtieri, afterwards in the Vatican Library. — *Montfaucon*, L'antiquité expliquée, Supplém. iii, T. 34. *Passeri*, Picturæ Etrusc. in vasculis, i, T. 1-3. *D'Hancarville*, Antiquités étrusq., ii, T. 41. *Dubois-Maisonneuve*, Introduction à l'étude des vases, T. 65. *Overbeck*, Griech. Kunstmythologie, ii, p. 437, T. vi, 13.

119. Apulian Crater: Paris and Helen (?).

The arrival of Paris in Sparta and his meeting with Helen were very variously represented by the artists of the later period. On the vase before us we see Helen leaning negligently against a pillar and conversing with Paris, who is identified by his Phrygian cap. Above Paris sits a Cupid with a wreath in his left hand; and to the left, above, is Aphrodite with the fan. Below, to the left, appears Pan with a fawn in front of him, and to the right, a little higher, is a Satyr, these deities of field and wood indicating that the lovers have met in the open air. — In the absence of any very distinct characteristic, this painting is open to other interpretations. Some authorities take the woman for Œnone, the first wife of Paris; others recognize in her Aphrodite, seeking to win Paris to her side before his famous judgment, or encouraging his passion for Helen. In the latter case, the figure with the fan is explained as Peitho or even as Helen herself, the prize beckoning to Paris from afar. — On the reverse is a

Bacchanalian scene, treated in the manner usual on vases of this class.

From the Gualtieri collection. — *Montfaucon*, Supplément de l'antiquité expliquée, III, T. 32. *Passeri*, Picturæ in vasculis, I, T. 15 et seq. *Pistolesi*, Il Vaticano descritto, III, T. 100. *Inghirami*, Pitture di vasi, II, T. 171. *D'Hancarville*, Vases d'Hamilton, IV, T. 24. *Millingen*, Peintures de vases grecques (*Reinach*, Bibliothèque des monum. figurés, II), T. 43. Comp. *Welcker*, Alte Denkmäler, V, p. 437. Sitzungsberichte der Münchener Akademie, 1868, p. 61 (*Brunn*). *Roscher*, Lexikon der Mythologie, I, p. 1962 (*Engelmann*).

121. Crater from Lower Italy: Comic Scene.

The painting on this vase reproduces with all fidelity in matters of costume a scene from one of the burlesque farces known as *Phlyakes*, which were in vogue during the third and second centuries at Tarentum and elsewhere in Magna Græcia. A richly-dressed lady, looking out of an upper window, converses with Zeus, who is fetching a long ladder in order to climb up to her. Zeus has a pointed beard, is old and ugly, and wears, according to the wont of burlesque-actors, a padded red garment (known as a *somation*), with reddish-brown sleeves and hose, and a tall headdress, looking like a burlesque of the royal diadem. Hermes, standing on the right, similarly dight with petasos and kerykeion, holds up a lamp towards the window, by way of lighting his lord on his nocturnal love-adventure. The identification of the lady, who is the object of the expedition, is not very certain. She is usually taken for Alcmene, who unwittingly received Zeus disguised as her husband Amphitryon. The circumstance that the aged king of the gods appears in his own person as he thus poaches on another's preserves, may be explained as an artistic licence of the painter, who was unable otherwise to identify the personages engaged with sufficient distinctness; or the painter may have had in view another form of the legend.

Winckelmann, Monum. inediti, II, T. 190. Mus. Gregor., A II, T. XXXI. Comp. Jahrbuch des deutschen archäol. Instit., I, p. 276 (*Heydemann*), where the remaining bibliography is collected. *Voelker*, Rhinthonis fragmenta (Halle, 1887), p. 19.

124, 125. Apulian Amphoræ.

The contemplative group of young warriors and women on this vase is interesting less from the indifferent situations it presents than from its faithful delineation of the costume and manners of the semi-Hellenized inhabitants of Southern Italy during the fourth and third centuries B. C. Comp. Amphora No. 182.

For No. 125: *Pistolesi*, Il Vaticano descritto, III, T. 98, 1. — For No. 182 : *Pistolesi*, III, T. 98, 2 and 3. *Millin*, Peintures de vases, II (*Reinach*, Bibliothèque des monum. figurés, II). T. 69.

127. Apulian Amphora, with volute-handles: Triptolemos, Funeral Scene.

The neck is adorned in front with luxuriant foliage, from which issues a head in a Phrygian cap. The principal painting represents the procession of Triptolemos, in elaborate detail. Demeter, holding a large torch in her left arm, presents the ears of corn to the youthful hero of Eleusis, who is to spread the knowledge of cereals throughout the earth. The winged chariot of Triptolemos is drawn by two huge serpents, one of which is being watered by a Hora (or Nymph). Another female figure with a torch, standing behind Demeter, is perhaps Hecate, appearing here as the companion and attendant of the goddess. At the top reclines Zeus with his eagle-sceptre, and before him stands Hermes, who has been directed by the king of the gods to accompany Triptolemos on his expedition. The flower-wreathed figure to the right is probably to be recognized as Kore-Persephone, conversing with a second Hora, who offers her a garland of flowers. — On the reverse is a sepulchral monument supported by columns, with the figure of a youth and his hound, surrounded by women and youths bearing funeral gifts in their hands.

Acquired from Prince Poniatowski for the Vatican Library. — *Visconti*, Opere varie, II, T. 1. *Pistolesi*, Il Vaticano descritto, III, T. 64. *Arneth*, Gold- und Silbermonumente zu Wien, Beilage 1. *Millin*, Peintures de vases, II, T. 31 et seq. (*Reinach*, Bibliothèque des monuments figurés, II, p. 62, where the remaining bibliography is collected). *Overbeck*, Griech. Kunstmythol., III, 4, T. XVI, 5, p. 552.

130. Stamnos: Troilos.

Troilos, youngest son of Priam, accompanied by his sister Polyxena, has gone to fetch water from the spring outside the city, taking a couple of horses also to water them; and is meanwhile surprised by Achilles, who has been lying in ambush. Troilos rides off as fast as he can, leading the other horse, but the swift-footed Achilles is close behind him and already stretches out his arm to seize him. Polyxena flees on the other side, having dropped the slender vessel, which lies on the ground before the horses. — On the reverse is a youth between a man and a woman, all three draped.

Mus. Gregor., II, T. XXII (A II, T. XXVII), 1. Comp. *Welcker*, Alte Denkmäler, v, p. 458. *Klein*, Euphronios², pp. 228 et seq.

132. Stamnos: Eos.

Just as Helios is conceived of as driving a chariot and four, so Eos, the winged goddess of dawn, is here depicted driving with a whip *(kentron)* and reins, a team of four fiery steeds. Beside the horses two names are inscribed, but unfortunately not very legibly (perhaps Kaloros and Phaëthon). In the background is a column supporting a tripod, the exact significance of which in this place is not very clear. — On the reverse is a Maenad between two Satyrs.

Mus. Gregor., II, T. XVIII (A II, T. XXIII), 2. *Gerhard*, Auserlesene Vasenbilder, II, T. 79. *Lenormant-De-Witte*, Élite céramograph., II, T. 109 A. Comp. *Welcker*, Alte Denkmäler, v, p. 482*. *Knapp*, Nike in der Vasenmalerei, p. 54.

133. Hydria: Apollo and the Muses.

The painting here stretches across the shoulder of the vase in a band bordered all round with narrow ornamental stripes. Apollo, with his seven-stringed lyre, stands beside a low tree, surrounded by six Muses, who seem to be peacefully conversing together. One of them holds a double-flute and two others have lyres. At this period the Muses were still represented merely as dignified ladies; the separate individualities are not yet distinguished by names and special attributes; and even the number nine, though already fixed in the early theogonic poems, had not yet established itself generally in the popular conception.

Mus. Gregor., II, T. xv (A II, T. xxi), 2.

134. Amphora with twisted handles: Hector's Farewell.

Hector in complete armour here reaches the goblet to the youthful-looking Hecuba, who is pouring a libation on the ground from a ewer. To the left is the aged Priam, holding a staff in his right hand, and covering his face (which is turned away from the spectator) with his left; in gloomy forboding he has averted his eyes from his son, as though he had a presentiment of his approaching death. The various figures have their names written beside them; 'Beautiful (or excellent) is Hector' is the inscription beside that hero. There is no doubt that the painter had in mind the last farewell of Hector, without aiming at reproducing every detail in the famous description in the Iliad. He has in fact utilized the current types of parting-scenes, and has thus allowed the woman offering the libation to retain a girlish appearance little suited for the bearer of the appended name. On the other hand, the grief-stricken figure of the old man so entirely corresponds with the situation of Priam, that we may accept without farther ado the indication given by the inscriptions, and recognize in this picture an appropriate reflection from the poem that inspired it. — The painting on the reverse is less carefully executed. A bearded man, with bald forehead, stands, leaning upon a tall crutch-handled staff, between two women.

Mus. Gregor., II, T. lx (A II, T. lxiv), 2. *Gerhard*, Auserlesene Vasenbilder, III, T. 189. Comp. Sitzungsber. der Münchener Akademie, 1868, p. 76 *(Brunn)*. Jahrbücher für Philologie, supplementary vol. xi, p. 552 *(Luckenbach)*. *Winter*, Jüngere attische Vasen, p. 27.

136. Amphora shaped like a wine-skin: Libation of a Victor.

This amphora, a so-called *Pelike*, had been broken in antiquity and mended with three bronze clamps. — On the front appears Nike (name appended), with a kerykeion in her left hand, filling a gilt goblet from her vase for a fully-armed warrior named Skeparnos. The circumstance that the goddess of victory herself pours out for him the wine, with which the grateful libation to the gods is to be made, marks him as victor in the fight. The old man on the right (with the name Oinys, *i.e.* Œneus) is apparently the father of Skeparnos. — On the reverse is a bearded man between two women, one of whom holds his sword, the other his helmet.

Mus. Gregor., II, T. LXIII (A II, T. lxvii), 2. An almost identical specimen, but with different names, is preserved in the British Museum (No. 721); comp. *Gerhard*, Auserlesene Vasenbilder, II, T. 150.

Room VIII.

The splendid collection of *Kylikes (Tazze)*, or flat and shallow vases, is the chief point of interest in this room; but vases of all shapes and periods have also found a place in it, the older specimens being to the right of the entrance, the later specimens (of Etruscan origin), to the left. Upon the elevated brackets in the corners are four tall over-decorated Apulian amphoræ (comp. No. 223), that in the front corner to the left being a specially prominent specimen. The principal painting upon this is a representation, with many figures, of the wrestling contest between Peleus and Thetis, besides which there are two friezes, one of marine animals and the other of young men and women bearing all manner of toilet-articles in their hands. The amphora in the hinder corner on the same side, with a painting of Europa and the Bull, is very similar in shape and decoration.

For the Thetis vase: *Passeri*, Picturæ in vasculis, I, T. 8-10. *Pistolesi*, Il Vaticano descritto, III, T. 89 et seq. *Millingen*, Ancient

Unedited Monuments, I, Pl. 10. *Overbeck*, Gallerie heroischer Bild-werke, p. 190, T. vii, 8. — For the Europa vase: *Passeri*, I, T. 4-6. *Pistolesi*, iii, T. 91 et seq. *Overbeck*, Kunstmythologie, ii, p. 436, T. vi, 15.

The side-walls of this room are hung with copies of paintings which decorated the interior of a tomb-chamber at Vulci, discovered by Alexander François in 1857, and were afterwards removed to the Museo Torlonia (alla Lungara) at Rome. These pictures, which date from the third century B.C., are among the most important remains of Etruscan painting, which has in them adapted Greek forms to national peculiarities. The gloomy and cruel character of a people that delighted in human sacrifices and gladiatorial combats here finds expression in the choice of bloody subjects. A few isolated personages from the Greek myths occur, such as Amphiaraos, Sisyphos, the aged Nestor, and Phœnix; and several of the momentous scenes from the legends of Troy and Thebes are represented; *e.g.* the Locrian Ajax *(Aivas)*, son of Oileus, in the act of tearing Cassandra *(Casntra)* from the foot of the statue of the god where she has sought sanctuary; the mutual fratricide of Eteocles and Polynices, the sons of Œdipus; and finally the grisly sacrifice offered by Achilles at the funeral pyre of his friend Patroclos (Iliad, xxi, 22; xxiii, 175 et seq.). In this last-named scene Achilles *(Achle)*, in presence of Agamemnon *(Achmenrun)*, thrusts his sword into the breast of a captive Trojan *(Truials)*. The shade of Patroclos *(hinthial Patrukles)* is also represented, in no way differentiated from the living, either in appearance or armour. Beside Patroclos is a female demon with outspread wings (*Vanth*; perhaps a goddess of death), while on the other side of Achilles the Etruscan Charon *(Charu)*, with hammer on shoulder, awaits his victim. The Telamonian Ajax and Ajax son of Oileus *(Aivas Tlamunus* and *Vilatas)* each drag another nude captive to the slaughter. The pictures on the other part of the wall, with subjects taken from Etruscan tradition, correspond with these scenes from the Greek epos. Thus, Ajax dragging the captured Trojan to death is balanced on the opposite side by Mastarna *(Macstrna)* cutting the bonds of a prisoner, Cæles Vibenna *(Caile Vipinas)*, a rescue explained by the adjoining groups, in which three unarmed men, perhaps the custodians of the prisoner, are being overmastered by three warriors. The Etruscan names are inscribed beside all the figures. According to a trustworthy tradition, Mastarna is the Etruscan name (or more strictly a title) of Servius Tullius, the successor of Tarquinius Priscus, who, before his accession, shared many campaigns with his faithful friend Cælius Vibenna. A famous incident from one of these campaigns is the subject of the picture before us. The next painting, the murder of *Cneve Tarchunies Rumach (i.e.* Cneius Tarquinius Romanus) by *Marce Camitlnas*, a pendant to the Theban fratricide on the other part of the wall, stands in relation to the preceding painting and seems to prove that the men from whom Vibenna was delivered were Romans.

The laurel-crowned form of *Vel Saties*, whose robe is richly decorated with figures of dancing warriors, also refers us to Etruscan soil. From the boy kneeling beside him, holding a bird, it has been supposed that this painting represents a priest and his acolyte.

Monumenti dell' Instit., vi, T. 31 and 32. *Noël des Vergers*, L'Étrurie et les Étrusques, iii, T. 21-30, pp. 47 et seq. *R. Garruci*, Tavole fotografiche delle pitture Vulcenti (Dissertazioni archeologiche, ii, pp. 57 et seq.). Comp. Bull. dell' Instit., 1857, pp. 113 et seq. Annali, 1859, pp. 353 et seq. *(Brunn,.* Dennis, Cities and Cemeteries[3], ii, pp. 503 et seq. *Corssen*, Sprache der Etrusker, i, p. 278, T. viii. *Deecke*, Etrusk. Forschungen, 3, pp. 246 et seq., 7, p. 45. *Gardthausen*, Mastarna oder Servius Tullius, pp. 29 et seq. *Bursians*, Jahresberichte für die Fortschritte der klass. Alterthumswissenschaft, 32, 1882, p. 382 *(Deecke)*. *Martha*, L'art étrusque, pp. 395 et seq.

At the end of the room is a marble bust of Gregory XVI., by De Fabris. In front of this is a table, the top of which is made up of innumerable fragments of ancient coloured glass. The *Six Table-Cases* below the windows contain works in glass and enamel, including diverse vessels in iridescent, greenish, and clear glass, some with raised ornamentation; beautiful miniature amphoræ (perhaps used as scent-bottles), ewers, and alabastra, in coloured smalt, such as are found in Etruscan graves from the beginning of the sixth century B. C. downwards. The manufacture of the last-mentioned seems to have flourished especially among the Phœnicians, under the influence of Egypt. The ribbon-like ornamentation was produced by drawing grooves or furrows in the surface of the vessel while still soft, filling these up with glass-threads of various colours, and finally re-baking and polishing the whole until the various glass-threads seemed to form a homogeneous mass with the ground-colour, which was usually blue, less often green or yellow. The process required the utmost dexterity and precision and bristles with difficulties, so that modern imitations have never been very successful. The ring-shaped beads with particoloured centres are similar but are generally of a higher antiquity (7-6th cent. B. C.). The so-called glass-mosaics 'a millefiori' (Nos. 231 A, 243 A) were produced by a different process, which reached a high perfection at Rome under the influence of Hellenistic models. These mosaics are formed of numerous little rods and threads of particoloured glass welded together in imitation of vegetable forms, mineral structures, or marble mosaics.

Most of these specimens were purchased by Pius IX. in 1875 from the Rossignani collection. The specimens previously in the museum are figured in Mus. Gregor., II, T. CIV et seq. (A II, T. XCVII). — For the Phœnician alabastra, comp. *Perrot-Chipiez*, Histoire de l'art, III, pp. 197 et seq., p. 734. *Frœhner*, La verrerie antique. pp. 18 et seq. *Helbig*, Homerische Epos[2], p. 32.

We begin our inspection of the separate vases on the left, following the numbering, which, however, reverses the chronological order.

144. Kylix: Rape of Persephone.

The interior painting shows Persephone seized and borne away by Pluto. Pluto's fillet, Persephone's diadem, earrings, necklace, and bracelets with pomegranates, and the other ornaments are represented by little gilded grains or balls applied in relief to the terracotta. Both the symbolical pomegranate and the exterior paintings corroborate the reference to Pluto. The ruler of the underworld appears seated on his throne, grasping his sceptre in his left hand, and adorned with a diadem and a bracelet of pomegranates. A youth in front of him offers him a pomegranate-blossom (in one picture; in the other it is a pomegranate), while another is about to place a garland upon the royal head. The drawing and costumes betray the non‑Attic origin of this kylix; it was probably produced by a Greek factory in Central Italy during the fourth century.

Mus. Gregor., I. T. lxxxiii, 2. *Overbeck*, Kunstmythol., III, 4, T. xviii. 12, p. 594. Comp. *Braun*, Ruinen und Museen, p. 826, 50. *Foerster*, Raub der Persephone, pp. 234 et seq.

152. Kylix: Triptolemos.

The interior painting, representing once more the young Triptolemos (name appended) in his winged chariot, is drawn carefully but freely, with a slight use of white pigment. The exterior paintings, representing a Nike on one side and a torch-bearer on the other, each flanked by two youthful figures, are, on the other hand, very perfunctorily executed (end of the fifth century).

Mus. Gregor., II, T. lxxvi (A II, T. lxxx), 2. *Gerhard*, Auserlesene Vasenbilder, I, T. 45. *Lenormant-De-Witte*, Élite-céramograph., III, T. 46. *Overbeck*, Kunstmythol., III, 4, p. 500, T. 15, 8.

154. Kylix: Æsop.

A dwarfish man, enveloped in a mantle from under which his staff projects, is here shown, seated upon a stone. His body is stunted and his head disproportionately large. The face is of a purposely exaggerated ugliness: the nose is long and crooked, the hair hangs in smooth, straight locks both before and behind, and the forehead is wrinkled, while the coarse whiskers and the beard sticking out in a point complete the picture of a man whose interest in other matters leads him to disdain to improve or to conceal the hard measure dealt out by nature to his outward appearance. With inquisitive attention he regards his companion — a fox with tail tucked in, who is seated upon a rock and gesticulates with his fore-paw as he speaks. We are evidently in the realm of the bestiaries, which even on Greek soil recognize reynard as the fugleman of the beasts. The misshapen man is no other than Æsop, the legendary founder of fables among the Greeks. Comp. No. 756, p. 29.

Mus. Gregor., II, T. lxxx (A II, T. lxxxiv), 2. O. Jahn, Archæol. Beiträge, T. 12, 2. p. 434. Comp. Braun, Ruinen und Museen, p. 828.

161. Etruscan Stamnos: Pluto and Persephone.

Pluto, with rough hair and short beard, is here shown in his chariot drawn by four fiery steeds, driving with the richly adorned Persephone to Hades. Beneath the horses the upper part of the figure of a bearded man, with round hat and herald's baton, projects from the earth; this is the courier, conducting his lord to the underworld. Persephone, who wears rich jewels and wreaths, stands calmly beside Pluto, so that this scene apparently represents not the first visit of the goddess to Hades but the return home (katagoge) which took place every year in autumn, in terms of the Olympian compact. Even in this painting several non-Greek peculiarities appear, and the painting on the other side of the vase belongs wholly to the domain of Italic conceptions. To the left is another bearded man (concealed from the knees downward), with petasos and herald's baton, looking up towards Hermes, who is clearly identified by his winged helmet, his long caduceus, and his winged sandals. Beside Hermes stands a youth with lance and hammer, perhaps an Italic warrior transferred by Hermes to the official of the underworld, who may be regarded either as a gate-keeper or as an escort of souls, like Charon. In any case the meaning of the scene remains doubtful. For the local Etruscan style of the vase, comp. p. 289.

Gerhard, Auserlesene Vasenbilder, ɪɪɪ, T. 240, p. 165. Comp. Archæol. Zeit., ɪv. 1846, p. 350. *O. Jahn,* Münchener Vasensammlung, p. ccxxxiv. *Foerster,* Raub und Rückkehr der Persephone, pp. 235 et seq. *Overbeck,* Kunstmythologie, ɪɪɪ, p. 604, T. xvɪɪɪ, 14.

162. Kylix: Sacrificial Scenes.

The interior painting shows us a boy with sacrificial utensils (a kind of basket and a bowl) in his hands, standing beside an altar. The upper part of his body is bare, according to the custom of acolytes at sacrifices, and his mantle is wound round his waist. On one side of the exterior is a ram, on the other a bull, each led by an acolyte towards a priest awaiting them in front of a temple, indicated by Ionic columns surmounted by an architrave (latter half of the fifth century).

Mus. Gregor., ɪɪ, T. lxxɪ (A ɪɪ, T. lxxv), 1. Comp. Compterendu de la commission archéol. de St. Pétersbourg, 1868, p. 164.

On the upper shelf, —

163. Etruscan Hydria: Decorating a Tombstone.

The crude errors in drawing and the hard and uncertain lines of the painting on this vase betray an inartistic hand, which, without due appreciation of its own limitations, has attempted to copy a model of the developed Attic style. Both this vase and No. 161 are probably to be regarded as Etruscan productions. To the right is a tall stele or tombstone, decorated with a band of palmettes, with a cornice surmounted by a pediment with a ridge-ornament. A youth is engaged in painting the ornament of the so-called cymatium on the moulding beneath the cornice. To the left is a two-horse chariot at the galop, driven by a bearded man. The relation of this to the stele is not very clear. Some authorities take it for a reference to a race in honour of the obsequies, while others regard the charioteer as the apotheosized knight, or, in harmony with the national Etruscan theories, as Pluto.

From Vulci. — Mus. Gregor., ɪ, T. xvɪ, 1. *Gerhard,* Festgedanken an Winckelmann, 1841, T. ɪɪ. Berichte der sächs. Gesellschaft der Wissenschaften, 1867, T. v, 5, p. 111 *(O. Jahn).* Comp. *Braun,* Ruinen und Museen, pp. 819, 43.

164. Kylix: Armed Ephebi.

In these groups of fully-armed youths and bearded men — sons going out to battle along with their fathers — the artist had no intention of representing any particular scene or any homogeneous subject; he was interested only in exhibiting the noble warlike forms in various positions, and one can trace his proud satisfaction with his own skill and success. These refined and elegant paintings must be counted among the best productions of the great kylix-painters; they are remarkably akin to the drawings of Brygos. The outlines are clear and vigorous, the details of the design executed with loving care, and the various weapons depicted with the fidelity of an expert. Observe especially the shields with their heraldic symbols, and the broad, ornamented shield-covers hanging from them.

Mus. Gregor., II, T. lxxxvi (A II, T. lxxxix), 2.

167. Kylix: Warriors arming.

The interior painting shows a nude youth beginning to don his armour; the right greave is already on, and he stoops to fasten the other. A bearded man opposite him holds the lance in readiness; behind, to the right, is the shield. On one side of the exterior a woman is about to pour out a draught of wine for a warrior, a youth converses with another man, and close by is a nude youth looking thoughtfully at his sword and shoulder-belt. In this painting also the chief interest of the painter as well as of the spectator lies, not in the subject, but in the variety of the forms and motives. The figures on the other side of the exterior are specially charming. One youth is seated, clasping his left knee with both hands; another is standing and holds his lance near the top; a bearded man is comfortably seated on a block of stone, his legs crossed and his chin resting on his right arm. All these positions and motions are met with in plastic art after the middle of the fifth century, and originated in the school of great painters, the most important of whom was Polygnotos.

Mus. Gregor.. ii, T. lxxxvii (A ii, T. xc). 1.   Comp. *Braun, Ruinen und Museen*, pp. 822, 45. Jahrbuch des deutschen archæol. Instit., ii. p. 171 *(Dümmler)*.

169. Kylix: Youths in the Palæstra.

This vase is certainly by the same artist as No. 167, and painted as a pendant to it. It shows the same slender forms, the same straight profiles, the same ornamentation, and the same refinement and elegance of execution. The pictures here introduce us to the Athenian palæstra; several youths, in various attitudes, are using the strigils or scrapers which served to remove the oil and dust from their bodies after the exertions of wrestling, etc.

Mus. Gregor., ii, T. lxxxvii (A ii, T. xc), 2.

Glass-Case.

On the top-shelf are a few VASES OF LOCAL ETRUSCAN MANUFACTURE, among which is a large ewer, with ornaments and animals engraved upon it in evident imitation of Oriental models; and a number of BLACK TERRACOTTA VASES *(bucchero nero)*, with shapes and plastic adornments apparently copied from metal-work. Among the latter is a vase in the shape of a flat box on a tall stand, surrounded with a raised garland of rays and bosses, and adorned on the upper rim with four projecting animal's heads with horns. The lid is decorated with engraved animal-forms, including a group of fishes, and has a handle in the shape of a horse. Another remarkable vase derives its shape from the idea of a man standing in a chariot and pair. In the top of the horses' heads are inserted elaborately adorned stoppers, while a number of small holes are perforated about their mouths, through which the liquid contents of the vase were poured. An erect figure, representing the charioteer, serves as handle.

The two last-named vases are said to have been found in the Regullini-Galassi Tomb. — Mus. Gregor., II, T. xcvi (A I, T. iv), 3; T. xcviii (A I, T. vi). Comp. *Martha, L'art étrusque*, pp. 463 et seq. *Birch*, History of Ancient Pottery[2], p. 450.

Two Black-glazed Vases of the Cales variety, without feet.

These vases (comp. p. 289), which present the form of the phialæ or pateræ used in religious rites, are provided in the centre with a projection like the boss of a shield (omphalos) for the purpose of lifting them. In one case this boss bears the head of a woman in relief. Round the boss is stamped a raised band, in which Ares, Heracles, Athena, and Dionysos appear one behind the other, each in a four-horse chariot escorted by Nike. Each chariot is preceded by a flying Cupid, and below each team appears a small animal (boar, dog, serpent, and goat). Vases with these or similar stamped reliefs have frequently been found; the earliest examples dating perhaps from the latter half of the third century B. C.

Gori, Mus. Etrusco, I, T. 6. Mus. Gregor., II. T. cii (A I, T. xxxvi), 1. Comp. Annali dell' Instit., 1871, p. 24 *(Klügmann)*; 1883, p. 67 *(Foerster)*. Bullet., 1884, p. 50 *(Henzen)*.

Bucchero Kylix, with human figures as supports.

The cup of this vase is supported at the sides by three moulded winged figures, in imitation of larger models in metal. Sixth century.

Comp. *P. E. Visconti*, Monum. sepolcri di Ceri, T. 9, 2. *Conze*, Zur Geschichte der Anfänge griech. Kunst, p. 8.

Bucchero Vase with an engraved heraldic design of a man between two horses, modelled on the well-known types found on the Greek geometric vases of the so-called Dipylon variety.

Mus. Gregor., II, T. xcv (A II, T. II). Comp. Annali dell' Instit., 1872, T. K. 19, p. 178 *(G. Hirschfeld)*.

On the second shelf, from left to right, —

Red-figured Pitcher : Menelaos and Helen.

On the capture of Ilium Helen flees from Menelaos, who threatens to punish her infidelity with the sword (see

p. 298, under No. 43), and seeks refuge at the statue of
Athena; in her terror she grasps the Palladium below
the shield with her left hand, and raises her right towards
Menelaos in supplication. Her beauty proves her protection; for Menelaos is overcome by the sight of her
loveliness, scarcely concealed by the Doric garment open
at the side; his former love revives, the sword falls from
his hand. Aphrodite herself has interposed; in a calm
attitude, holding her mantle to her breast, she stands
opposite the passionate Menelaos, and sends towards
him a little Cupid, to place a fillet upon the hero who is
about to bow to the supremacy of love and beauty. To the
left (and indicated by an inscription) is Peitho, goddess
of persuasion, a frequent companion of Aphrodite and a
personification of her might, who here appears in a merely casual connection with the composition. The principal
group, which recurs in practically the same form among
the metopes on the north side of the Parthenon, is without
doubt borrowed from some monumental painting of the
middle of the fifth century.

Mus. Gregor., II, T. v (A II, T. xi), 2. Comp. *Overbeck*, Gallerie
heroischer Bildwerke, p. 631, T. xxvi, 12. *Michaelis*, Parthenon,
p. 139. *Baumeister*, Denkmäler des klass. Alterthums, I, p. 746.
Jahrb. des deutschen archæolog. Instituts, II, p. 178 *(Studniczka)*.

Two Black-figured Vases by Nicosthenes.

The shape of these vases indicates clearly enough the
studio of the potter whose name they bear (comp. No. 10 a,
p. 293). On one side of the neck of the first is a representation in the archaic stiff mode of the bearded Dionysos
and a Mænad; on the other side is a woman between
two rearing lions, one of which she holds by the neck.
This latter scene is a painting, at this date already reduced
to a stiff conventionalized form, of the goddess of nature
and mistress of the lower animal-kingdom, erroneously
described as the Persian Artemis. The body of the vase
is decorated with warlike scenes of the usual type, in
which fully-armed hoplites and an archer take part. The

ornamentation of the second vase is more varied. On each side of the neck is a draped Nike in an attitude of haste; on each shoulder a pair of energetic pugilists; and on the body a frieze of animals, including griffins and Sirens. Each of the ribbon-shaped handles is adorned with a two-handled tripod, and the inner rim of the mouth with dolphins facing inwards.

Mus. Gregor., ii, T. xxvii (A ii, T. xxxiii). Comp. *Klein*, Vasen mit Meistersignaturen 2, p. 56, 8, and p. 62, 33.

Red-figured Pitcher: Persian Court.

The spout of this curiously shaped vase is decorated with an owl (the common symbol on Athenian coins), and the body with a picture of the Persian court, which here seems to have entered a semi-ideal sphere. The 'Great King' (named simply *'basileus'* or king in the inscription, according to the custom of those days) is clad in a sleeved chiton, mantle, and flapped Persian cap, and holds a long sceptre. A female form (indicated as the Great Queen by the inscription), similarly clad, approaches him, bearing a long amphora with pointed foot, while another woman, behind the king, gesticulates with her right hand as she speaks. This extraordinarily delicate drawing, in which only the feet are strikingly defective, may probably be referred to the period immediately after the Persian Wars (about 450 B. C.).

Mus. Gregor., ii, T. iv, 2. Ann. dell' Inst., 1847, T. v. Comp. *Heydemann*, Alexander der Grosse und Dareios, p. 18. Jahrbuch des deutschen arch. Instit., ii, p. 174 *(Dümmler)*.

The two adjoining vases of similar shape, which were probably made in the same studio and intended as companion-pieces, are ornamented at the spout with hovering Cupids. The principal painting on one of these exhibits three youths using the strigil; that on the other shows a woman, with a ewer in her left hand, presenting a goblet to a bearded man, while a second woman holds out her goblet to be filled.

Mus. Gregor., ii, T. iv, 1 and 3. Ann. dell' Instit., 1847, T. v. — All three vases were found at Vulci in 1836.

Capacious Pitcher: Cock-fight.

Two youths are on the point of placing their pugnacious game-cocks on the ground, ready to let them fly at each other when the word is given. The third youth standing by is perhaps the director of the fight or the umpire. Cock-fighting was a favourite pastime in ancient Athens, and was not only cultivated by private individuals but also found a place in public festivals. About the middle of the fifth century.

Mus. Gregor., ii, T. v (A ii, T. xi), 1. Comp. *O. Jahn*, Archæolog. Beiträge, p. 441. *Daremberg-Saglio*, Dictionnaire des Antiquités, i, p. 180.

Hydria: Heracles and Satyrs.

The antithesis between the mighty Heracles and the thievish, impudent, and cowardly race of Satyrs was frequently touched on in the early Attic satyr-plays. The beautiful painting before us presents us with a merry scene of this kind (middle of the fifth century). Heracles, alarmed by a noise, starts up from a hasty siesta on a platform of masonry. The rascally Satyrs have stolen his weapons and hastily take to flight with all caution as the hero awakes; they look behind them with anxiety, and one has let the quiver fall in his terror.

Millingen, Peintures antiques de vases grecs (*Reinach*, Bibliothèque des monmm. figurés, ii), T. 35. Mus. Gregor.. ii, T. xiii (A ii, T. xix), 1. Comp. Philologus, xxvii, T. ii, 2, p. 18 *(O. Jahn)*.

On the third shelf, —

A few Arretine Vases (comp. p. 289), including a small kylix, decorated with rosettes in relief, and a small jug with raised garlands, rosettes, and dolphins. A blackglazed kylix, with relief-ornamentation, of the so-called Samian or Megarean Variety, is proved by its inscription *(C. Popili)* and decoration to have been made in some Roman pottery, using the same models as the Arretine factories.

Mus. Gregor.. ii, T. ci, 4; cii, 2 (A i, T. xxxv, 4; xxxvi, 2). — For the 'Megarean' vases, comp. *Benndorf*, Griech. und sicil. Vasenbilder, pp. 117 et seq. Fünfzigstes Berliner Winckelmannsprogramm, p. 3 (Robert).

Vases in the shape of heads, such as were produced in Attica in imitation of early-Asiatic art from the close of the sixth century in great variety to serve as drinking-horns, goblets, cups, etc. Drinking-horn in the form of a ram's head; polychrome drinking-horn in the form of a mule's head; admirably modelled double head of Heracles and a negro; beautiful double female head; interesting vase, with a spout (now broken off) ending in a point, formed of a comic mask and a caricature head (5-4th cent.). The two ointment-flasks, in the shape of women, belong to an earlier period, and their strong leaning to oriental types indicates their origin in an Asiatic (Græco-Asiatic?) studio.

Mus. Gregor., ii, T. lxxxix (A ii, T. iv). Comp. Röm. Mittheil. des arch. Instit., v, pp. 320 et seq.

Red-figured Kylix: Jason at Colchis.

The large interior painting represents an adventure of Jason, of which nothing farther is known in literary tradition, but which is certainly not a mere invention of the vase-painter. Beside a tree on which hangs the (golden) fleece appear the head and scaly shoulders of the huge dragon, whose body we must imagine to stretch towards the left. From the jaws of the monster, thickly set with pointed teeth, projects the upper portion of the bearded Jason; the dragon has been compelled to disgorge the hero, rendered invulnerable by magic. Jason owes his safety to Athena, who stands by, leaning on her spear, with her owl in her left hand, and attentively observing the incident. — On the exterior of the vase are groups of men and youths conversing, in great variety of attitude and arrangement of drapery. These figures also are distinguished by delicacy of execution. In the paintings on this beautiful vase some authorities have sought to recognize the hand of Euphronios, who has once elsewhere made use of a precisely similar figure of Athena. But there is no doubt that this vase-painting has copied some work of the greater art; while the style of the exterior painting seems more akin to the work of Duris, which in many points resembles the later vases from the studio of Euphronios.

Monumenti dell' Instit., ii, T. 35. Mus. Gregor., ii. T. lxxxvi (A ii, T. lxxxix), 1. *Roscher*, Lexikon der Mythologie, ii, p. 85. Comp. *Flasch*. Angebl. Argonautenbilder, pp. 24 et seq. *Winter*, Jüngere attische Vasen, p. 42. *Klein*. Euphronios[2], p. 191. *Heydemann*, Iason in Kolchis, pp. 20 et seq.

On the lowest shelf is a very varied collection of vases, some of them specially interesting for their shape. These include several vases in the shape of animals (duck, deer, dove, stag, ape); small ointment-flasks in the Corinthian style, with the usual decorations (men dancing, warriors marching, hoplites fighting attended by their henchmen, groups of animals, etc.); a Corinthian box with lid bearing the picture of a hare-hunt, a favourite design from very early times; two vases of so-called Egyptian faïence (coloured and enamelled terracotta), a variety produced in Phœnician potteries, but also imitated in Greece at an early period.

Mus. Gregor., ii, T. ci; cv, 2 (A ii, T. xcvii). — For the Egyptian faïence, see *Perrot-Chipiez*, Histoire de l'art, iii, p. 732, T. vi.

174. Kylix: Warriors arming.

The interior painting exhibits a youth, apparently in haste, completely armed with the exception of one greave, which he is in the act of putting on. His aged father, who looks round (as though to someone calling him?), holds the helmet in one hand, while with the other he has taken down from the wall a bag which seems to contain some article of clothing. The shield lies on the ground, and a spear leans against the wall. On one side of the exterior are a youth removing the cover of his shield with the assistance of a boy; a bearded man girding on his sword, while a youth holds his helmet and shield in readiness; a youth polishing his spear with a cloth; and finally an armed youth putting on his second greave (like the figure in the interior), while his sword hangs on the wall and his helmet hangs on a hook. Similar scenes occupy the other exterior side: one warrior holds a piece of armour in his left hand, which he seems to have just cleaned with a cloth; another, arming himself, is fastening his right shoulder-piece. All the figures are charmingly conceived and carefully executed. The youthful figures on the exterior and interior are especially graceful and recall the compositions of the quattrocentists. We may refer these vase-paintings of about 480-460 B. C. to the hand of Brygos, to whom several peculiarities of type seem to point.

Mus. Gregor., II. T. LXXXI (A II. T. LXXXV), 2. *Gerhard*, Auserlesene Vasenbilder. IV, T. 270. Comp. Bonner Studien. p. 76 (*Dümmler*).

179. Kylix: Medea and the Peliades.

Medea, the Colchian sorceress, who followed Jason to Thessaly, devised a diabolical plot to wreak her vengeance upon Pelias, King of Iolcos, who withheld the sovereignty from Jason. Having acquired the power of restoring animals to life by boiling them along with magical herbs after they had been cut in pieces, she exhibited this miracle of rejuvenescence upon a ram, and thus prevailed upon the credulous daughters of Pelias to induce the aged king to submit his infirm body to the same violent procedure, so as to arise to new life in the form of a lusty youth. The present vase, dating from about 440 B. C., represents scenes from this legend in paintings probably designed under the influence of some tragedy. The absence of inscriptions and the fact that the various female figures are not sufficiently differentiated by their costumes unfortunately prevent us from identifying them with certainty and so explaining the details of the scenes depicted. In the interior painting we see the aged Pelias, seated upon a camp-stool, courteously receiving a majestic woman, probably Medea; to the right is a door, with one wing closed. In one of the exterior paintings appears the ram, on which the rejuvenating experiment has apparently been successfully performed. Whether the woman leading the ram or the figure behind with the vase represents Medea seems doubtful. The two other maidens, carrying caskets, are either two of the daughters of Pelias or attendants. On the other side of the exterior is the huge cauldron in which Pelias is to be boiled. One of his daughters conducts the feeble king, who seems to offer resistance. The maiden standing in a reflective attitude behind his stool is, to judge from her youthful appearance, presumably another of his daughters, seized with a presentiment of the threatening misfortune. Medea is probably to be recognized in the female figure beside the cauldron, who has wrapped her upper garment round her waist in the usual manner of sacrificing officials and holds the sword in her left hand, while she raises the right in an encouraging gesture.

Mus. Gregor., II, T. LXXXII (A II, T. LXXXVI), 2. Archæol. Zeit., IV, 1846, T. 40, p. 250. *Brunn*, Uebungsblätter, No. 17. Comp. *Braun*, Ruinen und Museen, p. 828, 56. Annali dell' Instituto, 1876, pp. 44 et seq. *(Schultz)*.

186. Kylix: Œdipos and the Sphinx.

In the interior painting we see Œdipos seated carelessly upon a fragment of rock, opposite the Sphinx, which crouches upon a low Ionic column. The letters in front of the latter (AITPI, *i.e.* κ]αι τρι[α) probably represent in an abbreviated form the famous riddle of the Sphinx, which seems to be taken here in a form differing from that usually accepted. — The paintings on the exterior present a company of drunken Satyrs, executed with a highly humourous and bold realism. One group, of especial originality, represents a Satyr raising his shoe to strike a boy-Satyr, who stretches his arms for help towards a third Satyr approaching with a wine-skin on his shoulders and raising his right hand as though to deprecate the anger of the first. The boy-Satyr is of lower stature than the others but is otherwise formed precisely like them, with but a scanty growth of hair on his head. It would

not be difficult to connect this group with the interior
painting, and thus to explain the latter as belonging to
some satyr-play dealing with the legend of the Sphinx.
Æschylos produced a play of this kind in 467 B. C. In
point of style, the drawings correspond very closely with
the work of Duris, so that if they are not actually by
that master himself they must be by some closely-related
contemporary.

Mus. Gregor., II, T. LXXX (A II, T. LXXXIV), 1. — For the interior painting: *Overbeck*, Gallerie heroischer Bildwerke, p. 34, T. I, 12.
Duruy, Histoire des Grecs, I, p. 97. Wiener Vorlegeblätter für 1889,
T. VIII, 6. *Hartwig*, Die griechischen Meisterstelen der Blüthezeit
des streng rothfigurigen Stiles (1893), T. 73. Comp. *Braun*, Ruinen
und Museen, p. 823, 46. Rhein. Museum, 43, p. 359 *(Dümmler)*.

189. Kylix: Midas.

Midas, King of Phrygia, was noted for his wealth as
well as for his ass's ears, which he is said to have received
in consequence of deciding a musical competition in favour
of Pan's pipes as against the cythara of Apollo. His varied experiences were frequently treated by the dramatic
poets of Attica. The writers of satyr-plays especially must
have found admirable material in the story of the drunken
Silenus who was captured in Midas's rose-garden and
conversed with the king on the vexed question of the
worth of life. The circumstances of the capture are
represented in several vase-paintings; and the interior
painting on the vase before us is probably to be connected
with the same episode. King Midas (recognizable by the
ass's ears), sceptre in hand, is seated on an imposing
throne, the back of which ends in a griffin's head, and
listens to a report brought to him by an attendant. The
latter is clad in a short coat, a Phrygian flapped cap, and
travelling shoes, and carries in his left hand a hooked
staff (perhaps of cane). His message probably announces
the capture of the Silenus. — The exterior is decorated
with wild figures of Satyrs and Mænads. These may perhaps be meant to recall the dance of Satyrs that took place
in the orchestra of the theatre beside Midas in a satyr-

play (comp. No. 186). The vase probably dates from the
last decades of the fifth century.

Mus. Gregor., II, T. LXXII (A II, T. LXXVI). 2. Archæol. Zeit., II,
1844, T. 24, pp. 383 et seq. *(Panofka).* Annali dell' Instituto, 1844,
p. 212, T. D, 3 *(Braun).* Comp. *Braun*, Ruinen und Museen.
p. 828, 55. Jahrbuch des deutschen archæolog. Instit., II, p. 112
(Heydemann).

196. Kylix: Group of Men and Boys.

The interior of this vase has been covered with a slip
of white pipe-clay, but the coloured drawing for which it
was thus prepared was never added. On the exterior are
groups of men and boys, revealing the style of Hieron
(comp. p. 286) both in conception and drawing. The
animated gestures of the groups indicate the different
degrees of favour with which the advances of the men are
received. One specially attractive group shows a youth
standing with animated gestures (of entreaty or refusal)
opposite a bearded man, who holds up a rabbit by the ears,
and appears to be angry with the youth; at the same time,
as if to make the latter jealous, he presents the animal
to another boy, who lays his right hand on his forehead
in his delight at the gift. The accessories of the charming painting are supplied by two dogs, a gnarled olive-
tree, and objects used in the palæstra (ointment-flask
and strigil) hanging upon wall-pegs.

Mus. Gregor., II, T. LXXX (A II, T. LXXXIV), 3. Comp. Arch.
Zeit., XLII, 1884, p. 249 *(P. J. Meier).*

201. Kylix: Heracles and the Tripod; Æneas quitting Troy.

The interior is occupied by a symposium-scene. A
bearded man, half-rising from his couch while his head,
heavy with wine, falls upon his shoulder, throws the
wine-lees from the bowl in his right hand towards a
fixed goal (as in the game of cottabos), while his left hand
reaches for a vessel of another description. Beside him
is a girl busily playing her flute. — One of the paintings on the exterior represents Heracles, seizing the

tripod and brandishing his club threateningly against Apollo, who endeavours to snatch the implement from him. Behind Heracles appears Athena, with lowered lance, raising her right hand to appease the disputants; and behind Apollo is Artemis, seeking to soothe her brother. On the other side is Æneas, carrying his father Anchises on his back after the fall of Troy, preceded by his wife, and accompanied by two companions armed in the Greek style, and a warrior in Scythian costume. The severe and careful drawing corresponds to some extent with the style of the earlier works of Euphronios (about 500 B.C.).

Mus. Gregor., ii, T. lxxxv (A ii, T. lxxxviii), 2. Comp. *Welcker*, Alte Denkmäler, iii, p. 272. *Overbeck*, Kunstmythologie, iv, p. 401, T. 24, 11.

209. Kylix: Scenes from the Comos.

In the interior is a man apparently about to place a flower upon an altar; on the exterior are eight youths parading the street after a merry banquet, with sticks, drinking-bowls, flutes, and crotala (castanets). The severe, but clever and refined drawing is closely akin to the style of Brygos (500–470 B.C.).

Mus. Gregor., ii, T. lxxviii (A ii, T. lxxxii), 2. Comp. Jahrbuch des deutschen archæol. Inst., vii, 117 *(Winter)*.

211. Black-figured Kylix with drinking-motto.

This vase is a specimen of an elegant variety, very popular between 560 and 530 or 520 B.C., the interior of which was decorated with a black-figured design (in the present case a Siren) and the exterior with a motto only. The motto on this vase runs: 'Take a good draught and may it do you good'.

Mus. Gregor., ii, T. lxiv (A ii, T. lxviii), 1.

218. Kylix: Love-Scenes.

In the interior painting a maiden converses with graceful gestures with a youth. The chair and the workbasket under the handles indicate that the scenes on the exterior take place in the women's apartment. Men and women are here grouped in animated conversation, but we are not able to interpret their gesture-language more particularly. The style of the drawing encourages us to place this vase among the later works of Hieron (comp. p. 286).

Mus. Gregor., II, T. LXXVIII (A II, T. LXXXII), 1. *Gerhard*, Auserlesene Vasenbilder, IV, T. 294 et seq., 1-4. Comp. *Klein*, Vasen mit Meistersignaturen[2], p. 163.

225. Kylix: Drinking Scenes.

The exterior paintings depict an Attic symposium, with abundance of detail. On one side are three men reclining upon couches; one seems to be drinking to another, while skilfully balancing a kylix in his other hand; the second is throwing the dregs from his goblet at a fixed goal (cottabos); the third is playing on the lyre and singing. On the other side a boy is engaged in drawing wine from a large amphora with volute-handles; a man, with a flute in his left hand, is reclining upon a couch and drinks to his companion, who is singing lustily, with his head thrown back in ecstasy, and beating time with his right hand to the music of the female flute-player standing before him. On the wall above the couches hang baskets, mantles, and a flute-case. The various vases forming a black-painted frieze below the painting are supposed to stand upon a table in front of the couches. — The interior painting represents the unpleasant results of over-indulgence in wine. A bearded man, reclining on a couch, with his head supported by his left arm, is retching, a process he has endeavoured to facilitate with the fingers of his right hand. A girl, probably a flute-player, not unaccustomed to render such services, holds his head with both her hands, and regards the sufferer attentively. The delicate and charming drawing unites with various motives in this composition to suggest the name of Brygos as its producer (ca. 470 B.C.). Comp. p. 286.

Mus. Gregor., II, T. LXXXI (A II, T. LXXXV), 1. Comp. *Klein*, Euphronios[2], p. 311. Bullet. dell'Instituto, 1834, p. 45 *(P. J. Meier)*. Bonner Studien, p. 74. *(Dümmler)*.

227. Kylix: Hermes as Cattle-Thief.

On the very first day of his life Hermes earned the right to be considered the patron of thieves and swindlers. The Homeric hymn relates how on the evening of the day of his birth he went secretly from Cyllene in Arcadia to Pieria on Olympos, drove off thence the golden-horned cattle of the gods, and, cunningly concealing their traces, hid them in a cave. The graceful scenes on the exterior of this vase relate how Apollo found the cattle, after long searching. On one side Apollo appears in a long mantle, a tall staff in his hand. The herd of cattle, found at last, is also seen in the painting on the other side, which must be regarded as continuous with this one. The discovery of the thief is likewise shown in this second painting. Maia, the mother of Hermes, stands with a gesture of angry astonishment at the entrance to the cave, where the boy-Hermes, clad in a chlamys, with the petasos on his head, lies unconcernedly, as though nothing had happened, in a peculiarly-shaped little bed (like a shoe). One of the cattle, however, snuffs the cradle and thus seems to betray that its inmate is not unknown to her. — The less important interior painting is another symposium scene. A youth, reclining on a couch behind a table, is playing the double-flute, while a bearded man, grasping a goblet in his left hand, lifts his right to his head as though in ecstatic admiration. The style of the highly original and admirably executed drawings points to Brygos (480-470 B.C.). Comp. p. 286.

Mus. Gregor., ii, T. LXXXIII, 1. *Lenormant-De-Witte*, Élite céramographique, iii, T. 86. Archæol. Zeit., ii, 1844, T. 20, pp. 321 et seq. *(Panofka)*. *Baumeister*, Denkmäler des klass. Alterthums, i, p. 681. Comp. *Braun*, Ruinen und Museen, p. 826. *Klein*, Euphronios², p. 85. Bonner Studien, p. 73 *(Dümmler)*.

228. Hydria: Heracles and Alcyoneus (below).

This vase belongs to a peculiar variety of hydriæ, dating from about the middle of the sixth century, and known as Cæretanian, from the place (Cære) at which most have been found. The non-Attic origin of this vase is

indicated clearly enough by the lighter colour of the terracotta, by the choice of ornamentation (frieze of bucrania or
ox-heads and woollen fillets, realistic ivy-wreaths, garland
of large lotus-flowers and palmettes), by the peculiarities of
costume, and, above all, by the character of the variegated
paintings, in which many points are engraved. The nearest
analogues to the latter are found on fragments of vases
from Cyme in Asia Minor, so that the vases found at Cære
may also be regarded as imports into Italy from the Greek
cities in Asia. Many peculiarities in the choice and conception of the subjects are also explained by this theory.
The principal painting depicts the combat of Heracles
with a giant of extraordinary ugliness, probably Alcyoneus, the herdsman on the peninsula of Pallene, whom
Heracles is said to have slain in his sleep. Heracles is
in the act of vigorously attacking the giant, who has just
risen from his couch; and behind the hero appears Hermes,
clad, contrary to the usual custom, in a long robe, hurrying towards him and raising his left hand in encour-
agement. On the reverse are a couple of wrestlers and
another pair of athletes about to engage in wrestling or
in a boxing-match *(pankration)*. — The exaggerated
animation of the movements, and the bold but somewhat
lax management of the outlines led earlier authorities to
place these vases among the productions of late-Etruscan
art; but since then we have learned to recognize these
characteristics, as well as many other so-called native
Etruscan peculiarities, as distinctive features of Ionic
art. Comp. p. 276.

Formerly in the Vatican Library. — Mus. Gregor., II, T. xvi. 2.
Berichte der sächs. Gesellschaft der Wissenschaften, 1853, T. 8. 2,
p. 143 *(O. Jahn)*. Comp. *Preller-Robert*, Griech. Mythologie, I, p. 72.
M. Mayer, Giganten und Titanen, pp. 172 et seq. Römische Mittheil. des archäol. Inst., III. p. 167 *(Dümmler)*.

230. Kylix: Warrior racing; Athena's Chariot.

In the interior painting is a flute-player, in the festal
garb of musicians, playing to a nude warrior (with helmet,
shield, and javelin), who is in an attitude of animated

motion, suggesting a race rather than a war-dance. On
one side of the exterior, the preparations of Athena and
Heracles to mount a chariot are depicted with a genre-
like minuteness of detail. The goddess, standing behind
the chariot, holds the reins in both hands; two horses have
just been harnessed to the chariot; a man and a youth, with
his chlamys tied round his waist like an apron, are giving
the final touches. Heracles leads a third horse from the
left and another attendant brings the fourth one from
the right. On the other side is a scene from the Comos:
seven youths dance along with various vessels in their
hands. Beside the paintings is the inscription ἐποίησεν,
'he made it', a factory-mark here apparently used by the
artist Epictetos (ca. 500 B. C.). Comp. p. 286.

Mus. Gregor., II, T. lxxxiv (A II, T. lxxxvii), 2. Comp. *Klein*,
Vasen mit Meistersignaturen[2], p. 113, 9. Römische Mittheil. des
archæol. Instit., v, p. 341.

232. Kylix: Voyage of Heracles, Death of Hector.

When Heracles was on his way to Erytheia against
Geryon (comp. p. 297), Helios assisted his passage to
the limits of the west by lending him the golden cup, in
which the sun every night sailed across the ocean from the
western extremity of the world to his rising-place in the
east. In the interior painting before us we see Heracles fully
armed sailing in the bowl-shaped vessel, without oars or
sail, over the tumbling waves of the sea, in which swim
cephalopoda and other fish. Comp. Hydria No. 97 (Apollo's
voyage; p. 311), which has a stylistic relationship to this.
— On the exterior the duel between Achilles and Hector
in presence of Athena and Apollo occurs twice. Apollo,
in the act of quitting the field, holds an arrow in his
hand (comp. No. 106, p. 315). In one of these scenes
Achilles fights with the lance and Hector with the sword,
in conformity with the description in the Iliad; but in
the other, Achilles is armed with the sword, while Hector's lance is shivered against the shield of his opponent.
The painter, therefore, has not tried to illustrate lines

from the Iliad, but has followed his independent fancy
in employing general types of duel-scenes to represent
the overthrow of the Trojan hero. The style of drawing
permits us to attribute this vase with certainty to the
industrious vase-painter Duris (ca. 480 B.C.). Comp.
p. 286.

Mus. Gregor., ii, T. lxxiv (A ii, T. lxxviii), 1. *Gerhard*, Auserlesene Vasenbilder, ii, T. 109, iii, T. 202, 2-5. *Roscher*, Lexikon der
Mythologie, i, p. 2204. Comp. Bonner Studien, p. 83 *(Dümmler)*,
and the references cited under No. 106, on p. 316.

237. Kylix: Theseus and the Marathonian Bull.

The circular field of the interior painting is here
skilfully filled by the figure of a galloping Centaur on
the point of hurling a huge block of rock. This motive
and the wounds on the breast and thigh indicate that
this figure has been borrowed from some larger composition dealing with the battle of the Centaurs and Lapithæ.
On one side of the exterior is Theseus, who has fastened
a rope to the horns and hind-legs of the bull and thus
brings him to the ground. To the left Athena is hastening
away as though horrified, and to the right is a boy holding a horse by the bridle, the latter a figure without
definite connection with the rest of the composition and
probably added merely to fill up the space. — The other
side is occupied by warlike scenes of the ancient type.
This vase clearly belongs to the earlier period of the red-
figured style, as practised by Oltos, Cachrylion, and their
school (ca. 510-490 B. C.).

Mus. Gregor., ii, T. lxxxii (A ii, T. lxxxvi), 2. Comp. *W. Müller*,
Theseusmetopen, pp. 29 et seq.

245. Slender Amphora: Mounted Archers.

The neck of this vase is adorned with a heraldic
group of two panthers, with a single head in common.
On one of the shoulder-panels appear three horsemen
with pointed caps, turning round to discharge their
arrows. They thus appear to be executing the well-known
manœuvre of the Scythian cavalry, who used to feign

flight and then, suddenly wheeling round, launched their arrows with more deadly certainty against their pursuers. On the other shoulder are three mounted hoplites with brandished spears, who must be regarded as the pursuers of the archers. The space below the horses on both sides is filled in with running animals, in the manner of the early Ionic pictures, in either case with two dogs pursuing a hare. Below the pictorial panels runs a frieze of animals, including a griffin. This vase has been supposed, from the presence of the archers, to have been made in some Greek colony near Scythia; and it is perfectly true that these types, afterwards used in the depicting of Amazons, were invented by the Ionic Greeks of Asia Minor. But they were conveyed at an early date also to the Italian colonies founded by the Asiatic Greeks; and it is therefore a moot point whether these and similar vases, which certainly still belong to the sixth century, were imported from Asia Minor or were manufactured in some Greek town in Italy, under Asiatic influence. Comp. p. 276.

Mus. Gregor., ii, T. xxix (A ii, T. xxxvi), 2. Römische Mittheil. des archæol. Instit., ii, T. ix, p. 172 *(Dümmler)*, p. 244 *(Von Duhn)*. Comp. Arch. Anzeiger, 1889, p. 51 *(Furtwaengler)*. Jahrbuch des deutschen arch. Inst., iv, p. 221 *(Schumacher)*. Bonner Studien, p. 256 *(Loeschke)*.

246. Kylix: Scenes from the Palæstra.

The interior painting exhibits a youth taking a run before leaping. In his hands are heavy *halteres*, or dumbbells to increase his momentum. The paintings on the exterior, which are framed by large palmettes, show three ephebi, of whom one takes aim with the discus in his outstretched hands, another holds the discus in his lowered left hand and seems to be speaking to the first, while the third is taking off his chlamys. On the other side are two youths in combat, and a third running and swinging a club before throwing it. The highly archaic bodily forms and the incised line about the hair (comp. No. 93, p. 311) point to the date 510-500 B. C., and various peculiarities of style suggest the attribution of these drawings to the school of Chelis. Comp. p. 286.

Mus. Gregor., II, T. lxx (A II, T. lxxiv), 1.

251. Black-figured Kylix by Tleson.

We possess a large number of similar vases by Tleson, son of Nearchos (ca. 550-530 B. C.), the only ornaments on which are the palmettes on the handles and the signature of the maker. No. 249 is the work of another of these 'small masters'.

Comp. *Klein. Vasen mit Meistersignaturen*[2], p. 73.

254. Kylix with both black and red figures.

The small group of kylikes, with the interior painting in black and the exterior figures left in the terracotta colour on an otherwise black-varnished surface, date from a brief transition period (ca. 520 B. C.), which immediately preceded the exclusive predominance of the red-figured style (comp. p. 285). The interior painting of the present vase shows Dionysos holding vine-twigs and a pointed drinking-horn. On the exterior, between large leaf-palmettes and ornamentally treated eyes, is a fully armed warrior stooping as he cautiously advances, on one side, and on the other, an armed youth, wearing a mouth-strap *(phorbeia)* and blowing a straight trumpet.

Mus. Gregor., II, T.lxix (A II, T.lxxiii), 3. *Klein*, Euphronios[2], pp. 297, 299.

256. Kylix with both black and red figures.

The foot, with the signature of the maker Pamphæos, does not belong to the upper part of this vase; but the style of the latter, and also of No. 254, agrees very well with the known tendencies of that vase-maker. Comp. No. 258 and p. 286.

Mus. Gregor., II, T.lxix (A II, T.lxxiii), 4. Comp. *Klein*, Vasen mit Meistersignaturen[2], p. 91,8. Bonner Studien, p. 201 *(A. Koerte)*.

258. Black-figured Kylix by Pamphæos.

Pamphæos, who flourished towards the end of the sixth century, worked quite in the severe spirit of the archaic vase-painters in producing his black-figured vases. The vase before us is a case in point. In the interior is a Gorgon's head; on the exterior, between large eyes, on one side is a front-view of a four-horse chariot (beside which is the signature), and on the other the combat of Heracles with Hippolyta, the Amazon queen.

Mus. Gregor., II, T. lxvi (A II, T. lxx), 3 a, 4 a, 4 b. Comp. *Klein*, Vasen mit Meistersignaturen², p. 90, 5.

266. Black-figured Kylix: Ajax and the Body of Achilles.

On the outside of this vase is the inscription: 'Hail, and drink'. The interior is decorated with a group occurring elsewhere in archaic paintings: the Telamonian Ajax hurries from the battle-field, bearing on his left shoulder the corpse of Achilles, which he has rescued from the enemy after a hard fight. The names of the heroes are inscribed beside them.

Mus. Gregor., II, T. lxvii (A II, T. lxxi), 2. Comp. *Overbeck*, Gallerie heroischer Bildwerke, p. 546.

275. Cyrenean Kylix: Prometheus and Atlas (?).

This vase comes from a pottery at Cyrene, in North Africa, which seems to have carried on a pretty large export-trade to Italy about the middle of the sixth century. It reveals numerous peculiarities in its technique, ornamentation, and choice of paintings. The panel intended for the picture is coated with a thin slip of yellowish-white pipe-clay, while red is freely used in the painting itself. Conspicuous amongst the rows of ornamentation on the exterior is a frieze of pomegranates. The lower segment of the interior painting is occupied by the upper portion of a column with lotus-flowers at the sides. To the right in the painting appears Prometheus (?), who is fastened by the hands and feet in a painful position to a column, while the eagle perches on his lap and plunges its beak into his breast so that the blood gushes on the ground. In contrast to this Titan, who suffers in solitude in the remote Caucasus, appears his brother

Atlas (?), who supports the globe in the uttermost parts of the west. The legs of the bearded Titan give beneath the weight of his burden, which rests on his shoulders in a formless mass. The serpent rearing its head behind Atlas is added merely to fill in the space. The picture deviates in more than one respect from the traditional methods of representing both Prometheus and Atlas; and the very juxtaposition of the two is itself remarkable. These figures have, therefore, been otherwise explained as two sufferers in Hades; that to the right as Tityos, whose liver was devoured by vultures, and that to the left as Tantalos, over whose head hung a rock threatening destruction. But this explanation also is attended with many difficulties. We have before us in short an independent pictorial tradition, for whose types no complete analogy can be found in any of the current traditions of the Attic legends.

Mus. Gregor., ii, T. lxvii (A ii, T. lxxi), 3. *Gerhard*, Auserlesene Vasenbilder, ii, T. 86. Wiener Vorlegeblätter, series D, T. ix, 7. Comp. *O. Jahn*, Archæolog. Beiträge, pp. 229 et seq. Archæolog. Zeit., xxxix, 1881, p. 217, 2 *(Puchstein)*.

Ninth Room: Collection of Bronzes.

The so-called 'greater arts' are but sparsely represented in this room. The few Italic or Etruscan sculptures which the collection does contain are, however, so much the more valuable to us from the fact that the total number of extant works of this kind is insignificant. They include the so-called Mars of Todi (No. 313), two figures of boys (Nos. 283, 329), and a series of statuettes in glass-case No. 198. Thanks to their characteristic individuality, they suffice to give us a fair idea of Etruscan or Central Italian art. The artists, destitute of all creative genius, have simply copied Greek models in the dryest and most superficial way, without vigour and without precision, and often depriving them entirely of their idealistic conception. Hand in hand with a keen observation of nature and a careful execution of details goes an astounding lack of comprehension of organic and vital unity. We again meet many of these peculiarities in Roman art, which was influenced in its early stages by that of Etruria. From the last century of the pre-Christian era onwards, the sculptures of Etruria cannot be distinguished from those produced in other parts of the Roman empire. The early Empire is represented in this room by a good portrait (No. 173), and the time of Hadrian by the remains of a colossal statue (No. 206). Another portrait-head (No. 257), dating from the time of the soldier-emperors, brings us down to the extreme limits of ancient art.

The importance of the collection is mainly due to its specimens of decorative and industrial art. From this point of view the objects found in Etruscan tombs (Cervetri, Corneto, Vulci, Orvieto, Chiusi) are as important for the period from the seventh to the second century B. C. as the discoveries at Pompeii are for the two following centuries. For the Etruscans furnished the dwellings of their dead not only with all kinds of earthenware vessels (p. 274), but also with all the weapons and metallic ornaments of the living, and even with kitchen utensils, table ware, and apparatus for lighting and heating. It is true that these equipments of the tomb are often made of very thin plates of metal and could not have been actually used in real life; but as they are faithful copies of the objects themselves, they replace the latter for our eyes quite as adequately as for the shade of the deceased.

The observer will be surprized to see what an important rôle was played by bronze in the domestic equipment of the ancient world. Numerous articles of the cuisine, of the toilette, and so forth, which we now make of wood or earthenware, glass or ivory, were then made of metal. And he will also be astonished to see the intelligence and imagination expended by the Etruscans on the modelling and adornment of the most common objects of the household, such as the modern decorator entirely despises, — and that, too, without in the slightest degree impairing their practical usefulness. The forms of organic nature are constantly borrowed, not only for the essential parts of the construction, but also for such accessories as handles, arms, and supports — a custom that reached Etruria from the most ancient centres of Eastern civilization through the Phœnicians and Ionians. Many of the forms used for dishes and goblets, for stands and candelabra, will appear perfectly familiar through their continued use in our own times, which, however, they have reached for the most part through later modifications of the Roman period.

Most of the objects in this room date back to the archaic period, in which the history of the industrial arts coincides with the history of art in general. The early stage of civilization known as the 'First Iron Age' is represented only by a few characteristic objects, such as the primitive vessels (Nos. 97, 222, 247) formed of separate sheets of metal fastened together by rivets (ca. seventh century B. C.). The origin of these vessels is still disputed, some authorities regarding them as products of native Italic workmanship, while others believe them to have been imported from the Orient.

In the immediately following period we know beyond a doubt that Etruria was profoundly influenced by Oriental civilization. It is admirably represented in this collection by the contents of a large tomb discovered near Cervetri in April, 1836, by the Abbé Regolini and General Galassi. The tomb, which is now almost wholly destroyed, was concealed in an artificial mound. It consisted of a long rectangular chamber, connected with a somewhat narrower chamber by a trapezoidal doorway, the lower half of which was closed by a wall. The contents of the first chamber, in the sides of which were two large semicircular niches, included several bronze vessels, the mouldering remnants of a chariot, a kettle-stand (p. 413), a bedstead (No. 155, p. 371), on which were a few human bones, a tripod (No. 157), and an incense-burner (No. 57). On the floor, near the bed, lay several small idols (No. 208, p. 381); against the walls leant eight richly decorated shields (No. 164, p. 373), in partial preservation, and some bundles of javelins and lances; on nails in the central part of the ceiling formed by the gradual approach of the side-walls hung some bronze cups and dishes. On the wall in the doorway stood two bronze kettles (Nos. 295, 314; p. 390) and two silver cups. The inner chamber contained the basin No. 158 and other vessels in bronze. On a stone bench, on which a corpse had been placed, lay several silver cups adorned with reliefs (No. 344, p. 399), and all the rich gold ornaments (comp. Nos. 332 et seq., pp. 397 et seq.) which had decked the corpse, almost every piece in its original position. Some of the cups found in this tomb were inscribed 'Larthia', which is supposed to be a female name; hence the jewelry of the inner chamber is believed to have adorned the corpse of a woman. It is quite possible, however, that the ornaments may have been those of a ruler who clothed himself with Oriental pomp; and it is certain that the military equipment of the outer chamber must have belonged to some such personage.

The fact that the Etruscan alphabet borrowed from the Greeks of Chalcis is used upon some of the vessels in this tomb proves that it cannot date much farther back than the close of the seventh century B. C. The curious and characteristic style of these objects can be explained by the historical events of the period. The Oriental (Asia Minor) origin of several of the shapes of the vases and of the motives of the ornamentation is incontestable. It does not, however, follow that the individual objects are themselves of Oriental — i. e., for the period under discussion, Phœnician — origin. The art of Asiatic Greece in the seventh and eighth centuries B. C. employed the same elements, and under its influence a similar style was early developed on Italian soil. As early as the second half of the eighth century the Chalcidians of Eubœa planted colonies on the west coast of Italy. The Phocæans also carried on a lively traffic with Etruria in the seventh and sixth centuries. The merchants of

Rhodes likewise appeared in the Tyrrhenian Sea at the same epoch, and indirect (viâ Syracuse), if not direct, relations existed between Corinth and the maritime cities of Etruria. Thus the Phœnicians, who had frequented these coasts at a much earlier period, soon saw themselves expelled from the Etrurian market. Their Carthaginian kinsmen, however, carried on a brisk contest with the commercial flotillas of Greece, and allied themselves with the Etruscans, who felt themselves threatened by the growing power and numbers of the Ionic settlements on the Tyrrhenian coast. The Phocæans were defeated at the battle of Alalia in B. C. 537. The Regulini-Galassi Tomb must have been constructed during this period of commercial rivalry between the Phœnicians and the Asiatic Greeks; and hence the provenience of each object found in it remains problematical. As regards the ornaments of gold, see pp. 394 et seq. The technical execution of the bronzes gives no clue to their place of origin. They all show the so-called 'sphyrelaton', or hammered system, which was universal in the earliest period of art; i. e. the reliefs, generally very low, which adorn the thin plates of metal, have been produced by the blows of a hammer from within or behind.

The same considerations hold true for the later days of the archaic epoch (550-450 B. C.), to which, e. g., belong the tripod No. 150 and the bronze mountings of Bomarzo (pp. 408 et seq.). The Greek influence continues in spite of the defeat of the Phocæans, though now penetrating by other routes, while the rôle of the Phœnician commerce is almost played out. The Greeks preserve their old market in Campania; the seaports of Sicily serve as intermediaries between continental Greece and Italy. The ever-present question with regard to the 'finds' of this period is whether the modifications of Asiatic Greek forms which they exhibit are due to the Italic Greeks or to the Etruscans themselves. In the second half of the fifth century the Etruscan metal industry, based, perhaps, on an ancient native technique, had reached a high stage

of development; its impulse came from the Orient.
Without showing any creative power, in the proper sense
of the word, it yet transformed its foreign models with
an original taste, marked on the one hand by a trait of
coarse realism, on the other by a tendency to mannerism
and the fantastic. The strongest characteristic of the
metal-work of the Etruscans was, however, its technical
perfection. At Athens, at the time of the Peloponnesian
War, the Tyrrhenian bronze vessels were highly extolled,
though, it is true, some of these may have been products
of Magna Græcia. Household utensils and lighting
apparatus were especially valued; and, as a matter of fact,
it is precisely these objects that are found in the greatest
abundance and of the most original workmanship in the
Etruscan tombs. The Vatican collection is particularly
rich in them.

Among the objects generally classed together under
the common name of **Candelabra** we may distinguish
three principal varieties, which, for the sake of brevity,
we may distinguish as candelabra proper, lamp-stands,
and thymiateria (incense-burners), though the candelabra may often have been used as incense-burners and
the thymiateria as lighting apparatus. Candelabra and
lamp-stands have nearly the same form, the invention of
which is certainly of Phœnician origin. It consists of a
tall and slender shaft supported by a three-limbed base
or stand. In the different varieties of this form, of which
the earliest specimens in the Vatican date from about
the middle of the fifth century, we can trace a gradual
evolution from the simple to the composite, from the
sober and severe to the elaborate and the fantastically
realistic.

The candelabra proper are usually $2^{1}/_{2}$-5 feet in height;
their supports, generally gracefully bent, are in the shape
of animal's feet (most often the paws of a lion), between
which hang palmettes. The shaft, tapering slightly towards the top, is sometimes round, sometimes four-
cornered, sometimes smooth, sometimes fluted like a

column; its lower part is often covered with foliage. At the top, on a low plinth, is a figure, serving not only as an ornamental finish but also as a handle. The candles are stuck sideways on spikes (generally four in number), projecting at right angles to the shaft below the figure. These spikes are fashioned to resemble lotus-blossoms, the bills of birds, and so on. Below them is often fixed a shield to protect the hand from the dripping wax.

The lamp-stands are generally smaller, averaging about $1\frac{1}{2}$ foot in height. The supports, often stiff and inelegant, are in the form of the paws of lions or dogs, or the hoofs of deer or horses, sometimes also that of human legs or small human figures. Between the stand and the shaft are often interposed other figures, sometimes treated with the severity of Caryatides, sometimes in a state of motion. The shaft is generally made like a column or imitates the stem of a plant. It is frequently ornamented with animate objects, such as a boy climbing, or a serpent, or a hedgehog or cat pursuing a bird. On the top of the shaft is a small receptacle for the burning oil (or incense), or a flat surface for a lamp, or a small cup with a spike for a candle in the middle. Small birds are often represented sitting on the edge of this cup, as if grouped round their nest or round a basin of water. Chains sometimes hang from it, weighted with little balls.

The thymiateria are much shorter and heavier in shape than the lamp-holders. On three lion's paws, often ornamented with figures, rests a base in the shape of a truncated pyramid, formed of three plates of metal tapering towards the top. From this rises a thick, undulating shaft, adorned with saucer-like ornaments, some opening upwards and some downwards. This shaft is surmounted by a vessel for the reception of incense. The prototypes of these stands, which were used in private houses as well as in temples, were of Semitic origin, and were imported (in forms probably modified by the Asiatic Greeks) both into Greece, where we often meet them as marks of sanctuaries, and into Italy. Their forms maintained themselves in various modifications down to the imperial epoch, and may be recognized in the countless stone and (so-called) marble candelabra of the Roman museums.

The crowded Bronze Room also affords an instructive picture of the rich variety of the Tyrrhenian **Domestic Utensils.** An advance in development can be traced in the various implements here, corresponding to that which we have traced in the candelabra and lamp-stands. The numerous pots and jars especially may be separated into two distinct groups, an earlier and a later. Those of the more ancient group (sixth to fifth century B.C.) are stiff and clumsy; the main body of the jar expands uniformly, and is surmounted by a straight round neck to which a simply formed handle is attached. The later examples (from the end of the fifth century B.C.) are of more animated and graceful contours; the body is more rounded, the neck much more slender, the lip moulded into the form of a clover-leaf — a form at once practical and tasteful. The handle rises in dainty curves above the vessel, and is decorated with numerous figures, like the handles of amphoræ. The varied forms of the handles, the feet, and the ornamentations of the feet are throughout of especial interest. As these parts were cast in solid metal, they have in many cases been preserved, when the thinner bodies of the vessels have fallen into fragments. Archaic forms predominate in their figured ornamentations; but this, owing to the conservative character of this branch of art-industry, is, of course, in itself no proof that any given example is of archaic origin. We continually meet with new and original variations, which, however, frequently lack the refined taste of their Greek models, and sometimes transform these models in a fantastic and arbitrary manner without reference to the primary idea.

In the excavations of the tombs of the last centuries of the pagan era other groups of monuments appear, which belong more to the art of designing than to that of sculpture — viz. the chased hand-glasses and cists.

The elementary form of the **Hand Glasses** was known

in the ancient metal industry from the earliest times.
Some are simple round bronze disks, which were placed
in flat cases or provided with a hinged cover.   Others
have handles, which were often ornamented in various
ways at their point of junction with the glass. These
handles end in an ornamental figure (most often the
head of an animal) or else in a smooth point, evidently
intended to be fitted into a socket or sheath of bone. In
the mirrors of a later period, numerous specimens of
which have been found at Palestrina, the disks are
frequently pear-shaped. The polished surface (especially
in the smaller examples) is often slightly convex; while
the backs (deviating from the usual rule in Greek mirrors) are ornamented with engraved designs, or even, in
a few exceptional cases (*e.g.* No. 326), with reliefs in
the style of the lids of folding mirrors.

These engraved designs, of which considerably more
than two thousand are still extant, enable us to institute
an interesting comparison between them and the designs
on the Greek vases — a comparison showing in the most
striking way the different spirit that obtained in Etruscan
and in Greek handiwork. Though these mirror-designs
are, like the vase-paintings, indirectly inspired by archetypes created by the 'greater arts' of Greece, we seek in
them almost in vain for the artistic finish, the fresh
individuality, the seldom absent delicacy and refinement
with which the vase-painters (especially those of the red-
figured Attic vases) copied and modified their models.
Thus, on the whole, in spite of the technical dexterity
evident in their admirable execution, they do not make
an altogether pleasing impression.

The Etruscan artificers used their patterns without
either pleasure or sympathy, often indeed negligently
and mechanically. They not seldom adopted subjects
without understanding them, and reduced well-conceived
motives to caricatures by unskilful adaptation to the space
at their disposal, or by unhappy attempts at modification.
The fact that among their works are a few admirable

examples of fine design and charming workmanship,
is explained by the close adherence in these cases to
Greek models, their Italian origin being betrayed only
by a few superficial additions and alterations, chiefly in
matters of costume (shoes, bracelets, bullæ, etc.). Great
differences may be observed in the style of the designs.
The majority reproduce models of the Hellenistic period;
a few show traces of the archaic forms of the sixth century;
while others again betray the influence of the great painters of the fifth century. We must therefore guard against
fixing the date of any specimen merely by its style. The
decorative art of Etruria, which at no time was independent, continued to follow archaic models even in the Hellenistic period; but this does not imply an intentional
imitation of antique styles. Patterns from different
epochs were used in juxtaposition with a perfectly
unconscious arbitrariness, such as is also apparent in the
mural paintings of the Roman period. Nevertheless, in
the style of execution, in the sometimes severe, sometimes careless drawing, in the choice of forms of ornament, in the arrangement of the often too numerous
figures, in the treatment of backgrounds, and so forth,
we may trace a chronological line of development, the
exact beginning and end of which have been, of course,
only approximately determined. Without doubt the great
majority of the Etruscan mirrors, which were found in
graves only in conjunction with vases of later local
manufacture, belong to the period between the end of
the fourth and the beginning of the second century.
The mirrors found in Præneste, illustrating a phase of
Latin art and often bearing Latin inscriptions, belong in
the main to the same period. Engraved mirrors dis-
appear from the furnishing of tombs at the time when
they were supplanted in everyday use by more practical
shapes, like those found at Pompeii. These last are circular bronze disks covered on one side by a thick coating
of silver and adorned on the other with ornaments in the
form of rings and circles.

Intimately connected in style and workmanship with the mirrors, and often found with them in the same tombs, are the **Cists**. These were formerly described as 'mystic' cists because they were supposed to have some connection with the Bacchic mysteries. This theory, however, is quite erroneous; these cases were used, as is proved by the strigils, salve-boxes, mirrors, hairpins, combs, and rouge-boxes frequently found in them, for containing the requisites of the toilet and the palæstra. At an earlier period wooden boxes, occasionally covered with metal plates, were employed for this purpose; but in the third century cists made entirely of metal came into vogue. These latter are usually round (more rarely shaped like a whetstone), and, according to a probable conjecture, reproduce the ancient *Ciste a cordoni*. The characteristic ornamentation of the cists may also be recognized in types which were imported from the East (comp. vol. I, p. 463, No. 620). The body of the cist is generally ornamented with engraved designs, very seldom (No. 327) with reliefs. The engraved cists come, with very few exceptions, from Præneste, and were probably manufactured either there or in Rome. Their designs, which are frequently of pure Greek character, demonstrate that the Greeks of Campania played a considerable rôle in this branch of industrial art. On the other hand the figures which adorn the points of attachment of the feet, and also those on the handles on the lids, exhibit a thoroughly Etruscan (Italic) character. They seldom rise above clumsy mechanical work, and reproduce the most hackneyed types, many of which are stiffly formal copies of archaic patterns. The manufacture of these cists seems to have ceased in the course of the second century B.C. Along with the mirrors, they are the last representatives of ancient Italic art. Like the 'greater arts', the Etruscan industry and the decorative art of the last republican epoch declined under the levelling influences of the Roman empire. Utensils of all kinds from this Roman period are also to be seen here, though in this respect the Vatican Museum cannot compete with the priceless treasures of the bronze rooms in the museum at Naples, where the industry of the imperial epoch can be more conveniently studied.

On the Rogulini-Galassi Tomb, see Bull. dell' Inst., 1836, pp. 56 et seq.; 1838, pp. 171 et seq. *Grifi*, Monumenti di Cere antica (Rome, 1841). *Canina*, Descrizione di Cere antica (Rome, 1838), T. 3, pp. 59 et seq.; Etruria marittima, T. 50-59, pp. 179 et seq. Mus. Gregor., I, T. cvii (A I, T. I). *Dennis*, Cities and Cemeteries, I[3], pp. 264 et seq. *Helbig*, Homerische Epos[2], pp. 29 et seq., 39 et seq., 91 et seq. Ann. dell' Inst., 1885, pp. 26 et seq., 92 et seq. *(Undset)*. *Gsell*, Fouilles dans la nécropole de Vulci (1891), pp. 419 et seq. — On Etruscan bronzes in general, comp. *Brunn*, in *Scheffler*, Ueber die Epochen der etruskischen Kunst, 1882. *Jules Martha*, L'art étrusque (Paris, 1889).

We begin our inspection to the left of the door, and first follow the wall.

11. Small Candelabrum or Lamp-Stand.

Up the shaft, which is adorned with oblique fluting and rests on three deer's feet, climbs a cock, pursued by a dog (?). On the rim at the top sit two pigeons. Comp. pp. 356 et seq.

Museo Gregoriano, I, T. xlviii (A I, T. lxxv), 4. *Dennis*, Cities and Cemeteries, II[3], p. 479.

12. Chafing Dish.

This large basin has movable handles and rests on three lion's paws, protruding from the mouths of griffin's heads. In antiquity, as among the southern peoples of to-day, apparatus of this kind were used for warming rooms. Comp. No. 145 (p. 370).

16. Ideal Woman's Head, from a statue.

This beautiful type reproduces a Greek original of about the beginning of the fourth century B.C.

Mus. Gregor., A I, T. lxxiv, 3.

17. Thymiaterion (incense-burner).

The low shaft supporting the cup for the incense is

thick and heavy in its proportions; the restoration is in great part arbitrary. Comp. p. 357.

Mus. Gregor., I, T. L (A I, T. LXXVII), 4.

18. Small Candelabrum.

The shaft, on which is a cock pursued by a cat, is borne by a nude figure of Eros in a thoroughly free style, wearing shoes and bracelets and holding an apple in his right hand. The support is formed of three lion's paws, issuing from griffin's heads (comp. No. 12).

Mus. Gregor., I, T. LV (A I, T. LXXXII), 5. Comp. *Friederichs*, Kleinere Kunst, No. 690.

22. Small Candelabrum.

Up the shaft climbs a youth, in a free style, holding a pruning-hook. On the edge of the socket sit dogs.

Mus. Gregor., I, T. LI (A I, T. LXXVIII), 2.

24. Small Candelabrum.

The support is formed by three human legs. A piece of drapery folded above these forms the transition to the smooth shaft, which is encoiled by a serpent.

Mus. Gregor., I, T. XLVIII (A I, T. LXXV), 3.

26. Crater (mixing vessel).

This vase has been reconstructed by a modern restorer with several ancient fragments. The handles, consisting of a young man bent backwards and grasping the tails of two lions couched on the brim of the vase, reproduce a highly archaic type of the art of Oriental Greece or Chalcis. The figure-subjects adorning the points where the handles are attached are also very interesting. One of these, in perfect preservation, represents Heracles, with his club, in combat with a female figure, armed with a lance-head and supposed to be the Italic Juno. Between lie the Cerynean hind and the head of the Erymanthian boar, the objects of Juno's attack. If this explanation is correct, the groups afford an interesting proof of a somewhat obscure myth, hitherto met on Italian soil only, in which Heracles (or rather his *Genius*, according to the Italic ideas) and Juno are coupled, first as enemies and then as friends. The figure-motives are borrowed from early Ionic art.

Mus. Gregor., I, T. VI (A I, T. LVI), 3. — For the types of the handles, comp. *Friederichs*, Kleinere Kunst, No. 1440. *Schumacher*, Bronzen in Karlsruhe, No. 527. Bonner Studien, p. 176 *(Fowler)*. — For the interpretation of the subject, see Ann. dell' Inst. arch., 1867, p. 357[2] *(Reifferscheid)*. *Roscher*, Lexikon der Mythologie, I, p. 2221 *(Furtwaengler)*, 2163 *(R. Peter)*.

28. Small Candelabrum.

Three women, bending backwards, bear a round base on their heads. On the base stands a Satyr, with a horse's tail, holding a wine-skin in his left hand, while in his right he has a cup ready for use in the game of cottabos (comp. No. 225, p. 343). On the head of the Satyr rises a fluted column, surmounted by a naked boy, who stands on one leg and holds the candle-socket high above his head, as if to place it out of the reach of the dog beside him.

Mus. Gregor., I, T. LV (A I, T. LXXXII), 7. Comp. Ann. dell' Inst., 1868, p. 229 *(Heydemann)*. *Dennis*, Cities and Cemeteries, II[3], p. 479. *Martha*, L'art étrusque, p. 528.

32, 33, 34. Convex Circular Shields.

Convex shields like these were frequently used for the decoration of the walls or ceilings of tombs. Some (No. 32; comp. also Nos. 111, 112) are adorned with a central boss in the form of a repoussé lion's head in bronze, attached by rivets. The lion's jaws are wide open; the eyes, cut in the metal, are filled with black and white enamel. The boss of the other shields (Nos. 33, 34, 113) is in the form of a bearded mask of a god, with short horns and animal's ears — the type of river-gods (Acheloos, Dionysos-Hebon). Comp. Nos. 112-114.

Found at Corneto-Tarquinii. - Mus. Gregor., I, T. XXXVIII (A I, T. LXXXV), 1-4. *Micali*, Monumenti per la storia (Florence, 1832), T. LI, 1-3 (Storia, III, p. 63). Comp. Bull. dell' Inst., 1829, p. 151 ; 1866, p. 327. *Friederichs*, Kleinere Kunst, p. 271. *Curtius*,

Bronzereliefs von Olympia, p. 8. *Benndorf*, Gesichtshelme und Sepulcralmasken, p. 367. *Helbig*, Homerische Epos[2], p. 438.

39. Bronze Pitcher.

The spout, situated above the body of the vessel, is in the shape of an inverted calyx. A lion is attached to the upper part of the handle in such a way that it seems to wish to drink from the vase. The date of the vessel is about the fourth century B. C.

Pistolesi, Il Vaticano descritto, III, T. 109. Mus. Gregor., I, T. VI (A I, T. LVI), 2.

3S, 40, 42, 44. Candelabra, of the ordinary shape.

Comp. p. 356.

Mus. Gregor., I, T. LIII (A I. T. LXXX), 3 and 5; T. LIV (A I, T. LXXXI), 3 and 5; T. LII (A I, T. LXXIX), 1; I, T. LII (A I, T. LXXIX), 3.

43. Pitcher in the form of a Woman's Head.

Vessels in the shape of a head have been made both in bronze and pottery from the earliest times. This example is of the Hellenistic period.

Pistolesi, Il Vaticano descritto, III, T. 109. Mus. Gregor., I, T. IX (A I, T. LIX), 1. *Dennis*, Cities and Cemeteries, II[3], p. 477.

54, 60. Two Candelabra.

These two lofty candelabra were evidently made as a pair. The shaft of each is adorned with a young warrior, controlling a rearing horse.

Mus. Gregor., I, T. LIII (A I, T. LXXX), 4. Comp. *Friederichs*, Kleinere Kunst, No. 705. Ann. dell' Inst., 1879, p. 123 (comp. *Duhn*).

57. Incense-Burner on wheels.

In a rectangular plaque of metal is inserted a basin, over which is a stirrup-shaped handle, with a small, cup-like recess on its top. The basin was probably intended as a receptacle for the glowing coals, while the hollow in the handle contained the incense or perfume. The plaque rests on the heads of four small human figures, in short coats, standing on the ends of the axles. It is ornamented with two pairs of erect lions in repoussé work, facing each other. Round the edge is a row of flower-calices like lilies, cut out of metal.

Utensils mounted on wheels are said to have been used in Solomon's Temple, while Homer tells of the golden wheels under the tripods of Hephæstos (Iliad xviii, 375) and of the 'rolling' silver work-basket of Helen (Odyssey, iv, 131). The custom of mounting vessels on wheels to make them easily movable seems to have reached the Greeks through the Phœnicians; and it is quite possible that the perfume-burner before us may be of Greek workmanship. The so-called 'kettle-carriers', often found to the north of the Alps, are of the same kind.

Grifi, Monum. di Cere, T. xi, 3. Mus. Gregor., i, T. xv (A i, T. xiv), 5 and 6. *Perrot-Chipiez*, Histoire de l'art, iv, p. 335. Comp. *Ateken*, Mittelitalien, p. 384. *Genthe*, Etrusk. Tauschhandel, pp. 61 et seq. *Furtwaengler*, Bronzefunde von Olympia, p. 40. *Helbig*, Homerische Epos [2], p. 108. Zeitschrift für Ethnologie, 1890, p. 72 *(Undset)*.

62, 64, 66. Bronze Mounts, in an Oriental style.

These fragments, along with Nos. 176, 177, 179, formed the adornment of some large object, such as the bed No. 155 or the chariot of which other remnants were found in the Regulini-Galassi Tomb. The reliefs, in an Asiatic style, pourtray panthers, lions, roe-deer (curiously curtailed and contorted), and an upright Sphinx of a very singular form. They are obviously not original Phœnician works, but Italic copies of Oriental models. Comp. p. 407.

Found in the Regulini-Galassi Tomb. — *Grifi*, Monum. di Cere, T. xi, 6-8. Mus. Gregor., i, T. xvii (A i, T. xxi).

67, 81, 82, 85. Decorative Bronze Disks, probably for the walls of a tomb.

Comp. *Grifi*, Monumenti di Cere, p. 144.

69. Etruscan Horn.

The shape of this instrument is that of the ordinary Roman trumpet *(tuba)* and the Etruscan horn *(lituus)*. It consists of a long tube ending in a curved and expanding 'bell'.

Mus. Gregor.. I, T. xxi (A I, T. lxxxiv). 8. *Dennis*, Cities and Cemeteries, II[3], p. 476. Comp. *Braun*, Ruinen und Museen, p. 797. *Müller-Deecke*, Die Etrusker, II, p. 213. *Gevaert*, Histoire de la musique de l'antiquité, II, p. 652. *Baumeister*, Denkmäler des klass. Alterthums, III, p. 1660 (Jan.).

70. Iron Lance-Heads.

Mus. Gregor., I, T. xxi (A I, T. lxxxiii), 6. 7.

83. Visor and Helmet.

Of the visor the only parts extant are the cheek-pieces *(paragnathides)*, united by a hinge; they represent the lower part of a bearded face, from the jaws to the middle of the nose.

Mus. Gregor., I, T. xxi (A I, T. lxxxiv). 2. *Benndorf*, Gesichts- helme und Sepulcralmasken, T. xiv, 5, p. 29. *Dennis*, Cities and Cemeteries, II[3], p. 476.

84. Italic Helmet, of about the fourth century B. C.

The shape of this helmet, with its peak in front and button on top, recalls that of a modern jockey-cap. The movable cheek-pieces, attached to the helmet by hinges, have been broken off.

Pistolesi, Il Vaticano descritto, III, T. 109. Mus. Gregor., I, T. xxi (A I, T. lxxxiv), 1. Comp. *Kemble*, Horæ ferales, T. xii, 5. *Friederichs*, Kleinere Kunst, p. 226, No. 1020.

91. Etruscan Suit of Armour, of about the fourth century B.C.

This armour includes a cuirass and a pair of greaves. The back and front of the cuirass faithfully reproduce the anatomical details of the body, as was customary in Greek armour from the fifth century downwards, and are meant to fit closely to it. They were connected with each other by straps passing through the rings attached to their edges.

Mus. Gregor., I, T. xxi (A I, T. lxxxiv), 3 and 9. Comp. *Vis- conti-Guattani*, Mus. Chiaramonti, T. a, I, 2, pp. 162, 324. *Friede- richs*, Kleinere Kunst, p. 2287.

94. Circular Shield.

This shield has precisely the same form as the Greek shields of the fifth and fourth centuries B.C. No. 4 is a similar example, battered, bent, and pierced with holes.

Mus. Gregor., I, T. xxi (A I, T. lxxxiv). Comp. *Schumacher*, Bronzen in Karlsruhe, No. 710. Olympia, IV, T. 62, p. 163 *(Furt-waengler)*.

Above, Etruscan Helmet.

This casque coïncides in form with a helmet now in the British Museum, which, according to an inscription on it, was taken by King Hieron of Syracuse from the Etruscans after his victory at Cumæ (B.C. 474) and was dedicated by him at Olympia.

Mus. Gregor., I, T. xxi (A, T. lxxxiv), first to the left. — On the example from Olympia, see *Kemble*, Horæ ferales, T. xii, 1. Comp. *Roehl*, Inscript. Græcæ antiquiss., No. 510.

Below the shield (No. 93) are a lance and a battle-axe (with modern shafts); above are two curious bronze sheaths (with modern handles), supposed to be the holders of fans or whisks.

These sheaths, with four others, were found in the Regulini-Galassi Tomb. — *Grifi*, Monumenti di Cere, T. vii, 5. Mus. Gregor., A I, T. xii, 15.

97. Vessel of Great Antiquity.

This vessel, resembling an amphora, has somewhat the same shape as the usual terracotta cinerary urns found in the so-called *tombe a pozzo* ('well-tombs'; see p. 445) and probably served the same purpose. It is composed of separate sheets of metal, fastened together by rivets and adorned with rows of parallel lines, zigzag lines, and small knobs in repoussé work. Round the middle is a ring with pointed nail-heads, to which the wire handles are attached.

Mus. Gregor., I, T. v (A I, T. liv), 5. Comp. *Friederichs*, Kleine Kunst, No. 1314. Ann. dell' Inst., 1885, p. 99 *(Undset)*. Bullet. di paletnologia ital., xiii, p. 78 *(Pigorini)*. *Martha*, L'art étrusque, p. 69.

98, 108. Small Candelabra, in a developed style.

The shafts rest on the heads of nude figures of girls, the style of which points to the second or third century B.C.

Mus. Gregor., I, T. LV (A1, T. LXXXII), 1, 2.

99. Pitcher.

The mouth is in the form of a bird's beak. At the lower end of the handle is a group of Eos and Cephalos; the upper part of the handle is adorned with a relief of a human form ending in a serpent.

Mus. Gregor., I, T. III (A1, T. LIII), 1. Comp. *Stephani*, Nimbus und Strahlenkranz, p. 61.

112-114. Circular Shields.

Comp. No. 32.

118, 120, 122, 124. Candelabra (4-5th cent. B.C.).

The shaft of No. 118 is crowned by a nude figure holding a pair of crotala in its hands, Nos. 120 and 122 by athletes, and No. 124 by a warrior. All these little figures show clearly their inspiration by Greek models, but have been modified by the influence of Etruscan conceptions.

Mus. Gregor., I, T. LIV, 2; LV, 1; LIV, 2; LV, 4 (A1, T. LXXXI, 2; LXXXII, 1; LXXXI, 1; LXXXII, 4).

132. Thymiaterion.

> The shaft, which is adorned with disks and bell-shaped cups, has been freely restored. The plate and hook at the top do not belong to it.

The legs on which rests the narrow three-sided pyramid supporting the shaft present a bizarre medley of Greek ornamental motives — a kind of mixture that seems to have appealed strongly to Etruscan taste. Each angle bears the upper part of a Silenus, with wings at the haunches and ending below in the paw of a lion.

Mus. Gregor., I, T. XLVIII (A1, T. LXXV), 5. Comp. *Hauser*, Neu-attische Reliefs, p. 124.

On both sides of the door leading to the urn-room hang ribbed paterae, without handles (Nos. 135, 136), a dozen of which were found in the Regulini-Galassi Tomb.

Grifi, Monum. di Cere, T. VII, 2, p. 144. Mus. Gregor., I, T. xv (A I, T. XIV), 2.

145. Brazier, with cover.

Of the same kind as No. 12.

Mus. Gregor., I, T. XIV (A I, T. LXIII), 2. Monum. dell' Inst., II, T. 42 D. Comp. Ann. dell' Inst., 1837, p. 166. *Friedrichs*, Kleinere Kunst, p. 190, No. 761.

We now return to the door by which we entered, and begin an inspection of the row of objects parallel with the wall and at a short distance from it.

150. Tripod.

This tripod illustrates the evolution that took place in Etruria during the sixth century B.C. of an early type of tripod that had been brought from the Orient to Italy through the Ionians. The lowest part of the stand consists of three lion's paws, resting on three flattened frogs. From each of the lion's feet rise three fluted shafts, the central one vertically, while the two at the side slope outwards and unite in a horseshoe clasp with the corresponding shafts of the other legs. The three feet are united below by horizontal braces, meeting in the centre in a ring adorned with three recumbent figures of Silenus. Each of the upright supports is crowned with volutes of acorns and palmettoes, bearing groups of two persons: Heracles and Juno (?), a man and a woman, two figures of Silenus with horse's hoofs. The types of these figurine are evidently inspired by Ionian models, but they have been used partly to express purely Italic conceptions; thus the first-mentioned group is very naturally believed to be a representation of the marriage of Juno and the Genius identified with the Greek Heracles. The curved or slanting supports bear groups representing a lion devouring a roe-deer, while the spaces between their tops are occupied by volutes with lotus-palmettoes and acorns in perforated work. The upper part of the tripod is modern. From the analogy of other similar utensils, we may believe that in its original state it consisted of a basin or receptacle for coals, above which was a gridiron for bearing pots and pans. The Etruscan tripods did not share the sacred character they so often bore in Greece, where they were mainly used as votive offerings and prizes at games; but retained their original character of braziers or cooking apparatus.

Mus. Gregor., I, T. LVI (A I, T. LXXXIII). Mon. dell' Inst., II, T. 42C. *Martha*, L'art étrusque, p. 526. Comp. Ann. dell' Inst., 1873, p. 162.

For an interpretation of the groups, see Annali, 1867, p. 360 *(Reifferscheid)*. *Roscher*, Lexikon der Mythologie, I, p. 2266 *(Peter)*. — Many similar specimens have been found at Vulci (Annali, 1842, p. 63; 1862, pp. 177 et seq.). One resembling that before us in all respects, and retaining the upper portion, was found at Dürkheim in the Rhenish Palatinate and is now in the museum of Spires. It is figured in *Lindenschmit*, Altertümer unserer heidnischen Vorzeit, II, 2, T. 2, and in the Westdeutsche Zeitschrift für Geschichte und Kunst, 1886, T. II, pp. 233 et seq. *(Undset)*. Comp. *Friederichs*, Kleinere Kunst, p. 191. Olympia, IV, pp. 127, 131 *(Furtwaengler)*.

On each side of the above-mentioned tripod is an unornamented bronze cauldron (Nos. 149, 151), one large, the other small, supported on three-legged iron stands put together out of antique fragments.

Found in the Regulini-Galassi Tomb. — Mus. Gregor., I, T. II (A I, T. XIII), 4 and 13.

155. Bedstead or Bier.

The bottom of this bed, which is the oldest extant specimen from classical antiquity, is formed of a lattice-work of thin bars of bronze, very similar to those used in the modern iron bedstead. At one end is a raised portion to serve as a pillow. Along the sides there was perhaps originally a border of metal or of wood covered with metal (comp. No. 62, p. 366).

Grifi, Monum. di Cere, T. IV, 6. Mus. Gregor., I. T. XVI (A I, T. XV), 8 and 9. Comp. *Braun*, Ruinen und Museen, p. 784. *Semper*, Der Stil, II², p. 218. *Helbig*, Homerische Epos², p. 124. *Baumeister*, Denkmäler des klass. Alterthums, I, p. 311.

156. Bronze Cauldron on a restored iron tripod.

The lower part of this specimen is modern and has been erroneously restored. The upper part is a portion of an amphora showing the same very archaic technique as No. 97.

Said to have been found in the Regulini-Galassi Tomb. — Mus. Gregor., I, T. II (A I, T. XIII), 11.

157. Small Tripod.

This tripod, of a still more archaic form than No. 150, reproduces a type that recalls models of Eastern Asia and is found (occasionally with iron rods) at several of the most ancient seats of Hellenistic civilization, in Cyprus, Olympia, etc. In each of the three lion's claws are fastened three vertical rods and two bent horizontal rods, with rings in their lower parts. The central vertical rods end at the top in the beaks of birds (or shrivelled swans' heads), and above the curved pieces between the side-rods are metal plaques with heads of oxen. The ring intended to support the basin is rivetted to these plates and to the beak-like tops of the central rods. The flat cauldron without handles which is at present on the tripod does not belong to it.

Found in the Regulini-Galassi Tomb. — Mus. Gregor., I, T. LVII (A I. T. XII), 5. Comp. Olympia, IV, pp. 126 et seq. *(Furtwaengler)*.

158. Cauldron with grip-handles, on an iron tripod.

The handles are in the form of lion's heads, turned inwards to the bowl, with open jaws and ears bent back like horns. They were evidently intended to hold the chains by which the vessel was suspended. The outside of the hemispherical cauldron is adorned with two rows of of winged bulls framed in twisted bands and with a rosette on the ground, the whole being in repoussé work. The vessel itself is an Etruscan production, but the handles have been copied from Greek, the ornamentation from Phœnician, models.

Found in the Regulini-Galassi Tomb. — Mus. Gregor., I, T. XVI (A I, T. XV), 1-5. *Canina*, Etruria marittima, I, T. LVII, 5. *Semper*, Der Stil, II², 5.

On the end-wall, —

164, 182, 190. **Round Shields.** Comp. Nos. 291, 304, 318.

The thinness of the metal plate used for these shields proves that they were never intended for practical purposes, but were meant from the first for sepulchral furniture. War-shields at the earliest period were made of layers of bull's hide sewn together and covered on the outside with bronze; and in imitation of this construction the shields before us consist of a round projecting boss in the centre surrounded by narrow concentric bands separated by rows of smaller knobs or bosses, and embellished with primitive repoussé work. Nos. 164, 190, and 291 are ornamented only with geometric patterns in a severe style, such as squares and rectangles filled in with parallel lines, zigzags, etc. On the other hand Nos. 182, 304, and 318 display rows of horses, dogs, running hares, scales, and anchors (?), enclosed in a plaited band, all of very primitive execution. These shields were most probably produced in Etruria after foreign models; recently they have been described as products of early Umbrian workmanship.

Found in the Regulini-Galassi Tomb. — *Grifi*, Monum. di Cere, T. XI, 1 and 3. Mus. Gregor., I, T. XVIII et seq. (A I, T. IX et seq.). *Canina*, Etruria marittima, T. 59. Comp. *Friederichs*, Kleinere Kunst, pp. 218 et seq. *Perrot et Chipiez*, Histoire de l'art, III, p. 870. *Helbig*, Homerische Epos², p. 313. Museo Ital. di antichità class., II, pp. 102 et seq. *(Orsi.)*

170. **Cabinet with Small Bronze Utensils.**

On the top-shelf are two curiously shaped bronze forks, discovered at Vulci. Fixed to a bronze socket, intended for the insertion of the wooden handle, is a ring, bearing in one case five, in the other case seven much bent prongs, together with an additional and smaller prong in each case. The lively imagination of the Italian

ciceroni has converted these objects into instruments of
torture, used by the pagans to lacerate the bodies of early
Christians; but in reality they served a much less truculent purpose. Forks of this kind are invariably found
along with other kinds of culinary and sacrificial implements, and were evidently used for turning over or
taking up meat, etc. The utensils called 'pempobola' by
Homer (Iliad, ɪ, 463; Od., ɪɪɪ, 460) probably closely
resembled these.

Mus. Gregor., ɪ, T. xlvii (A ɪ, T. lxv), 1, 3, 4. Comp. *Helbig*,
Homerische Epos[2], p. 355. Olympia, ɪv, p. 189 *(Furtwaengler)*.

On the second shelf are mirrors, strigils, supports of
various kinds, long pins ending in hands or animals' heads
(probably hair-pins), and ladles *(trullae, simpula)*. The
strigils or scrapers are formed of a narrow metal blade
fitted with a slender and curved handle, and were used
to remove dust and oil from the body after the exercises
of the gymnasium. The ladles resemble our toddy-ladles,
having a hemispherical bowl attached to a long handle,
and were used to ladle wine from the deep store-jars or
craters into cups or goblets.

For the strigils: Mus. Gregor., ɪ, T. xlvii (A ɪ, T. lxv), 2. — For
some of the supports: Mus. Gregor., ɪ, T. lxi (A ɪ, T. lxxi). — For
the pins: id., ɪ, T. lxvi (A ɪ, T. lxiv). — For the ladles: id., ɪ, T. ɪ
(A ɪ, T. lii), 1-3.

On the third shelf are handles of vases and other
attachments, of very various shapes. One very ancient
flask has a movable handle. The body of the flask is
made of bronze plates rivetted together and embellished
with studs, concentric circles, and four rude figures of
animals (apparently horses), all in repoussé work. Similar vessels have been discovered in tombs dating from
the so-called first iron age. Vases of the same shape are
also found among Cyprian pottery, while the ornamentation is Italian in origin.

Found at Cosa, near Vulci. — Mus. Gregor., ɪ, T. x (A ɪ, T. lx).
Semper, Der Stil, ɪɪ[2], p. 64. Comp. *Perrot et Chipiez*, Histoire de
l'art. ɪɪɪ, pp. 690, 830. Ann. dell' Inst., 1885, pp. 99 et seq. *(Undset)*.

172. Candelabrum.

The shaft is surmounted by a group of a warrior and a woman (Ajax and Cassandra?). Probably from the transition period at the end of the fifth and beginning of the fourth century B.C.

Mus. Gregor., I, T. LIV (A I, T. LXXXI), 4.

173. Fragmentary Statue of a Roman, from the Augustan period.

This statue reproduces the common type of a man entirely nude except for a small cloak on his left shoulder and arm, in the act of delivering a speech *(allocutio)*.

The abdomen, legs, and forearms have been broken off. Mus. Gregor., A I, T. LXXIV, 2.

175. Bronze Statuette of a Youth (fragment).

Skilful and vigorous in execution; dating from the Hellenistic period.

The head, the arms, and the right leg are broken off.

176, 177, 179. Reliefs in bronze repoussé.

Comp. Nos. 62 et seq.

187. Shutter with Engraved Mirrors. Comp. pp. 358 et seq.

The gilt mirror (freely retouched), in the middle of the shutter, is referred to the latest epoch of the industry (second century), both by the execution and by the invention of the motives. The subject of the design is uncertain. The lovers embracing in the centre, under a partly illegible inscription, are supposed to be Paris (or, according to a recent suggestion, Theseus) and Helen. The nude woman to the left is named *Alpan*, a name in which some authorities have sought to recognize that of Persephone. The name *Maristuran*, visible beside the nude and winged youth to the right, most probably indicated the god of war (Mars, husband of Venus). Other authorities are more inclined to identify this figure as a Cupid or as one of the Dioscuri. In the upper part of the picture, which is framed by a border of marine animals, appears a Fury, with serpent and torch. On the handle is a winged figure playing on the lyre, and identified as a Muse by the inscription *(Mus)*.

Found at Vulci in 1836. — Mus. Gregor., I, T. XXIII (A I, T. XCIII), 1. Ann. dell' Instit., 1851, T. L, p. 151 *(Braun)*. *Gerhard*, Etruskische Spiegel, IV, T. 381. Comp. Archæol. Zeit., XLIII, 1885, pp. 176 et seq. *(Marx)*. *Bugge*, Beiträge zur Erforschung der etrusk. Sprache, I, pp. 9 et seq.

Below, to the left, —

Mirror: Peleus and Atalanta wrestling.

According to the legend the maiden huntress of Arcadia measured her strength against Peleus at the funeral games held in honour of Pelias. Atalanta *(Atlnta)* wears nothing but a cloth upon her head and a close garment, with a wheel embroidered upon it, round her waist. Peleus *(Pele)* on the other hand is entirely nude; his clothes and ointment-flasks lie on the ground beside him. The delicate execution of the drawing strongly reminds us of the severe style of Attic vases of the first half of the fifth century B.C.

Found in 1837 at Vulci. — Mus. Gregor., I, T. XXXV (A I, T. CIII), 1. *Gerhard*, Etrusk. Spiegel, II, T. 224. Comp. *Braun*, Ruinen und Museen, p. 801.

Below, to the right, —

Mirror: Girl's Head looking towards the right.

The decorative motive is unusual but very happily chosen. The inscription is not perfectly legible. The style of the design is entirely free.

Mus. Gregor., I, T. XXVI (A I, T. XCV), 1. *Gerhard*, Etrusk. Spiegel, IV, T. 287, 3.

195. **Roman Helmet**, probably of the third century A.D.

This helmet is inscribed with the name of its owner, a soldier in the 12th urban cohort: *Aurelius Victorinus mil. coh. XII urb.* From other sources also we know that soldiers of the imperial epoch were in the habit of inscribing their name and corps upon their weapons, especially on their shields.

Mus. Gregor., A I, T. LXXXIV, 7. Comp. Archæologisch-epigraph. Mittheilungen aus Oesterreich, II, p. 117 *(Hübner)*. Ephemeris epigraphica, IV, No. 641 et seq., VII, No. 1166.

196. Shutter with Mirrors.

Above, to the left: Mirror with a figure of Chalcas. The augur *(Chalcas)*, a dignified personage with large wings and flowing hair and beard, is attentively examining the entrails of the victim, in order to unravel the future. The entrails of the slaughtered animal lie before him on a table; behind him, on the ground, stands a ewer. This winged figure, which recurs on the Ficoronian cist (p. 437), is no doubt a copy of some Greek original (of about the end of the fifth century); but it was first adopted to represent an augur in Central Italy, where some local association of ideas seems to have caused augurs to be conceived of as provided with wings.

Found in 1837 at Vulci. — Mus. Gregor., I, T. XXIX (A I, T. CII), 1. *Gerhard*, Etrusk. Spiegel, II, T. 223. Comp. *Braun*, Ruinen und Museen, p. 802. Gazette archéol., 1880, p. 112 *(Lenormant)*.

Above, to the right: Mirror, with a youth in a chariot with four winged horses, advancing towards the left. A band inserted in front of the charioteer's head bears a long Etruscan inscription of uncertain meaning, in which the name Achilles occurs. The drawing recalls Italic vasepaintings of the end of the third century B.C.

Found in 1837 at Vulci. — Mus. Gregor., I, T. XXXV (A I, T. CIII), 2. *Gerhard*, Etrusk. Spiegel, IV, T. 288 (comp. V, p. 65¹). Comp. *Corssen*, Sprache der Etrusker, I, p. 760.

In the centre: Mirror with Helios, Eos, and Poseidon (Neptune). Neptune *(Nethuns)* is seated on a rock, with the trident (pronged at both ends) in his right hand, and his left hand raised in a conversational gesture. Before him stands Helios *(Usil)*, a bow in his right hand, with his head surrounded by a nimbus, shaped like the aureole of later Christian art. Eos *(Thesan)* stands behind Helios

and lays her right hand familiarly on his shoulder. The
union in one group of these three divinities seems to
refer to the sun rising from the sea, preceded by dawn.
The top of the handle is adorned with the figure of a sea-
monster with a human body and legs ending in interlacing
serpents, with beards; in each hand is a dolphin. The
edge of the mirror is embellished with a border of an-
themia or small rosettes. This mirror, the design on which
seems to have been inspired by a Greek original of the
fourth century, is not older than the end of the third
century B.C.

Found at Vulci. — Monumenti dell' Instit., ii, T. 160. Mus.
Gregor., i, T. xxiv (A i, T. xcii). *Forchhammer*, Apollons Ankunft
in Delphi, T. 1. *Gerhard*, Etrusk. Spiegel, i, T. 76 (v. p. 65). Comp.
Braun, Ruinen und Museen, p. 801. *Corssen*, Sprache der Etrusker,
i, p. 259.

198.　Glass-Case to the left of the window.

Small Bronze Figures, of various kinds and diverse
　　origin.

Top Shelf: Statuette of the Etruscan Minerva, with
an owl on her right hand. Her ægis, which is shaped
like a gorget, is adorned with the Gorgon's head and also
with a half-moon and stars. Traces of wings remain on
the back of this figure.

Found in 1837 near Orte. — Mus. Gregor., i, T. xliii, 1 (A i, T.
cvi, 5). *Gerhard*, Gottheiten der Etrusker, p. 61, T. 4, 1. Comp.
Braun, Ruinen und Museen, p. 863. Ann. dell' Instit., 1872,
p. 225 *(Roulez)*.

Second Shelf: Statuette of a dancing Silenus, holding
a cup by the handle, as though about to play at cottabos
(comp. No. 225, p. 343). — Statuette of a girl, with her
right hand raised in an attitude of a prayer, on a base
bearing an Etruscan inscription.

The Silenus: Mus. Gregor., A i, T. cvii, 7. — Statuette of Girl
(formerly owned by Depoletti): Annali dell' Instit., 1864, Tav. d'agg.
T, 2, p. 412 *(Brunn)*. *Fabretti*, Corpus inscrip. italic., No. 2603 bis.
Corssen, Sprache der Etrusker, i, p. 634. *Deecke*, Forschungen und
Studien, i, p. 52. *Martha*, L'art étrusque, p. 509.

Third Shelf: Primitive votive figures, some with the pileus or high cap. Athlete with the discus in his left hand. Fine terracotta figure of a young man, with his left hand raised, in a listening attitude.

Fourth Shelf: Group of Heracles and the Nemean lion rearing on its hind-legs (a handle of a lid; after an archaic model).

For the votive figures, comp. Notizie degli scavi, 1888, p. 230 *(Helbig)*. — The athlete: Mus. Gregor., A I, T. cvii, 9. — Heracles: Id., A I, T. cvi, 8. Comp. *Roscher*, Lexikon der Mythologie, I, p. 2197 *(Furtwaengler)*.

201. **Low Bronze Seat,** very archaic in form.

Mus. Gregor., A I, T. lxxiv, 10. Comp. Zeitschrift für Ethnologie, 1890, p. 121 *(Undset)*.

202, 203. **Low Stands** *(craticula,* capifuoco), apparently used as a kind of gridiron.

Found in the Regulini-Galassi Tomb along with a third specimen in iron. — *Grifi*, Monum. di Cere, T. iv, 5. Mus. Gregor., I, T. lvii, 6 (A I, T. xii, 12). *Canina*, Etruria maritt., T. lix, 6. Comp. p. 457.

205. **Bronze Chariot.**

When this chariot was discovered its wooden parts had already mouldered to dust, but the upper metal rim and the floor of the body were still perfect, while most of the metal ornamentation and the iron parts of the wheels were still preserved, though in fragments. Thus the shape and size of the vehicle could be exactly determined. On these data the brothers Pazzaglia re-constructed the chariot in wood, covered it with metal plates, and fastened the fragments of the ancient bronze coating upon it with nails, many of which also were the originals.

The body of the chariot is too small to accommodate more than one person (or at most two, standing one behind the other), so that it was probably a racing chariot; or it may even have been specially constructed merely as an ex voto offering. Judging from its ornamentation, it appears to date from the fifth or fourth century B. C. The upper rim of the sides, which have a double curve, is studded with heads of nails, while in front is a winged male figure, ending in an arabesque of leaves (almost wholly a modern restoration). The head of this figure, which has its hair elaborately dressed, is surrounded by a nimbus of rays, which has led some authorities to identify it as the sun-god, and others as Phobos, god of fear. At each end of the inner rim of the chariot-body, towards the rear, is a mask of Medusa, and a similar mask adorns the peg or pin used to fasten the yoke. The pole ends in the beautifully executed head of a bird of prey (hawk or eagle) — a symbol of the winged speed of the chariot. The axles are decorated with lions' heads. The chariots used in Roman triumphs were probably formed like this.

The chariot is said to have been found among the ruins of Roma Vecchia in the Roman Campagna, and passed from the possession of the brothers Pazzaglia into the Appartamento Borgia. It was first figured by Piranesi on a separately issued sheet, then in the following: Vasi, Candelabri, etc., I, T. 13. *Inghirami*, Monumenti etruschi. VI, T. L', 5. *Visconti*, Museo Pio-Clementino, V, T. B, II and III. pp. 234. 252 et seq. Mus. Gregor., A I, T. lxxiv, 11. Comp. Beschreibung Roms. II, 2. p. 27. *Braun*, Ruinen und Museen, p. 806. *Stephani*, Nimbus und Strahlenkranz, p. 20. *Helbig*, Homerische Epos[2], p. 146. *Daremberg-Saglio*, Dictionnaire des antiquités, I, p. 1642.

206. Colossal Bronze Arm, found in the harbour of Cività Vecchia, the ancient Centumcellæ, along with a **Dolphin's Tail** (No. 200) and a **Bronze Shaft** (No. 174). These are evidently three fragments from one of the colossal statues of Neptune which it was customary to erect at Roman harbours. The shaft (of the trident) rested against the left arm of the god, while the dolphin reared itself at his feet, with its tail in the air. As the mole at Centumcellæ was built by Trajan, it has been suggested that these fragments belonged to a statue of that emperor as Neptune. The suggestion, however, is incapable of proof, though the fragments may very possibly date from Trajan's reign. The careful modelling of the arm (No. 206) gives us a high idea of the technical perfection attained by the Roman metal-workers; though even this has been somewhat over-praised.

Mus. Gregor., A I. T. lxxiv. 8 and 9. Comp. Bullet. dell' Instit., 1851, p. 30. *Braun*, Ruinen und Museen, p. 805. *Friederichs-Wolters*, Berliner Gipsabgüsse, No. 1615.

207. So-called Peter Cist.

Found about 1816 near Præneste, and at first in the possession of F. Peter, afterwards in the Accademia di S. Luca. Within the cist were found two alabaster and one wooden ointment-pot, a broken strigil, and a mirror.

This round cist (comp. pp. 361 et seq.) is supported on three animals' claws, above which are lions preparing to spring. The lid has two sea-monsters engraved upon it, and its handle is formed of a group of a Satyr and a nude woman. The body of the cist is adorned with engraved scenes from the palæstra, bordered at the top and bottom by a series of delicately executed double palmettes. Two pugilists, with hands enveloped in straps, stand on a piece of ground, represented as being uneven and planted with laurel-trees; to the left is an athlothetes or umpire, and to the right hangs a corycos, or sack filled with sand, used by pugilists to practice their blows. Near the sack stands a young man, holding boxing-straps, while from the flask in his uplifted left hand he drops oil upon his shoulders. A companion seems to be rubbing the oil in. Farther on is a Satyr playing the flute. Separated from these scenes by a clumsy Ionic column is a group of three figures, the significance of which cannot be made out in consequence of the absence of the central figure.

Guattani, Memorie enciel., VI (1815), T. IX, p. 65 *(Peter)*. *Gerhard*, Etrusk. Spiegel, I, T. VI et seq. Mus. Gregor., I, T. xxxvii (A I, T. xc), 1. Comp. *Jahn*, Ficoronische Ciste, p. 27. Ann. dell' Instit., 1866, pp. 150 et seq. *(Schöne)*.

208. Glass-Case in front of the first window.

Small Images in Black Terracotta (bucchero), including various types of female divinities, usually with long hair and rigid arms raised to the level of the chin. These crude and rough figures convey an excellent idea of the earliest period of Etruscan art, in which, however, foreign models already exercised an influence. Two small monkeys (also in bucchero), in the middle of the case, should be noticed.

Found in the Regulini-Galassi Tomb. — *Grifi*, Monum. di Cere, T. IV, 3 and 4. Mus. Gregor., II, T. CIII (A I, T. III), 3-10. *Dennis*, Cities and Cemeteries, I³, p. 267.

Small Ointment Flask, in black clay, inscribed with very ancient lettering.

Round the foot of this flask are inscribed the letters of a Greek alphabet, resembling the oldest Chalcidian alphabet which we know from other sources, but with two extra characters. This little vessel is thus of the highest importance for the history of writing. Arranged in a spiral round the body of the flask is an Etruscan syllabary composed of thirteen groups of syllables (bi, ba, bu, be, gi, ga, gu, ge, etc.).

This flask was found during General Galassi's excavations, but not in the large tomb (pp. 353 et seq.). — Mus. Gregor., II, T. CIII (A I, T. III), 2. *Dennis*, Cities and Cemeteries, I³, p. 271. Ann. dell' Instit., 1836, p. 136, T. *B*. *Canina*, Etruria maritt., p. 189. *Roehl*, Inscript. græcæ antiquissimæ, No. 534. *Corssen*, Sprache der Etrusker, I, p. 5, T. I, 3 and 4. *Müller-Deecke*, Die Etrusker, II, p. 526. *Kirchhoff*, Geschichte des griech. Alphabetes⁴, p. 135. Journal of Hellenic Studies, 1889, p. 187 *(Ramsay)*.

Foot of a Vase, with an Etruscan inscription in very archaic characters, which were first incised on the terracotta and then picked out with red paint.

In the possession of Gen. Galassi before passing to the Vatican Museum. — Mus. Gregor., II, T. IC (A I, T. XXXIV), 7. Comp. Annali dell' Instit., 1836, p. 199 *(Lepsius)*. *Abeken*, Mittelitalien, p. 361. *Mommsen*, Unteritalische Dialekte, p. 17. *Corssen*, Sprache der Etrusker, I, p. 444, T. 15, 2. *Bugge*, Beiträge zur Erforschung der etrusk. Sprache.

210. Thymiaterion (fifth or fourth centuries).

The shaft has been freely restored. The prism-shaped base rests upon four winged legs of animals, above each of which is a seated Sphinx.

Mus. Gregor., I, T. xlix (A I, T. lxxvi), 3.

222. Bronze Amphora of archaic workmanship.

This amphora, with its long straight neck and flattened body, recalls one of the typical forms of the terracotta cinerary urns of the so-called first iron age. It is formed of hammered bronze plates rivetted together; and round the middle of the body runs a ring of nails with pointed heads. Comp. No. 97 (p. 368) and No. 247 (p. 384).

Mus. Gregor., 1. T. v (A i, T. liv. 2. Comp. *Schumacher*, Bronzen von Karlsruhe, No. 432. Annali dell' Instit., 1885, p. 28. Zeitschrift für Ethnologie, 1890, p. 122 (*Undset*).

246. Glass-Case in front of the second window.

One large and several small **Pateræ**, bearing the Etruscan word '*suthina*', currently interpreted as meaning 'cinerary' or 'for the worship of the dead'. **Styli** (pens), **Feet**, and **Attachments of Vases**, including three specimens of a group in the archaic style representing Heracles and the Italic Juno disputing for the possession of the hydria (feet of a bronze cist).

Mus. Gregor., 1, T. lxi (A 1, T. lxxi). 8. Comp. Annali dell' Instit., 1867, p. 357 (*Reifferscheid*). *Roscher*, Lexikon der Mythologie, 1, p. 2263 (*Peter*).

Pair of Etruscan Clogs (very ancient).

The wooden soles are covered below and on the sides with thin plates of bronze, an admirable protection against the roughness and dampness of the ground, but somewhat wanting in point of elasticity. In order, therefore, to give the foot a certain mobility, each sole is made in two parts united by a hinge. The golden sandals mentioned in the Homeric poems were no doubt also made of wood and covered with a thin metal plate.

Mus. Gregor., 1, T. lvii, 7 (A i, T. lxxii, c). Comp. *Dennis*, Cities and Cemeteries, ii³, p. 484. *Braun*, Ruinen und Museen, p. 796. *Friederichs*, Kleinere Kunst, No. 1532. *Schumacher*, Bronzen von Karlsruhe, No. 204. *Helbig*, Homerische Epos², p. 1094. Monum. antich. pubblic. per cura dell' Accad. dei Lincei, 1 (1890), p. 275 (*Brizio*).

247. Bronze Vase.

A companion-piece to No. 222, but with flat-headed instead of pointed nails.

249. Weight in the shape of a recumbent Swine.

This bronze figure is filled with lead. The handle on the back and the figure C on the body reveal the use of this article.

Pistolesi, Il Vaticano descritto, ii, T. 109. Mus. Gregor., A i, T. lxxiv, 12.

254. Small Sacrificial Bull.

The garland round the horns and the band about the body show that the animal was destined for some solemn sacrifice. This little statuette may have been a votive offering.

256. Thymiaterion.

The prism-shaped base rests upon three winged lions' feet, the spaces between which are elaborately ornamented with palmettes. Above each of the feet of the thymiaterion and leaning against the angles of the base is the nude figure of a youth, with a garland on his long, flowing hair, his legs bent back, and his hand on his hips. The shaft has been freely restored. The thymiaterion probably dates from the fifth century B. C.

Mus. Gregor., i, T. li (A i, T. lxxviii), 3. *Martha*, L'art étrusque, p. 530.

257. Head of Trebonianus Gallus.

The coarse but characteristic execution, the short hair, and the fashion of the beard refer this head to the concluding years of the third century after Christ. It has been recognized as a portrait of the soldier-emperor C. Vibius Trebonianus Gallus (251-253 A. D.) from a comparison with coins. The laurel crown was restored in accordance with various traces of the original.

At one time in the Villa Mattei, afterwards in the Stanza dei Busti. — Monumenta Mathæiana, ii, T. 31. *Visconti*, Museo Pio-

Clementino, vi, T. CO, p. 234. Mus. Gregor., A i, T. lxxiv, 1. Comp. *Meyer-Schulze* on *Winckelmann,* Geschichte der Kunst, vii, 2, § 21. Beschreibung Roms, ii, 2, p. 192, 78.

281. Glass-Case in front of the third window.

Mirrors, one with the front (*i.e.* the mirror proper) shown; strigils; and fibulæ (safety-pins) of various shapes.

282. Glass-Case containing Metal Vessels and Rings.

A large number of the gold and silver vessels in this case were found at Vicarello, near Bracciano, in Etruria, where they had been left as votive offerings by wealthy patients who had used the thermal sulphur-springs. Several of them bear votive inscriptions; *e. g.* a silver cup is inscribed 'Apollini sancto Cl. Severianus D. D.' (*i. e.* dono dedit or dedicavit), and a small bronze-gilt amphora, with bacchic masks on the handles, is inscribed 'Apollini et Nymphis sanctis Nævia Basilla D.D'.

Comp. Corpus inscrip. latin., xi, pp. 496 et seq., Nos. 3285, 3288; and below, pp. 420 et seq.

THIRD SHELF. Bronze flask richly embellished with meanders, cymatia, and foliage, in repoussé and chased work.

Mus. Gregor., i, T. ix (A i, T. lix), 3. Comp. *Schumacher,* Bronzen von Karlsruhe, No. 221.

Among the silver and bronze rings are several seal-rings, some of which bear an emblem, others their owners' names.

283. Seated Bronze Statue of a Nude Child, with a bird in his hand.

A characteristic Etruscan touch is seen in the fact that the otherwise completely nude child wears a bulla suspended from his neck by a long chain as well as thick rings on his arms and right ankle. On the right leg is the Etruscan inscription: '*Fleres zersansl cver*', the meaning of which is doubtful. The statue, which may be referred to the fourth or third century, is evidently a votive offering, dedicated to the gods under whose protection the life of the child represented was to be placed. Comp. No. 203 (p. 271) and No. 329 (p. 393).

Found near the Trasimene Lake. — *Fontanini*, Antiquit. Hortæ, p. 146. *Montfaucon*, Antiquité expliquée, III, T. 40. *Dempster*, Etruria, I, T. 44. Mus. Gregor., I, T. xliii, 5 (A I, T. cvii, 8). *Conestabile*, Monum. di Perugia, T. 99 (73), 6, p. 450. *Martha*, L'art étrusque, p. 507. *Fabretti*, Corpus inscript. italic., No. 1930. Comp. *Corssen*, Sprache der Etrusker, I, p. 538. *Deecke*, Etrusk. Forschungen und Studien, II. p. 46.

285. Helmet, with delicate ornamentation.

Helmets were frequently made in whole or in part in imitation of human heads. In the present case a head of a Silenus has been adopted as a model both for the bald forehead with the hair in relief above it, and for the equine ears.

Mus. Gregor., A I, T. lxxiv, 6.

291, 304, 318. Ornamental Shields, of archaic workmanship.

Comp. No. 164, p. 373.

294. Shutter with Mirrors.

Below, to the right, —

Mirror : Heracles and Atlas.

In his expedition to obtain the apples of the Hesperides, Heracles was obliged to seek the aid of Atlas, and while the latter went off to fetch the apples, the hero took upon his own shoulders the burden of the heavens. When Atlas returned, he refused to resume his burden, but by the cunning of Heracles he was induced to undertake it for a little, until the hero should make a cushion to relieve the pressure. No sooner had Heracles secured the apples than he departed, leaving Atlas to fulfil his toilsome task. The mirror represents the close of the episode. To the right is the bearded Atlas *(Aril)*, bending beneath the weight of the starry heavens, which he supports on his shoulders and hands. On the left is the departing Heracles, carrying the apples and his club, and clad in the hide of the Nemean lion, the head of which hangs down behind. Heracles is represented as a young man, with the down of youth upon his cheek. The inscription beneath his right shoulder names him *Calanice*, from the surname Callinicos (or brilliant victor), which he bore even in the earliest Greek poems. To his right are a spear planted in the ground, and a conventional silphium plant, indicating that the scene of action is one of the Syrtes of N. Africa. The care and grace with which the whole, even the ornaments, are drawn, are not unworthy of a Greek artist. There is no doubt that the design was executed in close relation to some original dating from the middle af the fifth century B.C.

Found at Vulci in 1829 and afterwards in the possession of Feoli. — *Micali*, Monum. per servire alla storia[2] (1833), T. 36, III, p. 53. Mus. Gregor., I, T. xxxvi (A I, T. cv), 2. *Gerhard*, Etrusk. Spiegel, II, T. 137. Wiener Vorlegeblätter für archæol. Uebungen, VIII, T. 12, 2. Comp. *Braun*, Ruinen und Museen, p. 799. Athen. Mittheilungen des arch. Instit., I, p. 207 *(Curtius)*.

297. Patera with a small figure as handle.

The figure of a winged woman forming the handle is fastened to the vase by a group of palmettes above the head and by the tips of the wings, which are rivetted to the rim of the patera. The closest analogues for such handles are offered by the supports of Greek standing mirrors, which were often carved into figures. The attitude of the present figure, however, proves that it dates from the Roman period, though its Etruscan origin is indicated by the arrangement of the drapery round the body, the shoes, and the ornaments. Comp. No. 310, p. 388.

Formerly in the Vatican Library. — *Pistolesi*, Il Vaticano descritto, III, T. 107, 3. Mus. Gregor., I, T. xiii (A I, T. lxii), 1.

299, 302, 305, 309. Round Bronze Plaques, with repoussé ornamentation.

The heraldic lions rearing back to back and the rosette surmounted by a vegetable ornament in the

Egyptian style seem to imply the existence either of Phœnician models or of Oriental Greek models influenced by Asiatic art.

Found in the Regulini-Galassi Tomb. — *Grifi.* Monumenti di Cere, T. 6, 5. Mus. Gregor., I, T. XV (A I, T. XIV), 3 and 4. Comp. *Furtwaengler*, Bronzefunde von Olympia, p. 69.

308. Bundle of Spits.

The ten pointed rods united by a cross-piece passing through the eyes at their upper ends can hardly have been weapons of war; more probably they were used as spits or fire-irons for sacrificial or culinary purposes.

Found in the Regulini-Galassi Tomb. — *Grifi*, Monum. di Cere, T. V, 3. Mus. Gregor., A I, T. XII, 6 and 8. Comp. *Dennis*, Cities and Cemeteries, II³, p. 477. A similar bundle of seven rods appears among the bas-reliefs of the Tomba dei Rilievi at Cervetri, on the central pillar, to the right. *Noël des Vergers*, L'Étrurie, III, T. 1 et seq. *Dennis*, op. cit., p. 251.

310. Patera with a small figure as handle, like No. 297.

In the base of the small figure is a ring, by which the vessel could be suspended.

Found at Chiusi. — Mus. Gregor., I, T. XIII (A I, T. LXIII), 2.

311.   Shutter with Mirrors.

To the right, near the foot, —

Eos and Thetis before Zeus.

Zeus stands in the centre, grasping a thunderbolt in his left hand. Eos *(Thesan)*, mother of Memnon, and Thetis *(Thethis)*, mother of Achilles, each beseeches him to grant the victory to her son in the impending duel between these heroes. The father of the gods looks towards Minerva *(Menrva)*, whose decision is in favour of Achilles. The drawing bears evident marks of the later Etruscan local style (*i.e.* of the end of the third century B.C.).

Mus. Gregor., I, T. XXXI (A I, T. c), 1. *Gerhard*, Etrusk. Spiegel, IV, T. 396. Comp. Bull. dell' Inst., 1837, p. 73. *Braun*, Ruinen und Museen, p. 800. *Overbeck*, Gallerie heroischer Bildwerke, p. 529.

To the right, at the top, —

Mirror: **Ulysses and Tiresias.**

The descent of Ulysses to Hades and his interview there with Tiresias are here represented in a manner differing essentially from the Homeric description (Odyssey, XI, 82). The bearded Ulysses *(Uthuche)* is seated on the left, with drawn sword; before him stands Hermes, accompanying his words with a gesture of the right hand. The inscription *Turms Aitas* placed beside the god probably identifies him as Hermes Chthonios, the conductor of souls to the underworld. Leaning against Hermes and also supported by a staff appears the shadowy form of Tiresias (*hinthial Terasias*, "shade of Tiresias", according to the inscription), apparently in a kind of hypnotic slumber. The seer is represented with the traits of a young man. Ulysses has summoned him from the underworld by means of a sacrifice, and Mercury has brought him thence still sleeping. The style of the drawing recalls Greek vase-paintings of the fourth century B.C.

Monum. dell' Instit., II, T. 29. Mus. Gregor., I, T. xxiii (A I, T. xcix), 1. *Gerhard*, Etrusk. Spiegel, II, T. 240; Gottheiten der Etrusker, T. 6, p. 85. Comp. *Braun*, Ruinen und Museen, p. 799. *Overbeck*, Gallerie heroischer Bildwerke, p. 790. *Corssen*, Sprache der Etrusker, I, p. 271.

313. **Statue of a Young Warrior**, probably Mars, the Italic god of war.

Above his sleeveless tunic this warrior wears a cuirass, ending in a double row of lambrequins *(pteryges)*; on his head is a helmet (restored); and in his left hand was an iron spear, of which a few traces were found. This statue were found at Todi in 1835, enclosed by four stone slabs arranged like a kind of cist, amongst some architectural remains supposed to be those of a temple. It has therefore been suggested that it is the image of a god, which had been concealed from the iconoclastic zeal of the early Christians. No light is thrown on the subject by the dedicatory inscription in the Umbrian dialect, en-

graved in Etruscan characters on the middle of the cuirass
in front: *Ahal Trutitis dunum dede* (*i.e.* 'Ahala Trutidius
donum dedit', *i.e.* A. T. presented this). The head is
devoid of expression, and the statue is far from being a
masterpiece, though it is of great value for the history
of art, in view of the limited number of Italic bronze
works that have come down to us intact. The figure is
made in six parts (head, torso, arms, and legs), which
vary both in point of execution and in their proportions.
The Italic (Etruscan?) sculptor did not use Greek models for all the parts, as is especially evident from the
inadequate modelling of the torso; but his work on the
whole seems to have been inspired by some Greek original of the middle of the fourth century. In the absence
of comparative data to enable us to fix a more definite
period, the statue may be referred to the third (or perhaps
the second) century B.C.

Mus. Gregor., I, T. XLIV et seq. (A I, T. CVIII et seq.). *Rayet,*
Monuments de l'art antique, II, T. 68 (livraison II, T. VIII). *Baumeister,* Denkmäler des klass. Alterthums, III, p. 2044, T. 89. Comp.
Bull. dell' Inst., 1835, p. 130; 1836, p. 65; 1838. p. 113. — For the
inscription, see *Aufrecht und Kirchoff,* Umbrische Sprachdenkmäler,
p. 392, T. IX a. *Bücheler,* Umbrica, p. 174.

To the right and left of the preceding, —

295, 314. **Two large Bronze Cauldrons,** upon modern
iron tripods.

Each of these has five handles, formed of lions' heads
with long necks, by which it could be lifted or suspended.
These handles were manufactured by being hammered
upon a core, and then filled up with an earthy substance.
Handles in the shape of lions' and griffins' heads seem
to have been popular with the Oriental Greek artists from
the seventh century onwards; and the fashion was afterwards adopted by the Graeco-Italian and the Etruscan
artists.

Grifi, Monum. di Cere, T. V, 2. Mus. Gregor., I. T. XV (A T,
XIV). I. *Canina.* Etruria maritt., T. 57 C. Comp. Olympia, IV, p. 121
(*Furtwaengler*).

323. Glass-Case containing Small Bronzes.

Mirrors. Handles and feet of vases. Domestic utensils. Roman balance, constructed on the principle of the
modern steelyard, with a long beam, carefully graduated,
on which the weight could be moved backward and forward, while the article to be weighed was suspended from
one end by means of a hook or in a scale. In the present
instance, the weight is shaped like a bust. — The hands
(above) in hammered bronze embellished with gilded nails
are explained as ornaments from Roman standards or
(more probably) as votive offerings.

For the balance: Mus. Gregor., A I, T. LXXII a. — For the hands:
id., I, T. LVII, 3 (A I, T. LXXII b). Comp. *Braun*, Ruinen und Museen, p. 796.

326. Shutter with Mirrors.

In the middle, —

Mirror with relief of Eos and Cephalos. Comp. p. 359.

The winged Eos is here flying through the air carrying her beloved Cephalos, whose arm rests upon her
shoulder. The want of flexibility in the drawing, and
the method of indicating flight (or rapid springing gait)
by bending the knees of Eos, indicate that the Greek
original of this composition belonged to the art of the
sixth century B.C.; though the date of the mirror itself
may be very different. The shoes of Eos and the aureole
of rays round her head are probably additions due to the
Etruscan artist.

Discovered in 1840 near Vulci. — Mus. Gregor., I, T. XXXVI (A I,
T. CV), 1. *Abeken*, Mittelitalien, T. 7. Mon. dell' Instit., III, T. 23c.
Gerhard, Etrusk. Spiegel, II, T. 180. *Martha*, L'art étrusque, p. 544.
Comp. *Braun*, Ruinen und Museen, p. 798. Arch. Zeit., XL, 1882,
p. 349 *(Furtwaengler)*. *Roscher*, Lexikon der Mythologie, I, p. 1272.

Detached Glass-Case.

Antiquities from Pompeii.

The glass, terracotta, and bronze articles in this
case were discovered, according to the inscription, on

Oct. 24th, 1849, in excavations made at Pompeii in presence of Pope Pius IX. It is, however, very possible that several of them were previously placed in the spot where they were 'found', according to a formerly not uncommon practice when ceremonial excavations were to be made. Thus a Pompeiian origin cannot be considered as absolutely established in all cases. The beautiful **Marble Equestrian Relief,** with a horseman plying his whip, is certainly not Pompeian. It is an original Greek work, of about the end of the fifth century, and was probably a votive offering from the victor in a horse-race.

Tyndaris in Sicily is said to have been the real place of discovery. — *Avellino,* Dilucidazione di un antico basso-rilievo di marmo, scoperto in Pompei (Naples, 1850). Comp. *Friederichs-Wolters,* Berliner Gipsabgüsse, No. 1206. *Reisch,* Griech. Weihgeschenke, p. 52.

In front of the third window, —

327. **Oval Bronze Cist.** Comp. p. 361.

Found at Vulci in 1834. Within it were found two broken bone combs, two hair-pins, an ear-pick, two little glass vessels with rouge, and a mirror (said to be the 'Durand Mirror' reproduced in *Gerhard,* Etrusk. Spiegel, II, T. 181).

The body of the cist is adorned with stamped reliefs of battles with the Amazons, a kind of decoration seldom found on cists. A series of beautiful groups, nearly all of which also occur on Greek monuments of the fifth century, is repeated thrice round the cist, while the small space left over is filled in with a fourth repetition of part of the stamp. That the artist who modelled the stamp at least was a Greek, is proved by the delicate borders of palmettes on each side of the design; but that the bronze plate embellished by the reliefs was not employed for a cist until a later date in Etruria (or Campania) is evident from the clumsiness with which the rings are fastened to it. The late construction of the cist (third century) is farther demonstrated by the decorations of the lid, on which the heads of a woman and of a bearded man with

pointed ears (a Nymph and a Silenus) appear twice amidst
an elaborate arrangement of foliage and flowers. The
handle (in cast metal) is formed of two swans, whose
tails touch each other, with respectively a nude man and
a nude woman reclining at their ease upon them.

Mus. Gregor., I, T. XL-XLII (A I, T. LXXXVII-LXXXIX). Monum.
ed Ann. dell' Inst., 1855, T. 18, p. 64. Gerhard, Etrusk. Spiegel,
I, T. 9-11. Comp. Bull. dell' Instit., 1834, p. 9. Braun, Ruinen
und Museen, p. 797, 16. Annali, 1866, p. 163 (Schoene). Martha,
L'art étrusque, p. 534. Schumacher, Praenestinische Ciste zu Karlsruhe, 66.

328. Fine Bronze Amphora, tapering to a point and
supported on a circular stand, which perhaps did not
originally belong to it.

The ornamentation is very tastefully adapted to the
structural conditions of the vase. The shoulder beneath
the neck is fluted, and farther down, the widest part of
the body is embellished with a zone of delicately-executed
palmettes, bordered by wavy lines. At the upper attachment of each handle is a pair of couchant deer, licking
their hind-legs; and at the lower end of each is a seated
Silenus with hoofs, one drinking eagerly from a large
cantharos, the other lazily laying his hands on his paunch.
If this vase be not itself an original Ionian work of the
sixth or fifth century, it has been produced in close connection with some model of that character, and conveys
a high idea of Etruscan workmanship in bronze.

Mus. Gregor., I, T. VIII, 4 (A I, T. LVIII, 2). — A vase closely
resembling the above, and evidently from the same pottery, was
found near Schwarzenbach, in the principality of Birkenfeld.
Comp. Archäol. Zeit., XIV, 1856, T. 85, pp. 161 et seq. Friederichs,
Kleinere Kunst, No. 674.

**329. Seated Figure of a Nude Child, with a Bulla
round his neck.**

An Etruscan inscription of four lines is engraved
upon the left arm, most of which has been broken off.
At one time, when a mythological signification was
assigned to all figures, this statue was believed to

represent the miraculous child Tagès, who, according to
the Etruscan legend, rose from the earth one day while
Tarchon was ploughing in the vicinity of Tarquinii. There
is, however, no doubt that it is really the votive statue
of some child of noble birth, like No. 283 (p. 385). In
the present statue, as in many others, we may note the
mingling, peculiar to Etruscan art, of unskilful clumsiness in the modelling of the details, with a high degree
of lifelike realism.

Found about 1770 near Tarquinii; afterwards in the Vatican
Library. — *Fea*, Storia dell' arte, ɪ, p. 312. *Micali*, Antichi popoli
Ital., ɪɪɪ, p. 64, T. 44. *Pistolesi*, Il Vaticano descritto, ɪɪɪ, T. 110.
Mus. Gregor., ɪ, T. xɪɪɪ, 4 (A ɪ, T. cvɪɪ, 5). Comp. *Braun*, Ruinen
und Museen, p. 804. *Fabretti*, Corpus inscript. Italic., No. 2334.
Corssen, Sprache der Etrusker, ɪ, pp. 348, 458.

330. **Large Brazier,** like No. 145.

Upon the ashes, which still remain from antiquity,
lies a pair of tongs, furnished with wheels, which kept
them above the coals and allowed them to be handled
more easily. There are also two fire-rakes, with hooked
ends, shaped like a hand bent at the wrist.

Found in 1833 at Vulci. — Mus. Gregor., ɪ, T. xɪv (A ɪ. T. ʟxɪɪɪ). 1.
Comp. *Braun*, Ruinen und Museen, p. 795. *Friederichs*, Kleinere
Kunst, p. 190.

Glass-Case containing Gold Ornaments.

In the circular case in the middle of the room are a
large number of the more precious objects discovered in
Etruscan tombs. The glazed compartments at the top
contain the gold and silver articles from the Regulini-
Galassi Tomb (p. 353), some of which possibly date as far
back as the seventh century B.C. Our attention is at once
attracted by the technical perfection exhibited in the
large plates of thin gold, which covered the corpse de-
posited in the inner tomb-chamber. The figures in relief
which embellish these were first stamped and then covered with small gold points (granulated); while their geometric ornamentation is partly in filigree (*i. e.* in fine

gold wire) but chiefly in granulated work, *i. e.* outlined
by means of minute grains of gold, sometimes as fine as
dust, soldered or stuck on to the gold plate. Several very
ancient fibulæ, ornamented in the same style and bearing
Etruscan inscriptions, seem to prove that this granulated
work was adopted at a very early period by the artists of
Central Italy. But the large ornaments from the Regulini-
Galassi Tomb must be considered, not as native imitations, but as foreign importations; for at that date the
Greeks and Phœnicians imported largely into Etruria
(p. 355). The gold ornaments have a style of their own,
in which the forms are modelled conventionally and
without severity, yet at the same time with a certain
regard for realism; they seem to be the products of an
art, which, though powerfully affected by a foreign influence, sought out independent paths, yet had not yet
learned to express its national character in adequate
forms. It has been more than once assumed that these
ornaments are of Phœnician origin, on the ground that
the palmette-decoration and several of the figure-designs
are demonstrably borrowed from the Semitic art of Asia
Minor. But this theory is negatived by the fact that among
the products of the workshop where they were made are
numerous fibulæ, a kind of ornament that is nowhere else
found among Phœnician works. Moreover an entirely
un-Semitic system of decoration is apparent in the developed forms of the geometric ornamentation, such as
the cross with hooked arms, the complicated meander, the
zigzag lines, etc. No certain proof can be adduced that
the 'granulated' mode of working was especially affected
by Phœnician goldsmiths. Traces of a very early use of
grains of gold in this manner may indeed be detected on
some of the objects found at Troy; but no granulated
works of the perfection displayed by the specimens from
the tomb at Cære are met with earlier than the seventh
(or at the very earliest, eighth) century B.C., to which
date belong works discovered at Rhodes (Camiros) and
in Lydia and also a few isolated (therefore probably im-

ported) articles found in Cyprus and at a few other points in the Hellenic world. We are therefore led to the conclusion that this style of art was probably first developed in one of the auriferous districts of Asia Minor, which had preserved the traditions of the goldsmith's craft from the so-called Mycenian epoch. From Asia Minor also are derived the types of the Chimæra, the winged horse, the winged woman, and the nude man contending with the lion — the last a type that differs widely from the draped dæmones, represented on the monuments of Mesopotamia. We cannot, it is true, determine in detail which of these figures were invented in North Syria and which in Lycia and the Greek colonies in Asia Minor. But it is highly significant that the gold ornaments found at Rhodes display the same union of motives from Oriental Asia and from Asia Minor and the same union of stamped and granulated work. It must, however, remain undecided for the present whether the combination and development of these various elements took place independently in Rhodes, or on the adjacent coast of Asia Minor, or in Lydia, or among the Ionians in Phocæa, or simultaneously and in a similar manner at several of these points.

Among the discoveries in the tomb at Cære, a distinct category is occupied by the silver bowls (mostly gilded) adorned with hammered reliefs. Their dry, constrained style, and still more their choice of types, reveal a very close connection with Egyptian art. Assyrian influences also appear more or less distinctly (p. 399). On the other hand, precisely similar vases have frequently been found in the island of Cyprus. We may therefore conclude that the bowls from the Regulini-Galassi Tomb were produced in some place under Phœnician influence, possibly in Cyprus itself. That island, like Phœnicia generally, was long merely an Egyptian province, until it passed into the power of Assyria at the close of the eighth century B.C. But the Assyrian influence in the domain of art could only have gradually affected the previous Egyptian tendencies in the course of the seventh century B.C. It has been supposed that the bowls showing exclusively or mainly Egyptian motives are older than those showing Assyrian motives; but the varying traditions of different factories would themselves adequately account for these differences. Moreover, a Greek spirit makes itself apparent in the lively conception and the transformation of imported motives into genre subjects. That spirit played an important part in the development of Cyprian art; and it is possible that some of the articles were made with the direct collaboration of Greek workmen.

For the origin and style of the gold ornaments, comp. *Langbehn*, Flügelgestalten der ältesten griech. Kunst (1881), pp. 77 et seq. Ann. dell' Inst., 1885, pp. 74 et seq. *(Undset)*. *Helbig*, Homerische Epos², pp. 39 et seq. *Daremberg-Saglio*. Dictionnaire des antiquités, I, pp. 795 et seq. *Dumont-Chaplain*, Céramiques de la Grèce, pp. 139 et seq. Jahrb. des deutschen archäolog. Instit., II, pp. 90 et seq. *(Dümmler)*. Athen. Mittheil. des Instit., XII, p. 9. *(Studniczka)*. — For the silver bowls, comp. Ann. dell' Instit., 1876, pp. 199 et seq. *(Helbig)*, pp. 268 et seq. *(Fabiani)*. *Brunn*, Kunst bei Homer, pp. 17 et seq. *Curtius*, Archaische Bronzereliefs, p. 12. *Langbehn*, op. cit., p. 98. *Helbig*, Homerische Epos², pp. 26 et seq. *Perrot et Chipiez*, Histoire de l'art, III, pp. 750 et seq. *Dumont-Chaplain*, op. cit., I, pp. 113 et seq. *Roscher*, Lexikon der Mythologie, I, p. 1755. Olympia, IV, pp. 99, 141 *(Furtwaengler)*. American Journal of Archæology, III (1887), p. 322 *(Marquand)*. Museo ital. di antichità class., III, p. 870 *(Orsi)*.

We may now proceed to a detailed examination of the cases.

332. Rings; Small Fibulæ; three large **Earrings**, each with a pendant ornamented with four lions' heads; three small **Golden Spirals**, apparently to be used as hairclasps. Below are small **Gold Plates** of various shapes, as in the next compartment.

Grifi, Monum. di Cere, T. III, 1. Mus. Gregor., I, T. LXXV (A I, T. XXVII), 8 and 12. — For the hair-clasps, comp. *Helbig*. Homerische Epos², p. 243. Olympia, IV, pp. 58 et seq. *(Furtwaengler)*.

334. Numerous Small Gold Plates, for sewing upon garments, most of them with holes at the corners.

The different pieces, which are exactly fitted to each other, are of different shapes: some are like the calyx of

a conventional lotus; several are embellished with stamped ornaments (*e. g.* a draped woman with wings, lion
turning his head, human masks, etc.). It is, however, difficult to examine them carefully in their present position.

Grifi, Monum. di Cere, T. IX. Mus. Gregor., A I, T. XXV. Comp.
Arch. Zeit., XLII, 1884, p. 113 *(Furtwaengler).*   *Martha,* L'art
étrusque, p. 561.

336. Silver Vases.

A bowl with two handles and one without handles
are inscribed *Larthia,* which may be either the nomina-
tive form of the feminine name *Larthia* or the genitive of
the masculine name *Larth.* On a small amphora is the
inscription *Milarthia, i. e.* 'this (is the property) of
Larth(?)'. Stirrup-shaped handle ending on each side in
a griffin's head, with the two attachments, each adorned
with two crouching two-headed lions.

Grifi, Monum. di Cere, T. VII. Mus. Gregor., I, T. LXII (A I,
T. XIX). *Canina,* Etruria marittima, I, T. LIV. — For the inscription,
comp. *Pauli,* Etrusk. Studien, II, p. 59, IV, p. 71.

338. Double Chain of twisted gold wire, the ends of
which are formed of two lions' heads. **Two Large Amber
Beads,** set in a gold band ornamented with a meander-
pattern in granulated work, and four empty settings —
apparently a fragment of a large breast-ornament. **Large
Breast Ornament** *(hormos),* consisting of 16 hollow
double truncated cones, adorned with incised lines, and
12 (originally 16) flattened spheres, strung alternately
on a cord.

Grifi, Monum. di Cere, T. III. Mus. Gregor., I, T. LXIV and
LXXVII (A T, XXVI and XXXI). *Canina,* Etruria marittima, T. LV.
Comp. *Helbig,* Homerische Epos[2], pp. 268 et seq.

340. Rings, Earrings, Fibulæ. The largest of the last
(in the middle) is covered with triangles and crosses with
hooked arms designed in grains of gold. Two smaller
fibulæ of the same shape show meander-patterns.

For the fibulæ: Grifi, Monum. di Cere, T. VI. Mus. Gregor., I,
T. LXVII (A I, T. XXVI). Comp. Ann. dell' Inst., 1885, p. 29 *(Undset).*
Athenische Mittheil. des archäol. Instituts, XII, p. 9 *(Studniczka).*

342. Gold Pectoral.

This gold plate, as its shape shows, covered the breast from throat to waist, and was meant to be sewn upon the ordinary garment or upon a special piece of cloth. It is covered with stamped figures arranged in rows; the geometric ornaments separating or framing the rows are formed of fine gold points. In the outermost row are goats, repeated over and over again; then winged animals probably intended for griffins in spite of their leonine heads; then chimæras (not yet with serpents as tails), winged horses, lions with their heads turned and a conventional flower (palmette) issuing from their jaws, browsing stags, draped and winged female figures holding a kind of palmette in their hands, instead of the more usual animals; then more 'griffins', draped and winged women of another kind, looking like bees, lions, more female figures like those last mentioned, and finally griffins. The centre of the pectoral is occupied by an oval, the lower part of which is filled in with 'Phœnician' (Syrian) palmettes, while above are successive rows of griffins, winged women with palmettes, lions, and (at the top) four repetitions of a group of a nude man grasping a rampant lion with both hands. For the technique and style of this remarkable ornament and for the origin of the various types, comp. pp. 394 et seq. The group of the nude man with the lion is a free variation of the well-known Babylonian-Assyrian representation of the draped and usually bearded lion-taming dæmon, here, however, deprived of its symbolical signification.

Grifi. Monum. di Cere, T. i. Mus. Gregor, i, T. LXXXII et seq. (A i, T. XXVIII et seq.). Comp. the references cited above, p. 397.

344. Silver Vases with reliefs.

At the top: **Flat Dish,** gilded except on the rim. The inside of the dish is occupied by an animal-piece in the Egyptian style. Two lions have overcome a bull, while a bird of prey hovers overhead with outspread wings; the four papyrus-stalks localize the scene. This medallion is surrounded by two bands of designs. The first represents a lion-hunt. A powerful lion stands with its paw upon a nude man stretched upon the ground (a frequently recurring motive in Egyptian art); two comrades of the fallen hunter, armed with spear and bow, threaten the animal from the right, while behind them are two mounted attendants, each with a pair of horses. To the left is a retreating horseman, turning in the saddle to launch his arrows against the lion. In front of him is a wild goat leaping from a height. Farther on, between two palm-trees, is a group, well-known in Assyrian art, of a man plunging a dagger into the body of a rearing lion in front of him. — The outer band is occupied with a long procession of foot and horse soldiers, interrupted at one point by a war-chariot with two horses. For the style and origin of these vessels, comp. pp. 396 et seq.

Grifi, Monum. di Cere, T. v, 1. Mus. Gregor., i, T. lxvi (A i, T. xxiii). *Canina*, Etruria maritt., i, T. 56. *Perrot et Chipiez*, Histoire de l'art, iii, p. 768.

To the left, —

Silver Vase with reliefs (much damaged; gilded like the preceding).

The interior design displays a group, borrowed from Egyptian art, of a king slaying a fettered captive. Beside the latter are traces of another figure. Round this central picture run two bands with processions of foot and horse soldiers variously armed, like those on the preceding vase.

Grifi, Monum. di Cere, T. x, 2. Mus. Gregor., i, T. lxv (A i, T. xxii), 1.

To the right, —

Silver Vase with reliefs (broken; gilded).

In the interior is another animal-piece from Egypt; a cow suckles her calf (beside which there are traces of another calf) in a lofty papyrus-thicket, above which fly marsh-birds. The next row (of which only fragments are preserved) shows a procession of soldiers. This is also the subject of the second or outer frieze, in which appear horse-soldiers, archers, and a chariot with two horses.

Grifi, Monum. di Cere, T. x, 1. Mus. Gregor., I, T. LXV (A I, T. XXII), 2. — Interior picture: *Perrot et Chipiez*, Histoire de l'art, III, p. 790.

Silver Bowl with reliefs.

On the outside are two friezes of armed warriors on foot, on horseback, and in chariots. In the upper row the procession is twice interrupted by a seated lion, above which hovers a bird of prey. On the bottom of the bowl (outside) is a lion seated between two men, with one large and two small birds hovering overhead. — The interior is also adorned with reliefs. The central medallion repeats the group of a cow suckling her calf; and the first encircling band contains the usual soldiers and chariots, with the addition, however, of two forage-waggons drawn by mules. Half of the upper band is occupied by a warlike procession, the other half by a religious scene in the Egyptian style. Two men are seated upon cubical seats, with cups in their hands; a woman between them is in the act of pouring wine into the cup of one of them; three women to the left, with baskets on their heads, recall the women bearing gifts for the dead, who are so frequently represented on Egyptian monuments. The bodies of the women are, moreover, drawn as if naked, in the Egyptian manner, the garments supposed to envelope them being indicated merely by dotted lines on each side.

Grifi, Monum. di Cere, T. VIII and IX. Mus. Gregor., I, T. LXIII et seq. (A I, T. xx et seq.). *Canina*, Etruria maritt., I, T. 56, 2 and 3. Comp. *Perrot et Chipiez*, Histoire de l'art, III, pp. 780, 785.

345. Large Fibula.

This remarkable specimen, which was long erroneously taken for an ornament for the head, is in reality an elaborately ornamented fibula (brooch), the general form of which has been developed from the disk-shaped fibulæ found in the earliest cremation-tombs of the so-called first iron age. From its large size it seems to have been worn rather as an ornament than to fasten the garment. It consists of a broad oval disk, joined to another pear-shaped plate by means of two metal rods or bars. On the back is a long pin, the pointed end of which fitted into the tube concealed by the larger disk. The execution and style of decoration of this brooch closely correspond with those of the large pectoral (comp. p. 399). The oval plate is embellished with five pacing lions and with a double border of Phœnician rosettes united to form a chain. The two connecting rods are richly adorned with zigzags in granulated work; from their ends hang pendants in the shape of palmettes. The ornamentation of the pear-shaped plate consists of six rows of winged quadrupeds (griffins?) in stamped work and seven rows of small ducks, made in the round. Its lower end shows a human mask in the Egyptian style, which seems to have been used with the same typical significance in this art that the Gorgon's head had in Greek art from the end of the seventh century B. C.

Grifi, Monum. di Cere, T. II. Mus. Gregor., I, T. LXXXIV et seq. (A I, T. XXXII et seq.). *Canina*, Etruria maritt., T. 54, 1 and 2. *Martha*, L'art étrusque, p. 110. Comp. Ann. dell' Instit., 1885, p. 30 *(Undset)*, and the references cited above. p. 397. Another proof that this fibula is not of Semitic origin is the fact that a companion-piece has been discovered near Ponto Sodo (now in the Antiquarium at Munich), decorated with figures of warriors, birds, and lions, in a geometric style closely resembling that of the so-called Dipylon vases (*Micali*, Monumenti per servire alla storia, 1832, T. 45, 3, III, p. 66). — For the typical use of the masks, comp. *Furtwaengler*, Bronzefunde aus Olympia, p. 71.

Two Bracelets.

Each of these consists of a strip of thin gold, decorated at the edges with meanders and triangles, and divided into six panels by narrow meander-patterns. In each panel are three female figures in long drapery, joining hands; between them, and filling up the background, are plants with long stalks crowned with palmettes (conventionalized palm-trees). At each end of the gold strips is a double plate of gold, bordered with a double plaited band, and with essentially the same decoration on both sides: between two rearing lions stands a draped figure holding conventionalized plants, while to the right and left a man is on the point of plunging a dagger into the back of each lion. At the corners of the double gold plates are knobs in the shape of a human head, while gold chains are fastened to the upper edges for the purpose of securing and fitting the bracelet. These bracelets in their foreign character reveal more markedly than any of the other ornaments a dependence upon some non-Greek model.

Grifi, Monum. di Cere, T. III, 4. Mus. Gregor., I, T. LXXVI (A I, T. XXX). *Canina*, Etruria maritt., I, T. LIV, 4-7. *Fontenay*, Les bijoux anciens et modernes (Paris, 1884), pp. 264 et seq.

The lower (horizontal) shelves of the case exhibit **Ornaments of various periods.** The rich variety of these affords a direct testimony to the Oriental love of splendour which characterized the Etruscans and which is also apparent in their portrait-statues. They also show to what a pitch of excellence the ancients had attained in all branches of the goldsmith's art — in repoussé work, wire-drawing, filigree and granulated work, chasing (work with the graver), and niello (enamelling upon gold). All these processes are here represented by admirable examples, which have frequently been taken by modern Italian goldsmiths as models and have not always been equalled. Most of these ornaments were exclusively intended for the decoration of the dead; they had the same shape and the same significance, but not the same intrinsic value, as the corresponding ornaments worn by the living (comp. p. 352).

It cannot be in all cases decided which of these articles were manufactured in Etruria itself. The Etruscan jewellers seem to have reached an advanced stage of skill at an early period, but the forms of the fibulæ, rings, earrings, bracelets, and breast-ornaments are wholly of early-Greek origin, so that these ornaments, though found in Etruria, may frequently give us an idea of the precious objects described by Homer. Indeed, some of the most

beautiful specimens, which are practically identical with
specimens found in Greek tombs, must be regarded as
actually Greek originals. Even the numerous wreaths of
golden leaves find their archetypes on Greek soil. They
were very generally used in Etruria for the decoration
of the dead, which perhaps casts a side-light upon the
customs of the living; and, indeed, the *Coronae Etruscae*
are said to have served the Romans as models for the
wreaths with which they used to decorate their triumphing generals. The bullæ, however, are of genuine Italic
execution, and perhaps were invented also in Italy. These
hollow lockets, sometimes round, sometimes heart-shaped,
are made of thin gold and adorned with reliefs or repoussé work. They were so to speak a distinctive national symbol peculiar to the Etruscans, which was borrowed from them by the Romans. The reliefs on the later
specimens usually reproduce Greek types in a crude and
often unintelligent manner, forcibly adapting them to the
limited space and to Etruscan taste, in the same way as
we have already had occasion to notice in the poor
designs on some of the mirrors.

331. **Gold Wreath** of thickly-placed oak-leaves. **Gold
　　　Necklace** of small beads strung together, with
　　　pomegranates hanging from them. **Gold Rings,**
　　　with engraved symbols.

　　Mus. Gregor., I, T. LXXXIX (A I, T. CXXX); T. LXXIX (A I,
T. CXXIV), 5.

333. **Gold Laurel Wreath.** Thin **Gold Diadem** in the
　　　shape of two twigs bent to meet each other,
　　　with myrtle-leaves in green enamel and myrtle-
　　　berries in coloured enamel.

　　Mus. Gregor., I, T. XCI (A I, T. CXXXII), 1 and 2. Comp. *Frochner,*
Musées de France, T. 35. *Fontenay,* Les bijoux, p. 392.

335. **Seven Golden Bullæ,** to be strung on a cord and
　　　worn round the neck.

On three of these bullæ recurs the figure of a bearded
man working on a helmet with a hammer (Hephæstos

forging the arms of Achilles). On two others is a warrior brandishing his sword above an unarmed and nude youth who has fallen to the ground. On the remaining two appears a mare licking a nude child who has seized her teats and is about to suck them; adjacent is a nude man, who appears to be stroking the animal, while his left hand grasps the child's left arm that is slightly extended towards him. This scene probably illustrates the myth of Hippothoon, son of Alope, who was exposed at birth and nourished by one of the mares of his father Neptune. The nude man, in that case, is the shepherd who found the child. These bullæ were discovered at the same time as the necklace which is placed beside them and dates from the same period, *viz.* about the second century B.C. The separate parts of the necklace are decorated with alternate figures of a seated Sphinx and heads of the Medusa (in the later, nobler style, which depicts the Gorgon as a woman with flowing hair and a necklace).

Found in 1837 at Vulci. — Mus. Gregor., i, T. lxxxi (A i, T. cxxvi), 1. Comp. *Panofka*, Atlas und Atalante, pp. 17 et seq. Compte-rendu de la commission archéol. St. Pétersbourg, 1864, p. 169. *Heydemann*, Pariser Antiken, p. 13.

337. **Elegant Chatelaine of small chains,** from which hang heads, female masks (including one of the Medusa type), flowers, and buds.

Mus. Gregor., i, T. lxxx (A i, T. cxxv), 4.

Golden Fibula, two **Flat Buttons,** embellished with a relief in the developed archaic style, representing a Mænad holding a lyre and a serpent. Three round **Disks,** with a beautiful female head in profile (fourth century type). — **Three Bullæ,** with relief of a young warrior, struck by lightning and falling backwards; probably Capaneus, whom Zeus smote with a thunderbolt beneath the walls of Thebes.

Mus. Gregor., i, T. lxxi (A i, T. cxix); lxviiia (A i, T. cxvi); lxixb (A i, T. cxvii). — For representations of Capaneus, comp. *Benndorf*, Heroon von Gjölbaschi-Trysa. p. 193.

339. **Fragments of Necklaces. Earrings** of the type known as *orecchini a baule*, which have been with considerable probability identified with the earrings, adorned with grains of gold, mentioned by Homer. Comp. the similar specimens, Nos. 341, 345.

Mus. Gregor., I, T. LXXII (A I, T. CXXI). Comp. *Fontenay*, Les bijoux, pp. 91 et seq. *Helbig*, Homerische Epos[2], p. 273. *Martha*, L'art étrusque, p. 567.

341. **Earrings. Wreath of Gold Leaves. Necklace** of acorns and calves' head, a somewhat clumsy design.

The necklace was discovered in 1837 at Vulci. — Mus. Gregor., I, T. LXXVIII (A I, T. CXXIII), 5.

343. **Seal-Rings. Scarabæi** (stones in the shape of beetles like the Egyptian scarabæi). Large **Bulla**, suspended by a simple chain (found in a cinerary urn at Ostia).

Mus. Gregor., I, T. LXXVIII (A I, T. CXXIII), 4.

345. **Earrings** *(orecchini a baule*). **Wreath of thickly-set oak-leaves.** Graceful pair of **Earrings**: beneath a disk, decorated with semicircles and groups of dots in granulated work, hangs an amphora between two chains. Similar **Earring**, the disk being decorated with a rosette and the amphora replaced by a cock in enamelled gold. Greek work of the third century B.C.

Mus. Gregor., I, T. LXXIV (A I, T. CXXII). Comp. *Fontenay*, Les bijoux, pp. 109, 114. *Martha*, L'art étrusque, T. 17 and 9.

Two Brooches or similar ornaments (one in fragments). These admirably delicate works are inlaid with gems and recumbent figures of Sileni (in gold repoussé with granulated work). Two Sileni are perfect, the third is only partly preserved. These are certainly Greek works, a little earlier in date than the earrings mentioned above.

Found in 1837 at Vulci. — Mus. Gregor., I, T. LXXIII a and LXXI c (A I, T. CXXI a and CXIX c).

Two Large Gold Bullæ, with the relief of a chariot with four winged horses, apparently on the point of descending to earth. The bearded man and the younger long-haired figure with a shield are perhaps Zeus and Athena, about to enter the contest with the giants. The style of the relief, the dotted background, and the wavy ornaments surrounding the scene prove that the bullæ do not date farther back than the second century B.C. — A third **Bulla,** of similar size and kind, and probably belonging to the same necklace as the preceding, shows a relief of a different group. A draped woman and a nude youth are shown seated and embracing each other (perhaps Venus and Adonis). Beside them, to the right, is a Cupid.

Found in 1837 at Vulci. — Mus. Gregor., 1, T. lxxviii (A 1, T. cxxiii), 2 and 3. Comp. Bulletin de l'acad. de Bruxelles, 1842, p. 258 *(De Witte)*. *Braun,* Ruinen und Museen, p. 792. *Martha,* l'art étrusque, p. 572.

Chatelaine with golden animals' heads and square settings for gems. Several small **Gold Fibulæ** of various shapes, some decorated with small figures of Sphinxes.

For the chatelaine: Mus. Gregor., 1, T. lxxx (A 1, T. cxxv), 1. — For the fibulæ: 1, T. lxix (A 1, T. cxvii).

X. Corridor.

The glass-case by the window contains bronze articles, including several bits for horses.

Comp. *Gozzadini,* De quelques mors de cheval italiques, pp. 17 et seq.

By the wall, opposite the entrance, are some additional fragments of the bronze mountings already mentioned under No. 62 (p. 366). On one of these is a winged lion standing on its hind-legs, with a human head crowned with lotus-flowers (Sphinx), and on another is a woman holding a conventional flower.

Grifi, Monum. di Cere, T. vi, 7 and 8. Mus. Gregor., 1, T. xvii (A 1, T. xvi).

Fragments of two large **Bronze Shields,** of the same kind as the shields with exclusively geometric decorations mentioned under No. 164 (p. 373).

Also from the Regulini-Galassi Tomb. — Mus. Gregor., A I, T. xii, 3.

Patera with a statuette as handle.

The handle is formed of the statuette of a nude woman adorned with necklaces and bracelets (Venus), who holds a mirror before her face with her left hand, while she arranges her hair with her right. Beneath the small flat pedestal of the statuette is a ring by means of which the patera could be suspended, thus apparently superseding the original structural purpose of the statuette, which was intended to hold the patera upright. This vessel, like the companion-pieces Nos. 297 and 310 in the ninth room (pp. 387, 388), dates from the last century B.C.

Found in 1834 at Vulci. — Mus. Gregor., i, T. xii (A i, T. lxi).

Bronze Mountings, ornamented in repoussé work.

These eight metal plates, of which five retain the original length of 0,438 mètre, while three are broken, doubtless formed the mountings of a cist, though it is now impossible to fit them together with certainty. The rows of lotus-buds and lotus-palmettes on the three purely decorative plates are distinctively Greek in character; the figure-subjects are obviously inspired by the archaic Ionian art of the sixth century, though they include certain alien elements, probably added in some Italic studio working from the Ionian models.

The first and third bronze plates are similar. Each displays three repetitions of a group of four women and five men meeting (probably warriors returning). All the men have one arm raised as though saluting or addressing their companions; the foremost warrior grasps a club in his lowered right hand, and the fourth, armed with a spear, leads two horses, one of which is decorated with trappings. The second and fourth plates likewise resemble each other and present a sacrificial scene, also repeated thrice upon each. To the right a god clad in a long garment (Dionysos?) is seated upon a folding-stool; Hermes, identified by his winged sandals and his petasos, advances towards him, with a lance in his right hand. Farther to the right, near an altar, a bald Silenus, with swine's ears and equine tail and hoofs, holding a cup in his left hand and a sacrificial knife in his right, awaits the approach of the two victims (deer or goats, notwithstanding their long legs?), which are being brought in solemn procession by five other Sileni of the same type. The foremost of these Sileni bears an axe (?), the second plays the double flute, the third carries a wine-skin, the fourth an amphora, while the fifth has a knife (?) in his right hand and three objects like sticks in his lowered left. The seventh plate is even more interesting, though the series of scenes upon it, illustrating the war of the gods and the giants, is unfortunately imperfectly preserved. To the left is a stooping man with wide-spread legs (probably a Satyr, though his left foot is like a man's); more to the right are two giants, whose legs are curiously enveloped by a double tendril issuing from the ground, so that one of them is almost brought to his knees; facing the giants is a god (Hephæstos), half obliterated. The following subjects succeed from left to right. Hermes, recognizable by the petasos and armed with a spear, has seized a kneeling giant by the throat and disregards his appeal for mercy. The costume of this giant (short tunic and cuirass) is distinctly seen. Near this group another giant lies dead beneath a fragment of rock; above his head two closely united warriors (Artemis and Apollo) press forward, each brandishing a sword in the right hand, and extending the left towards a giant who has just been overthrown by another god (Poseidon?). Zeus launches his thunderbolt against a giant, who in the impotence of terror throws himself upon the ground. Next to Zeus is Hera, wearing a pointed cap, who sets her foot upon the body of a vanquished foe; while in front

of her Athena seizes a giant by the shoulder and brandishes in her right hand an arm which she has torn from
the body of another enemy. In the forefront appears
Heracles, girt with the lion's fell, holdinghis bow in his
extended left hand and swinging his club in his right,
while before him a giant has sunk to his knees. On
the extreme right was another warrior-god (Dionysos
with the thyrsos-spear?), of whom only the legs and
the right hand holding a spear adorned with ribands
are seen.

Found at Bomarzo (1832?). — Mus. Gregor., I, T. xxxix (A I,
T. lxxxvi). Antike Denkmäler, herausg. vom archäolog. Institut.
I, T. 21. Comp. Mayer, Giganten und Titanen, pp. 339 et seq.;
Römische Mittheil. des arch. Instit., III. p. 176 (Dümmler). The
fragment of another metal band, moulded from the same stamp as
the first and third of the above-mentioned, is reproduced as frontispiece in Panofka, Collection Pourtalés. Other fragments of replicas
of these bands may be seen in the Museo Kircheriano (comp. p. 434)
and in the Musée du Louvre. Comp. Schumacher, Pränestinische
Ciste zu Karlsruhe, pp. 57 et seq. Bulletin de la Société des Anti-
quaires de France, 1892, p. 150.

The case to the right contains a number of comparatively uninteresting fragments of Roman sculpture in
marble and bronze. Among the marble sculptures may
be mentioned a Hygieia and an Asclepios, on the second
shelf from the bottom; and among the bronzes a statuette
of Heracles resting and a Dionysos in the archaistic style,
on the third shelf.

On the floor and on stands along the wall are leaden
water-pipes with inscriptions (comp. p. 428).

Found on the Via Aureliana, near Trajan's aqueduct, in 1850.
Comp. Lanciani, Le acque e gli acquedotti di Roma (Rome, 1880),
pp. 249 et seq.

Room XI.

In this room are three Etruscan sarcophagi ornamented
in front with interesting bas-reliefs: No. 43, Etruscan
ceremonial procession with musicians; No. 97, Ma-
gistrate and his retinue; No. 119 (of nenfro), Murder
of Clytæmnestra, Sacrifice of Iphigenia, Mortal duel

between Eteocles and Polynices, the Theban brothers, Telephos and the infant Orestes. The room also contains Etruscan cippi (tombstones); inscribed slabs; farther on, a number of very antique vases, including several large platters and store-jars without handles *(pithoi)* in red terracotta (known as 'Red Ware') with stamped reliefs; Etruscan vases of black terracotta (bucchero), with reliefs in the Oriental style; a cinerary urn (a so-called *canopus*), the top of which reproduces a human form, etc.

For No. 43, comp. *Dennis*, Cities and Cemeteries, II[3], p. 454. — No. 119: Mus. Gregor., I, T. xcvI (A II, T. c). *Brunn-Koerte*, I rilievi delle urne etrusche, I, T. 80, II; 83, 2 and 3, II, T. 20, 6. — For the inscribed slabs: Mus. Gregor., I, T. cv et seq. (A II, T. cv et seq.). — For the vases, II, T. xcIx et seq. (A I, T. II and xxxIV). — For the red ware, comp. *Birch*, History of Ancient Pottery[2], pp. 455 et seq. Arch. Zeit., xxxIx, 1881, p. 40 *(Loeschcke)*. — For the canopus, comp. Museo Ital. di antichità class., I, p. 320 *(Milani)*.

On the walls are copies of mural paintings from the tombs at Corneto, arranged in the following order, beginning to the right of the entrance. Painting from the tomb known as the *Grotta del Morto* (lamentation for the deceased, and dances); from the *Grotta delle Bighe* (funeral games and dances); from the *Grotta della Caccia del Cignale* or *Grotta Querciola* (festival with dancing and music); from the *Grotta delle Iscrizioni* (games); from the *Grotta del Triclinio* (banquet); from the *Grotta del Barone* (military games; horsemen). Each sheet of canvas contains the paintings from a single wall of the tombs. These frescoes date back to the earliest development of Etruscan painting (from the close of the sixth century B.C.), and all of them were executed under the influence of Greek models (the earliest from Ionian models, the others from Attic models). Some of them may even have been painted by Greek artists in Italy, who have consulted Etruscan tastes in some details. The painting of Pluto and Persephone, above the door, is of much more recent date. The original, found in the Campanari tomb, is now destroyed.

Mus. Gregor., i, T. xcix-civ (A ii, T. xci-xcvi). — The Campanari Tomb: Monum. dell' Instit., ii, T. 53 et seq. Comp. *Braun*, Ruinen und Museen, pp. 807 et seq. *Dennis*, Cities and Cemeteries, i³, pp. 325, 373, 306, 364, 318, 368, 465. Ann. dell' Instit., 1859, pp. 325 et seq., 1866, pp. 422 et seq. *(Brunn)*, 1863, pp. 336 et seq., 1870, pp. 5 et seq. *(Helbig)*. *Woermann*, Geschichte der Malerei, i, pp. 101 et seq. *Martha*, L'art étrusque, i, pp. 377 et seq.

Room XII.

The cabinet in the middle of this room contains a series of antique bronzes, the most important of which are the large vases and platters, some with Etruscan inscriptions.

From the tomb of the Herennii at Bolsena (Volsinii), and acquired by Pius IX. from the Marchese Ravizza's collection. — Comp. *Corssen*, Sprache der Etrusker, p. 360, T. 8.

Statuette of a Haruspex, or examiner of the entrails of victims. The haruspex, who has long hair and no beard, wears a pointed cap *(tutulus)* and a close tunic without sleeves, on which is an Etruscan inscription (on the left leg). Above the tunic is a pallium with a wide border, fastened in front with a fibula.

Discovered in a tomb near the Tiber. — Mus. Gregor., i. T. xliii, 2. Comp. *Dennis*, Cities and Cemeteries, ii³, p. 478. *Corssen*, Sprache der Etrusker, i, p. 641. *Martha*, L'art étrusque, p. 506.

Relief-Bust of a God, with pantheistic symbols, a coarse work of a late period. The bearded deity, of a type suggesting the representations of the god Silvanus, holds a pine-cone in his right hand and in his left the branch of a tree round which a serpent is coiled. An eagle is perched upon his shoulder; and on his breast appear a star (or a wheel, a common symbol in the East for the sun) and a relief of Mithras, with an amphora and a boar's head below. The bust evidently represents some Græco-Roman deity, furnished with various symbols of the cult of Mithras comp. vol. i, pp. 478 et seq.); this fusion of gods and cults of the most diverse character was common during the close of the imperial epoch. —

Close by is a **Similar Bust**, of still cruder execution and
almost barbaric in conception; the god here wears a
sleeved tunic and a Phrygian cap, and holds in his right
hand a pine-cone and in his left a staff (or torch?), round
which a serpent coils.

Both busts are supposed also to have come from Bolsena. —
Comp. Revue archéol., 1892, ii, Pl. x, pp. 189 et seq. *(Cumont)*.

Upon the cabinet, —

Stand made of bronze plates.

This stand consists of a lower part like a truncated
cone, surmounted by two large spheres, on which rests
a small cauldron (comp. No. 31, p. 296 . The repoussé
ornamentation in the Oriental style corresponds with this
very archaic shape. The peculiarities in the former are
probably to be accounted for by the fact that the stand
is neither a purely Phœnician nor a purely Greek work,
but an imitation manufactured in Italy, perhaps in Etruria itself. The cauldron is ornamented with two friezes,
one consisting of bulls and pacing lions, the other of
winged lions and griffins in the archaic 'Phœnician' style,
and with a row of palmettes, quite unique in character.
Each of the spheres is embellished with two rows of
lions and bulls. On the truncated cone the above-mentioned peculiar palmette-form recurs in four bands; then
lions and bulls attacking each other; then lions, griffins,
and a Sphinx ?; and finally winged lions and winged bulls.

From the Regulini-Galassi Tomb. — *Grifi.* Monum. di Cere, T. xi,
2. Mus. Gregor., i, T. xi (A i, T. xvii). Comp. *Semper,* Der Stil [2],
ii, p. 74. *Martha,* L'art étrusque, p. 109. Olympia, iv, p. 135
(Furtwaengler).

The glass-case in front of the window contains ivory
articles, stili pens, and dice. We should also notice
the two halves of a round casket, with crouching Sphinxes
and a group in relief representing a beardless, long-
haired man in a short garment, between two rearing
lions (probably a Phœnician work).

From the Regulini-Galassi Tomb. — Mus. Gregor., ii, T. cvi
(A i, T. viii), 9 and 10.

A small adjoining chamber is fitted up to represent an Etruscan tomb *(tomba a camera)*. Two lions in nenfro lie in front of the entrance as guardians of the dead. Along the walls in the interior are stone benches, on which the corpses were laid, surrounded by vases and various articles of daily life. Similar articles are hung on the walls.

The lions were discovered at the entrance of a tomb at Vulci. — Mus. Gregor., A II, T. CI, 6.

The Museo Kircheriano and the Pre-historic Museum at the Collegio Romano.

The **Museo Kircheriano** derives its name from the German Jesuit priest Athanasius Kircher (1601-1680), a native of the neighbourhood of Fulda, who became a professor in the Collegio Romano about 1635. At Rome he indulged his mathematical and historical tastes by the formation of a collection of curiosities, which, besides natural productions of all kinds and specimens of all branches of artistic industry, included also a few unimportant antiques. It was not until the eighteenth century that this collection, chiefly owing to the exertions of Bonanni and Contucci, assumed more and more the character of a cabinet of antiques; and about the same time (ca. 1738) it acquired its chief treasure, the Ficoronian Cist.

During the suspension of the order of the Jesuits (1773-1823) the Museo Kircheriano was more and more neglected in favour of the great papal collections in the Vatican and at the Capitol. But in the present century the famous archæologist Giuseppe Marchi turned his attention to the neglected museum; under his auspices the section of Christian antiquities, the collection of leaden missiles for slings, and that of water-pipes received large additions, while the treasure-trove of Vicarello and the celebrated graffito of the 'Caricature Crucifixion' were also added to the museum under his management. The Collegio Romano and its collections became the property of the state in 1870; and since then the Museo

Kircheriano has been completely re-arranged on a scientific system. The Græco-Roman and Christian antiquities have been combined in a special section by Ettore de Ruggiero (in the rooms to the left of the entrance'. The ethnographical specimens were transferred to the Museo Nazionale Preistorico ed Etnografico, opened in 1876, a collection that already, under the management of Luigi Pigorini, has risen to the rank of a museum of the first class, and is still constantly receiving additions. In 1876 it received an acquisition of more than usual value in the extensive sepulchral treasure of Præneste (pp. 446 et seq..

Bonanni, Musæum Kircherianum (Romæ, 1709). *Contucci*, Musei Kirkeriani in Romano, S. 1. Collegio Ærea notis illustrata, Rome, 1763. *Brunati*, Musei Kirkeriani Inscriptiones Ethnicæ et Christianæ (Milan, 1837). *Ettore de Ruggiero*, Catalogo del Museo Kircheriano; parte prima (Rome, 1878). Comp. *Justi*, Winckelmann, II, 1, p. 128. *Luigi Pigorini*, Il Museo nazionale preistorico ed etnografico di Roma, 1881; secunda relazione, 1884. Nuova Antologia, XXXIV, series III (1891).

According to the present interim arrangement, the Museo Kircheriano occupies the saloon to the left of the principal entrance and the two adjoining rooms. The Prehistoric Collections are arranged in the vestibule and in the south half of the long suite of rooms on the east side of the building. The north half of this suite and the entire north façade is given up to the third section of the museum, consisting of the Ethnographical Collections. (A plan for the use of visitors is in preparation.)

Museo Kircheriano.

Room I.

Terracottas.   Marble Sculptures.   Miscellaneous Antiquities.

The specimens are not arranged strictly in the order of their catalogue-numbers. We begin our inspection to the left of the entrance. Among the numerous terracotta reliefs, the decorative use of which has been described on p. 269, the following may be noticed: —

40. Terracotta Plaque: Egyptian Landscape.

Two arches supported on pilasters form a frame for a fantastic landscape on the Nile at the time of the inundation. To the left, on the river-bank, is a round hut with a stork standing upon it; near the hut is a woman reclining on a litter; in the foreground a hippopotamus is wading in the stream, while a crocodile lies stretched upon a gigantic water-plant. To the right, in the background, is a square hut, with two storks upon the roof; on the Nile is a boat rowed by two Pygmies; more in the foreground are a crocodile and an aquatic bird. Nos. 54 and 90 are fragments of similar reliefs. In their general character these pictures recall other landscapes of the banks of the Nile due to Alexandrian art, particularly the base of the statue of the Nile vol. I, p. 28).

The numerous replicas of this subject differ from each other in various details. Comp., *e.g.*, *Gori*, Inscript. antiquæ in Etruriæ urbibus extantes, I, T. 19. *Combe*, Terracottas in the British Museum, T. xx, 36. *Campana*, Opere in plastica, T. 114. Comp. *Woermann*, Die Landschaft in der Kunst der alten Völker, p. 300. — A fragment of a similar terracotta is preserved in the Museo Etrusco of the Vatican (see above, p. 273); a complete specimen is to be seen in the Palazzo dei Conservatori (vol. I, p. 449).

72. Terracotta Plaque: Victories sacrificing a Bull.

Comp. Nos. 117, 151, 161-166, etc., in the same room.

This group, which recurs in reproductions with numerous variations and in all varieties of material, is here treated in a purely decorative style. Comp. above, p. 12, No. 729.

100. Terracotta Plaque: Hierodouli.

Two hierodouli, or temple-servants, with curious calathos-shaped headdresses from which they have been taken for wingless goddesses of victory , are dancing one on each side of a palladium. This is another of the numerous

motives current in the Roman decorative art of the first
century of the empire.

Comp. *Campana*, Opere in plastica, T. 4. *Müller-Wieseler*,
Denkmäler der alten Kunst[2], II, 2, T. 20, 214a, p. 151.

107. Terracotta Plaque: Gladiators and Beasts in the Circus.

The architectural background to the left is here formed
by a building supported on columns, from the windows of
which a woman and a young man are gazing with lively
interest on the scene. To the right is a gateway, upon
which several egg-shaped objects are placed (comp. vol. I,
p. 244); and beyond this is a Corinthian column surmounted by a female statue. Between the columns of the
groundfloor of the auditorium appears a lioness, springing upon a helmeted gladiator, who is defending himself
with sword and shield against a lion, that, issuing from
the gateway, attacks him on the other side. Another
gladiator, in a low hat, pursues the lion and plants his
lance in its neck. Below the lion is seen the nude figure
of a man lying prone on the earth.

Campana, Opere in plastica, T. 93, to the right. Comp. Bull.
dell' Instit., 1884, p. 159 *(P. J. Meier)*.

130. Terracotta Plaque: Decoration of a Herma of Dionysos.

A Satyr and three women are here engaged in decor-
ating the herma of the bearded Dionysos, and in making
preparations for a bloodless sacrifice. One of the women
to the left) bears a hydria on her shoulder and a kind of
situla bucket) in her right hand; the second woman holds
a basket of fruit, from which the Satyr is taking a bunch
of grapes; and the third to the right) grasps a vine-
shoot.

Campana, Opere in plastica, T. 44.

On the floor, beneath, —

Sepulchral Altar, of marble hollow), with a top
resembling in shape and decoration the gable-roof of a

temple. Each corner of the top is adorned with an eagle, and on the pediment is a wreath. On the front of the altar appears Pluto, raising the resisting Proserpine to his four-horse chariot, the reins of which are held by a Cupid; beneath the horses' fore-feet coils a snake. The empty space below was meant for the epitaph. The sides of the altar are decorated with laurel-branches.

Bonanni, Mus. Kirch., T. xxvi, 116. *Montfaucon*, L'antiquité expliquée, i, T. 38. *Overbeck*, Kunstmythologie, iii, p. 644, T. 18, 3.

Cabinet 11. Terracottas.

On the second shelf from the bottom is a bas-relief of a family banquet; on the third is Ganymede with the eagle.

On the floor, to the right of the cabinet, —

Sarcophagus of a Child, in marble, decorated with reliefs.

In the middle of the front is a laurel-bush, to the left of which is a child with a goose, and to the right an infant playing with a toy-carriage (or perhaps with a go-cart to aid him to walk?). More to the right is a closed carriage drawn by a team of mules; within are a man and woman, the latter holding a baby on her lap. To the left is a similar carriage, with another group of father, mother, and child, while a Cupid hovers above the mules. It is obviously the same child the child whose remains reposed in the sarcophagus, that figures in all four scenes, which represent four different episodes in his short life. Bas-reliefs of the same kind, composed of a series of scenes from the lives of children, occur also on other sarcophagi dating from the imperial epoch.

Found at Rome in 1723. — *Montfaucon*, L'antiquité expliquée, supplement, v, T. 42 et seq. Beschreibung Roms, iii, 3, p. 493. Comp. *De Ruggiero*, Catalogo, p. 53, No. 173. — For similar children's sarcophagi, see Archæol. Zeitschrift, xliii, 1885, pp. 209 et seq. *(Wernicke).*

Above the sarcophagus, —

1. Etruscan Cinerary Urn, in terracotta.

On the front appears the duel of the Theban brothers, a subject that recurs times without number on vessels of this kind. A woman (portrait of the deceased reclines upon the lid, holding a leaf-shaped fan in her hands. The polychrome colouring of the head and fan is admirably preserved.

For the representations of the Theban brothers. comp. *Brunn-Koerte*. 1 rilievi delle urne etrusche, ii, pp. 32 et seq.

Cabinet III.

The middle shelves contain numerous **Silver and Bronze Vases**, found in 1852, along with thousands of coins (see p. 422), near *Vicarello*, on the banks of the Lago di Bracciano. The inscriptions engraved on these vases prove that they are votive offerings dedicated to Apollo and the Nymphs in gratitude for restored health by visitors to the neighbouring thermal springs of the Lago di Bracciano, which were celebrated in antiquity comp. above, p. 385). Beside the shallow vases and goblets, the visitor should notice the small broken silver vessel, on which is a relief of Pan holding a basket of grapes in his left hand and a thyrsos in his right. But the most interesting objects on the third shelf from the bottom) are FOUR SILVER VASES IN THE FORM OF MILESTONES. Upon these, in four columns, are inscribed the names and lengths of the various stages on the journey from Gades Cadiz to Rome, the total distance being added at the foot. Two of the itineraries give the total as 1811 thousand paces, while on the other two a slightly different number is given. The vases, which are of different sizes, date from different periods the largest from the latter half of the second century, the smallest from the third century after Christ. They are votive gifts from patients who had come from the South of Spain to Rome, and thence to the Lago di Bracciano.

Marchi, La stipe tributata alle divinità delle Acque Apollinari.
Rhein. Museum, IX (1854), pp. 21 et seq. *(Henzen)*. *De Ruggiero*,
Catalogo, pp. 102 et seq., Nos. 402-410. *Friedlaender*, Sittengeschichte Roms in der Kaiserzeit, II, 6, p. 17. Corpus Inscriptionum Latin., XI, Nos. 3281-3292.

On the bottom-shelf, —

Leaden Book.

Each cover of this book bears a bust in relief in the
centre, the front cover a veiled woman, the back cover
a bearded man. Within the covers were seven very thin
leaden leaves, originally fastened by a hinge but now
exhibited separately. They are inscribed on both sides
with an unintelligible series of Greek, Latin, and Italic
letters, while in the upper third of each page are scratched
two human or animal figures, or two symbols. The source
of this book is not quite clear. The style and the writing
are both very remarkable, but the article is held to be
genuine and is believed to be a mystical book of the
Basilidian Gnostics.

Comp. *De Ruggiero*, Catalogo, pp. 63-79, No. 199.

On the same shelf, —

Leaden Tablet with a Love-Charm.

The character of the writing seems to refer this tablet
to about the middle of the last century B.C. The pathetic
prayer of the jealous mistress runs somewhat as follows:
— "As the dead, in whose grave this tablet is laid, can
neither speak nor converse, so may Rhodina be dead to
M. Licinius Faustus, and be unable to speak or converse
with him. As the dead have no access to god or man, so
may Rhodina have no access to M. Licinius; may she be
to him no more than the dead that lies buried here. O,
Father Pluto, to thee I devote Rhodina, that she may ever
be hateful to M. Licinius Faustus. And I devote also to
thee M. Hedius Amphio, C. Popillius Apollonius, Ven-
nonia Hermiona, and Sergia Glycinna."

Found in 1852 in a tomb in the Vigna Manenti on the Via
Latina. — Comp. Corpus Inscriptionum Latin., I, No. 818; VI, No. 140.
De Ruggiero, Catalogo, p. 61, No. 195.

On the same shelf, —

Two Leaden Weights; one hexagonal (381 grammes; perhaps Sicilian', with a Greek inscription name of the market-inspector); the other square (602 grammes), and inscribed Ἰταλικόν on one side, and Δίλιτρον (i. e. bilibra = two-pound) on the other, and bearing the names of a consul (Julius Clatius Severus) and of an agoranomos (ædile).

The bilibra is said to have been found near the Fori dell' Astura, between Porto d'Anzio and Capo Circeo, the other weight near the Lake of Albano. — Comp. *Secchi*, Campione d'antica bilibra Romana (Rome, 1835). *De Ruggiero*, Catalogo, p. 58, Nos. 191 et seq. Annali dell' Instituto, 1856, p. 51, 1865, p. 191 *(Schillbach)*. Inscriptiones Græcæ, Siciliæ. et Italiæ, ed. Kaibel, Nos. 2417, 2418. Monumenti antichi pubblicati per cura dell' Accad. dei Lincei, I, pp. 157 et seq. *(Gamurrini)*.

The table-cases contain a rich collection illustrating the **Roman Coinage,** including specimens of the *aes rude* (uncoined pieces of bronze) and the *aes grave signatum* (early Italian coins cast in moulds, as well as of minted coins from their first appearance down to the imperial epoch. Most of them were found in the magazine for votive offerings at the Lago di Bracciano comp. p. 420, thus proving that the baths of that region were frequented at all ages. These cases also contain numerous engraved gems and specimens of vitreous paste.

Comp. *Marchi*, L'aes grave del Museo Kircheriano (Rome, 1839); La stipe tribulata alle divinità delle Acque Apollinari (Rome, 1852). *Mommsen*, Geschichte des röm. Münzwesens, 1860. *R. Garrucci*. Le monete dell' Italia antica, 1885. — For the engraved and paste gems: *De Ruggiero*, Catalogo, pp. 220 et seq., 246 et seq.

On the wall, —

229. Terracotta Plaques: Mourning Penelope, Ulysses and Eurycleia.

These two reliefs, evidently companion-pieces, are reproductions of models perhaps of paintings dating from about the middle of the fifth century. On one Penelope, seated upon a chair below which is placed her work-basket, is shown plunged in melancholy thoughts, in the same attitude as in the well-known statue (vol. I, No. 92, p. 54). Behind her stands the nurse Eurycleia. While his faithful wife thus abandons herself to despair, the much-travelled Ulysses has already returned home disguised as a beggar. This is the subject of the second relief, which represents with great dramatic expression how Eurycleia, while washing the feet of the supposed stranger, recognizes him as her master by a scar. In her joyful surprize, the aged nurse has overturned the basin of water, but before she can rise to her feet or utter a cry, Ulysses has grasped her and stopped her mouth, while he anxiously looks round to ascertain that no one has seen and understood her agitation. Behind Ulysses stands the shepherd Eumæos (restored below the knees), clad in a chiton and goat-skin, and holding in his left hand a traveller's staff and in his right hand a small bowl. Near the chair of Ulysses a dog lies sleeping, a detail doubtless suggested by the story of the faithful Argos, which was the first to recognize his master (Odyss., XVII, 291). The artist, without binding himself too closely to the account in the Odyssey, has here obviously aimed at representing Ulysses at the moment of his return, surrounded by all the retainers that had remained faithful to him.

Thiersch, Epochen der Kunst[2], p. 430, 4. *Overbeck*, Gallerie heroischer Bildwerke, pp. 805 et seq. *Welcker*, Alte Denkmäler, V, p. 231. *Winckelmann*, Monum. inediti, I, T. 161, p. 217 (Ulysses and Eurycleia). *Campana*, Opere in plastica, T. 71 and 72 (two extra attendants appear on the relief of Penelope, to the left). *Baumeister*, Denkmäler des klass. Alterthums, II, p. 1049. Comp. Annali dell' Instit., 1867, p. 334 *(Helbig); 1872,* pp. 293 et seq. *(Conze).* Sitzungsberichte der Münchener Akademie, 1868, p. 78 *(Brunn).* Jahrbuch des Arch. Instit., II, p. 171 *(Dümm'er).*

221. Terracotta Plaque, with the so-called Persian Artemis.

The winged goddess is here indicated as mistress of the lower animal world by a lion and a panther rearing themselves beside her. This motive was commonly employed in Greek art to represent Artemis. The purely decorative type here used was popular among the Hellenic peoples from a very early antiquity.

Comp. Beschreibung Roms, II, 2, p. 21. For the type, comp. especially *Studniczka*. Kyrene, pp. 135 et seq. Bulletin de Correspondance hellén., 1891, p. 106 *(Lechat)*.

256. Terracotta Plaque: Bust of Demeter.

The goddess is here represented with long rippling hair. In her two hands, symmetrically raised, are bunches of wheat-ears and poppies. A serpent coils round each of her arms.

Comp. *Campana*, Opere in plastica, T. 16. *Overbeck*, Griech. Kunstmythologie, III, pp. 510, 514, T. 16, 8. Comp. Bull. dell' Inst., 1866, p. 233 *(Benndorf)*.

Cabinet IV.

This cabinet contains votive animals in terracotta to the left on the second shelf from the top, a sow with her litter), small ivory figures, numerous dice, and all kinds of bronze utensils and glass articles. Among the last (third shelf from the bottom, to the right are the fragments of a vase with medallions in shallow relief representing marine subjects fishers, bathers, boatmen .

For the glass vase: *De Ruggiero*, Catalogo, p. 253, No. 7.

On the wall, —

281. Terracotta Plaque.

Four Cupids bearing a garland of fruit.

Comp. *Campana*, Opere in plastica, T. 15. *Benndorf und Schœne*, Bildwerke des Lateran, p. 365, No. 553.

290. Terracotta Plaque: Busts of Four Gods (two replicas and part of a third .

Mars, with a helmet, and Zeus. with his sceptre, face each other, as do also Athena, with helmet and ægis, and Hera, who is distinguished by her diadem and her mantle brought up like a veil over the back of her head.

Campana, Opere in plastica, T. 3 (below).

315. **Modern Terracotta Plaque: Hephæstos and Athena** (after the E. frieze of the Parthenon). Only the lower portion of Athena is preserved.

This plaque, at one time taken for a Greek original and even for one of the sketches made by Pheidias for the Parthenon, was produced in Italy between 1830 and 1840, along with similar plaques now at Paris and Copenhagen. All these plaques were made from reductions of casts taken direct from the Parthenon frieze by Choiseul-Gouffier in 1784.

Waldstein, Essays on the Art of Pheidias, pp. 258 et seq., T. XIII. Comp. Röm. Mittheil. des Arch. Instit., I (1886), p. 60 *(Von Rohden)*. Revue critique, 1886, I, p. 405 *(S. Reinach)*.

Cabinet V.

Terracotta Lamps.

The floor of the recess at the end of the room is embellished with a **Mosaic** representing a pillar with a basket before it, a thyrsos leaning on the basket, a garlanded mask, and 'to the left' two flutes, the whole contained in a rich landscape.

The sculptures in the recess are for the most part unimportant. Among them may be mentioned, —

91. **Marble Statuette of a Goddess of Nature** 'to the left'.

The head with the drapery upon it, the mural crown, the throat, and both hands are restorations.

This statuette resembles archaic figures in its stiff attitude, with feet set close together and forearms projecting. A long veil, reaching to the ground, hangs from the back of the head, which must originally have worn a wreath or diadem. Above the sleeved chiton is a heavy mantle, embellished with four raised bands in imitation of embroidery, which was probably represented on archaic temple-figures by means of wood-carving or repoussé work. The free style of the motives in these bands contrasts with the general character of the statuette, and suggests that they are of later origin. The first band shows the busts of a veiled woman and a young man (Selene and Helios). The faces of both have been restored. In the second band are the Graces, in the usual attitude with arms interlaced: in the third is a semi-nude Nereid upon a sea-goat, her veil floating in an arch above her head; and in the fourth are three winged Cupids with attributes which cannot be clearly distinguished.

These reliefs doubtless symbolize the three regions of the world (sky, earth, and sea , of which the goddess is conceived as the mistress. Like the Ephesian Artemis (comp. vol. I, No. 347, p. 249 , whose artistic type has certainly inspired the artist of the present statuette, the goddess here represented is a goddess of Nature, local to Asia Minor, whose images, transformed by the Greeks, are frequently but erroneously taken for those of Aphrodite Urania.

Comp. Denkschriften der Wiener Akad. der Wissenschaften, XIX (1870), pp. 41 et seq. (*Jahn*, Europa). Berichte der sächs. Gesellschaft der Wissenschaften, 1868 (*Jahn*, Codex Pighianus), pp. 177 et seq. *Von Sacken*, Antike Sculpturen des Antikencabinetts in Wien, pp. 29 et seq., T. 11. *Friederichs-Wolters*, Berliner Gipsabgüsse, No. 1551. *Froehner*, Collection H. Hoffmann, T. 23. — In a small bronze of the same type (present locality unknown; cast in Berlin, catalogue No. 1772) the head is adorned with a diadem apparently formed of groups of heraldic animals, like the head of the Artemis at Munich (*Friederichs-Wolters*, Berliner Gipsabgüsse, No. 450).

Relief in Coloured Marble in the centre of the recess .

A young man here stands with his horse in front of a large gateway. Most of the figure of the youth and part of the hindquarters of the horse are carved in the yellowish-grey part of the marble: the remainder of the relief is red. This work recalls the funeral bas-relief in the Villa Albani (No. 780; p. 15), the figure on which was at one time taken for Antinous, and which stands in close relation to an Argive bas-relief of the Doryphoros of Polycleitos. To judge from the architectural ornamentation forming its background, and from the nature of the marble,

the relief before us is one of the purely decorative reliefs
that were popular at the close of the Hellenistic period.
The execution is Roman.

For the bas-relief in the Villa Albani, comp. *Dietrichson*, An-
tinous, p. 192. — For the Argive bas-relief: Athen. Mittheil. des
Arch. Instit., II, T. 13. *Friederichs-Wolters*, Berliner Gipsabgüsse,
No. 504.

Cabinet VI.

Roman Lamps.

On the wall, —

335. **Terracotta Plaque.** Comp. No. 130.

336. **Fragment of a Terracotta Plaque: Scene in the
Theatre.**

The wall (proscenium, decorated with projecting
Corinthian columns between which hang garlands, seems
to belong to a house rather than to a temple, if we may
judge by the smallness of the door in the centre. On an
altar to the left is seated an actor with the mask and
dress of a slave, who has apparently (in the play) taken
refuge at this sanctuary from some impending punishment.

A complete example of this scene is figured in *Campana*,
Opere in plastica, T. 98. Ann. dell' Instit., 1859, T. O, p. 389.
Schreiber, Culturhistor. Bilderatlas, T. III, 4.

337 (338, 353, 402, 405, 406, 420). **Fragments of
Terracotta Plaques: Palæstra.**

Between Corinthian columns appear hermæ, amphoræ (338), statues of victorious athletes with wreath
and palm-branch (420, to the right), some indicated as
pugilists by the cæstus on their hands (337; 420), and
figures of Heracles with the club and lion's hide
(353; 420).

Campana, Opere in plastica, T. 95, comp. T. 91 and 96.

362. **Terracotta Plaque: Theseus and Ægeus.**

This relief was formerly supposed to represent Nestor
offering a draught to the wounded Machaon (Iliad, XI,

624 et seq.); but its true explanation is to be found in
the legend of Theseus. Theseus, brought up at Troizen
far from his native land, has returned to Athens and
dwells near his father Ægeus, without being recognized
by him. Only the sorceress Medea, second wife of the
old king, is aware of the young stranger's origin; and
with numberless artifices she persuades her husband to
poison him. But at the decisive moment Ægeus recognizes his son by the scabbard of the sword which he
himself had left at Troizen. This is the moment of the
bas-relief. Theseus, seated on a chair, is already raising
the goblet to his lips, but the aged Ægeus springs forward and seizes the cup with his right hand, while he
grasps his son's arm with the left. A young woman standing by regards the scene with interest.

Campana, Opere in plastica, T. 68. *Combe*, Terracottas of the
British Museum, T. xII, 20 (with additional figures). Comp. *Overbeck*,
Gallerie heroischer Bildwerke, p. 421. Ann. dell' Inst., 1863, p. 459
(*Rutgers*). Arch. Zeit., xLIII, 1885, pp. 282 et seq. (*Michaelis*).
Baumeister, Denkmäler des klass. Alterthums, III, p. 1794.

Cabinet VII.

On the top-shelves: **Leaden Water-pipes**, some of
which come from Ostia. The inscriptions upon them
sometimes denote the workshop where the pipes were
made, sometimes the proprietors of the conduit they
formed part of.

On the two lowest shelves: **Projectiles for Slings**,
an extensive collection including some specimens of
Greek origin. From remote antiquity both the Greeks
and Romans had corps of slingers in their armies;
and the projectiles used by these, either in the form of
round stones or according to a later usage' of pieces of
lead shaped like olives, have been discovered in great
numbers near all places that have sustained a siege
of any length. These missiles frequently bear inscriptions; sometimes the name of a nation or city, sometimes the name of a general or the number and surname

of a legion, and occasionally jests, military toasts, or threats and insults addressed to the enemy. A large number of the specimens in this cabinet date from the battles fought in Picenum, especially near Asculum, during the Social War (91-88 B.C.); others were found near Perugia, which was besieged by Octavianus and defended by Lucius Antonius in B.C. 40. The makers of spurious antiquities have frequently turned their attention in this direction also; and several forged specimens of leaden projectiles are exhibited here.

For the leaden water-pipes, comp. *De Ruggiero*, Catalogo, pp. 142 et seq. *Lanciani*, Le acque e gli acquedotti (Rome, 1880). — For the leaden missiles, comp. Corp. Inscript. latin., I, pp. 188 et seq., IX, pp. 361 et seq. Ephemeris epigraphica, VI *(Zangemeister)*. *Bergk*, Inschriften römischer Schleudergeschosse (Leipsic, 1876). *De Ruggiero*, Catalogo, pp. 82 et seq.

On the wall, —

417. Terracotta Plaque: Pelops and Hippodameia.

Comp. above, p. 273.

Mentioned by *Winckelmann*, Monum. inediti, No. 117 (p. 159).

6, 7, 8. Three Etruscan Cinerary Urns, with figures on the lid and reliefs on the front, representing the hero known as Echetlos.

Comp. above, No. 774, p. 40.

Cabinet VIII.

On the second shelf from the bottom: **Large Bronze Tablet**, with an inscription in the Faliscan dialect, dedicated to Minerva. The inscription derives enhanced interest from the fact that we have very few examples of this dialect, which is the nearest congener of Latin. It runs as follows: *Menerva · sacru | La · Cotena · La · f · pretod · de | zenatuo · sententiad · voutum | deded · cuando · datu · reeted | cuncaptum; i.e.* 'Sacred to Minerva. Lars Cutenius, son of Lars, praetor, has accomplished this vow by decree of the senate. It has been accomplished as it had been promised '? .'

Found at Santa Maria de Falerii, one half in 1860, the other half ten years later. — *De Ruggiero*, Catalogo, p. 56, No. 188. *Zretaïeff*, Inscrip. Italiæ inferioris dialecticæ (Moscow, 1886), p. 26, No. 70. Corpus inscript. latin., XI, No. 3081. *Deecke*, Die Faliskor, p. 156.

On the third shelf: **Iron Collar**, hanging from which is a little metal label bearing the following inscription: *fugi, tene me, cum revocaveris me dm.* (domino) *Zonino, accepis solidum*, i.e. 'I have run off, catch me, if you restore me to my master Zoninus, you will receive a solidus'. The small size of the collar and the nature of the inscription clearly show that the collar was not intended for a slave, but for a dog or other domestic animal.

De Ruggiero, Catalogo, p. 137, No. 508. *Bruns*, Fontes iuris Romani, p. 274 (promissiones populares, No. 2).

127–129 'on the wall'. **Terracotta Plaques: Satyrs gathering and pressing grapes.**

Comp. No. 363 in this room.

Campana, Opere in plastica, T. 39, comp. T. 40. *Combe*, Terracottas in the British Museum, T. 33, 67.

434. **Terracotta Plaque: Contests of Amazons and Griffins.**

Comp. *Campana*, Opere in plastica, T. 78 and p. 217 above.

Cabinet IX.

Terracotta Lamps.

In the recess next the door, to the left of Cabinet X, —

Base of a Marble Candelabrum.

On the upper surface of this triangular base is a round hole in which the marble shaft of the candelabrum, or rather thymiaterion (comp. p. 357), was stepped and secured by a wedge. Its three sides are embellished with reliefs of Cupids carrying a sword, a shield, and a helmet — the arms of Ares in the original sense of the composition. The upper corners are ornamented with projecting rams' heads, and below are winged feet of animals, between which palmettes are inserted, as in the case of bronze thymiateria.

Bonanni, Mus. Kircher., T. I, 40. *Montfaucon,* L'antiquité expliquée, T. 50. — On bases of the same kind, comp. *Hauser,* Die neu-attischen Reliefs, p. 109; and above, vol. I, p. 263, No. 374.

34. Small Herma-Head.

This head, a mediocre work of the Roman epoch, reproduces a type of young man, invented during the former half of the fifth century.

Cabinet X.

Antique Terracotta Vases.

On the third shelf: Small **Ointment Flasks**, one of great antiquity, in the form of a helmeted warrior's head, and another reproducing an archaic head of Heracles, both in colours. At each corner of the same shelf is a **Patera,** with three painted fish, a variety belonging to the latest period of South Italic (perhaps Campanian?) ceramic art.

For the archaic ointment-flasks, comp. Gazette archéol., 1880, p. 145 *(Heuzey).* Röm. Mittheil. des Archäol. Instit., v, p. 320 *(Reisch).* — For the patera, *Furtwaengler,* Berliner Vasensammlung, pp. 963 et seq.

Room II.

Bronzes.

The statuettes and fragments of statues in the cabinets in this room include almost nothing of importance, and the authenticity of several specimens, among the earlier acquisitions of the museum, is doubtful. The present (provisional) arrangement of the collections prevents a large number of the specimens, including most of the mirrors, from being properly seen; while the various types of utensils, handles, etc., though copiously represented here, may be more conveniently studied in the Museo Gregoriano. Only a few of the more important articles are therefore here mentioned.

Cabinet I.

Head of Apollo, at the top, to the left.

This bronze represents the god as a graceful and sentimental youth, a type dating from the post-Praxitelian age.

Comp. *Winckelmann,* Geschichte der Kunst, v, 5, § 27; vii, 2, § 20. *Overbeck,* Griech. Kunstmythologie, iv, p. 120.

Bronze-gilt Head of a Young Man, on the same shelf, to the right.

This head, crowned with a diadem, is entirely Roman in conception. It probably represents a Genius.

Comp. *Winckelmann,* Geschichte der Kunst, vii, 2, § 20.

Pear-shaped Mirror, on the second shelf from the bottom, to the right.

This was found at Palestrina and bears Latin inscriptions of the second century B.C. The design on the mirror shows a bearded and garlanded Silenus, with clearly-defined swine's ears ¡ *Marsuas)* leaping and waving an aspergillus in his right hand. On a pedestal to the right stands a richly-ornamented crater. In the background, to the left, is a small goat-footed Paniscos *Painsscos* as the misspelled inscription has it, who imitates the Silenus with burlesque gestures. Beside the left leg of Marsyas is the inscription ⁄to be read from the top downwards¸: *Vibis Pilipus cailavit, i.e.* 'Vibius Philippus engraved this'. This artist has obviously contented himself with copying an earlier model.

Monum. dell' Instit., ix, T. 29, 2. *Gerhard-Koerte,* Etruskische Spiegel, v, T. 45. Comp. Bullet. dell' Instit., 1867, pp. 67 et seq. *(Benndorf).* Corpus Inscrip. latin., xiv. No. 4098.

Cabinet II.

On the fifth shelf, to the left: **Small Bronze Relief.** This relief, on which Heracles is represented advancing towards the right, holding his club in his raised right hand, is a Greek work of the sixth or fifth century B. C. It probably formed the decoration of a casket.

Comp. *Roscher*, Lexikon der Mythologie, I, p. 2150. *Olympia*, IV, p. 105 *(Furtwaengler)*.

On the same shelf, —

Two Bronze Statuettes of Philosophers (?), seated and holding caskets containing scrolls.

To judge by their execution these statuettes date from the end of the antique period, and have, moreover, been freely retouched by a modern hand.

Comp. *Winckelmann*, Werke (Donaueschingen, 1829), II, p. 204, (Fernow's ed.), II, p. 110, (Hoffmann's ed., 1847), II, p. 180.

On the sixth shelf: **Votive Hands, Bronze Utensils, Feet of Vases, Handles, and Figures on Lids,** including an **Acrobat** walking on his hands.

For the figures on lids: *Micali*, Antichi monum., T. 56, 1. Comp. Sitzungsberichte der sächs. Akademie der Wissenschaften zu Leipzig, 1878, p. 132 *(Heydemann)*.

On the fifth shelf, to the right, —

Archaic Etruscan Bronze of a Ploughman.

A man, clad in hat, chiton, and an animal's skin, is ploughing with a hook-shaped plough, drawn by a span of oxen, with the yoke on their necks, fastened behind their horns. The plough is composed of a strong hook-shaped piece *buris,* to which the share *vomer,* is fastened by means of rings, while the stilt *(stiva)*, a continuation of the buris, is furnished with a cross-piece for the hands to grasp. This group was at one time believed to represent Tarchon, who, according to the Etruscan legend, discovered the mysterious child Tages while ploughing (comp. above, p. 391); and it was assumed (quite erroneously) that the small statuette of Athena close by belonged to the group. The animated though somewhat clumsy group is in reality merely a votive offering from some ploughman, who wished to have his daily task represented plastically.

Found near Arezzo. — *Gori*, Museo Etrusco, I, T. 200. *Micali*, Antichi monumenti (Florence, 1810), T. 50. Monumenti per servire alla storia (Florence, 1833), T. 104. *Baumeister*, Denkmäler des klass. Alterthums, I, p. 13. *Daremberg-Saglio*, Dictionnaire des antiquités, I, p. 355. *Martha*, L'art étrusque, p. 510. Comp. Beschreibung Roms, III, 3, p. 496.

Cabinet III.

In the left section of the cabinet, on the third shelf from the bottom: **Fragments of a Bronze Band,** ornamented in repoussé work. These are portions of a replica of the Bomarzo bronze-mountings, now in the Etruscan Museum at the Vatican (see pp. 108 et seq.).

On the fourth shelf, —

Fragment of a Greek Mirror-Case, with relief of Athena combating a giant, in delicately-executed repoussé work.

Athena, in full armour, and wearing a helmet with a triple crest, advances rapidly to the right, thrusting her spear (broken off) against the giant Encelados (head wanting). The giant has wings almost completely broken off) on his shoulders; his legs below the knees end in serpents; and his thighs are covered with scales. The hide of a beast is wrapped round his left arm, while his right hand raises his sword in defence rather than in attack. The figure of the giant with legs ending in serpents presents a superficial resemblance to the later representations of the battle of the gods and giants, such as, *e.g.*, in the reliefs on the altar from Pergamum now in the Berlin Museum; but the severe style of the relief as a whole refers it to an earlier period, about the middle of the fourth century.

Journal of Hellenic Studies, IV (1883), p. 90 *(A. H. Smith)*. *Roscher*, Lexikon der Mythologie, I, p. 1606 *(Kuhnert)*. Comp. Berichte der sächs. Gesellschaft der Wissenschaften, 1879, pp. 131 et seq. *(Heydemann)*. *Mayer*, Giganten und Titanen, p. 396.

On the fifth shelf: **Small Cist,** with feet formed like comic actors (wearing masks and each carrying a basket in the left hand'. The handle on the lid represents a fully draped woman seated on the ground and holding a parasol over her head. This figure recalls the type of Greek women current in the fourth and third centuries.

Found at Bolsena. — Comp. Ann. dell' Instit., 1866, p. 179, No. 56 (Schoene).

On the sixth shelf: **Groups of Warriors**, two tiny archaic statuettes forming companion-pieces to each other. These groups were used to adorn some very antique Italic helmet, and were placed on each side of the plume or crest. The adjoining group of a **Young Man with long hair**, leading a rearing horse, dates from the same period and was used for a similar purpose.

Comp. Ann. dell' Instit., 1874, pp. 46 et seq. (Helbig).

On the eighth shelf, —

Three Feet of a Cist, with a relief in the free style: Poseidon pursuing a young warrior (evidently a giant) over the sea.

The head of Poseidon is of a type that clearly reveals the late-Etruscan origin of the group. The god holds his trident in the left hand, and with the right seizes the shield of his foe. A marine monster, with a fantastically shaped head, bites the left thigh of the giant, and another monster of enormous size rears itself beside his head.

Found at Palestrina. — Gori, Museo Etrusco, I, T. 124. Inghirami, Monum. etruschi, III, 3, T. 17. Müller-Wieseler, Denkmäler alter Kunst, II, T. VII, 86a, p. 113. Comp. Ann. dell' Inst., 1866, p. 191 (Schoene). Overbeck, Griech. Kunstmythologie, III, p. 332. Mayer, Giganten und Titanen, p. 390.

On the same shelf are **Three Feet of a Cist**, with the nude figure of a winged woman, arranging her hair. On each side are different attributes (mask of an animal; ointment flask).

Comp. Schumacher, Prænestin. Ciste zu Karlsruhe, p. 27.

In each corner of the end-wall is a candelabrum, surmounted by figures, of the kind described above (pp. 356 et seq.). In the cabinet are Etruscan and Sardinian bronzes, miscellaneous Egyptian antiquities, and a bearded head in the Assyrian style, cut out of a relief.

In front of the first window, —

Small Bronze Statue of Dionysos.

The god is here represented as a nude youth, with an ivy-wreath in his curly hair, his left arm enveloped in a nebris and his feet shod with sandals. His left foot rests upon a small panther. In his right hand is a thyrsos and in his left is another attribute. This work reproduces a type invented in the Hellenistic period; but judging from the heavy treatment of the forms, which have not been touched by the chisel, it seems to be merely a modern cast of an antique bronze.

Musei Kirkeriani Acrea, II, T. 22, p. 95 *(Contucci)*. Comp. *Winckelmann*, Kunstgeschichte, VII, 2, § 20. — First recognized as a modern replica'by *Helbig*.

In front of the second window, —

Nude Figure of a Child, of the Roman period.

The slightly stooping attitude of this figure shows that it was intended to support a large basin in its outstretched arms. It is a mediocre and purely decorative work, probably from the garden of some Roman villa.

Musei Kirkeriani Acrea, II, T. 20, p. 87 *(Contucci)*.

Upon the cabinet between the windows: **Three Small Candelabra and a Thymiaterion and a Small Tripod.**

In the glass-case to the right of the entrance, —

Candelabrum. Comp. p. 356.

The shaft, up which a dove climbs, rests upon the head of a nude youth, who holds a discus in his lowered right hand, while he shades his eyes with the left. The base is formed of three draped human legs. Comp. No. 21, p. 363.

In the same case: **Various Candelabra and Lamps,** chiefly of the Roman period.

In the middle of the room, —

Antique Bronze Chair, inlaid with silver.

The left arm of this chair ends at the top in an ass's head and is ornamented at the bottom with a garlanded bust of Silenus; the right arm ends at the top in a swan's head and has no plastic decoration at the bottom. An ornamental border of meanders and rosettes inlaid in silver runs round the seat of the chair.

Comp. the bronze bisellium in the Palazzo dei Conservatori, No. 553, vol. I, p. 413.

Mithras Group, in marble.

A poor work, which cannot be of earlier date than the middle of the third century after Christ.

Comp. vol. I, pp. 478 et seq., No. 615.

Ficoronian Cist: the Argonauts in the country of the Bebryces, in Bithynia. Comp. the photograph hanging to the left of the door.

This cist, justly celebrated for the artistic beauty of its engraving, may be regarded as the finest specimen of its kind, all the more as it exceeds other cists in point of size, though in shape it exactly resembles them (comp. p. 361'. The cist rests upon three lion's paws, treading upon frogs (one foot restored); and the junction of these with the body is decorated with a group of Cupid, Heracles, and Iolaos. The handle on the lid is another group of three figures: a beardless man, with a collar, star-spangled mantle, and sandals, who, in spite of the absence of any characteristic attribute, may be regarded as a Dionysos of a late-Italic type, is supported by two Satyrs, recognizable by their pointed ears, equine tails, loose garments of skins, and the wine-vessels. (A drinking-horn was probably held in the restored hand of the Satyr to the spectator's right.) On the metal plaque, serving as a base for this group and rivetted to the lid, the following verse is inscribed in letters whose shape refers them to the middle of the third century B.C.: *Novios Plautios med Romai fecid, Dindia Macolnia fileai dedit,* i.e. 'Novius Plautius made me (*i.e.* the cist) at Rome; Dindia Magolnia presented me to her daughter'. Dindia Magolnia was a Præncstine, as her name shows. The lid itself is richly chased. Towards the centre arc two lions and two griffins, rampant and facing each other, and between them is a bull's head. In the outer circle is a series of hunting-scenes, in which men and youths (some of a very pronounced Italic type are hunting two boars, a stag, and a hind. The animated composition and the fresh and careful drawing recall the Greek vase-paintings of similar subjects, though hardly any of these are of equal excellence. The engravings on the body of the cist attain an even higher artistic level, while their subjects are more attractive. At the top and bottom are broad ornamental bands in the conventional style of the Hellenistic period, consisting of highly developed flowers and palmettes interspersed with these; in the upper band are heads of Medusa; and in the lower band, pairs of heraldic Sphinxes seated facing each other. The zone between these bands is filled in with a composition the subject of which is borrowed from the story of the Argonauts.

In the course of their voyage to Colchis in search of the golden fleece, Jason and his companions landed on the coast of Bithynia; but Amycos, King of the Bebryces, prevented them from using a spring of water, and challenged them to a boxing-match, an exercise in which he had hitherto defeated all visitors to his coasts. Among the Argonauts was Polydeuces (Pollux), who accepted the challenge, and. thanks to his wonderful skill, overcame the barbarian king. The chastisement of the vanquished forms the centre of the composition before us. Polydeuces, exerting all his strength, fastens Amycos by the arms to a tree, which affords the purchase for his own left arm. Both adversaries wear cæstus (the ancient substitute for boxing-gloves), which cover the forearm and

are furnished with straps (comp. p. 227. Anger and
exertion are clearly expressed on the face of Polydeuces,
chagrin and disappointment on that of Amycos. The
mantle and shoes of Amycos lie beside him to the right.
Lower, at the foot of the tree, sits the young attendant of Pollux, apparently asleep, with his master's
cloak thrown over him and holding his master's shoes
and strigils; and beside him are an oil-flask, hanging
from a strap, and the hoe which has been used to mark
out the boxing-ring and to soften the earth. To the
right stands Athena, protectress of the Greeks in their
combats with barbarians, characterized as goddess of
battle merely by the spear in her left hand and by the
aegis, bordered with serpents and adorned with the Medusa's head and several stars. She is richly clothed and
ornamented; in her hair is a coronet of golden leaves
placed close together, resembling the coronets that have
been found in large numbers in Italian tombs. Above
Athena appears a flying Nike, bearing the crown and
fillet of victory to Polydeuces. This main group is
flanked on each side by a pair of spectators. Seated on
an amphora to the left and leaning with both hands on
his spear in a proud attitude, is a bearded man, probably one of the Bebryces, as his hair and facial type
resemble those of the king. The bearded personage seated
beside him, with large wings, pensively supporting his
chin with his arm, is generally taken for Sosthenes, the
local dæmon, who had predicted the victory of the Argonauts. To the right of the central group sits a young
Greek, distinguished from his companions by a garland
and by a bracelet of Italic form. This is doubtless Jason,
the leader of the Argonauts. The bearded man standing
in an easy posture behind Jason is probably Heracles,
whom a later tradition describes as taking part in the
expedition of the Argonauts. His back is turned to the
spectator. To the right of all these figures is a scene of
disembarkation from the ship Argo, which has been
beached in an opening among the rocks. From the stern

flutters a streamer. A young Argonaut seated on the
fore-deck watches the place of combat, a companion behind him lies stretched on his back asleep, and a third
busies himself with a provision-sack, for a banquet is to
celebrate the victory. Another youth, carrying a small
cask by a handle and a basket from which hangs a piece
of cloth, descends from the deck by means of a ladder
leaning against the ship; while on the ground beside the
ladder sits another armed youth, apparently fastening
his shoe.

This group of Argonauts, which stands in immediate
relation to the combat of Polydeuces, serves as a transition to the scene at the fountain, whose water the Greeks
may now enjoy undisturbed. The spring issues from a
lion's mouth, placed high up on the rock. Beneath the
falling water is placed an amphora; an Argonaut is in
the act of quenching his thirst from a large cup, and a
similar cup hangs on the rock to the left for the use of
passers-by. A pot-bellied Silenus, seated on a stone
near the spring, complacently patting his rotund stomach,
regards the youth to his left with a mocking and mischievous air, indicating that this gesture is a burlesque
of the gymnastic exercise of the latter. The young Greek,
however, quite unmoved, continues to deal lusty blows
against the sand-bag (or wine-skin) suspended from a
tree, a favourite method of practising for the boxing-
ring (comp. p. 381). Farther to the right another
Argonaut is endeavouring to make an amphora full of
water stand upright by thrusting its pointed end into
the soft earth. Above, in a niche of the rock, the youthful genius of the place reclines in a graceful attitude,
wearing a bulla suspended from a collar, in the Italic
style, and holding a fluttering tænia in his right hand.
Still farther to the right are two Argonauts in confidential
converse, one laying his arm with a friendly gesture round
the neck of the other, who stands with a somewhat
nonchalant air. The latter is probably to be identified as
Castor, the second Dioscuros, from his sailor's cap. An

amphora lies on the ground between the friends. This charming group has been used at once to separate and to unite the scene at the spring and the scene of the punishment of Amycos; for that no great space is supposed to separate these scenes is proved by the fact that upon this amphora sits one of the spectators of the principal group.

This composition, with its numerous figures, thus forms a homogeneous and carefully considered whole, that possesses an enduring charm and well repays minute study, both by the abundance of its attractive motives and by the conscientious execution of details. The landscape, for example, is as delicate as a miniature. There is no doubt that the composition as a whole is a reproduction of some large Greek painting (about the beginning of the fourth century); but it is equally certain that the actual engraving before us is the work of an artist of the beginning or middle of the third century, i.e. of the period to which the borders framing the principal subject belong. This artist has used his model with a certain independence; without diminishing the general unity of the whole, he has not only given to various details, such as the ornaments and utensils, the shapes current in his own day, but he has even modified entire figures in the spirit of the contemporary types (e.g. the Athena and the Nike). The winged male figure, which we have already seen representing Calchas on a mirror of this epoch (comp. No. 196, p. 377), may also be an addition by him, for the idea of giving wings to a genius must have been very familiar to an artist working in Italy.

The delicate and loving carefulness of the drawing seems to prove that it was executed by a Greek; though it must be admitted that there is scarcely a trace of Greek inspiration either in the feet or the lid of the cist. It has been suggested that Plautios may have carved the group on the lid without being the artist of the engravings, for the inscription that mentions him appears on the metal plate forming the plinth of that group. But it is quite obvious that Plautios was the proprietor of the studio whence the cist was issued, and that the inscription was not added until the cist was completed. The most probable explanation seems to be, therefore, that the makers of cists were in the habit of purchasing the cast figures that adorn the lids and that could be made in quantity (another replica of the group in question is extant), while they themselves executed the engravings on the sides of the cists. The mention of the place *Romai* would seem to suggest that the artist was not a native of Rome but had gone thither, perhaps from Præneste or Campania; or he may even have been a Greek, in accordance with his artistic style. We may recall in this connection that a certain Marcus Plautius, a Greek born in Asia Minor, flourished about this period or a little later, and that his paintings in the temple of Ardea won him great fame and the right of citizenship.

Found in 1738 in the great necropolis of Præneste near the church of S. Rocco, and acquired a few years later by Ficoroni, who presented it to the Collegio Romano (*Justi*, Winckelmann, II, p. 128). — Musei Kirkeriani Aerea, I, T. 1-9. *Gerhard*, Etruskische Spiegel, I, T. 2. *Marchi*, La cista atletica del Museo Kircheriano (Rome, 1848). *Broendsted*, Den Ficoroniske Cista (Copenhagen, 1847). *E. Braun*, Die ficoronische Ciste (Leipsic, 1849). *Baumeister*, Denkmäler des klass. Alterthums, I, p. 454. *Roscher*, Lexikon der Mythologie, I, p. 527. Wiener Vorlegeblätter für archäologische Uebungen, 1889, T. XII. *Martha*, L'art étrusque, p. 537. Comp. *O. Jahn*, Die ficoronische Ciste (Leipsic, 1852). Ann. dell' Instit., 1862, pp. 15 et seq. *(Brunn)*; 1866, pp. 151 et seq., p. 203 *(Schoene)*. *Mommsen*, Röm. Geschichte, I⁷, pp. 446, 478. Corpus inscrip. lat , XIV, No. 4112, and pp. 328 et seq.

Room III.

Early Christian and Mediæval Antiquities.

Along the walls are **Tombstones, Reliefs from Christian Sarcophagi, Marble Sepulchral Tablets**, and a few **Jewish Monuments**.

Comp. *Von Schultze*, Archæolog. Studien über altchristliche Monumente (Vienna, 1880), pp. 256 et seq.

Beneath a large vase in the centre of the room, —

125. So-called Caricature Crucifixion.

On the S.W. slope of the Mount Palatine, on the site of the former Vigna Nussiner, are a number of apartments which were excavated in 1856, and are regarded by some authorities as a Pædagogium, or school for the imperial slaves, and by others as a guard-house. This 'graffito' was discovered scratched on the stucco in the second of the three small square rooms adjoining the semicircular exedra. It seems to date from the first half of the third century, though some authorities refer it to the reign of Hadrian. It exhibits a man with an ass's head, nailed to a cross and clad in the colobium (or short tunic worn by slaves and freedmen) and trunkhose; to the left stands a beardless man in a similar costume, raising his left arm in an attitude of prayer towards the crucified. In front of him is the inscription: Ἀλεξάμενος σέβετε Θεόν, *i. e.* 'Alexamenos worshipping his god'. The drawing is evidently a caricature made by one of the imperial servants in mockery of a Christian companion. We learn from Tertullian and other sources that the Christians and Jews were believed, even during the third century, to adore a god with an ass's head.

Garrucci, Il crocifisso graffito in casa dei Cesari, 1857. Comp. *Becker*, Spottcrucifix (Breslau, 1866). *Fr. X. Kraus*, Spottcrucifix vom Palatin (Fribourg, 1872). Realencyclopædie der christl. Altertümer, II, pp. 774 et seq. *Garrucci*, Storia dell' arte christiana, VI, p. 138. *Daremberg-Saglio*, Dictionnaire des antiquités, I, p. 1375.

In the cabinets are **Christian Terracotta Lamps** and **Mediæval and Oriental Curiosities.**

The door opposite the entrance to the third room leads to the **Ethnographical Museum,** which occupies the entire north portion of the building and the north half of the long east corridor. The south half of this corridor contains some of the prehistoric collections, the objects of Italic origin occupying the rooms opening from the corridor to the outside (east), while the rooms on the

side next the inner court contain objects from abroad.
Following the systematic arrangement of the museum,
we begin our inspection at the door to the right (E.) of
the main entrance and opposite the special entrance to
the Museo Kircheriano.

Prehistoric Museum.

In the vestibule are a few models of prehistoric con-
structions in stone. Glass-Case I. **Models of Four
Megalithic Monuments** (known as Specchia, Truddhu,
Pietra Fitta, and Dolmen), from the Terra d'Otranto,
near Lecce. — Case II. **Model of a Sardinian Nurago**,
one of the tower-like monuments used by the primitive
Sardinians as refuges in times of danger; though some
authorities regard them as fortifications erected by Phœnician settlers.

Gazette archéologique, VII, pp. 30 et seq. (*Lenormant*). *Perrot-
Chipiez*, Histoire de l'art dans l'antiquité, IV, 22 et seq., 51 et seq.

To the left of the door leading to the long E. corridor: **Tomb of Stone Slabs**, dating from the close of the
first iron age. This tomb, found in the province of Novara,
contained several primitive terracotta vessels. — To the
right: **Small Tomb**, of much later date. This was found
in a necropolis in the province of Massa-Ferrara, where
the civilization of the first iron age seems to have long
survived the dawn of history.

In the next portion of the Museum, forming the south
(right) part of the east corridor, the exhibits are grouped
according to the great periods of prehistoric civilization
(stone age, bronze age, iron age), the objects of each age
being subdivided according to their place of origin. The
last room, at the south end, contains the Treasure of
Præneste, which marks the transition from prehistoric to
historic times.

The first two sections, immediately adjoining the
vestibule with the tombs, are devoted to the stone age.
The third is occupied by the monuments discovered at

the prehistoric *stazioni* (settlements) on the Monti Lessini, by the aid of which we may trace the continuous development of prehistoric civilization from its rise to its most recent period.

In the three following rooms the bronze age is represented, chiefly by the discoveries made in lake-dwellings and 'terremare' mounds containing prehistoric remains, in Venetia, Lombardy, and the Emilia.

The next (seventh) section contains various objects from both the bronze and the iron ages. In the cabinet to the left of the exit are a number of bronzes from Sardinia, including the **Statuette of a Warrior**, clad in a tunic, hose, and cuirass, and wearing a helmet with two projecting horns; in his right hand is a fragment of his sword(?) and in his left his shield, furnished with a handle of a curious form. On his back this warrior bears a small carriage, to the pole of which is attached a wicker work-basket.

Mémoires de l'académie des inscriptions, T. xxviii, p. 579 *(Barthélemy)*. *Winckelmann*, Kunstgeschichte, iii, 4, § 45; Werke, ii, T. 6 (Fernow's ed.), Atlas, i, No. 21 (Donaueschingen's ed.), or Werke, ii, T. 24 (Hoffmann's ed.). Gazette archéol., vii (1881), T. 24, pp. 133 et seq. *(Robion)*. *Perrot-Chipiez*, Histoire de l'art, iv, p. 68. Comp. Beschreibung Roms, iii, 3, p. 495.

The three following sections contain articles of the first iron age, arranged according to the necropoles of North, Central, and South Italy. The most interesting exhibits are the *Tombe a Pozzo*, or 'well-tombs' (Rooms VII and VIII), transferred hither bodily, with their contents, from the burial-places in West Etruria. These are tombs for cremation, in the shape of a well or pit, with black cinerary urns of clumsy shape, usually covered with a flat cup by way of lid, and containing crescent-shaped razors, simple fibulæ, and small ornaments in amber, bone, glass, etc. The **Cinerary Urns** in the shape of huts (comp. p. 267) date from the same primitive stage of civilization. These are represented here by several specimens, one of which comes from Corneto (in the small glass-case to the right in Room 10).

Treasure of Praeneste.

All the articles exhibited in Room XI were brought from a tomb discovered in February, 1876, by the brothers Bernardini, at Palestrina (Praeneste), near the church of S. Rocco. The tomb was in the form of a rectangular trench, with walls lined with slabs of tufa, and was perhaps originally covered by a stone roof ($17^3/_4 \times 12^3/_4$ ft.); its depth was fully $5^1/_2$ ft. An elongated cavity in the floor of the tomb contained a few mouldering bones along with the golden shield (No. 1) and three fibulae, — obviously the remains of the corpse buried here and of the ornaments that adorned it. Most of the other articles were placed near the walls of the tomb; they seem to have been the sepulchral equipment of a single wealthy man, probably a powerful chief. We are at once struck with the resemblance of these objects both in the choice and shape to those found in the large Regulini-Galassi Tomb at Caere pp. 353 et seq.. We find the same bronze utensils, showing the same Oriental style in their ornamental reliefs; the gold and silver articles reproduce the same types from Asia Minor and display the same perfection of workmanship; the silver vessels decorated with reliefs are of the same kind in both tombs (pp. 394 et seq.). The wealthy princes of Praeneste had evidently not only the same manners and customs but also the same commercial relations as the chiefs of Caere. In point of date, the tombs cannot be separated from each other by more than a few decades; while it is difficult to say which is the earlier. Probably the tomb at Caere is the more ancient, in spite of the much more simple construction shown by that at Praeneste.

Comp. Bull. dell' Instit., 1876, pp. 117 et seq. *(Helbig)*. Annali, 1876, pp. 197 et seq.; 1879, pp. 1 et seq. *(Helbig)*. Notizie degli scavi di antichità, 1876, pp.113 et seq. *(Ccnestabile)*. *Fernique, Etude sur Préneste* (Paris, 1880), pp. 125 et seq., 172 et seq. — On the similar discovery, the yield of which is now partly in the Palazzo Barberini, comp. Archaeologia, XLI, 1 (London, 1867), pp. 3 et seq. *(Garrucci)*. *Fernique*, pp. 173 et seq. — On the style and origin of the various articles, comp. the references cited at p. 397.

Since the re-arrangement of the museum, the articles found in this tomb have been placed by themselves in a large glass-case, and the numerical order of the catalogue has occasionally been disregarded, in order to place the more important specimens in a better light. But in the following description it has been found convenient to adhere to the numerical order for each shelf.

Middle Shelf.

To the left, on the side next the entrance, —

1. **Plaque in dull gold, in the form of a parallelogram**, the gem of the collection. This is divided lengthwise into two equal portions by a raised round moulding; and the ends are bordered with similar mouldings, decorated with meanders and ending in lions' heads.

Each part of this plaque has four rows of small figures soldered to it, making 131 in all. These figures are each formed of two halves, made in stamps, and are decorated with minute gold points. In the outermost row are 15 birds with human heads, recalling the famous Harpies, so frequently represented in the archaic art of Asia Minor; the second row consists of 11 small lions, with human heads on their backs (a unique type on the model of the Chimæra or similar monster); in the third row are 12 standing lions, and in the fourth are 12 seated lions. The central moulding is decorated with 9 couchant lions, turning their heads backwards, with animals' heads (goats?) rising from their backs, a type invented before or at the same time as the Chimæra-type. On the four external rows are four small horses on each side. The plaque was evidently intended to be sewn to cloth, and was probably used as a breast-ornament (or, according to some authorities, as an ornament for the head). The remarks made at pp. 391 et seq. with reference to the similar jewels found in the Regulini-Galassi Tomb are applicable also to the style and origin of this ornament.

Monum. dell' Inst., x, T. xxxɪa, 1. Comp. Bull. dell' Inst., 1876, p. 126. Annali, 1876, p. 259 *(Helbig)*, 1885, p. 46 *(Undset)*. Notizie degli scavi, 1876, p. 115. *Langbehn*, Flügelgestalten der ältesten griech. Kunst, p. 81.

2. **Brooch in dull gold,** called *Fibula a Cornetti.*

Monum. dell' Inst., x, T. xxxɪa, 7. Comp. Bullettino, 1876, p. 122. Annali, 1885, p. 29 *(Undset)*.

3. **Plaque in dull gold,** with a toothed border.

On the plaque are flying water-fowl, lions, and Sphinxes, all in stamped work and ornamented with small golden drops.

Monum. dell' Inst., x, T. xxxɪ, 2. Comp. Annali, 1876, p. 249.

4. **Cylinder of thin gold plate,** ornamented with delicate granulated work and two rows of small lions at the sides. — Nos. 5 und 6, to the right, are similar cylinders, but less richly ornamented.

Monum. dell' Inst., x, T. xxxɪa, 4.

On the other side of the shelf, in the compartment to the right, —

9. **Thin Bracelet in dull-gold.**

The stamped reliefs represent birds with women's heads and outspread wings. The style is the same as that of the above-mentioned jewels.

Monum. dell' Inst., x, T. xxxɪa, 5. Comp. *Langbehn*, Flügelgestalten, p. 82.

16, 17. **Silver Brooches** (safety-pins).

These somewhat complicated but highly practical fastenings resemble No. 1 in style and technique. They consist of two parts; on the outside of one part are three small handles and on the inside two long pins to be thrust into the garments meant to be pinned together; on the outside of the other part also are three bent portions, the first and last of which are hollow and serve to receive and fasten the pins of the other part. The two parts are united by clasps, ornamented with figures on the lower part of the brooch. When the fibula was first discovered, the various parts were all united to form one whole, and the use of the article was long unknown. One of the specimens, however, was accidentally broken and the interior mechanism was thus exposed to view. The body of one of these pins is ornamented with winged Sphinxes in the round, that of the other with lions having double human heads, and bodies covered with small golden drops. The golden buckle of Ulysses, described in the Odyssey (xix, 225), was probably constructed somewhat after the fashion of these.

Mon. dell' Instit., x, T. xxxi, 6 and 7. Annali, 1879, T. c, 9, pp. 15 et seq. Comp. Annali, 1876, pp. 249 et seq. *Helbig*, Homerische Epos[2], pp. 277 et seq. *Langbehn*, Flügelgestalten, p. 82. *Fontenay*, Les bijoux, p. 326.

18. Fragments of Small Silver Animals.

These perhaps formed part of an ornament like No. 1.

In the part of the case facing the window, —

20. Two-handled Goblet in dull gold.

A group of two sitting Sphinxes is soldered to the upper part of each handle.

Monum. dell' Inst., x, T. xxxia, 6. Comp. Bull., 1876, p. 124.

23. Silver Crater, gilded on the outside.

On the edge are six half-serpents (silver covered with gold leaf) serving as handles.

The body and foot of this vase are ornamented with reliefs that show the influence of Egyptian art. At the top, at the point where the handles are attached, is a band of geese; in the two next bands are foot-soldiers, cavalry, and chariots; while the fourth shows lion-hunts and rustic scenes. In the last we see a man in Egyptian costume brandishing his sword against a rampant lion, upon which a dog is springing, a realistic adaption of the heraldic arrangement borrowed from Asia Minor; two lions attack a bull, while a horseman, fleeing at the

galop, turns round in his saddle to launch his arrows
against them; a woman gathers grapes from a vine wind-
ing itself between two palm-trees; a man tills the soil
at the foot of a palm-tree, while two horses browse beside him; a huntsman brings back his game hanging on
a pole; to the left are three oxen browsing between a
palm-tree and a papyrus-plant. The medallion at the bottom, surrounded by these friezes, displays a lion triumphantly placing his paws upon the body of a man; above
hovers a sparrow-hawk. This union of warlike and rustic
scenes suggests an interesting point of resemblance to
the shield of Achilles as described by Homer; and, indeed,
silver vessels of this variety present numerous analogies
to that shield.

Monum. dell' Instit., x, T. xxxiii. Comp. Annali, 1876,
pp. 252 et seq.

24. **Deep Bowl in silver gilt,** adorned on the inside
with two rows of reliefs of bulls and horses,
birds and trees.

This cup was found adhering to a much rusted iron
axe-head, upon which a portion of the exterior design
has been imprinted.

Mon. dell' Instit., xi, T. ii, 8.

25. **Flat Silver Bowl,** adorned inside with gilded reliefs.

In the centre of this cup is a medallion framed by a
circle of pomegranates, succeeded by two rows of scenes,
with an outer border formed by a serpent covered with
scales, the Egyptian emblem of the cosmos. To the left
in the medallion is a long-haired nude man, bound hand
and foot to the trunk of a tree. A warrior in Egyptian
costume (in the typical attitude usually adopted for victorious kings) is dashing forwards and seems to transfix
with his lance a fleeing man, whose right heel is seized
by a jackal. In the small remaining space at the foot of
the medallion is another nude figure, apparently crawling
on the ground, with its left heel seized by a dog resem-

bling a jackal. The victorious warrior has been explained
as Horus, son of Isis and avenger of Osiris, triumphing
over the army of Set-Typhon, the spirit of darkness. The
captive man is Typhon himself, and the jackal is Anubis,
the faithful companion of Horus and usually represented
by that emblematic animal.

The band next to the medallion is occupied by eight
horses, above each of which fly two birds. The following band is broader and much more interesting. It
presents a series of distinct but related scenes, illustrating the adventures of some legendary hero, and evidently
reproducing motives borrowed from Assyrian art. The
first scene shows us a chariot and pair issuing from a
city, the walls of which are symbolized by two towers.
The charioteer leans forward to urge on the horses, and
beside him stands a man armed with a battle-axe, while
a quiver is attached to the side of the chariot. The warrior shows the type of the Assyrian kings and is sheltered
by a royal parasol. In the second scene the chariot has
halted and the charioteer is alone; the king is kneeling
behind a tree taking aim with his bow at a stag standing
before him on a mound. The third scene shows the king
on the mound pursuing the mortally wounded quarry,
from whose breast the blood gushes. The fourth scene
is laid in a forest, in which a huge palm-tree is conspicuous. The horses are unharnessed and stand near the
chariot, while their driver feeds them from a three-legged
crib. The royal hunter is engaged in cutting up the
stag, which hangs from a tree and has already been deprived of its head. In the fifth scene the king, shaded
by his parasol, is seated on a chair, offering a sacrifice
before eating. In front of him rises an altar on which lie
a crater and a ladle, while close by is a second and larger
altar, from which ascends the smoke of a sacrifice (evidently the slaughtered stag). Above appear the moon
and the winged sun-disk, the two deities to whom the
sacrifice is offered. To the left the scene is closed by a
wooded hill on which are a running hare and a browsing

stag. At the foot of this hill and close to the altar is the mouth of a cave, from which projects the head of a huge ape, with pendant tongue (?), lying in wait for his prey. In the sixth scene the ape appears with a human form and very shaggy, recalling the descriptions left us by the ancients of the monsters dwelling in the interior of Africa. He stands upright in a menacing attitude, holding a stone in one hand and a branch in the other. In the air hovers a winged goddess (perhaps Astarte, goddess of the moon) bearing high above the dusty road the chariot and its inmates (represented on a very small scale). The connection of the two motives is clear. The king, proceeding on his journey, has been attacked in rear by the gorilla, but the goddess bore her pious protegé aloft. In the seventh scene the chariot has returned to earth. Rescued from the sudden attack, the royal archer now pursues the monster and has already overtaken him and overturns him with the horses. In the eighth scene, the king, above whom hovers a sparrowhawk, has alighted from his chariot and proceeds to give the *coup-de-grâce* with his axe to the now defenceless monster. The ninth scene shows the hero's return to the city, whose towers thus form the beginning and end of the famous adventure. A patera (now in New York), with exactly similar scenes, was found at Curion, in the island of Cyprus. It is therefore highly probable that the scenes illustrate some once popular legend from Assyrian or Cypro-Phœnician mythology; but it is exceedingly questionable whether, as has been recently suggested, the hero of the adventure can be identified with Cinyras, the legendary priest-king of Cyprus.

Mon. dell' Instit., x, T. 31, 1. *Perrot-Chipiez*, Histoire de l'art, III, p. 759, No. 643. Comp. Bull. dell' Instit., 1876, pp. 126 et seq. Annali, 1876, pp. 226, 269, 276 et seq. *(Fabiani)*. *Helbig*, Homerische Epos², p. 22, Fig. 1. *Clermont-Ganneau*, Études d'archéologie orientale, l'imagerie phénicienne et la mythologie iconologique chez les Grecs, Paris, 1880 (Journal Asiatique, 1878, pp. 232 et seq., 444 et seq.). American Journal of Archæology, III (1887), pp. 322 et seq. *(Marquand)*.

26. Fragmentary Silver Bowl, adorned inside with reliefs, like No. 25.

The imitation of Egyptian models is proved in the case of this cup not only by the choice of subjects, but still more by the rows of hieroglyphics engraved below the central medallion and also framing both the medallion and the exterior frieze. The types borrowed from Egyptian art are in many cases removed from the groups of which they originally formed part; in many cases also they have been transformed; and the symbols of the ancient ideographic script have been used on this cup merely as ornaments, without any reference to their meaning. In the medallion in the centre we see the ordinary type of the Egyptian Pharaoh, triumphing over his foes. The king (or Osiris?), between whose legs is a lion (symbol of power), brandishes an axe in his right hand, while his left hand, in which are his bow and arrows, also seizes the hair of the enemies kneeling before him (three heads are distinguishable). Above him hovers the sparrow-hawk with an ostrich-feather (symbol of justice) in its talons. The field of the medallion above is occupied with cartouches of hieroglyphics. To the right stands Ammon-Ra (Horus), the god with a sparrow-hawk's head, handing to the king a feather or palm, the symbol of victory. The bearded male figure behind the king, to the left, is perhaps Anubis; he bears a corpse on his right arm, and drags another along the ground with his left hand, which also holds a palm-leaf fan. Below the row of hieroglyphs on which this group stands is a doubled-up figure on the ground, probably a conquered enemy like that on No. 25. The motives in the frieze surrounding the medallion are borrowed from the legend of Osiris. Four boats (one only partly preserved) float between four bouquets of lotus-flowers, from each of which emerges Isis suckling the infant Horus. On one of the boats Osiris appears bearing the uræus-serpent and sun-disk, between two figures of Horus; on the second the sun-disk, resting on the sacred scarabæus, separates two figures of Harpocrates (*i.e.* the infant Horus), represented as seated upon a lotus-flower, with a scourge in his hand, and one of his fingers in his mouth, after the manner of children. The two remaining boats have similar groups. The Phœnician inscription engraved in very small letters on the medallion just above the wing of the hawk should also be noticed; *Esmunjai ben Asto* seems to have been the name of the maker (or owner) of the bowl. This is a proof that the bowl came into the possession of the princes of Præneste from a Phœnician source, and offers a pregnant hint towards determining the origin of the whole class to which it belongs (comp. pp. 396 et seq.).

Mon. dell' Instit., x, T. xxxii, 1. Annali, 1876, pp. 258, 266 et seq. *(Fabiani).* Notizie degli scavi, 1876, T. ii. Gazette archéologique, 1877, T. v, p. 18 *(Renan).* Perrot - Chipiez, Histoire de l'art, iii, p. 97, No. 36 (p. 773). Corpus inscript. Semiticarum, fasc. iii, T. xxxvi, No. 164. Comp. Ann. dell' Instit., 1876, pp. 203 et seq. *(Helbig),* pp. 266 et seq. *(Fabiani). Helbig,* Homerische Epos[2], p. 23. — A bowl found at Salerno closely resembles the above; see Mon. dell' Instit., ix, T. xliv, 1.

The **Blue Glass Bowl** (No. 38, on the same shelf) was found inside the preceding, and, apart from the coloured mosaics, is undoubtedly one of the most ancient glass vessels found in Italy.

27. Elegant Iron Dagger.

The hilt is incrusted with amber, adorned with a chequer-pattern in silver. Near the hilt lies the lower part of the silver sheath.

Monum. dell' Instit., x, T. xxxi, 4 Bullett. di paletnologia ital., ix, T. 3, 11, p. 101 *(Pigorini).* Zeitschrift für Ethnologie, 1890, p. 19 *(Undset).*

28. Similar Dagger, in its sheath.

On each side of the silver sheath are two rows of raised figures. On one side only a few traces of animal-figures can now be distinguished. In the upper row on the other side appear horses(?), oxen, and a man on his

back defending himself with his sword against a lion;
in the lower row are stags, at which a kneeling archer
is shooting, and a Centaur, with human legs in front,
brandishing a bough in his left hand. These motives
indicate a non-Semitic source (comp. pp. 395 et seq.);
they find their analogues on monuments in the island of
Rhodes and elsewhere in Asia Minor.

Monum. dell' Instit., x, T. xxxi, 5. Comp. Bullet., 1876, p. 123.
Annali, 1876, p. 249.

In the part of the case facing the entrance, in the
third compartment to the right, —

45-49. **Carved Ivory Plaques**, probably used to cover
some wooden article. Traces of gilding and
colour are distinguishable.

These plaques reproduce Egyptian motives almost
exclusively, in a broad and lax style that we may ascribe
to the Phœnicians. The art of using ivory for incrusta-
tion was popular in the Semitic east from a very remote
antiquity. Plaque No. 45, probably from the sheath of
a dagger or knife, is adorned with various subjects, including an Egyptian boat with a rower at each end; a
seated male figure, facing a low altar to the right, which
is approached by two women, one carrying some in-
distinguishable object, the other a bowl and ewer. More
to the right is a large crater upon a tall support, behind
which is a third woman, in an attitude of adoration.

Monum. dell' Inst., x, T. xxxi, 3. Comp. Bull., 1876, p. 124.
Annali, 1879, pp. 6 et seq. *(Helbig).* *Perrot-Chipiez*, Histoire de
l'art, iii, p. 853.

The plaques Nos. 46-48, ornamented with figures of
warriors, musicians, horsemen, and war-chariots, are
perhaps fragments from a casket; as are also the fragments No. 53 (in the next compartment to the left), ornamented with flowers and buds in the conventional
Egyptian style.

Monum. dell' Instit., xi, T. ii, 1-6. Comp. Annali, 1879, pp. 6
. et seq. *Fernique*, Etude sur Préneste, p. 178.

In the part of the case facing the exit, —

To the left: 31. **Bronze Stirrup-shaped Handle**, with plated reliefs.

On the outside are various groups of lions and men, in a lax and careless style, also two horses treated heraldically, rearing opposite each other on either side of a conventional tree in the Assyrian style. The designs on the inside are, on the other hand, as delicately executed as those on the golden plaques (pp. 417 et seq.). In the middle is a row of lions and on each side a row of horses forming a rectangle, the whole enclosed by a plaited band. The details are rendered indistinct by oxidation.

Monum. dell' Instit., xi, T. ii, 9. Comp. Annali, 1879, p. 11.

To the right: 84. **Fragments of Primitive Vases.**

These potsherds, which were not found within the tomb but in the earth above it, are fragments of vases adorned with geometrical designs, which were the earliest imported from Greece.

Upper Shelf.

On the side facing the entrance, —

To the right: 72. **Archaic Tripod** of bronze and iron, of the same Ionian type from Western Asia as No. 157 in the Museo Gregoriano (p. 372).

The three bronze feet are shaped like hoofs, with a claw behind. From each rise three iron shafts or legs one straight, the other two bent outwards, which are connected by bronze ties decorated with engraved zigzags and circles. The bronze cauldron is soldered to the top of the three straight uprights, and also shows traces below of a central support, now wanting. At the points where the shafts meet the cauldron is a standing dog in bronze; and above each point of junction of the bent shafts is the nude figure of a man with long hair and Satyr's ears, resting his hands upon the edge of the cauldron, and looking into the interior. All these figures, which are nailed to the cauldron, exhibit a thoroughly primitive art. They may have been actually made in Central Italy, but they certainly imitate models borrowed from Asiatic Greeks.

Monum. dell'Inst.,x, T. xxxi a, 2. Annali, 1879, T. C, 8. Comp. Annali, 1876, p. 250; 1879, p. 15 (Helbig). Olympia, iv, p. 127 (Furtwaengler).

74. **Large Bronze Cauldron** with handles adorned with a lotus-flower, flanked with heads of oxen.

Monum. dell'Inst.,x, T. xxxii, 4. — For similar handles, comp. Olympia, iv, p. 146 (Furtwaengler).

In the part of the case facing the window, —

At the sides: Two curiously-shaped bronze tubes filled with wood and decorated with primitive human figures and small animals. These tubes are supposed to have formed part of a bed.

Comp. Monum. dell' Instit., x, T. xxxi a, 8-11.

To the left: **Low Cauldron,** supported by three ribbon-like feet attached to it by rivets.

Annali dell' Instit., 1879, CD, 7.

In the centre: **Two Craticula, or Gridirons.**

Annali dell' Inst., 1879, T. CD, 4. Daremberg-Saglio, Dictionnaire des antiquités, i, p. 1557. Comp. above, No. 202, p. 379.

81. **Base in thin bronze.**

This truncated cone is ornamented in an Oriental style, with four winged animals erect on their hind-legs and springing. It is crowned with a kind of chaplet of leaves, the outer edge of which is bent outwards like a basin, so as to suggest that this support was used as a brazier or torch-holder. But it is more probable that this implement is of the same kind as that in the Museo Gregoriano (p. 413), and was possibly used to support the cauldron in the shelf below. 'Hypothemata' of this kind are known to us both among Asiatic and Greek

works of art of the eighth and seventh centuries B.C.; and
these may very possibly have served as models for the
present specimen, which seems to be of Italic manufacture.

Monum. dell'Instit., xi, T. ii, 7. Comp. Annali dell'Inst., 1879,
p. 9 *(Helbig).* — Similar chaplets have been found near Marion
(Polis tis Chrysokou) in Cyprus and in the course of the German
excavations at Olympia. Comp. Olympia, iv, T. 68, 810, p. 125
(Furtwaengler).

Bottom Shelf.

Fragments of a Cauldron in hammered bronze, of
a highly archaic type.

Two human busts (cast in bronze), with birds' wings
and tails added without any organic harmony, are fastened
with rivets at two opposite points on the rim. On their
backs are rings through which passed the chains or cords
by which the cauldron was suspended. Six griffins were
originally placed between these busts, and five are still
more or less intact. These griffins are made of thin
bronze plates, hammered on a wooden shape and then
filled in with some solid material. The eyes were
inserted in white and dark-blue vitreous paste. The shape
of the heads recalls the most ancient type of griffin
adopted in the art of the Asiatic Greeks. Even with
reference to the shape of the cauldron and the style of its
decoration, we learn from literary tradition and the yield
of excavations, that their analogues are to be sought for
in the art-industry of the Greeks of Asia Minor during
the seventh century B.C.; so that we may probably ascribe the origin of this specimen to that same source.

Monum. dell'Inst., xi, T. ii, 10. Comp. Annali, 1879, p. 12. —
For similar winged busts found at Olympia: Archæol. Zeit., 1879,
T. 15. Olympia, iv, T. 44, 783 et seq., pp. 115 et seq. *(Furtwaengler).* — For similar heads of griffins found at Olympia: id.,
ibid., T. 45, 792 et seq. — An analogous vase with support was
found in a tumulus in La Garenne near Châtillon-sur-Seine, in Bur-
gundy; see Olympia, iv, pp. 114 et seq., where all other literary
allusions are cited.

To the right, —

Fragments of a Bronze Shield of the same kind as those found in the Regulini-Galassi Tomb (comp. No. 164, p. 373). The present specimen was adorned with human figures. The remains of three such shields were found attached to the walls of the tomb.

Also, on all three shelves, —

Fragments of Utensils and Weapons in wood and bronze, **Fragments of Phœnician Vases**, in terracotta covered with a blue glaze, and (behind) several **Handles,** mostly adorned with figures of animals.

For the handles, see Monumenti dell' Inst., x, T. xxxii, 5-7.

Index.

The figures generally refer to the consecutive numbers of the Handbook. The volume and page are given where the reference is to the introductory sketches or to the monuments described in pp. 286-292 of vol. ɪ and pp. 264-459 of vol. ɪɪ. The names of artists are printed in italics.

Heracles (comp. Hercules).
— and Alcyoneus, II, p. 344.
— and Athena, II, p. 311, p. 346.
— and boar, II, p. 297.
— and Geryon, II, p. 297.
— and Hippolyta, II, p. 350.
— and lion, II, p. 299, p. 300.
— and Nessos, II, p. 289.
— and bull, II, p. 295, No. 31.
— and Triton, II, p. 299.
—, on a mirror, II, p. 386.
—, voyage of, II, p. 346.
Heraclitos 694.
Hercules (comp. Heracles) 412.
— Musarum 413; I, p. 312.
— and Juno (bronze group), II, p. 364, p. 370, p. 383.
— Victor 134.
Herder 887.
Hermæ (statues composed of a head, or of a head and bust, placed on a quadrangular pillar corresponding to the height of the human body) in gymnasia 825; II, p. 97, p. 427.
—, leaning 811.
Hermaphrodite 181, 931, 1065.
Hermes (Mercury).
— with the child Dionysos 79; comp. Praxiteles.
—, herma 864.
—, heads and hermal busts 695, 707, 975.
—, reliefs 212, 213, 399, 439, 449, 515, 675, 760, 790, 851, 893.
—, statues 61, 145 (so-called Antinoos of the Belvedere), 332, 871, 936; II, p. 268; (so-called) 509, 521, 939.
—, on mirrors, II, p. 389.
—, on vases, II, p. 290, p. 314 (No. 103), p. 319, p. 320, p. 328, p. 344 (stealing cattle), p. 345.
Hero, votive relief dedicated to a 813.
Herodoros 380.

Herodotos 380.
Herons (on a cratera) 1061.
Herse 116.
Hesiod (?) 36.
Hesione 848.
Hesperides 420, 784.
—, apples of the 784, 558-560, 613; II, p. 386.
Hesperos 797, 860.
Hestia 742, 851.
Hieroduli (temple attendants), II, p. 417.
Hierogrammateus 146.
Hieron, painter of vases, II, p. 286, p. 341 (No. 196), p. 343 (No. 218).
Hilæra 384.
Hind 910.
—, mosaic 962.
—, Cerynæan 420, 917; II, p. 363, No. 26.
Hippocrates 792.
Hippodameia 336; I, p. 449 (?); II, p. 273, p. 429.
Hippolyta 420; II, p. 350, No. 258.
Hippolytos 416, 678.
Hippomenes 566.
Hippopotamus 47; II, p. 417.
Hippothoon, II, p. 405.
Homer 36 (?), 480-482, 495-497.
Hoop 740.
Horæ 347, 709 (?), 747, 779, 1058 (?); II, p. 320. Comp. Seasons.
Horus on portraits of the Diadochi 249.
— of Dionysos 249.
—, military 5, 786, 787.
—, signal, II, p. 366.
— of plenty, see Cornucopia.
Horrea Lolliana, I, p. 312.
Horse, in bronze 615.
—, torn by a lion 611.
Horsemen, relief of, II, p. 392, p. 426.
Hortensius, Q. 748.
Horti Serviliani 694.

Printed by Breitkopf & Haertel at Leipsic.

www.ingramcontent.com/pod-product-compliance
Lightning Source LLC
Chambersburg PA
CBHW032010110726
47901CB00004B/1031